POZ

Christopher Koehler

Harmony Ink

Published by
HARMONY INK PRESS

5032 Capital Circle SW, Suite 2, PMB# 279, Tallahassee, FL 32305-7886 USA
publisher@harmonyinkpress.com • http://harmonyinkpress.com

This is a work of fiction. Names, characters, places, and incidents either are the product of author imagination or are used fictitiously, and any resemblance to actual persons, living or dead, business establishments, events, or locales is entirely coincidental.

Poz
© 2015 Christopher Koehler.

Cover Art
© 2015 Paul Richmond.
http://www.paulrichmondstudio.com
Cover content is for illustrative purposes only and any person depicted on the cover is a model.

ISBN: 978-1-63216-368-4
Library Edition ISBN: 978-1-63476-052-2
Digital ISBN: 978-1-63216-369-1
Library of Congress Control Number: 2014948397
First Edition January 2015
Library Edition April 2015

Printed in the United States of America
∞
This paper meets the requirements of
ANSI/NISO Z39.48-1992 (Permanence of Paper).

Poz is dedicated to the memory of Spencer Cox (March 10, 1968—December 18, 2012). Spencer worked tirelessly as a member of ACT UP throughout the worst years of the AIDS epidemic to effect change and further advances in HIV treatment, including working with the FDA to speed the approval of HIV medications and other important contributions. But when I knew Spencer, I didn't know he was a hero.

ACKNOWLEDGMENTS

AS ALWAYS, I'm happy to thank Tricia Blocher, coach and all around good people, for knowing the fiddly rowing details I don't. Likewise, Whitney Powell helped me with crucial information about high school rowers applying for college and early admissions for athletes. Chillbear, as he always does, helped me with police procedural details without asking me too many questions. Any errors belong to me, not him.

No writer can ever let acknowledgments slide by without thanking his beta readers. As always, my husband read over my manuscript with careful attention to detail, but I get to thank Brandilyn and Posy Roberts, too. *Poz* also went into a gamma round, so thanks too to Becky Condit. *Poz* was in great hands with these four.

Lastly, I'm once again blessed by having Elizabeth North as my publisher. She didn't think this was an outlandish idea for a novel and encouraged me to go for it. *Poz* is the result.

AUTHOR'S NOTE

ACCORDING TO the Centers for Disease Control and Prevention, rates of HIV infection are again rising for young gay and bisexual men. The Real Story Safe Sex Project, started by Brent Hartinger, author of *Geography Club* and the rest of the Russel Middlebrook stories, is a new way to educate this vulnerable group.

The Real Story Safe Sex Project

HIV/AIDS is still a serious disease, and gay and bi guys are at high (and rising) risk of catching it. But many people don't seem interested in talking about it anymore.

So the Real Story Safe Sex Project takes a new, hopefully more entertaining approach: remind people about HIV and safe sex using entertainment and popular culture, especially projects involving your favorite fictional gay and bi characters.

Hartinger launched the Real Story with *Two Thousand Pounds Per Square Inch* using a character from his own Russel Middlebrook series. You can download the story for free on the Real Story's webpage, http://brenthartinger.com/therealstory/ (last accessed August 2014).

So how can you help?

A bunch of ways.

(1) Help spread the word. Tell people what the Project is all about. Follow the Real Story Safe Sex Project on social media to see the latest contributions to the effort. If you're a journalist or a blogger, consider writing about us.

(2) Volunteer. This entire project depends on people's willingness to help out. So are you a graphic designer? A proofreader? Do you have

some other skill you think might help the project? Check out the Real Story's webpage for volunteer opportunities.

(3) Create a Real Story safe sex story. This is the heart of the project—the reason it exists in the first place. So if you're an author or a filmmaker (even an unpublished or unproduced one), consider creating something on the subject of safe sex. You can use entirely new characters or existing characters from a book, TV show, or movie you created (and/or control the rights to). Then upload your short story or video to your favorite media platforms and tell your fans about it!

The only requirements the project has are that (1) the project be available in as many platforms as possible for free; (2) that it promote safe sex, preferably among gay and bi teens and twentysomethings; and (3) that you mention "The Real Story Safe Sex Project" on the cover if it's an e-story, and include a link to the project in the body of the work.

Check out the Real Story's webpage for complete details, http://brenthartinger.com/therealstory/

PROLOGUE

April, my senior year

"HEY, REMY," Michael said as he walked up. "Coach says hands-on in fifteen."

I looked up at my guy. The warm San Diego sun shone behind his head, giving him a halo to match the one I always saw when I looked at him, at least now. I can't believe there was a time I couldn't see how amazing he was. I smiled at him. I couldn't help it. I tipped my head up, and he obliged. I lost myself in his kiss, my eyes closing as his lips brushed against mine, softly at first but with increasing ardor. He knelt next to where I sat, driving all thoughts of my homework right out of my mind as he held my face lightly.

"All right, you two. Get a hotel."

We broke apart, foreheads touching and cheeks blazing. "Sorry, Howie," I said.

Our cox'n rolled his eyes. "You two are so sickeningly sweet together, I need insulin. At least I know you'll be relaxed and won't rush the slide."

"It's not like I nailed him in the bathroom," Michael said dryly.

"As hot as that visual is, I need you two to bring oars down to the beach. Then wait by the boat," Howie said. "I have to go herd the rest of the squirrels."

We each grabbed four oars and headed back down to the beach. We weren't supposed to carry that many at a time, and if Coach Lodestone caught us, he'd huff and he'd puff and he'd threaten to blow the house down, but one of the things I'd learned over the last year was that his bark was far worse than his bite. Mostly he would grouse that we'd scratch the paint on the blades of the oars, but we were careful, Michael and I.

After we set the oars against the slings holding the boat, we scampered back up to where we'd stashed our gear, and never mind what Howie said about waiting by the boat. I'm on a fearsome cocktail of drugs, and I needed more sunblock before I was on the water. Naturally Michael helped with those hard-to-reach places, like that spot right between my shoulder blades where my unisuit always managed to gape. I really didn't want to take chances with a burn. The Crew Classic only had two kinds of weather: rainy and miserable or sunny and hot. Fortune favored us this year. It was sunny. During rainy years, boats sometimes filled with so much water they had to be pulled from the chop by the Coast Guard. Rowing shells were meant to keep water out, not hold it in. Crew Classic legend held that after one particularly bad year, a crew was forced to abandon ship right in the middle of Mission Bay. The cox'n, who was last aboard, stood in her seat and bowed to the referees' tent and the Jumbotron cameras before executing a perfect dive into the chop. Then the safety launch plucked her from the water. That was cox'ns for you.

Sunblock applied, we still managed to be back at the boat before Howie returned to our knot of rowers with the last of the stragglers. So did Coach Lodestone.

"Nice of you to join us, gentlemen." Coach Lodestone looked over his sunglasses at the laggards as they joined our cluster. "I trust you didn't make Howie look too hard for you."

"No, sir."

"Good, good, because I'd hate to inconvenience anyone by requiring punctuality for this race, the last of their high school careers for five of your boatmates." Once he was sure he had their full attention, he continued. "This has been a good season for this lineup. Yes, we had some issues last fall, but head racing has never been our focus, and I think this spring has helped us—you—click as a crew. The weather is amazing, some of the best I've ever seen as a rower or as a coach. This is it. Make the most of it, and most of all, enjoy it."

Coach Lodestone put his hand in the middle of the cluster. Nine other hands swiftly followed his. "The worst thing is to cross the finish line with regrets, so make yourselves proud, because I'm proud of you."

"All right, enough chitchat," Howie barked. "Find your places aaand hands-on! Ready… aaand up to shoulders! We're rowing the *Helena Sundstrom* today. It's a solid boat, so try not to suck."

The junior crew of the Capital City Rowing Club had bought it off CalPac College last fall. It was no longer stiff enough for collegiate competition but still had plenty of life left in it, and we were lucky to have it.

The weather might have been perfect, but the water of Mission Bay still had a chill in it, pleasant in the heat of the afternoon. We waded out until we were knee-deep so we wouldn't scrape the boat on the sand when we climbed in. We took our oars from the junior varsity rowers who had kindly volunteered to bring them to us.

"Bow pair in!" Howie called from the shallows once all the oars were in their oarlocks. The oars acted like outriggers, lending a certain stability to the boat. It wasn't easy to roll an eight, but it could be done.

"Engine room, climb in." The four rowers in the middle of the boat clamored in. That figured. They were meat that moved the boat, but could they not climb in without the racket? Just once?

"Seven, your turn! Hold it steady, bow six. We'll tie in once we're on the water.

"Stroke, if you'd be so kind?"

He meant me. Howie was tiny. He was the only one who could see where we were going, but he brought no power to the boat. He was supposed to be small. That said, this race standardized cox'ns' weights. He had to carry a sandbag to bring him up to the minimum weight, and to prevent any cheating, race officials weighed all sandbags at the end of the race. What? Cox'ns bleeding sand out during the course of a race to give their crews an advantage? If they thought they could have gotten away with it.

So while we rowers might've been knee-deep in the water, Howie was waist-deep. I carried him from the shallows and set him in the boat's stern. He fiddled with his cox box, the small device that counted strokes and powered the boat's sound system.

"Your turn, Remy."

I climbed in last. Stroke didn't have to be super strong. I just had to hold a beat and not allow myself to be rushed by the seven people sitting behind me. I wouldn't be, and I knew I had seven great rowers behind me, Michael among them at seven. Together we made the stroke pair, and did we ever take flack for that.

All traces of his snarkiness gone, Howie started issuing commands as the *Helena* pulled away from the beach. From now until the boat was washed and back in slings after the race, his word was law. It might sound silly or mystical, but I already felt the power coursing through the carbon fiber of the oars and the shell. It was Howie's job to remind us how we rowed for the next thirty minutes of our warm-up and race, and he was brilliant at it. Soon we would click, eight bodies moving as one under the guidance of Howie's voice, the oars creaking as we pulled them through the water, bending under the strain of our bodies.

My last thought as we sat at the ready, waiting for the countdown, Sea World in the background, was that I'd almost thrown all of this away.

We were in San Diego at the Crew Classic, the last and biggest race of my rowing career with the juniors program of the Capital City Rowing Club. It was the end of my senior year of high school, and everything was golden. It would become one of my favorite memories.

It wasn't always like that. At one point during the previous year, I had doubted I would make it, and I don't mean qualifying for a seat in a boat for San Diego. I didn't say things like that out loud anymore because everyone told me I was melodramatic, and maybe I was. But that didn't change the fact that it was true. I wasn't entirely out my junior year, and I made a lot of stupid decisions that hurt a lot of people, most especially myself. I hurt Michael and my brother too, and I didn't think I would be able to make it up to them anytime soon. Or maybe I wouldn't have to. They seemed to have forgiven me.

I still had to forgive myself.

This was something I struggled with every day.

CHAPTER
ONE

The end of my junior year, approximately one year earlier

WHEN ALL this started, my older brother Geoff didn't know I was gay, at least not to my knowledge. I'd called him "Goff" when we were really young because I couldn't pronounce his name. He'd called me "Germy" because he couldn't say Jeremy. He still calls me Germy, even though everyone else calls me Remy. I still called him Goff, so I guess that was fair.

Goff was thirteen minutes older—we were twins of the fraternal variety—and he milked that older bit like a Holstein cow. Thirteen minutes, but you would have thought it was thirteen years. Anyway, he played football. He looked out for me, or at least tried, but he was and is straight as a plank. We wrangled a lot, still do actually, but he saved me from a lot of homophobic hassling, sometimes at the hands of his own friends, without even knowing I was gay, which was pretty cool of him.

"Teammates," Goff would say. "They're not my friends, not if they're giving you shit."

He was a good guy when he wasn't being an asshole.

That said, Goff never understood a fundamental part of me, at least not until I came out to him. I guess that was my fault, though. How could he, when I'd never told him I was gay? But how could I, when I couldn't have borne losing my brother? He was my twin, the person I was closest to in the world. Losing him would've meant losing a part of me. We fought like cats in a gunnysack and it drove our parents crazy, but they never understood that we went to the trouble of irritating each other because we loved each other. We certainly weren't going to tell each other that. We were (and are) teenage males. Dad was a shrink. Dr. Babcock should've gotten that but didn't.

So anyway, Goff missed a major piece of who I was and everything that went along with that. Now I wouldn't say all teenage boys were sex-obsessed, just every one I've ever encountered. But he had all the sex he wanted and had no idea what it's like not getting it. For me, it was not being gotten. So I was horny as hell in high school and about to burst. That was the start of all my problems, I guess.

Our family lived in Davis, an über-liberal organo-groovy college town about seventy miles from San Francisco. Davis had bought into Cesar Chavez's grape boycott, which I read about in history class; it made itself a nuclear-free zone, which was kind of a joke when UC Davis boasted a particle accelerator of its very own. Besides, what good would the declaration of being a nuclear-free zone have done? Protect the city if the US and the USSR had nuked each other? There were three major Air Force bases around the city during the Cold War. There'd have been a bright blue flash and then nothing. Good luck with that nuclear-free zone. The city was also a declared sanctuary for undocumented immigrants. I could go on, but why bother? A homecoming prince even brought his boyfriend to prom one year. As a gay kid, I should've been golden in a city and high school like this.

But someone forgot to send my parents that memo, or at least my mother. Mom was a smart woman—she majored in chemistry in college and went on to become a drug rep for a pharmaceutical company after she decided getting a Pharm.D wasn't for her—but she was oblivious sometimes, especially where Goff and I were concerned. Of both our parents, she in particular was loud with the compulsory heterosexuality messaging, things like telling me I was morally obligated to take some unpopular (read: fat with braces) girl to the prom. She said it was my "gentlemanly duty" or some such bull, but Goff and I both knew it was because she herself had been fat with braces in high school. She wasn't doing it deliberately—trying to make me miserable—but she succeeded admirably.

Women in Mississippi had taken their girlfriends to prom, or at least tried. Hell, even in Davis a few years ago, the aforementioned homecoming prince took his boyfriend, but my mom? She thought I had to make life better for every desperate and dateless girl out there, just to restore some cosmic balance because her life sucked during high school. Why didn't she get that this was my life, my one-way ticket through high school, not her do-over?

When I said things like that, her response was, "I think you can take one evening out of your life to make a difference in someone else's." Given the essentially obligatory service hours necessary to get into college these days, I thought I already had.

My boyfriend could've plowed me on the table at Thanksgiving, and she would have still said that. If I'd had a boyfriend. Well, there was Mikey Castelreigh. He wanted to be my boyfriend. I tended to think of him more as a kid brother even though he was only a year younger. I felt like there was a big difference between a sophomore and a junior in high school, however. Mikey looked like he missed the puberty train. I had a left hand. What I needed was a close friend who was gay. Mikey fit that bill very well.

Even at good ol' tolerant, GSA-sporting Davis High, it wasn't easy being different. We were still teenagers. Being smacked on the ass with the gay wand when I was born didn't change that. I wanted to think Mikey understood that. I think what Mikey didn't get was why we couldn't be friends with benefits. Uh… because it would have been like blowing my brother? If I had a brother who swung that way. But then, as has been pointed out to me many times, I also saw what I wanted to see and not always what was really there. Or boats. I saw rowing-related things very clearly. It was life that tripped me up at every turn.

But telling my parents? Like that would ever happen. Hear that flapping noise? That was the pigs flying out of my butt, which would happen right before I'd tell my parents I liked the cock. I never got the best vibe off them where that was concerned. Sure, they had gay and lesbian, even trans, friends, but it was different when it was their kid, you know? They were on a need-to-know basis where my life was concerned. Coming out? Survey says: No!

Goff told our parents about a lot of things that went on his life—whereas I told them very little—but then he and I had very different relationships with them.

"So how's that working for you, Goff?"

"Shut it."

I smiled, but it was really more of a smirk. "Still think having the olds know every single detail's harmless?"

"You're really kind of a dick sometimes, you know that?"

"Everybody has to be something, I guess."

"Really? I thought you were more of an asshole."

He had no idea what he was doing to me with this conversation. I mean, the homoerotic subtext was barely sub. Sure, Mikey and I were going to die laughing about it later, but right then I had to bite my tongue, and that was kind of painful.

I looked at him for a few moments, totally expressionless. Just long enough that he'd gone back to his homework. Just long enough to make him squirm. "What? You're creeping me out."

"I could've sworn I heard you say stop sleeping in your bed when you sneak out to see your girlfriend."

Mom and Dad never checked on me. Ever. I never gave them a reason to. Goff? Too many. Neither of us was stupid enough to think pillows under the blankets would fool them, but me in his bed? Physically we were nothing alike, but at least I made breathing sounds. We had a Jack and Jill bedroom setup where our bedrooms met in a common bathroom. We locked the bathroom door leading into the hallway and put the pillows in *my* bed, I moved to his, and he was out of there. He always showed his gratitude.

"You… that's harsh, man."

"Times are hard."

Goff threw down his pen. "Why're you doing this?"

"Because it's almost summer, which means fall's not that far away, which means neither is the prom, and it's never too early to present a united front."

"You're really twisted, you know that?"

I shrugged. "And you know she'll try to get you to take someone besides your girlfriend, since you quote-unquote haven't been dating that long."

"They're not that bad," Goff said, sighing.

"Have it your way, but don't come whining to me when Mom does exactly that." It's not that I was smarter than Goff. I wasn't. But I was smarter in different areas, like sneaking. It was like he didn't have an ounce of guile in him. Apparently I received both our shares. Somehow, and despite getting him into endless trouble as children, he still trusted me. Maybe it's because as we grew older, I got him out of scrapes, at least when I knew about them in time.

Maybe I shouldn't have complained. Goff got the same kind of nonsense from our parents too, and never mind that he had a girlfriend.

She wasn't even a cheerleader. She was super sweet and amazingly intelligent. He met Laurel because I brought her home to study for AP Biology I. It took him a few months of whining like an Irish setter, but they eventually took to studying each other's biology. I knew this because Goff was too chickenshit to buy his own condoms, so I had to buy them for him.

Speaking of shit of whatever species, Goff was in it because a teammate was caught dealing molly. Goff's friend slash teammate was busted by the cops at a team party. Oddly enough what our parents freaked out about was that Geoff had alcohol on his breath. He blew a 0.12 as a matter of fact. I think that was half again the legal limit. Yeah, hi, Mom and Dad, he was at a party where the host was busted for dealing *Ecstasy.* You maybe want to focus on the larger picture? Or maybe they were, because I knew for a fact my brother didn't and wouldn't take drugs. Anyway, Goff couldn't fart without them breathing down his neck for a while.

But if I'd known about the party, I'd have told him to watch his step, because rumors of drug-dealing by members of the football team had been flying around school for weeks. At the very least, he might've limited himself to a beer or two instead of getting trashed. Then Goff could've told the olds, "Sorry, Mom and Dad, I know it showed bad judgment, but I planned to call Germy to come and get me." And I'd have absolutely covered for him. For that matter, he could have gotten trashed, and I'd still have picked him up if he had warned me in time to cover for him.

Weirdly enough, they were totally permissive where I was concerned. They thought I was a late bloomer and hoped the talks they gave Goff about sex applied to me, too, because they made me sit down and listen to every single one of them, not that they contained anything I needed to know. But the last one? I couldn't take it anymore and I cranked up the sarcasm. It bugged Dad, I knew that for sure, and I was pretty sure I managed to irritate Goff, and never mind the fact that he was sick of those talks, too. Goff already knew not to get his girlfriend pregnant and to make sure *he* was in charge of *his* birth control.

Except for the condom buying. I was in charge of that.

"Could you maybe shut up, Germy? This is bad enough without your sniping."

Dad nodded. "Please listen to your brother. I get that you may be too old for these, but you're not making this easier on any of us. If you stop, I promise this will be the last one."

"You've said that every time, Dad. Yet here we are, another ho-hum day in paradise listening to these riveting talks," I said acidly. "I think we've got a lock on the prevention of premature grandparenthood. Not much else, but babies are definitely one sexually transmitted parasite we can rule out. Maybe someday we can move on to spirochetes."

"Jeremy…," Dad said in that warning tone of his. It held a hint of a threat, but what did I care? I'd heard it all my life and it had long since ceased to have the desired effect. It was more proof that I was the changeling, the odd Babcock out.

These things were so stupid. Take today's lecture. Please. Dad actually had the nerve to refer to the labia as a butterfly. How the hell was I supposed to keep a straight face when confronted with that? Dad was going on about female anatomy again, trying to help Goff—and presumably me—locate the female G-spot. I would never need to know, and based on the noises issuing from Goff's room of an evening, he already knew exactly where to find it. What I needed—what we both needed—was basic information on sexually transmitted infections. Anatomy had been covered in eighth-grade sex ed.

Yet this was vintage Dad, blithely charging ahead, with Goff in tow more or less willingly and me digging in my heels every step of the way. I could not say Dad never heard, if only because sound waves did stimulate his auditory nerves. It never changed his behavior, however, and trying to persuade Dad was like arguing with the wind for all the good it did, at least not once he had a notion fixed in his mind. Mom had some facility in managing him, but then, she had more experience. Goff and I were only teenagers, so what did we know? I was convinced that was how Dad's thought processes ran. The bizarissimo part of it all was that Goff was the good twin whereas I questioned everything, fighting anything I thought absurd with tooth and claw. I had even overheard Dad say as much when he thought he was unobserved. Yet Dad—both parents, really—kept Goff on a shorter leash.

I thought this different treatment was because of our different sports, I really did. Football? Sure. Everyone knew the deal, or thought they did. What they really knew was the reputation that came from a bunch of idiotic movies. Goff sure wasn't like that, and most of his football friends weren't, either. But crew? They had no idea about crew, not really, and never mind the stupid amounts of parental involvement my club required. No, when Mom and Dad were in college, rowers were pale, muscular gods and goddesses who walked the campuses, ate obscene amounts of food after their early-morning practices without gaining a pound, and stuck mainly with their own kind. They told me as much. That my club's juniors program practiced in the afternoon must have thrown them off my scent, because I had a tan despite the sunblock.

Seriously, I got away with murder. Or at least I did the summer before my senior year, and the person I killed—or almost killed—was myself. After that? I lived on Cellblock Q.

CHAPTER
TWO

SPRING WENT in either direction in the Sacramento Valley, sometimes on a daily basis. One year we had to wear parkas into June because it kept raining, but other years the weather was a mixed bag with warm weather one week and thunderstorms the next. That year, lightning and hail added a certain zest to rowing. It definitely gave me an appreciation for what crews in the Midwest and Southeast routinely put up with. This year, we lucked out. Spring was spring-like: cool in the morning but warming up nicely by lunch.

I sat outside at lunch with the rest of the rowing geeks, or at least those of us from Cap City's junior crew who did not assort themselves into some other clique. There weren't that many of us, and we fit on a couple of picnic tables under some trees on the quad. I never felt like I belonged anywhere else, so I sat with my crewmates by default. I lacked Goff's popularity. Seriously, my brother could go anywhere and be welcomed. He was a jock and top of the heap in that group, so yeah. He earned good marks too, so other than the hardcore geeks and LARPers who hated jocks as part of the order of things, he always had a table with the brainiacs, too. Sometimes they were not sure what to make of him, but his outgoing personality smoothed the way.

I wished I could be that kind of chameleon. The jocks could not figure me out, because crew did not fit into their canned hierarchy. Or maybe they just took their cues from some of the coaches who disliked the fact that there were jocks they did not control. I was just a rower; I did not want to get involved in the politics. I couldn't. As long as *my* coaches kept me from having to take any kind of mandatory PE, I was happy, and I got enough exercise at the boathouse, thanks all the same.

Because I displayed actual muscle development, the people in my AP and honors classes could not make heads or tails of me, either. I took the same classes. We studied together sometimes. But other than Laurel and a few of her friends, I could not get the time of day from that crowd. Even then I had to be careful because if I spent too much time with Laurel, Goff would think I was putting the moves on her. It was another reason to come out to him. I thought some of the athletes from the more intellectual sports like cross-country or swimming might be able to deal, but no. It was me and the other rowers, even if the majority of them were JV. Most of the guys in my boat went to other schools, which sucked. I wished I could say I got tired of their mangy butts, but when I was on my own at school, I had to admit I missed them.

Or maybe that was just the nature of high school, and I was melodramatic. Or maybe I was socially awkward? Regardless, I hung there in the background like wallpaper, basically invisible unless I did something tacky, in which case *everyone* noticed me, but not in the good way.

I'd never admit this, but I kind of envied Mikey. For starters, he was a lot more social. Or maybe he was a lot more grounded? He knew who he was, never mind that he was only a sophomore. Some people were like that. I didn't begrudge him that, but I wished I could figure out who I was. I think Mikey sat with me so I did not sit by myself. He told me I was the only person he knew who could be so alone in a crowd. Or maybe he had a crush on me. It could've gone either way. The motives of sophomores were dreadfully obscure, so I was not inclined to argue.

As I listened to people chatter, I wished I could tell Goff about me. I was pretty sure he knew something was up. What was worse was that it was starting to come between us. Goff sensed something. He had to, if only because I was out to my team and rowers gossiped like there was a prize for it. I knew I was the sensitive twin, but he was not stupid. The thought of telling him scared the crap out of me. My parents were worthless, so he was all I had. What if I told him and he freaked? Then I'd be alone. We had been there for each other since before we were born, and I couldn't face things without him. Couldn't face *life* without him, really. But if I didn't tell him, that might happen anyway.

"You're quiet," Mikey said.

Caught red-handed. "Just thinking."

He nudged my shoulder. "About?"

"My History Day project." Junior year in California meant US History, and since Davis was basically Lake Wobegon—all the children were above average—we had to participate in History Day. If we made an A on our projects, it went in the grade books as a double A, meaning we could skip a test—including the final—or replace a grade. Not bad.

Mikey made a face. "Is this what I have to look forward to?"

"Only if you take honors US History." I said that, but we both knew he probably would. People who didn't live here didn't really understand what it was like. Parents didn't apply academic pressure. They didn't have to. We internalized it and did it to ourselves.

"What's your topic again?"

"The Fourth Amendment's protections against unreasonable searches and seizures in the electronic age, specifically whether or not the police need warrants when it comes to using texts messages as evidence in criminal proceedings. You see—"

"That's enough." Mikey held up a hand. His smile took the sting off it. "Anything about the NSA? That's topical and sounds like it relates."

I shuddered. "Oh God no. For one thing, the legal analysis is all over the place. For another, federal judges are issuing contradictory rulings. It's just not something I want to touch."

For a lie to avoid telling him what I was really thinking about, History Day wasn't bad. It helped that I actually had to work on it.

"I was going to ask if you wanted to hang out after practice this weekend...."

I thought as much. "We can always do homework. Your place or mine?"

"Let's play that by ear, 'kay?" Mikey said. "Whichever house is quieter."

I bumped his shoulder. "We need to go. Weight training, remember?"

"Like I could forget." Mikey rolled his eyes. "Tons of fun. Oh wait!" he said as I rose from the picnic table. "Are you driving today?"

"Yep. You need a ride?" We went through this ritual almost every day. I always drove to practice because the boathouse was in West Sacramento, about fifteen miles away. Goff and I shared a car, but his practice was at school, so I drove to practice and then drove back by school to pick him up. That had been one of the conditions of Mom and

Dad buying us a car. If Goff had already gotten a ride home, he texted me. Mikey didn't live that far from us, and he always chipped in for gas.

"Yeah." Mikey sighed. "Until I get my own car…. I'm sorry to keep mooching off you."

"You're not mooching, and besides, our coaches keep hassling us to carpool, right?" It was true, they were all over that, and besides, between Cap City, UC Davis, and CalPac, parking was at a premium. Cap City's junior crew was the low spot on the totem pole. The more people we crammed in our cars, the less we had to listen to Coach Lodestone bitch about it.

Mikey smiled shyly. "Great, I'll meet you by your car after seventh period."

"What about weights? I'll see you in about ten minutes."

"Then, too." I could only smile and shake my head as he walked away.

THE STATE required PE through the tenth grade, but rowing counted for independent study PE and got the junior varsity crews off the hook. After that, no one had to take PE, but I rowed so I might as well have gotten some credits for it. All any of us required was our coach's signature on some form for the athletic department and we were covered. Easy peasy, right?

Wrong. Some of the coaches of other teams resented the fact that we existed. That was the only reason I could think of for their opposition. Naturally, the coach who oversaw weight training for all the independent-study athletes was one of the noisiest in his opposition. I thought he should take it up with Coach Lodestone. Instead he made passive-aggressive comments during weight training.

Whatever. It was not like I was all that fond of weights. I only lifted to make the boats move faster. It was funny. I had a goal. I lifted for a reason. But every day I trudged to the locker room, quashing my fight-or-flight responses. It was not much of a mystery. It was the locker room. Actual hell for the high school closet case was any place with naked guys. I wanted to look. No, I had to look. I couldn't help it. It was a biological compulsion. I kept my head down, trained on my locker, my duffel bag, my feet, anything but the guys around me, all of them smokin' hot. I couldn't look, not openly. I was afraid, because if I looked, I'd react, and my own flesh would betray me. I knew there were other gay guys at school, if only because my best friend was dressing out the next row over. I'd even sensed other eyes on me when I dressed out for PE, but I could never look around, because if I did, I'd get hard at the wrong time and then someone would know.

I was out to the guys on the crew, so I wasn't a total closet case. Mikey certainly knew, but I didn't look at him. It would've been like looking at my brother. Kind of. Anyway, I didn't look at them, they didn't hassle me. We were all friends, and you don't perv on your friends. The moral economy of the boner and all that. Besides, our lockers were in different rows. As for the other guys who lifted this hour? I had excellent peripheral vision, and some of them had starred in my fantasies this whole school year. Living on the edge, you know?

"Hey, man."

I met Francisco's eyes on the way out of the locker room. "Hey."

"More hoops. Couldn't you just squeal?" Francisco was as enthusiastic about this as I was. Cisco was a good guy and one of the other varsity rowers at Davis High from my boat.

"If we pull anything this close to the Crew Classic, Lodestone will kill Robertson."

Coach Robertson, our babysitter for the next hour, wanted us to warm up by shooting hoops.

Cisco grinned. "From your lips to God's ears. I'm so ready for all this to be over."

"No kidding." And I wasn't. Overtraining was no joke. After the Crew Classic, I was either going to sleep for a month, get sick, or both.

With that cheerful thought, we put minimal effort into the warm-up. We both knew there was a better way to warm up, and it was called an ergometer, the specialized rowing machine that dominated our sport, and we accepted no substitutes. Also, that would've been functional training for us, and I wasn't exaggerating. The Crew Classic was in two weeks, and all the rowers were hovering on the edge of overtraining. Lodestone knew it was a fine line, and he was being ultracareful. The question was, was Robertson?

After that warm-up, we shuffled into the weight room to do our thing. The cool thing about this section was not only that it was full of rowers, but it was full of *all* the rowers, both boys' and girls' junior crews. A lot of the men's crews looked upon the women's crews as prime dating material, and I didn't blame them. I'd noticed that rowers stuck to our own kind when dating. Who else understood the demands on our time? "I can't, I have crew" didn't sound like an excuse or a cop-out when you said it to another rower. Me, I regarded the presence of the women as the social hour. I didn't think my teammates realized how many of the ladies liked the other ladies. Oh well, they'd figure it out. Maybe.

At least resistance training was somewhat mindless, so long as we watched our form. At this point, I and my fellow rowers were using weight machines rather than free weights because the machines made it a little easier to let go. Machines may not have provided as good a workout as free weights, but this close to the biggest spring race, we were as strong as we were going to be. We weren't trying to build, just trying to maintain and avoid injury.

As soon as I could during weights, I got in my zone. Coach Robertson hated iPods in the weight room but was too lazy to do anything about them. I could appreciate sloth when it worked for me. Since I loathed the death metal the meatheads listened to, I dialed up a dance or alt rock playlist and tuned out. Abject misery wasn't anything I needed to share with anyone, not even my teammates. I could always pull an earbud out if it was time to visit. People assumed I wasn't paying much attention if I had my earbuds in, simply because they weren't. That often worked to my advantage.

Once in a while, I watched Mikey lift. You could tell from looking at people and the mistakes they made who'd make varsity soon and who never had a chance. He was a sophomore, and it was the end of the school year. Physically he might not have looked like much yet, but he was an ape on the ergs, pulling with a strength disproportionate to his size. Seriously, some of the guys in the varsity boats needed to be scared for their seats. They weren't, but they should be. He was an erg ninja, all stealthy and smooth, whispering in for the kill. I couldn't figure out why nobody had noticed him yet. I was fast, faster than he'd be for a while, but I had a feeling it was a good thing next year was my senior year. As soon as Mikey's stroke in the boat matched his up-and-coming erg scores? He'd row varsity.

Sometimes, however, I felt eyes on me, and when I did, they usually belonged to Mikey. Yeah, he liked to stare at me. On the one hand, it was kind of cool. The guy seemed like he was into me. Ego candy always tasted good. On the other hand, could he not look away once in a while? Maybe in the showers? I think I would have liked it better if I knew the candy didn't want to eat me back. It wasn't like I was going to say anything. I might have imagined it, and when you were a closeted gay guy in high school and your best friend was another gay guy, you kind of let things slide.

I used the leg press to practice starts at the beginning of the stroke: explode off the foot boards for a hard start. Bend those oars, dammit. My quads were ripped, nice to look at, I guess, but getting them to that point had been brutal.

"Get off that."

I looked up to see one of the meatheads from one of the sportball teams. Goff would have known which one. "Go away, Stephens. I'm using it."

"I want to use it." Stephens actually looked confused, like no one had told him no before, which I knew for a fact wasn't true. Word got around school, after all.

I nodded toward the dry-erase board behind me with my chin. "Get in line."

"Do back squats. They'll give you a nice ass. Whoever's fucking it will appreciate the effort, fag."

Ever been in a room when all conversation stopped? I'd thought it was just a figure of speech. I stared up at him. The only noise in the room was the swamp cooler and a radio playing in the background. I felt rowers around me, my tribe.

"That's pretty big talk for someone who can't figure out how to use a rubber. Do you need lessons?"

Probably not the best thing to have said to someone when I was basically trapped in a weight machine, but he had a lot of hostile witnesses. Stephens glared at me.

"Is there a problem?" Coach Robertson said, finally taking an interest in the fact that one of his jocks had made a feeble attempt at homophobic bullying.

"No, Coach," Stephens grunted.

"Too bad you didn't have the kind of aim you gave Missy during that last game before the play-offs. You might not have bungled the shot at the championships," I stage-whispered as I pulled myself up and out of the leg press.

Coach Robertson whipped his head around to glare at me while Stephens turned beet red, but there wasn't anything either could do to me because nothing I'd said was untrue. Stephens *had* bungled that shot, he *had* cost the team a shot at the state championships, and he *had* knocked up his girlfriend.

"If you were on my team, I'd never let you get away with that. Your coach will hear about this," Coach Robertson said.

"Will Vice Principal Gutslinger hear about Stephens's homophobic comments and your lack of reaction?" Cisco said.

"Class dismissed," Coach Robertson growled, waving us all out.

We all headed back to the locker rooms before the bell rang. I lacked the energy to care. It wasn't like this was the first time I'd heard crap like that or that the teachers hadn't done anything about it.

I didn't have a lot of time to shower off, but I managed to dawdle. I didn't dare risk wood. This was turning me into a nutcase. What was I saying? It already had. It was the same thing every day. First, changing and being afraid of my body's betrayal. Then weights, and finally the terror of the shower. Why couldn't I do this? They all knew I was gay and were okay with it, or most of them. So why couldn't I shower? Or maybe they only tolerated me because I didn't shower at the same time? I locked my throat so I didn't scream, but I wanted to and one of these days I would. I banged my head on my locker door instead. Yesterday I had pretended I had to go to the bathroom to kill time. My teacher for my next class had threatened to call my parents—again—if I was tardy too many more times.

By the time I got into the showers, Mikey was there waiting. He wasn't obvious or anything, but I doubted it was a coincidence. Once or twice might've been, but almost every day strained that to the breaking point. I seriously could not imagine what he saw in me.

"Dude... Remy, it's okay. It really is," Mikey said softly.

All I could do was stare at his face. I shook my head slowly, unable to speak. Mikey looked at me sadly as I washed myself as fast as I could without looking down.

But if I didn't look down, I thought as I ran to sixth period, *how do I know how big he is?*

CHAPTER
THREE

SO THAT was my life—school, crew, and casual homophobia in the People's Republic of Davis. None of this addressed my present predicament. I was almost done with my junior year of high school, and I still had this tiresome condition: still a virgin, no boyfriend, and no hope of landing one. I didn't have any proof, but I had the strangest feeling that Mikey would be more than ready to step up, but that was... weird, like my younger brother or something. If said younger brother was getting cruisy. Also, I knew I needed him as a friend, and a friend he'd stay for as long as my left hand worked. Besides, if he became my boyfriend, then people would've known I leaned that way, too, no matter how on the down low we kept things. I wasn't ready for that.

And yet.... Sure, I made noises about keeping him as a friend and thinking of him as a brother, but I was drawn to Mikey so strongly. I mean, how could I not have been? I was so lonely, and he was the only other person I knew for sure was gay. I mean, he was in the Gay Straight Alliance, and since he wasn't straight.... Then there was my undeniable attraction to him. Were I to be honest with myself, it didn't matter to me that I was a year older or he a year younger. It was like he had a hook in my nose. He could've led me anywhere. I guess it was a good thing he was such a (ahem) straight arrow. I drove myself a little crazier every day with this.

Thank God I had rowing or I would've been a total mess. No matter what else happened in my day, I always counted on the ritual of crew, starting with meeting Mikey at my car. Davis High had an open campus, meaning we could leave school whenever we weren't supposed to be in class. Lunch in town? Sure. Drive yourself to a doctor's appointment? Not a problem. Every so often some group of parents launched a campaign to close the campus, but a bit of digging revealed that their kids were the ones abusing the privilege and bringing themselves to the attention of the police. Nice try, assholes, but don't punish the rest of us because you failed Parenting 101.

Anyway, crew. I knew we were going to be worked like the dogs we were, and I never cared. That was not quite true. I cared a lot, because I looked forward to it, even needed it. In some ways the boathouse was home. I knew everyone and everyone knew me. We all contributed to something greater than the parts of the whole.

I always felt the annoyances of the day melt as we hit the road for the boathouse. It was the beginning of the ritual. Some of us changed at school, but most changed at the boathouse. The women always took the singles house, the boathouse that held the single-person boats; the men the fours house, the boathouse that held the four-seaters of various configurations.

Mikey and I changed near each other. Cisco wasn't too far away. Unlike the locker room at school, it did not matter because we had all known each other for so long. Even the new guys were absorbed quickly. I think one of the recent additions looked at me changing just after school started and said, "You're gay?" like he had a problem with it. I stood up as I was pulling on my Lycra shorts and said, "Yeah, so what?" The fact that I was taller, more muscular, and filled out my shorts better shut him down pretty quickly.

It was the ritual.

Then we took oars to the dock and started to warm up while we waited for our coaches, at least those of us who were smart did, usually with a light jog or on the rowing machines. After group exercises and warm-ups, our coaches posted the boatings. Even within the varsity squads, where a rower sat in a boat changed from practice to practice as, like in my case, Coach Lodestone moved his rowers about to see who rowed better where and which combinations of men moved boats faster. Lodestone only stopped moving us right before races, and even then he still sometimes made last-minute tweaks to lineups.

The ritual.

I came alive at the boathouse. I had given up trying to help other people understand, although my dad claimed he saw a faraway look in my eyes when I talked about rowing. I knew that had been why he'd gone to bat for me when Mom had threatened to make me quit when I'd had some trouble with my grades in the ninth grade.

"Dina, I've never seen him passionate about anything. He's passionate about this."

"But—"

"Not this time. We'll hire a tutor."

I'd learned to manage my time better, and it all sorted itself out, more or less. That was the first time I recalled Dad going to bat for me. Actually, it was the last time I remembered Dad going to bat for me. I tried to remember that when Dad worked my nerves, as during those birth-control lectures. That made it easier to remember.

Sometimes people asked me why I did it, why I put up with the demands on my time, and in all honesty, crew devoured all that free time, burped in my face, and then demanded more. I never got enough sleep, and yes, my grades suffered, even though I had dragged them back up to acceptable levels and qualified for the AP/honors track. I had no real social life and no outside interests beyond crew and whatever else I had to do to appear well-rounded on college-entrance essays.

I've talked to masters rowers, the adult members of Cap City Rowing. They took the morning shift at the boathouse. Some of them get the same distant look in their eyes talking about the sun rising on the water, the same look Dad thought he saw in my eyes when I spoke of the sun setting over those same waters. I wish I knew how to tell people that's why I did it, that's why I sacrificed everything. That was why we all did it. We bent our backs, we ripped the skin of our hands to shreds on the oar handles, we worked our muscles until we felt nothing but the blunt pain of lactic acid, we forced our heart rates up beyond our aerobic thresholds until we felt that sharp stab in our lungs only to let our pulses fall to do it again and again and again, we pushed ourselves beyond exhaustion, all in the hope that when we did it tomorrow, it might be a little easier. Because when the cox'n cried "Way 'nough!" and we gunwaled our oars and let the boat run beneath us as we looked up into the setting sun, our senses dulled with fatigue, we knew we had done our best and the sun had blessed us. Only then did we feel satisfaction.

That was why I rowed.

Only other rowers understood that.

That was the ritual of crew.

It was after one such practice, when I was still flying from the high I got from a perfect row, that I conceived the idea that helped me solve the problem of my annoying V-card.

The Crew Classic was the next weekend, but the boats left the next day. The trailer carrying them couldn't exactly drive fast, and San Diego was a long way south as it was. With the Grapevine and the pass through the Tehachapis to contend with, the truck pulling the boat trailer could only drive slow and steady.

Cap City operated under the assumption that if we rowed it, we rigged it, or de-rigged it, as the case was that afternoon. Fortunately, with both the gentlemen's and ladies' squads, as varsity men and women were called, the de-rigging went fairly quickly. Since both Coach Lodestone and Sabrina Littlewolf—the ladies' coach—planned to row a mixed double just for fun while they were down there, I was de-rigging a boat for them. The perks of being a varsity rower and the coach's pet, I guess.

The boathouse yard was controlled pandemonium—if that wasn't an oxymoron—and so the stranger's presence wasn't really an issue. No one on the junior crew knew all the masters rowers anyway, so what was one more person wandering around? That no one paid him the slightest heed probably irritated him, but no one else thought anything of it. We were busy.

Soon enough, Stranger Guy showed up in my peripheral vision, a faculty highly developed from not looking at people in locker rooms. For one thing he was hot. College age, if I had to guess, and definitely fit. The tight polo shirt he wore left little to the imagination, not that that stopped me. I already imagined a lot. He looked like he was making his way toward me. I was working by myself, and I wasn't rushing back and forth under the command of a cox'n.

I didn't want to look like I'd been watching him, because that would give the game away, but it's not like I'd been all that effective with the wrench I was allegedly employing to loosen the bolts on the riggers of the double, either. How many times did the wrench have to slip off the bolt before I could say that I was officially paying no attention at all to the de-rigging?

"Uh… excuse me?"

I pretended to be concentrating on the task at hand, but I felt his eyes on me. "Oh, hey."

"Is this the Capital City Rowing Club's boathouse?" Stranger Guy was a little shorter than me, but a lot more built, more like a lacrosse player or a wrestler than a rower. He also had the bluest eyes I'd ever seen, the kind that made you think someone wore tinted contacts, but no, they looked like his real eyes.

I shook my head. I was so glad I had a boat between us, because parts of me were sitting up and begging. "Yeah." My voice cracked. I coughed. "Yes, it is. Can I help you with something?"

"I'm looking for the Adaptive Rowing program. Do you know anything about it?" He smiled, like he'd noticed me noticing him.

"Adaptive rowing…. I'm not sure if either of the coaches are here yet, but you'll want to talk to either Nick Bedford—I think he's still in charge of it—or Brad Sundstrom." I absolutely could not breathe around either man, and the cool thing was that both men were gay, so neither could bust me for it because the chances were high both had been there themselves. Not that I appeared on their radar, and even if I had, I'd never have done anything. They wouldn't have either. They were both married, and I respected that. Their husbands or partners or whatever term they preferred were super nice guys, too. I wanted that for myself; I didn't want to break up someone else's. No, all I could do around them was stare discreetly and hope they never caught me.

Stranger Guy kind of rolled his eyes at me, like I hadn't answered his question, and maybe I hadn't. I didn't know. I found it hard to think when I looked at him. "Okay, next question. Where do I find those guys? If they're here, that is."

Guess I hadn't answered his question. I felt myself turning red. Maybe he'd think it was a sunburn? "Oh, sorry! The adaptive rowing program is housed in the singles house. It's on the other side of this building. Just follow this sidewalk," I said, pointing, "turn left at the corner and keep going. Just a couple of things. If you're not used to boathouses, boats have the right of way and 'heads up!' means duck because you're about to be hit with a boat."

"Heads up. Got it," Stranger Guy said. "What's the other one?"

"The women's teams change in the singles house, so if the door's even partially closed, make a lot of noise and knock before entering." By the end of a given year, the boundaries of who changed where got a little casual, particularly at regattas. The thrill had worn off, let's just put it that way. With the Crew Classic coming up, we'd be changing behind vans or holding towels up for each other, eyes averted. But Stranger Guy? He'd better not peek.

"Thanks for the warning," he said. "I'll go see what I can find, and thanks."

He smiled at me, and I swear my knees weakened. "No problem."

I got back to work, or at least tried. I had lost a certain amount of manual dexterity after talking to Stranger Guy. I finally set the wrench down and stilled my hands. I took a deep breath and exhaled, trying to regain my composure. I looked up to see Stranger Guy leaning against the boathouse watching me, a half smile on his face, one eyebrow raised. He wasn't just watching me, he was eye-fucking me. I knew the signs because I'd done it enough myself.

Then I realized why. After practice, I'd pulled the top of my unisuit down to cool off. Stranger Guy stared right at my chest, pecs, abs, and light dusting of hair. Like I always did, I flushed red from my forehead all the way down my chest. I felt it all heat up. I might as well have been standing there in my underwear. Boxer briefs might actually have covered more, come to think of it. There would be no hoping my blush would be mistaken for a sunburn, not this time.

I swore Stranger Guy laughed as he turned around and went about his business. *Screw you, too, buddy.* The humiliation was enough to break whatever spell Stranger Guy and lust had put me under. I yanked the straps of my uni up and got back to work, anger steadying my hand as I loosened the bolts. But who was I angrier at, Stranger Guy or myself? After all, he'd just walked up and looked me up and down. I was the one who'd started panting. Was this the kind of thing that got easier when you grew up? I sure hoped so, because this was torment, pure and simple, and the tormentor was me.

I had finished de-rigging the double. I'd wrapped the riggers with bungee cords so they'd stay together in the bottom of the boat trailer on the trip to San Diego. I had already placed the bolts and their washers and nuts back on the boat, just where they were supposed to go. It probably didn't make a whole lot of difference. If a bolt got lost, it'd just be replaced, but I did what I'd been trained to, and that was carefully match nuts to the bolts I'd taken them off of. But I had to tighten them down. Too loose and the vibrations of the truck would cause them to fall off during the drive, resulting in one or both coaches fussing at me. Too tight, and——

"You know, pulling the top up just makes it hotter."

I jumped, startled like a cat. "Jeez!"

Stranger Guy took a step back, but looked no less amused. "Sorry, didn't mean to scare you like that."

He looked anything but sorry. He had that same half smile and some kind of look in his eye that could've had me naked in minutes if I weren't so terrified. "Thanks for the directions. I found what I… wanted. My name's Josh."

Suddenly I had the feeling he wasn't talking about adaptive rowing anymore. My breath caught in my chest, like my ribs had turned into steel bands and I couldn't get any air.

"I'm—" I coughed. "—um, Remy."

"Well, Um Remy, it's great to meet you. Hopefully I'll see you around."

Stranger Guy—Josh—walked backward for a few moments to maintain eye contact, smirking. All I could do was stare. I was pretty sure my mouth hung open.

Then Josh turned around, and I snapped out of it. What had just happened? The wood in my uni knew what had happened. So why couldn't I believe it? I glanced down at the double I had just de-rigged. There was a small piece of paper that hadn't been there before.

I stared at it for what felt like forever, hardly daring to breathe, my pulse roaring in my ears.

I snatched it up before anyone else saw it. Was it… it was. A scrap of paper with a telephone number, just a number, no name. Davis, judging by the area code, and I doubted I'd ever forget his name anyway.

I should've thrown it away. I was terrified. However grown-up I felt, however ready I thought I was for this, reality hit me. I was a juvenile, a high schooler, contemplating an adult's game, and there was no way I was prepared for something like this. If I'd been asked earlier that afternoon, I'd have said yes. Right then? I think I could've thrown up. I wanted to blow chunks right there in the boatyard. I also wanted to run home and hide. But I couldn't, could I?

I was just a kid, but the thing was, Goff and I were first asked what our majors were when we were fourteen. Weird, right? Even though we were not identical, we'd had that in common from an early age. We had used it to our advantage, too. Earlier this year, we'd gotten fake IDs, although neither of us had had the balls to use them for anything. I think Geoff had toyed with the idea of buying beer for football parties but wasn't sure it was worth the hassle if he got caught. After that party with the molly bust, I couldn't blame him. Me, I'd always contemplated going to a gay club, but after my encounter at the boathouse with Josh, I threw that idea out. My reaction told me that was the last thing I was ready for, at least right then. A gay club? Jeez. I'd be terrified.

But I'd always looked old for my age, and now that I was about done with my junior year? I probably could've passed for a college student, and maybe not just a freshman. At least, that's what I hoped. Either that, or Josh was a pervert preying on underage guys, and maybe Coach Bedford or Coach Sundstrom needed to be told ASAP. I had no way of knowing.

"Hey, Remy! You about done?" Mikey said, walking up.

I'd never been more grateful to see him in my life. I shoved the slip of paper in my uni. "You bet. As soon as we get the word, we're out of here."

AS UNNERVED as I was, it's not like I dropped the pedal and drove home at ninety miles per hour to take a Silkwood shower. If nothing else, congested traffic at that time of day on the causeway connecting West Sacramento to Davis meant I was lucky to go fifty. That wasn't to say I didn't feel that scrap of paper burning against my skin as I drove, or that I didn't play Depeche Mode's "Strangelove" on a loop most of the way back to Davis.

I guess I was lucky everyone in the car knew my hang-up with eighties music, because no one threatened me with grievous bodily harm. Either that, or we'd been worked hard enough that no one had the energy to protest. My mind raced in overdrive as I kept coming back to the words "I'm always willing to learn/When you've got something to teach," only it was Josh I heard saying, "I'll make it all worthwhile."

As we pulled into Davis High's parking lot, Mikey made a face and grabbed for my iPhone. He switched it from "repeat" and changed the song. "That's enough of *that*."

I swapped out the two rowers I'd given a ride to for my brother. Goff waved his hand in front of his face. "Whoa, Eau de Sweaty Rower."

Mikey rolled his eyes but let me field that one. "Good thing football players never sweat or roll around like dogs on the lawn."

"Yes, but a water sport. Can't you guys rinse off when you're done? Maybe jump in the river?" Goff rubbed his eyes. "Seriously, I'm tearing up."

"Dude, if you'd ever come out to the boathouse, you'd never, ever say that," Mikey said.

"He's not kidding. Our coaches had the water tested. They refused to tell us the results, but the waiver our parents signed was longer the next year." Honestly, Goff played a sport that put him at risk for traumatic brain injuries, so he lacked all ground to stand on. Where did he get this stuff? Oh, wait....

We dropped Mikey off, and Goff and I drove home.

"Good practice?" I said, meeting his eyes in the rearview mirror.

He roused himself enough to reply. "Yeah. You?"

"Short and hard, then de-rigging."

He groaned. "That's right, you leave day after tomorrow. Loser."

"Shut it. You'll have the bathroom to yourself."

I parked the car in front of the house. We grabbed our gear and trudged inside. A quick round of rock-paper-scissors-lizard-Spock determined that Goff would be showering first. I flopped onto my bed, not caring about dried sweat or anything else. I'd trudge downstairs after my shower and shovel food into my face to fuel my homework hours, but right then I needed to think. I pulled Josh's number out and stared at his blocky, masculine handwriting. I did not know what I expected, to be honest. Numbers that burned themselves into my retinas before the paper consumed itself in a puff of flame? Numbers that twisted and turned before my eyes, resolving into a message that told me to abandon all such notions lest I get myself into trouble? It was just a plain scrap of paper, but it held my attention in a way few other things had.

My reactions were all over the place and not even consistent. In one way, it turned me on. It represented physical evidence that some guy was hot for me. The sight of me half-dressed had revved someone up enough to make him do something about it. The sight of me fully dressed in my uni made it more intense for him. That feeling went right to my gut, curling around my spine and groin and warming me in a way I'd never felt before. It felt... powerful. Sexy. Like maybe this gay thing could work out after all, like maybe it wasn't just going to be me and my hand for the rest of my life. Because even if nothing happened with Josh, the very fact that he'd slipped me his number now meant that someone else later on might find me worth his time, too, even if I did not understand why. I was just Remy, after all.

But that slip of paper with Josh's number scared me, too, and I knew I should've thrown it away before I'd left the boathouse. I hadn't even turned seventeen yet and wouldn't for another two months or so. When he'd asked me my name, I should have said, "Jailbait," and called him out as a fucking pervert. Hello? Look around, Josh. Notice how the boathouse is crawling with what are obviously teenagers? Just because I looked like I might've been an assistant coach didn't mean I was. But I always thought of the perfect thing to say… later. Even if on some level I needed to keep it, by keeping it I was playing that grown-up game. Sometimes acting older than my years could be good, but sometimes it could be scary, and right then it frightened me as much as it drew me in. The Voice of the Beehive had been so, so right, and oh how I wanted those scary kisses.

Finally, those numbers were seemingly my only link to an actual gay adult. In a weird way, that paper represented a lifeline to a world I knew would one day be mine, and when someone tosses you a life preserver, you don't throw it away.

CHAPTER
FOUR

I COULDN'T say the timing of the Crew Classic was great. Finals and AP tests weren't too far in the future, but between the trip down and back, I'd be missing only one day of school—leaving hours before dawn on Friday morning on charter buses rented by Cap City, we re-rigged and practiced late Friday afternoon, raced all weekend, de-rigged on Sunday afternoon, and then drove north on Sunday night. We studied when we could on the drive and in between racing and spectating, because there was no way on earth we weren't cheering each other on. I mean, come on, we were a team.

I also could not say what made this particular regatta a "classic." There had only been forty or so. Forty. My parents had furniture older than that, only those were called antiques. Some of my friends lived in houses older than that. Did that make those homes "classics"? There were cars on the road older than that. That didn't make them classics, it made them rolling slag heaps that had been grandfathered into passing California's stringent air-pollution laws. I thought about things like that on the trip south when I wasn't studying, eating artificially flavored and colored crap, or just generally being a teenager.

Sure, the club dues were expensive, but they paid for things like this. Of course, there were the parent chaperones to contend with, and they watched us like hawks. I was secretly proud of the fact that the junior crew kept its collective nose clean. The big scandal a few years ago was that some of the rowers had TPed and egged someone's house. Sure, it had been a huge mess to clean up, but considering what other kinds of trouble teenagers could be getting into—drugs, alcohol, unplanned pregnancies—toilet-paper omelets looked great in comparison.

Our coaches kept us pretty busy, and between fatigue and our grade requirements, we didn't have the time or the energy to get into real trouble. So we rode in chartered buses, pretended to do our homework, and ate gross food under the very watchful eyes of chaperones. The boys' and girls' teams weren't even staying near each other. They weren't taking chances, our coaches and parents.

I sat next to Mikey. I contemplated telling him about Josh, but didn't. Once I woke up for the day, I meant. Too many people around. Just because we all had headphones on or earbuds in didn't mean we were listening to music.

Somewhere south of Bakersfield, I'd had enough. I belched loudly and flopped over in my seat, right across whatever he was reading.

"That's disgusting."

I grinned up at him. "So?"

He considered me. "Is there something you want?"

"I'm bored. Entertain me."

It was automatic on his part, I was sure, but Mikey put one arm on my chest like it was no big deal. I tensed a little but didn't say anything. Instead I analyzed how I felt. It wasn't that bad. It felt… nice, actually. Once I got over my freak-out, I kind of relaxed into it.

"Entertain you?" Mikey said. He started brushing my bangs off my forehead. "How am I supposed to do that?"

"I don't know," I said happily. "I'm sure you'll think of something. You're Mikey."

"You could always call me Mike, you know."

I looked up at him. Where'd that come from? "I could…," I said, drawing the word out.

"Or you could keep on being the same annoying Germy we all know and loathe." Mikey sighed. He looked so serious as he looked down into my eyes, like there was something he wanted—no, needed—to tell me but couldn't right then. I couldn't discern what was on his mind, which confused me. Usually I knew what he was thinking, or could at least guess, but not this time. His hazel eyes held something different, something new. I noticed hidden depths there I had never seen before. I had no names for the things I saw, but I knew they were important, or would be some day. All I could do was stare back, although it made me increasingly uncomfortable, like he saw into my soul to the real me.

I noticed other things. His fingers were carding through my hair, his arm still on my chest, and I liked it. I reached up to touch his face—

"All right, you two lovebirds, break it up," someone called as he shuffled by, and the mood was broken.

Mikey and I blinked. I sat up in a hurry. The bus had stopped at some truck stop on the 5 in the middle of nowhere. Mikey stood and joined the line of people walking off the bus. He didn't look back, leaving me to wonder what had just happened, and more than that, what it meant.

I WISH I could say I wouldn't spend the rest of the weekend obsessing over our weird exchange, but I knew that's exactly what I'd do, at least during idle moments. Thankfully there weren't too many of those, but really, I had to wonder what was going on. Was I leaking pheromones or something? Because until this past week, people had proven pretty resistant to my so-called charms. When I looked in the mirror, I still saw plain ol' Remy. Whatever, I was just grateful I had a major regatta to distract me, because if nothing else, I would be too exhausted to spin my wheels over it. Or so I hoped.

Speaking of wheels, the bus pulled into the race venue midafternoon on Friday, or at least as close as it could get, before heading out for the houses where the boys' and girls' teams would be staying, where parent chaperones/volunteers would unload our gear for us and leave it in a huge heap for us to sort out. They were fantastic, but they couldn't be expected to do everything, right? All we kept was our backpacks, plus some workout clothes. We still had plenty of time to fit in a practice row, or go for a run, or check out the race venue. I planned to do all three.

For such a major regatta, the venue itself didn't occupy a lot of real estate, just a few blocks along Crown Point Shores on Mission Bay. The view of the bay was incredible, and the houses overlooking it? I bet they cost millions, but for that weekend I almost wished I lived up there. At the very least, I'd get a bird's-eye view of the entire venue, like the judges' stand and VIP enclosure at the halfway mark right on the beach and the Jumbotrons bracketing them on either end for the less exalted spectators seated in the grass. Across the main walkway from the judges' stand and VIP pen were the vendors and food booths. Sometimes during the weekend, I'd hit the official T-shirt stand. I always bought one for Goff (he always got a baseball cap, too), and this year I planned to buy a shirt for Laurel. Goff might've been my primary antagonist, but he was also my brother, and we were closer to each other than anyone else, and Laurel was such a sweetheart. Oh yeah, and Mom and Dad. They footed the bill for this adventure, after all, and they needed something to show for having one of their spawn in crew.

I had another reason for checking out the venue. I'd developed this weird ritual over the years. One of the first things I did at any regatta was walk as much of the course as I could. It wasn't too long before I heard footsteps behind me.

"Wait up, Remy."

I glanced over my shoulder and there was Cisco. Most of our boat trailed along behind him, along with a few of the junior varsity, the smarter ones. That included Mikey. "You walking the course?" Cisco said.

"I'm out here, aren't I?" *Seriously, don't ask stupid questions.*

Cisco flicked one of my ears. "Don't be an ass."

"Ow!" I rubbed the shell of my ear. "That goes for you, too."

"So what do you think?" Cisco asked me as we gazed out at the course.

I snorted. "What do I think? I think it looks great… right now."

And it did. The weather was gorgeous. With any luck, it would hold, but on the coast the weather could change with minimal provocation. I'd seen it turn nasty in the middle of a race weekend, and this was only my third Crew Classic. So had the Cap City coaches, according to the stories they told. All the rowers had had to sit through those stories enough times that we could sing along as our coaches recited them.

I looked at Cisco and the rest of our boat slyly. "Know what else I think? I think we need to get the JVs up here and make *them* identify what'll turn rough if the weather goes to hell."

Jack, our three seat, grinned. "Excellent idea." He turned to the junior varsity rowers. "Front and center, children!"

They looked at each other nervously. As a rule, Cap City's junior crew didn't haze, but I guess they thought there was a first time for everything.

"Now, now, none of that," I said. "We're walking the course to see what could potentially bite us in the ass during the race, especially if the weather turns feral."

"But you guys have all been here before," one of them said.

Cisco nodded. "Yes, we have, but every year's different."

"And if the weather turns, it won't matter whether we have any experience here or not, it'll be entirely new and definitely unfriendly," I said. "So c'mon. All the way to the start line, or as close as we can get. You'll see what I mean. Pay attention to the course. See if you can spot any potential problems."

"Knowledge is power. Seriously, if you're prepared for potential problems, you won't be spooked when your cox'n calls them out," Jack said.

Mikey nodded. I think he was as close to a team captain as the JV had. "It can't hurt. Let's humor them."

"So what do you see?" Cisco said.

"The sidewalk ends," one of the JVs said. "This is as far as we can go."

As far as observations went, this was along the lines of noticing an aircraft carrier bearing down on you. The sidewalk gave out around the five-hundred-meter mark. If we kept walking, we'd get wet.

"So. This is where the sidewalk ends. There's a bit of a breeze, but it's a gorgeous afternoon, right?" I nodded encouragingly. "So take a look out there. Tell me how big you think those swells are."

We all looked out to the bay, or to the sheltered part of it that we could see, that part that we'd be racing on tomorrow. Our backs were to the bridge over the bay.

"One foot, maybe?" Mikey said.

Cisco shrugged. "That's as good a guess as any. I wouldn't be comfortable sculling out there, not even in an open-water craft."

I turned around and pointed to the bridge. "We were looking at sheltered water. Over there is the rest of the bay and eventually the ocean. So what happens if the wind comes up? What kind of chop do you think we're going to get at the five-hundred-meter mark? What kind of crosswind?"

"Point made," Mikey said. The rest of his squad nodded.

"This is why I walk the course, or at least what of it I can get to," I said, "even on a course I'm familiar with. Or take a course like Lake Natoma. It's in our backyard, relatively speaking, but the conditions change depending on what the runoff from the Sierra Nevadas is or what the dam operators have been doing to the water levels. It changes within a season."

So we walked back to where we expected our boat trailer to park, trying to spot potential problems to set the less experienced rowers' minds at ease with possible solutions to different contingencies. We couldn't predict everything, but that wasn't the point, not for my race-course walks and not for taking the JVs with us. I did it as part of my race preparations, and Cisco wanted to include the junior varsity to allay their anxieties.

Cisco caught up to me afterward. "Let's see if the novice coaches cotton on to this."

"I wonder if Lodestone or Littlewolf have mentioned anything about this to them?" I said. "I guess that'd be a way to find out if they think it's of any value."

"Even if they don't, we get value out of it, and that's all that matters," Cisco said. He paused. I could tell he was building up to something. "So… what's up with you and Mikey?"

I thought about that for a moment. "I have absolutely no idea."

"So the bus…."

"Your guess is as good as mine." Interesting that people—okay, one person—were asking me about it already. We hadn't even been off the bus more than a couple of hours.

Fortunately, the trailer and re-rigging awaited us all. Normally re-rigging's a chore, but at that moment? Never happier to get my chores done.

AFTER THE gentlemen's crew fit an hour or so of light rowing in, we made it back to our temporary accommodations. The team had rented what looked like mansions, and I assumed the girls' teams found themselves in similar accommodations somewhere in the vicinity of Mission Bay. I hadn't had time to text my friends on the ladies' crew yet. Anyway, we stayed in huge places, eight or ten rooms at least, plus a lot of floor space. I was sure the neighbors loved the buses showing up, but at least they didn't stick around long after dropping us off.

Our gear was in an enormous heap, but the other squads had saved us some room. Or maybe it was the coaches and chaperones. Whatever. I was too tired and hungry to care at that point.

Food me, already.

Team dinners…. I hated to say it, especially given how much I loved my team, but I hated team dinners. I've heard some stupid saying about a committee being a creature with forty-eight legs—that was three varsity boats, eight rowers each, two legs apiece—and no head. That pretty much summed up team dinners. With food allergies, dietary preferences, and people acting like princesses thrown in, we were lucky we managed to eat at all. It was not like I believed in very much at all or for very long, but all I could say was thank God or whomever for the parent volunteers who cooked all the nights we were down there. They spared us all of that. Not only was cooking in cheaper than eating out—and this sport was freakin' expensive enough as it was—but it tasted better. So that first night down there, they fed us pasta, lots and lots of pasta.

After dinner the varsity rowers cycled through the showers to clean the bay off of us. Saltwater didn't feel all that good when it dried. Most of us headed to bed after that. Most of us. I waited until things were quiet and then texted Mikey.

R: *You awake?*

He must've been because he replied almost immediately.

M: *Yep.*
R: *Feel like talking?*
M: *Meet U upstairs on the roof.*
R: *???*
M: *There's a patio up there.*
R: *OK*

Five minutes later, there we were, both dressed in sweats to ward off the evening chill. Mikey's devoured him, making him look somehow vulnerable.

"Hi," Mikey said softly.

I had a feeling it wasn't because we were trying not to get caught by our chaperones.

"Hi." I waved diffidently. I carefully lifted up a deck chair and set it next to his. "So…."

"So?"

I sighed. "Are we okay?"

"What do you mean?"

No, that wasn't evasive or anything. "I feel like we've been avoiding each other since the bus."

Mikey sighed. "I don't get you."

"Cut the crap, junior—"

He put his hand over my mouth. "No, I mean I don't get what you want. At school, we're friendly, but you almost seem like you don't want to be around me sometimes. Then you lie down in my lap on the bus. You have to admit those are some pretty mixed signals."

"You're my friend. You are, Mikey." I didn't say anything for a few moments. "Maybe that's because I'm still trying to figure out whether we're supposed to be friends or something more. But I don't want to lose you as a friend." I thought for a minute. "I can't."

"Me neither." His voice was barely above a whisper.

I picked up his arm and tugged on it until he got the hint and climbed into my chair, into my lap. I might not have known between friend and boyfriend, but I needed to hold him, and maybe he needed to be held. I put my arms around him and rested my head on his shoulder.

"But Remy?"

"Yeah?"

"If we're friends or something else?"

"Yeah?"

"Could you at least call me Mike? Mikey's a six-year-old's name."

CHAPTER
FIVE

WE EVIDENTLY fell asleep up on the roof, because that's where one of the chaperones found us when we were late for breakfast. We stumbled downstairs, red-faced as all of the men's squads—novice, junior varsity, and varsity—turned to face us and gave us that slow applause thing. Mikey's coach glared at him, but I could tell Lodestone was faking it, if only by the eye roll he gave me. That didn't mean I wasn't going to hear about it later, however.

Our tardiness aside, breakfast was a hurried affair because Saturday was a busy day for races. All the heats took place on Saturday, as well as repechage for the losers. Since conditions could vary so much from heat to heat due to things like wind or tides, and since only the top two finishers from each heat went on to the finals, regattas that included heats typically also included a heat for the fastest of the "losers," and that was the repechage round. A two-thousand meter race might not take long—typically between six and eight minutes (and the crew better have had mechanical issues like a broken oar for that eight-minute time)—but it took a lot out of a crew, and more than one heat in a day meant rest, rehydration, and careful management of nutrition and electrolytes in between. By late morning, it wasn't unusual to find crews flopped out under their boats, half-asleep.

That's exactly what I did between my heats, only I couldn't sleep. How could I, with Mikey churning in my mind? Well, Mikey and Josh, if I were being strictly honest. All I could do was rest under the boat with my eyes closed and my earbuds in so I looked like I was out cold, but then, weren't all closeted teens masters of camouflage? Or semicloseted, in my case. I had no idea what to do, none whatsoever. I tried telling myself that I didn't have to *do* anything, that simply because Josh gave me his number didn't mean I had to call him. Likewise, just because Mikey—Mike—and I were trying to find our way, it didn't necessarily follow that we had to jump right into anything. I was almost seventeen. He would turn sixteen just before school let out for the summer. The problem was, I didn't—couldn't—listen. I felt a stress, a pressure, driving me forward.

I took the slip of paper with Josh's number out of my wallet. It was well-worn after being looked at so many times by now, but that didn't matter. I had memorized the numbers, and I could have recited them backward in my sleep. I'd even entered them in my contacts list and then password protected my phone. In fact, I'd used Josh's number as the password. That password protection more than anything might trip me up by proclaiming I had something to hide. I'd never protected my phone before, but between that number and Grindr, I didn't want Goff or anyone exploring my phone anymore. Yeah, I'd downloaded Grindr. It was all a part of my plan to see what was out there. I had no intention of setting up a profile. Not yet, at any rate, and there was no way I could've done anything at the regatta even if I hadn't been too afraid to. I didn't just have parent chaperones and coaches keeping an eye on me, I had the entire junior crew. I was even too nervous to stop by the Gay+Lesbian Rowing Federation's booth, and my crew knew I was gay. Fooling around? Ha!

But I did load Grindr once. Holy hell. My phone almost exploded.

I DIDN'T sleep or play possum all the time. I watched races I wasn't in, like those of colleges I wanted to attend. Coach Lodestone told me he had been in contact with coaches at those schools all year. My performance at the Youth Nationals later this summer would clinch any deals and possibly secure an early admission or two, but I knew there had been eyes on me during the heats. Since I had not known who, when, or where, I had managed not to freak out, but it had been added pressure. If any of those coaches had joined Lodestone to watch my races, they had disappeared by the time those races ended, saving me from mortification, but only temporarily. Lodestone took me around to meet all of them.

I also watched Mikey's races. I had my eye on him, and not just because I was trying to figure out what we were to each other. I stood next to Lodestone while Mikey raced. I liked him as a person, but more important, I respected him as a coach. Then there was the undeniable hotness factor. Okay, I came into my height early, but Lodestone? He rowed at the University of Washington, and the Huskies grow them big up there or something. Lodestone was not only way over six feet tall, but Goff once told me Lodestone looked more like he was built for certain positions in football that took bulk and muscles than for crew, which needed lean strength. I mean, his shoulders were out to there. Also, he was hairy in all the right places, like beard-shadow-right-after-shaving hairy. It was awesome. He was also straight as a plank. The only thing that kept me from hating his girlfriend was that she was not only brilliant, but she was sweet as she was smart. I mean, she was deaf, and I'd started learning some basic sign language—she was that beautiful a person. Or I had that big a case of hero worship for my coach. It could've gone either way.

Lodestone watched the races and didn't acknowledge my presence. I didn't take it personally. This was his job, after all. "Do your prerace walk while you were waiting for the trailer?" he said eventually.

At least he knew I was there. I lived for these moments with my coach. It felt like he treated me as an equal, even if only for a little while. "Coach. Please."

He laughed. "What was I thinking? Of course you did."

"And dragged most of my boat along for the ride. Something new this year, though."

"Oh?" He finally glanced down at me.

"Cisco dragged Mikey and some of the other junior varsity with us."

Lodestone didn't say anything for a moment. "Interesting. What do you think they got out of it?"

I glanced at my watch and then checked the schedule. I looked out at the water, squinting through the glare of the afternoon sun. There they were. There he was. "He's varsity next year."

"Oh, you think so, do you, Coach Babcock?" Lodestone said, laughing.

I flushed. "No, seriously. If you haven't watched him on the ergs, you're falling down on the job—"

"Strong words, oarsman."

I stood my ground. "They're true, sir. His numbers have dropped steadily this season. At the same time, his erg technique has improved. He's a match for anyone on our squad."

"Ergs don't float." Lodestone's voice was quiet, almost too quiet, like he was getting angry or I'd just overstepped my bounds, but dammit, he was the one who'd encouraged me to watch and analyze other rowers. If he didn't like the results, he had only himself to blame.

"No, they don't, but boats do, and you're watching his *right now*, same as me. Tell me you don't see someone who's better than most of his boat," I said, "and he's in the A boat."

Lodestone stayed silent, watching the rest of the race through binoculars. I didn't have any, so I could only follow Mikey until they passed beyond my ability to make out any useful detail.

"Perhaps I was too hasty in my dismissal," Lodestone said, dropping his binoculars at last. "You've given this a lot of thought, and more importantly, you've been watching his form." He eyed me appraisingly. "And here I thought you'd just been watching his body."

I turned red, and not just red, scalded lobster red. Even as a kid, I had blushed hard. "Guess you heard?"

"You could say that." Lodestone put his arm across my shoulder, laughing. He had a ready laugh, at least with me. "Remy, if you don't want anyone to know, you shouldn't cuddle on the team bus. Then there was breakfast this morning. If it's any consolation, the entire girls' team thinks it's adorable. The boys' team is a bit more divided. Varsity backs you, like it always has. Junior varsity? That's another issue, but word on the street is there's more than one rower who's simply jealous."

"Aww, jeez." I had only thought I couldn't be any more embarrassed. "Wait… of who, me or Mikey?"

Lodestone snickered. "Like I'd tell you. Just enjoy it, okay? That's part of the fun of being young. Now, about your outspoken advocacy…."

"Hey, you taught me to watch other rowers and made me ride in launches to observe," I said.

"Yes, but I never thought it'd come back to bite me in the ass this soon."

THE REST of the weekend passed in a blur of lactic acid and fatigue. The ladies' crews fared well, and while two of the three gentlemen's boats advanced from their heats, we were handed our asses in the finals. Some of it was the weather, which had turned overnight, some of it was our boys getting sick, and some of it we were just overmatched. What that might have done to my chances at recruitment, I couldn't say, but by the end of the weekend, I was too tired to overthink it. I knew Lodestone was disappointed, but the fact was we rowed the best races we had in us. Sure, we were let down, who wouldn't be? But we had no regrets, and that was the important thing. Mikey's junior varsity boat placed second for their cup. He kept muttering that second place meant first loser, and I made a note to myself to cut that off at the ankles as soon as I had a chance. That kind of talk was poison.

As it turned out, between the chaos of de-rigging and loading the trailer and then piling on the buses and hitting the road, I didn't have that chance for some time. We ended up avoiding sitting with each other. As it turned out, that bothered me. Were we friends or not? If so, why the hell weren't we sitting together? The messed-up part of it was that we spent the trip firing texts at each other. It would've been easier if we'd just sat next to each other.

Then there was all the eye-fucking. Jeez, we were stupid.

R: *Lodestone told me there was a bunch of people on your squad who were jelly of one of us.*
M: *WHO???*
R: *He wouldn't tell me :-/*
M: *A-hole*
R: *IKR?*
M: *We should've sat together and then looked around 2 see who gave us the stink eye.*
R: *Too late now unless we want 2 cause more talk.*
M: *I don't care.*
R: *Me neither.*
M: *You wanna?*

I got up and evicted Mikey's seatmate with the excuse of needing Mikey's help with my History Day project. I got a notebook out and turned the overhead light on for effect because I'm sneaky that way. Not that I ended up looking at it or anything.

"Hi," I whispered as I got comfortable.

He looked at me, his eyes soft. "Hi."

I nudged my leg up against his. I was too tired to try for subtlety, but he didn't seem to mind.

We never even looked around. Mikey fell asleep, head on my shoulder. It didn't take me long to join him. That's what came of exhausting ourselves for forty-eight hours, I guess.

THE PROBLEM with falling asleep was that I didn't study. The problem with the timing of the Crew Classic in early April was that those of us in our junior year had barely a month's lull in school before we took the last set of exams before AP tests and then finals. Maybe the junior varsity didn't need to worry too much about AP tests, but I sure did. Those tests made a difference for me. Same with my grades. This was the last hurrah for me, because the results of both would determine which colleges I could apply to and would have a chance of getting into. My less than stellar grades sophomore year needed papering over. I ate stress for all three meals each day after the Crew Classic, and it didn't stop until school let out. I swore I lived on acid blockers. Fortunately, the Crew Classic was the last regatta of the school year, and Lodestone knew the score. The juniors on the gentlemen's crew didn't exactly coast, but the intensity wasn't what it had been for me, at least until school ended.

As much as possible, I put all thoughts of Mikey, relationships, Josh, and my plan on the back burner. I'm not sure Mikey understood why, but right then, I didn't care. I couldn't. Goff was lucky. Laurel was in the same boat he and I were, and the three of us turned our dining room into a homework gulag. Mom and Dad were good sports about it, too. They kept the house quiet as a tomb for us and put all thoughts of entertaining on hold so we didn't have to move anything out of the dining room. We did our best to repay them by keeping the mess under control and removing anything related to tests and projects we had finished, and by expressing our earnest gratitude for any and all homemade food. I know teenagers had the rep for being selfish, self-centered, and immature, and there was truth to that, but I'd like to think the three of us showed our better selves to Mom and Dad during that high-stress time.

Finally the school year and regular rowing season ended, and not long after that, Goff and I turned seventeen. Then the hard work began. Some of us on the Cap City junior crew, myself included, had qualified for the Youth National Championships, so summer break? Sure, I'd be taking a class at City College, but I'd be logging many, many meters in a single without worrying about the fuss and bother of school. I just kept telling myself this was a once-in-a-lifetime opportunity, but between crew and a summer job at the boathouse, I should've forwarded my mail to the port, because I would see more of the Cap City boathouse than I would the Babcock house.

Mikey and I met up for lunch about a week after school got out. I think we both slept that entire week, save for a few text messages.

"So what's the plan for this summer?" Mikey asked over Chinese food.

I shrugged. "Not much of one, really. SAT prep to boost my scores. A class at City College to pad my college applications and make next year a little easier. And, oh yeah, sculling until Lodestone takes pity on me and puts me out of my misery. You?"

Mikey snorted. "Which means never. He won't rest until you're standing on the podium at the Nationals."

I groaned and slumped down in my seat. Mikey responded by kicking me under the table. "None of that. You know you want it just as much, or you wouldn't put up with it."

"Ow." I rubbed my shins. "You've got sharp toes."

He rolled his eyes. "Suck it. What're you taking at City College?"

"US Government. It's required and it's only a semester, so I might as well get it over with. You?" But him telling me to suck it? So not the thing to say, especially since I had seen him in the showers, because that was exactly where my mind went.

"US History," he said around a mouth full of sweet and sour chicken. Keep it classy there, Mikey.

"No AP History?"

He shrugged. "I'd rather get it over with this summer, and I can still take the AP test."

"Good point. I kind of wish I'd done that, now that you mention it." I thought about it some more. "It might've made last year easier."

"That's kind of what I'm hoping after watching you. You seemed pretty stressed."

Stressed did not even begin to cover it, but it was not all academics. How could I tell him what I really wanted to do was lure him into a dark corner? And that was new. I'd need to examine that sometime, maybe after I was done examining him.

Talk turned away from academics to rowing. Big surprise, since we both had it bad. We made plans to get up early in the morning and scull, and by early we meant 7:00 a.m. or so. That gave us time before classes started. It was also what passed for a relaxed summer in education-obsessed Davis.

It would make for a pleasant few weeks, at least until Cap City's various learn-to-row camps started, along with the ongoing adaptive rowing clinics. Lodestone had asked me to help coach the junior crew's learn to row, but I'd already been tapped by Coach Sundstrom to help with his adaptive program, and that would be my summer job. Besides, Lodestone pretty much owned my ass as it was, since the only way I wouldn't embarrass myself at the Youth Nationals would be long hours in a single while he cracked a whip, possibly literally.

Once camp, classes, and SAT prep started, I'd be busier than a one-armed fan dancer. I kept telling myself that it would be a *different* kind of busy than the school year. Sometimes I thought my delusions were the only thing that pulled me through. I wished I could have said that Goff was the smart one, but he planned to spend his summer the same way. The only difference was that he followed a different schedule—SAT prep in the morning, followed by working out and classes in the afternoon, and his job in the evening.

The summer looked to be a long one.

CHAPTER
SIX

SUMMER CLASSES at City College had started the week before, and already Mikey and I had midterms to study for. That was the joy of compressed summer sessions. Neither of us wanted to face any of the libraries that were open, so one Thursday we opted for my house, specifically my bedroom. We curled up on my bed, head to toe, bracketed by the head- and footboards. Mikey wrapped his arm around my feet, and I wrapped mine around his. We were cozy and studying. With snacks and drinks within easy reach, we were set for the afternoon. Since the subject matter overlapped—American government and the first half of the US history sequence—we took turns quizzing each other.

I guess it looked suspiciously like sixty-nine, but neither of us went there. Goff must've, however, because when he barged in without knocking, he stopped dead. "Oh. I didn't… that is, I—"

I looked up from my notes, mildly annoyed by the interruption. "Yes?"

By that time Goff had turned bright red. "I didn't mean to interrupt anything, guys. I'm sorry. I didn't know you two were—"

"Studying?" Mikey said, one eyebrow arched, clearly amused.

I seriously thought my brother was going to swallow his tongue. "Uh… yeah. Studying."

"Is there something I can help you with?" I said.

Goff—or should I have called him Goof?—looked relieved. "I'm heading to work, but the car's low on gas. If I leave you a twenty and take the scooter, will you promise not to hate me?"

In addition to the car, our parents had also bought us a Vespa to share, figuring that between the two we could and would make it work.

"Sure, no sweat. Thanks for the warning. I may bike to SAT prep tonight and then gas the car up tomorrow on the way to the port if that's okay. I'll drop it off before class."

Goff looked relieved. "I just didn't want to leave you in the lurch with a car low on gas. See you guys later."

Mikey and I waited until his footsteps faded and then burst out laughing. "You realize he thinks we're dating, right?" Mikey said.

I nodded, still snickering. "That look on his face? Priceless."

"I guess I'm out to him," I said. "Or he thinks I am."

"How do you feel about that?"

The thought frightened me, but also relieved me a little. Of course, this assumed he hadn't heard anything around school, which as I thought about it had to be a near-impossibility. "I'd have to tell him sooner or later, but honestly? I've hated keeping it from him. But just because you and I are affectionate doesn't mean we're together."

"True."

I went back to my studying, but I felt Mikey's eyes on me before he picked up his book. Then I started thinking about us, about our dancing around the possibility of actually dating, along with our affection toward each other on the trip to San Diego. We had certainly been an item, even if only an item of confusion. We never figured out who we had made jealous, but my feelings where Mikey was concerned were still conflicted.

I looked back up at him. "You ever think about being together? Going out, I mean."

"Yeah." Mikey closed his book and met my eyes. He had the most amazing hazel eyes. How come I had never noticed that? "But I'm saving myself for the right guy at the right time if that makes sense."

And apparently that wasn't me, despite our weekend in San Diego, despite everything that led up to it. Apparently it had all been in my head. Given my pre-Crew Classic ambivalence about being out and about with Mikey, I couldn't figure out why I felt like he'd just kicked me in the stomach. But that's what it felt like—like I should be vomiting blood.

I faked a smile. "Me too, I guess."

"Remy, are you okay?"

I smiled at Mikey and forced myself to meet his eyes. "Why wouldn't I be?"

"Just checking."

We both went back to our studying, but there was a weird current in the air. Uh... duh?

"So," I said eventually, "did I ever tell you what happened while we were de-rigging for the Crew Classic?"

"No, as a matter of fact, you didn't. You been holding out on me?"

I snorted. "You could say that. Some guy came up to me wanting information about the adaptive rowing program."

Mikey thought for a moment. "As I recall, you were about half-dressed while you were de-rigging the double for Coach Lodestone. I can't wait to hear how this sorted out."

"Dude, we were all half-dressed."

"The girls weren't half-dressed."

"Whatever. Do you want to hear about this?"

"Yes, I think I do."

So I started in on Stranger Guy's story. "Anyway, after I told him where to find the adaptive-rowing info, I looked up from de-rigging, and he was just leaning against the boathouse staring at me." I shook my head at the memory, hoping I could hide the wood I felt growing.

"Are you serious?" Mikey said. "You didn't show him yourself?"

"Of course not, I was de-rigging a boat." I shook my head. Honestly, where did he get this stuff?

"Was he hot?" Mikey asked.

"Totally."

Mikey leaned forward and smacked my forehead.

"Ouch! What was that for?" I rubbed the spot he'd smacked.

"Because a hot guy asked you for directions and then turned and watched you, and *you kept de-rigging a boat*. You're hopeless."

Was he for real? "Okay, so what should I have done?"

"Followed him? Offered to help him out?" Mikey sighed. He gave me a funny look, one I couldn't decipher. His eyes looked bright, but he wasn't crying. Whatever. Why did people have to be so confusing? I realized then that I would never figure Mikey out.

"Okay, but with what? I'd already given him perfectly clear directions to the singles house, and I'm pretty sure that's where Coach Bedford keeps the adaptive rowing program."

"Oh, for the love of…. You know, for someone who's so desperate to get laid, you sure are dense," Mikey snapped. "To answer your question, anything he wanted."

I guess Mikey was right, but what I failed to understand was his attitude. He stared at me like he was sad but also kind of angry. What the hell? He literally just shot me down for a relationship or even casual dating. One of these years, I might learn to keep my mouth shut, because apparently no good ever came of me talking. Boats made so much more sense.

What confused me the most, however, was Mikey's vibe. I'd never felt this kind of hostility from him.

THERE WAS a wonderful eighties band called Toy Matinee. It produced only a single eponymous album, and the band never received the attention it deserved, at least in my opinion. But with tracks devoted to Vaclav Havel, Salvador Dali, and Madonna? I was all over it. I lived my life through eighties music. Why think when I could find a lyric to express an idea for me? Toy Matinee wrote very intelligent lyrics. No wonder they didn't last long. "Last Plane Out," the one song that got any airplay, contained a lyric that held special meaning for me: "Greetings from Sodom, how we wish you were here…." Actually, I thought the entire song was brilliant, but that part especially. *Greetings from Sodom!* I could see it on a postcard. There was also a song on the album called "There Was a Little Boy," and one line in particular jumped out at me: "… he finds what he needs with an older boy," and it looked like that would be coming to pass for me.

Yep, I was going to call Josh. Eventually. As soon as I found my balls, because the entire thought scared the crap out of me. But what had been the purpose, I asked myself over and over, of keeping his number—let alone entering it into my phone—if I never intended to use it? I could say whatever I wanted about a lifeline to the one adult gay man I knew of, but couldn't I just as easily have gone and bought a copy of *Instinct* or *DNA* or *Out* or something? I didn't think those were kept behind counters or anything like that. But maybe those weren't the same, and I was just stalling.

So I set myself a deadline of when I would call Josh because otherwise I knew I never would. I promised myself that I would call him the following Monday, which made it four days after Mikey went rogue on me and allowed me to get through my midterm without thinking about any of it. Compartmentalization was my friend. The only problem was once I had finished my exam. Then I faced a weekend of adaptive rowing while ignoring Mikey and strange looks from Lodestone, to say nothing of Goff.

"Where's Mikey?" Goff said. We were standing in the kitchen on Sunday afternoon, the only time we were both free at the same time all week.

How was I supposed to explain to Goff that what he had seen not only didn't mean what he thought it did, but also that I had done something—I didn't know what—to alienate Mikey? Thinking about it still stung.

"At home, I guess."

"I thought you two were…."

"Were what, Goff?" I looked at him with wide-eyed, vacuous innocence. I didn't intend to make this easy on him.

"Were, uh… you know," he said urgently.

"No, I really don't."

Turning redder by the second, Goff grabbed my arm, dragged me out of the kitchen, and threw me into the downstairs bathroom, closing the door behind us. Then he switched on the fan, just to cover anything we said.

"You know damn well what I mean, *Germy*. I walked in, and you two were crawling all over each other."

"We were not." I laughed. "We were *studying*. If you think that's sex, Laurel must be very frustrated. Also, why do I keep buying you condoms?"

"Don't try to distract me." Goff shoved me against the door.

"Damn, that hurt! Knock it off," I said, pushing him back.

Goff held up his hands. "Okay, I'm sorry. I didn't mean to hurt you, okay?"

It was a good thing Goff hadn't meant to hurt me. I'd hate to feel intentional damage. I had forgotten just how strong my brother was. I rubbed the back of my head where it had hit the door. "Next time you want my attention, just rack me, okay? It won't hurt as much."

"I said I was sorry."

I sighed. I had no idea why we were even going through this farce. Goff had to know the answer to what he was asking. I mean, how could he not? "What do you really want to know?"

Like I couldn't have guessed.

"Remy… are you gay?"

I looked at him closely. He looked miserable, and that was one thing I hadn't expected. I glanced at the floor. Somehow I couldn't look my brother in the face. "Yeah, I think I am," I said softly.

"You know it's okay, right? With me, I mean?"

My throat felt thick, and it was hard to breathe, like I was starting to cry. I didn't want to cry. I didn't want to talk about this. I didn't want to be gay, even though I knew I was. I hadn't chosen this, but right at that moment, it didn't matter. It set me apart from everyone I knew, everyone but Mikey, and he wasn't speaking to me.

I jumped when I felt him touch my face, but Goff lifted my chin up so he could see my eyes. "It's okay."

"How can you say that?" I said thickly. "You're not gay. You don't have to worry about Mom and Dad freaking out. Your future is what you think it will be. Mine? I have to face losing everyone."

I heard him sniffle. "Not me. You'll always have me."

Then he grabbed me and held me. I hesitated, but then I hugged him back. I didn't know how long we were in the bathroom sobbing into each other's shoulders, but it didn't matter. That's why we had each other.

"Thanks," I said when I looked up at last.

He snickered. "Guess I should've listened when you said you really weren't interested in Laurel."

"Jackass." I shoved him. Then I glanced in the mirror. "We look awful. Neither of us has the coloring for this."

Goff laughed weakly. "You're horrible."

"I know." I hesitated. "Thanks, Goff. You don't know how much this means to me."

"I think I do. You've had my back for so long. I've been waiting to have yours." Goff paused. "You seem like you're made of ice, like you don't need anyone, but it's not true, is it?"

I shook my head. "No, but when you're hiding something…."

"No hiding anymore. You've got me and Mikey, and I know for a fact Laurel won't care. She's said as much—"

"Mikey and I aren't together, remember?" I laughed. What else could I do?

"Really? But I saw—"

"I know, but we're just friends, I promise. Or I think we *were* friends. I'm not sure what's going on. We were pretty tight at the Crew Classic, and I honestly thought we were heading for more, but turned out I was wrong." That cut like a knife, and I was tired of that, but I didn't have the first clue what to do. Pounding on his door was out, since Mikey had made his feelings clear. So was imitating John Cusack in that eighties movie in which he stood outside his love interest's house blasting some Peter Gabriel song on an impossibly large tape player, if only because I didn't make a fool out of myself very well.

Goff looked at me through narrowed eyes. "But why's he mad at you?"

"I really don't know, and I'm too tired to care right now. It'll sort itself out or it won't, but I do know one thing...."

"Yeah?"

I nodded. "If he wants to row this summer, he'll pull the stick out of his butt. He's too young for a key to the boathouse."

Goff laughed. "You were always a practical one."

"Guilty as charged, I guess." Then something occurred to me. "We've been in here long enough to raise suspicions."

"I guess, but we really don't talk like this anymore, do we?"

I would never have expected Goff to say something like that, but maybe that only showed how long it had been since my brother and I had shared anything. "I'll try to be more open in the future."

Goff cocked his head. "You think it's because—"

"The closet wraps everything in secrets. I have to think about everything I say. It's a relief that you know." It was, too.

"What about Mom and Dad?"

I shook my head. "I have to tell them in my own time." I shuddered, and not for effect. "Can you imagine Dad's response? He can barely stand me as it is."

"Remy...." Goff looked so sad. "That's not true. You can't say things like that."

"You've always gotten along better with them than I have, especially Dad. You know that. Just... please don't say anything."

"They won't hear it from me." I could tell he was troubled by what I'd said, but it was the truth and it always had been. He'd never wanted to see it, and I hated bringing it up. He was the one person in the world I was closest to. I never did understand why some people didn't get along with their brothers or sisters, but then, I bought my brother condoms, so we clearly had an unusual relationship in the first place.

Just before we left the bathroom, Goff elbowed me. "So, if you and Mikey aren't an item, I guess I won't have any competition for the rubbers."

"It's not looking that way, is it?"

MONDAY CAME and went, and naturally I never called Josh. I was too busy chewing my liver out about the entire thing. I knew I had a reputation for ice water in place of blood and nerves of steel. I'd heard it from Goff and Mikey, among others. But a lot of it was talk. A good rep meant a lot of avoided nonsense, but I had always liked to imagine there'd been a bit of truth to it. So where was that kernel? It was Friday night right before SAT prep, and I only had flop sweat to show for my efforts. That was me, a legend in my own mind.

Okay, enough was more than enough. I pulled out my phone.

R: *Hey, remember me? It's Remy from the Cap City Boathouse. I gave you directions.*

Then I turned my phone off and spent the next two hours learning how to boost my SAT scores.

CHAPTER
SEVEN

OH, JOSH remembered me, all right. First of all, my phone lit up—lit up like Times Square on New Year's Eve—when I turned it back on after class. *Buzz buzz buzz!* with a bunch of incoming text messages.

J: *Hey, pretty, of course I remember U ;-)*

...

J: *U there?*

...

J: *Text me back, brah.*

My hands shook as I read them. Crap. I should have told him I was going to be in class. This was what I'd wanted, right? So why was it so hard to breathe? By that point I figured I should just wait until I got home to reply. It wasn't like I had any hot plans for the night. Goff probably did so I was pretty sure I'd be left alone, especially if I told our parents I had to study. That wouldn't have even been a lie. I always had to study. And sleep.

I couldn't remember the ride home. I guess I hadn't done anything stupid since I made it home alive. I fixed a snack and took it upstairs with me, and then cleaned up. As I suspected, Goff was in the bathroom at the same time.

"You're getting ready for bed?" He sounded surprised.

What could I say? "It's been a long day."

"Did you just whine?" He nudged me with his shoulder.

"Probably. All I want to do is crawl under the covers and sleep for a week." At this point, I probably couldn't have slept even with a face full of sedatives. I wanted to do something under the covers all right, but as close as Goff and I were, there were some things we did not share. "Unfortunately I have to be up bright and early and ready to scull until I achieve perfection, and then help with a learn-to-row clinic I was drafted into."

I must have made a face, because Goff gave me a look of purest concern. "I thought you liked luring innocent young lads and lasses into a life of torture and rowing."

"This is an adult learn-to-row clinic, actually." I had to smile at Goff's phrasing, because he was right. "I'm just doing it because I get paid. One of the masters coaches is in charge. I'm just driving a boat."

"You're coxing?" Goff laughed. "This I have to see."

"You know where the boathouse is. Come watch."

"Don't you get too far out on the water to see much?"

I'd taken my contacts out by this time, so I looked over my glasses at him. "First day. We won't get that far," I muttered darkly.

I could tell by his smile that he was thinking about it. "Can I bring Laurel?"

"Of course." I gave him a look. He knew how much I liked her. "The more the merrier. If the water's calm, you might even be able to hear me doing a bad job of keeping my temper. The real fun, however, will be the coaches trying to do the same thing, and they'll have powered megaphones. You'll hear them loud and clear."

Goff pulled out his phone. "I'm telling Laurel about this right now."

"The more I think about this, the more it says something sad about us all that this is the most entertaining thing we can come up with." I shook my head.

"Remy, we're under eighteen. We can't drink, we can't get into clubs—okay, you and I can, but our friends can't—and we're not the type to spend the summer stoned. Let's face it, Davis in the summer is quieter than a grave. Watching you not blowing your stack, or better yet, not screaming and swimming for shore? Best game in town."

I had to admit Goff was right. It just sucked to hear it put so bluntly. "Okay, there's nothing I can say to that, but Goff?"

"Yeah?"

"Don't you dare wear as much aftershave as you're pouring into your hand. Some on the cheeks, some further south, and that's it. The idea is to make her go hunting for that elusive scent, not to choke us all in a cloud of it."

I was the recipient of the one-fingered mudra of contempt, but he poured about half of it down the drain and then followed directions. "Why am I taking advice from a gay virgin?"

"Because I'm right," I said around my toothbrush.

"And that's the most annoying part. Sleep well, Germy, don't wait up." And with that, my brother finished dressing. Then he was out the door and I had the bathroom to myself.

I padded back into my bedroom and locked my door. This wasn't something I wanted company for.

I climbed into bed and pulled out my phone. I didn't see any point to putting it off. I mean, I'd already jerked Josh's chain enough.

R: *Sorry, not ignoring U on purpose. In class this evening*

Josh responded almost immediately.

J: *Ah, the joys of summer school. Whatcha taking?*

Damn. He would ask. What would they call US government at UCD?

R: *Poli sci. Just basic US government*
J: *Were we a bad boy and flunked poli sci 1a?*

I started getting over my fear. The weird thing was, I was pretty into it already.

R: *If I say yes, will you punish me?*
J: *Whoa. Don't waste any time, do U ;-)*

R: *Did I mistake your intentions when U were eye-fucking me at the boathouse?*

Josh didn't reply right away. Maybe I had misread him. I was about to apologize when he texted back.

J: *Sorry. Had to ditch roommates. No U weren't wrong. Wanted to nail you against wall then&there*
R: *Could tell*

He was killing me with this.

J: *So. Wanna meet?*
R: *When/where?*
J: *Tomorrow?*

I thought about that. My Saturdays were pretty busy, but I could probably get away after dinner. Studying—my eternal excuse.

R: *I have 2 study, so library?*
J: *Perfect. Shields?*

Shields was the main library at UC Davis. Despite a renovation in the nineties, it was still a labyrinth, full of dark corners and out-of-the-way bathrooms. I could only imagine what Josh had in mind.

R: *I can be there by 7*
J: *Meet U on 3rd floor by men's room. Wear uni?*
R: *Yes 2 meet no 2 uni*
J: *Buzzkill*
R: *Goodnight, Romeo*
J: *LOL C U 2morrow*

LATE THE next night, I shut my bedroom door behind me and leaned against it. I managed not to slam it, but only just. Goff had taken Laurel to the movies, and my parents were asleep. I'm surprised my heart pounding in my chest didn't wake them up.

I couldn't believe I had done what I had just done. My head spun from it all, and I needed to talk to someone desperately. Even if he hadn't been busy, I was not sure this was something I could share with my brother. He had my back, but this involved my front. I did not need to know what he and Laurel did with theirs; he probably didn't want to know what I did with mine. That left one person I could talk to.

Mikey.

One problem with that.

Either he or I was going to have to suck it up and call the other one. Suck. Maybe that was a poor choice of words in the present circumstances, but dammit, I needed to debrief with my best friend or former best friend or best enemy or whatever he was, especially since I would probably see Josh around the boathouse when he was helping out with the adaptive rowing program in some capacity or other.

And because I knew this—I would hook up with Josh again.

So it looked like I would be texting Mikey, even though I was not the one who went psycho.

R: *I called Stranger Guy. I really need to talk.*

And then what? Suddenly I didn't know what to do with myself. I knew there would be no way I could focus long enough to study, either US government or SAT prep. I took a shower for lack of anything better to do. Maybe that would relax me enough to sleep.

When I got out, Mikey had blown up my phone, and I breathed a sigh of relief. A huge sigh. An epic sigh. Never mind the shower, the fact that Mikey still cared enough to reply relaxed me.

M: *Where are you? You can't just say things like that and disappear.*
R: *Shower. Can U meet? Would U rather text?*
M: *Can U come over here?*
R: *B there ASAP.*

I texted Goff where I was going and then pushed the Vespa down the block before I started it. It occurred to me that my brother and I barely told our parents anything but stayed in almost constant contact with each other. It was a twin thing, and Mom and Dad had learned to work with that. If they wanted to know where one of us was, they asked the other.

When I got to Mikey's house, he had already opened his bedroom window and removed the screen. His parents had to know what the ladder on the side of the house was for—didn't they?—but either they didn't mind or they were truly clueless. Regardless, I had other things on my mind, and quick and lithe as a cat, I was up and in Mikey's room in moments.

I'd barely set my feet on the carpet before he grabbed my arm and pulled me over to his bed. "Well?"

"Hello to you, too."

He waved that away. "Yeah yeah yeah, I missed you. We've kissed and made up. Now start talking."

I started at the beginning with the texting—why revealing what a chickenshit I was mattered, I didn't know, and besides, he probably already knew—but a part of me thought that if Mikey hadn't been such a psycho, we wouldn't—figuratively speaking—have had to kiss and make up, and could be in a relationship of our very own already, and might therefore actually have been kissing.

"So we met tonight."

"Ohmygod where?" Mikey gasped.

"Shields Library."

His jaw dropped. "He nailed you in a bathroom?"

"No, he didn't nail me," I said testily, "and lower your voice, unless you want your parents listening in." Honestly, this would've gone so much better if he'd just let me talk. "Can I just finish this?"

"Go on, go on, but this is killing me. Talk faster."

And my nerves were back. "I don't know how I made it through today. I was a nervous wreck. I mean, scared all day—"

"You? Scared?" Mikey laughed. "That's novel."

"Yeah, me. Scared. Any more clever remarks? Can I continue?" Maybe Mikey didn't know me that well after all.

Mikey made a "keep talking" gesture with his hand. "Yes, scared all day, and it got worse the closer I got, like I was going to puke the entire bike ride to campus. I almost turned around every time I stopped at a stop sign or red light. Even once I was in the library, I thought about bailing."

I looked up at Mikey, expecting to see him laughing or something, but he only looked concerned. "By the time I found where Josh said to meet, I felt like I was going to pass out." I sighed. "But I did it. I actually did it. I held another man's dick in my hand. He held mine."

"And?" Mikey whispered.

I laughed. It almost sounded bitter to my ears. "And I'm doing it again. It's way better than whacking off."

"But that's all you did, mutual j/o?"

I nodded. "That and kissing."

"What was that like? Kissing a guy?" He looked entranced.

I leaned forward and kissed him on the lips, just a brief kiss. "Magical."

Mikey blinked. "So—" His voice cracked, and he coughed to clear it. "So what made the difference? You almost turned around; you were so nervous you were sick to your stomach. Why'd you change your mind?"

"Josh's jaw dropped when he saw me." I smiled at the memory. Definitely a confidence builder. "Okay, I wore a tight T-shirt kinda sorta on purpose."

"You mean like the one you have on now?"

I looked down. I guess it was tight. They all fit like this one. Maybe I was growing again? "About, yeah. Maybe shorter? If I moved, you could see skin."

Mikey blushed. "Wow. Um… maybe you could show me some time. I mean, maybe Josh was nervous, too."

"Could be." I wondered what Mikey was getting at. If his signals were any more mixed, he would have needed to use a blender for a transmitter. "But I guess weight training is good for more than moving boats, because he sure got off on my muscles."

"You really don't know, do you?" Mikey had a funny look on his face.

I cocked my head to one side. "Don't know what?"

"Don't worry about it, Remy. Just keep lifting so you make the boats go faster."

I knew right then that I would never understand Mikey, and possibly never understand any other man, either. But that might have been okay. As I had learned that night, they seemed to like what they saw.

"You know what the best part of it was? Hands down?"

Mikey shook his head slowly.

"The exhilaration. I've never felt like that before. I can't describe the feeling of power that came from holding him, from holding Josh's dick. In that moment, I realized something. I could control him absolutely."

Mikey opened his mouth, but snapped it shut. He looked worried or something.

"What?"

He tried again. "That's… not what I expected you to say."

I shrugged. What could I say to that? I wasn't a mind reader. "I think it's time to get you a fake ID, too."

"Wait, what? Too?" Mikey looked like a whiplash victim.

I nodded. "I've got a fake ID. Geoff, too, but let's leave him out of this."

"Because I look soooo mature?"

"Yeah, that part might be a bit tricky, and the photochopping could be expensive. I'll help pay for it since this is all my idea."

"Okay, now for the why?" Mikey said, his tone indicating that he was humoring the crazy man.

"So we can get you into clubs. Some of them have eighteen-and-over nights."

Mikey looked at me like I was stupid. "I want to do this… why?"

"Well Jesus H Christ, Mikey. I'll need a wingman if I'm going to find guys at clubs. I figure it's safer than online," I said. He wasn't getting it, but it was plain as daylight to me. "Then, too, you might want in on the action, amiright?"

The silence, as they say, deafened. Mikey stared at me for a long time. Like, long enough to make me squirm.

"You sicken me. Get out."

I stared at him. I could not be hearing this. "What the—?"

"Get. Out."

I stood up. "Could you please make up your mind? You want me, you don't want me, but apparently you don't like the idea of me finding anyone else either. I don't know what the hell that's about."

Mikey didn't say anything, but I'd never seen him so furious. His arms were crossed over his chest, and he was shaking he was so mad.

"You said you were saving yourself for the right guy at the right time. For a while in San Diego, I'd thought—no, I'd hoped—that was me. Then you made it clear it wasn't." I almost told him how that had hurt, but then I realized it was not any of his business, not anymore. Besides, now I was every bit as furious as he. "You can't have it both ways, you know."

And with that, I climbed out the window. He could close it behind me.

The problem with having ridden the Vespa over was that I couldn't take my anger out on the pedals. No, I had to sit there sedately on the seat, puttering my way home. Whoever heard of taking a mad out by speeding furiously through the streets on a Vespa? No one, that's who.

But what the ever-living hell? I couldn't figure out what Mikey wanted. He'd turned me down, but he was angry—no, sickened—that I found affection somewhere else.

Whatever, Mikey. I don't need you, anyway.

CHAPTER
EIGHT

AFTER THAT, I found myself alone for much of the rest of the summer. Not alone, strictly speaking. I was around people all the time, whether it was in class at City College or in my SAT prep course or at the boathouse sculling balls to the wall in preparation for the Nationals, but those were alone in a crowd. No besties or anything, no one to talk to who knew me.

Mom even noticed one day. "Where is everyone?"

I looked up from my reading. "What do you mean?"

"You've never been one for a lot of friends, Remy, but you're usually with *someone*. For the last week, however, it's just been you. Is something wrong? Are you and Mikey fighting?"

She sounded really worried. "No, Mom. We're both just really busy this summer."

"I know, sweetie, but you used to study with each other. Lately it's not even that."

"I know. His summer school and my practice for Nationals and everything else don't really overlap." I couldn't really tell her the truth, but I smiled to throw her off the scent. "We'll get it all sorted out eventually. We still talk and see each other at the boathouse."

"That's something at least." She shook her head. "This overscheduling you kids do to yourselves. I never thought I'd be telling my children to slow down. Isn't it the other way around?"

I had to laugh. "Welcome to Davis."

"I know, but it's not healthy, is it?" But she laughed, too.

"Probably not, but hey, college'll be easy, right?"

"It would have to be." She kissed the top of my head. "Don't forget to sleep sometime."

"I think I've got it on my schedule."

Mom shook her head. "That'd be funny if it weren't true."

Goff knew the score, so he and Laurel tried to include me in their activities, or some of them. They meant well and I loved them both for it, but who wanted to be a third wheel? I tagged along, but seeing them being a couple just rubbed it in that I wasn't. Josh hardly counted.

Speaking of, Josh and I saw a fair amount of each other—under certain circumstances—and it beat doing it myself, but we weren't in any sense of the term in a relationship, and neither of us thought we were. As much as I longed for the walking-hand-in-hand, trading-letter-jackets, going-steady boyfriend, my ideas about casual changed a lot over the summer, and I realized that Mr. Right Now would do while I waited for Mr. Right.

I hadn't lied to Mom when I told her I saw Mikey at the boathouse. We just ignored each other in a painfully obvious fashion. Even Lodestone noticed it one morning before practice. He only raised an eyebrow in comment as the gentlemen's crew prepared for the morning's row.

I shook my head. "Don't ask. It's too stupid for words."

"At least you recognize it. Do I want to know?"

"Not unless you find it amusing that he doesn't want to go out but doesn't want me to see anyone else." My voice might've dripped a certain amount of contempt.

Lodestone made a face while my teammates tried to stifle their laughter.

"Yep, that about sums it up."

"So…. Throwing yourself into sculling, are you?"

I raised one eyebrow. "You noticed."

"You've gotten a lot faster lately, for what it's worth."

I saluted him. "Right now? Everything."

"I'm sorry you're going through this," Lodestone said, putting a hand on my shoulder, "but if you're up for it, I'll keep doing everything I can to help you transmute this lead into gold at the Nationals."

"I'm all yours, Coach."

He smiled at me. "You always have been, you know."

"So people tell me."

Lodestone rewarded me with two hours in hell, and I loved every minute of it. I managed to keep even with the four on some of the pieces. They hated me, and they should've. There were four of them in one boat, four people and four oars. There was one of me in a tiny boat with two much smaller oars. They lumbered along. I set the water ablaze, with Cisco and Jack in a pair nipping at my heels. I'd always hated the pair. The pair was just like the big boat we'd rowed in San Diego, only a tiny slice of it—one oar per rower and not much boat. They were tippy and temperamental, and I'd rolled them before. I was at one with my single, and it showed. Lodestone wasn't shy about using me or Cisco and Jack to berate the four. We grinned at them; they gnashed their teeth.

SAT PREP finished and I retook the SATs, raising my scores by a decent amount. Goff, too. Laurel pretended ours were on par with hers, which we appreciated. She was polite that way. I doubted I would take them again after that. They had reached a respectable level, and I knew I could do only so much. My grades, my AP test scores, and my various community-college courses along with community service projects via crew and school clubs would have to make up for any deficiencies. I couldn't be all things to every admissions officer. No one could, except apparently Laurel. As I told her, it was a good thing she was beautiful inside and out, and thank goodness Goff didn't have to glower at me anymore. Now that I was out to him, he knew I wasn't putting the moves on his girlfriend.

After the prep course and the SATs were done, all that was left in my summer were twice-daily training for Nationals and my explorations of what my dick was good for. As it turned out, it was good for all kinds of good times. I was reasonably discriminating within the bounds of being young and having fun. It's not like I had turned into a tomcat or anything. I kept my dignity, but as I had the time or the urge, I went looking.

Josh and I continued our discreet encounters, and we both had fun, but that was all it ever was—fun. So I branched out because I wanted to have *more* fun. I nosed around some of the quote-unquote gay dating sites, but they were only dating sites if you wanted your dates to last an hour or less. Adams2Steves.com struck me as the best game around insofar as everyone there admitted it was a game and played accordingly. I put up a profile, lying through my electronic teeth about age and everything related to that sort of thing. The one thing I insisted on was "drug and disease free/UB2." I never replied to messages unless the profile stated that. Mine did, and I expected that in my playmates. A lot of guys around my alleged age seemed to have time on their hands during the summer, mostly college students I presumed, since that was what I appeared to be. They were there when I wanted them, and that was what mattered.

I'd never deleted Grindr from my phone after San Diego, and that turned out to be a great source for college guys. There was something oddly compelling about it, too. It felt like walking into a store. I could point to anyone and say, "Yes, Shopkeeper, I'll have that one." And I could. Josh had taught me that much. I apparently checked off a lot of guys' boxes. I didn't think I was all that special, just some guy who looked older than he was through an accident of heredity and who happened to be built up through his choice of recreational pastime/obsession. People couldn't help how old they looked, but anyone who felt like putting the time in could make the most of what he or she had. That struck me as fairly democratic, and who knew how long rowing would hold my interest? I mean, it wasn't a varsity sport at most colleges anymore and hadn't been for years. If I got to college and couldn't sustain my studies and crew, there could be only one choice of which I'd vote off the island. I could always pick crew back up after I graduated. But if I didn't row? I knew I'd be about as active as a rock, and then I wouldn't look like I did, and presumably the interest on Grindr would dry up.

Goff knew I slipped out at night on occasion, but then again, so did he. I suppose he thought I'd met someone, and since I'd always been fairly closed-mouth, he didn't seem to think too much of it. I didn't burden him with the details that I'd met several someones and rarely saw them more than once or twice. What was the point? It's not like I could date any of these men. If they found out I was in high school, they'd panic. If my parents found out I was seeing someone in college, they'd freak out. They didn't even know I was gay. It was a bad situation all the way around, and I knew it. I couldn't really face the thought of telling my parents and trying to make it better, however. There was no point, since Mikey had already rejected me, but damn, I had thought coming out to Goff would have put an end to the secrets between us.

Then complications ensued with Josh. Ensued? More like exploded. I was just glad that I escaped injury from the hot shrapnel.

One afternoon before practice, I was putting my single in slings. Something had been off with one of the riggers during the morning practice, and I refused to go through another practice with a gimpy rigger.

A shadow fell across the boat, blocking my sight. I looked up, irritated and ready to rip into whomever it was, only to see Josh. I smiled instead.

"Hey, pretty," he said. He wore street clothes, so I assumed he was here to do something related to his internship with the adaptive rowing program rather than to work out or row.

"What's up?" I stretched the slight crick in my back. Why the slings for singles had to be so low to the ground I would never know, but given that the sport selected for reasonably tall people even at the juniors level, I failed to see why equipment manufacturers couldn't scale things up a bit.

Then I noticed his neck and stopped hearing a single word he said. Red blotches everywhere. He looked like he'd been attacked by an Electrolux or mauled by a Hoover.

I must have made the right responses back because he continued on to wherever he was going. The moon? Hell? It could have been anywhere, but my vote was for hell.

I knew Josh and I weren't exclusive. We had never discussed it, for starters, and I was hardly the poster boy for monogamy. Josh and I had also never dated in any formal sense of the term, if only because of the fact that dating traditionally took place in locations other than public bathrooms, as hot as that could be. Even I knew that much about actual dating, despite Mikey's probably realistic assumptions about my fixed focus on crew to the exclusion of everything else.

That wasn't what had made my jaw shatter on the floor.

It was the total lack of discretion. Under the circumstances, I valued discretion highly. It was a courtesy I gave to Josh and expected in return. While closeted in many areas of my life and thus practiced at hiding, I was new to all of this relationship business, even a relationship as casual as the one I thought I shared with Josh, and so disguising emotions when my first and current flaunted the evidence of another inamorato in front of me took more skill than I possessed right then, not with everything else demanding my attention.

I must have stared after him for a good five minutes.

"Hey, Remy," Lodestone said when he walked into the boathouse. When I didn't reply, he said, "Are you okay?"

That snapped me back to myself. That was exactly what I needed—a test of my emotional fortitude in front of a coach as perceptive and intelligent as Peter Lodestone.

"What? Oh. Hi, Coach." I blushed. Could I be any dopier? "I'm fine. Just lost in space."

He frowned at me. "Is everything all right?"

"Yep, just some trouble with one of the riggers, but I've about got it fixed."

I went back to work, but I felt Lodestone's eyes on me the entire time. Even when I left, I was sure he watched me all the way down the dock.

I SPENT my free time for the next several days hooking up with guys I found on Grindr, like it was some sort of payback to Josh for his infidelity. Only I didn't tell him, because I was being discreet. How was that for messed-up logic? What I had not realized was that I had not left my distraction on the dock and that Lodestone had been connecting the dots. In other words, as usual, I failed to notice anything. When something bothered me, I just sculled longer and harder. But one afternoon at practice a few days later—those of us going to Nationals were well into two practices a day by then—I noticed Josh talking to Lodestone on the dock. I saw the two of them grow increasingly agitated. I heard voices but did not and honestly could not care. I was about as emotionless as a block of wood at that point.

I stopped sculling and watched them. Then I saw Lodestone grab—literally grab—Coach Sundstrom and drag him into the argument, because by that time I'd figured out they were fighting. I assumed the only reason it hadn't turned physical was because Lodestone could've folded Josh into a pretzel and Sundstrom sported even more muscle, but Josh looked furious. Then Sundstrom blanched. I'd never seen that before—a grown man with a tan actually turn white. It was something to see. So was two men—two big men—against one. The glances out to me told me not only were they fighting about me but also that I'd better get back to work. So I did. I'd already seen enough, and I had better things to do, like concentrate on sculling. Once again, compartmentalization was my friend, and I'd become very adept at shoving things aside that had nothing to do with rowing. In two weeks I would be competing against guys my age from all over the country.

In any event, the shit had not finished hitting the fan when I got off the water, not by a long shot. As I carried my single back to the boathouse, I saw Lodestone talking to a cop. Coach Sundstrom paced nearby, looking like he was about to dismember someone. The sudden weight in my stomach told me all I needed to know. I did not even need to see them glance over to me. Real subtle, guys. How about playing me a fanfare while you're at it?

As I went back down to the dock to pick up my oars, Jack pulled me aside. "Dude, what's going on?"

"I have no idea," I said wearily.

Jack shook his head. "You didn't do anything weird?"

"Life is getting baroque, but last I heard that wasn't a crime, so no." I tried to think what might have gone down while I was sculling, but couldn't think of anything. Yet two of the Cap City coaches had practically mauled my not-boyfriend on the dock, and now there was a police officer waiting for me. Cops automatically made me worry. Damn, had they figured out what I had been doing all summer? I mean, I'd lied on two hookup sites…. Shit. Maybe they would still let me row at the Youth Nationals.

"Leave him alone," Cisco said. "We've got our own equipment to deal with."

Cisco shot me a sympathetic look as he went back down to the dock to get their own oars while Jack trudged into the eights house where the pairs were stashed so he could wipe the water off of their boat.

Meanwhile, I was alone in the singles house wiping down my boat when Lodestone, Sundstrom, and the cop cornered me. Maybe not intentionally, but when they got between me and the exit, they might as well have. I swallowed the lump in my throat.

"I am so sorry," Coach Sundstrom said, "Remy, is it? I had no idea Brennan would ever do something like that, or we never would've taken him on as an intern. When Nick finds out about this, he's going to kill the guy with his bare hands." The cop coughed. "Sorry, Officer. That's just a figure of speech."

"Understood," he said with a slight smile. "Actually, Mr. Babcock, I just wanted to talk—"

I frowned, although what I really wanted to do was puke. "Am I under arrest?"

"Oh no! Of course not, Remy! I just need to talk to you about Mr. Brennan and your relationship with him." The cop looked very embarrassed, and suddenly I knew the feeling. "I want to re-emphasize that you're not in any trouble and that you haven't done anything wrong, but I need some basic information and a detective down at the station will need to ask you some more questions, but that's all."

"Oh, okay, but I have to warn you, I've been out there sweating for a couple of hours and I don't smell very good." But if I wasn't under arrest, why was it three against one?

"I can get you into the CalPac boathouse," Lodestone said. "They have showers in their locker room. Will that be all right, Officer? Because he's right, sweaty rower is a unique smell you're probably not ready for."

The cop nodded reluctantly. "If it doesn't take too long."

"He'll be quick, and Remy? Expect an e-mail from me later, because I need to talk to you, as well." I calmed fractionally, but if I weren't in any trouble, why did Lodestone look like he wanted to murder me?

THE UNIFORMED officer had been correct. He had asked only basic questions, like my age and where I went to school. He skirted around the edges of my sexual orientation, but we both knew the answer to that. As it turned out, he had saved the hardball questions for Detective Jeanette Nakimoto.

"Thank you for coming in this afternoon," Detective Nakimoto said as she sat down in the interview room I had been cooling my jets in for the better part of an hour, an hour I had spent conjuring one nightmare scenario after another, each worse than the one before.

At least I'd had the chance to clean up, rehydrate, and eat, otherwise I would have been a lot less cooperative. Who knew, maybe the officer and the detective knew that. "I didn't think I had much choice."

Nakimoto sighed. "I'm sorry if we gave you that impression, but the reality is that we need your help if this case is going to stick."

"Really? Then the only way you're going to get that help is if you leave my parents out of this. I'm not out to them." I already did not like the direction this was heading, and if the good detective forced me to come all the way out, then she would find out just how uncooperative I could be. And I still felt like puking.

"I see," Nakimoto said.

"Do you? So far, I've been put on the spot in front of my teammates, and rowers gossip worse than old women, so this will be all over my rowing club by tonight, if it isn't already. My coach seems like he's ready to kill me, and someone I've been involved with has not only humiliated me publicly but has also been dragged off in chains," I said, trying to stop the wavering in my voice. "On top of it all, I've got a major competition in two weeks, and all of this is nothing but a distraction, a distraction I don't need. So why don't you go ahead and tell me why I should cooperate?"

Detective Nakimoto said nothing for a few moments. She only watched me long enough to make me squirm. "Okay, it was never our intention to make things bad for you. We were responding to a report of a potential crime of a sexual nature against a minor, and for that I can't and won't apologize, but I can see now that we should've handled it differently."

"You think?" I sniffled, but only because the air conditioning was so cold. At least, that was what I told myself. But "crime of a sexual nature against a minor"? Holy—damn. That sounded horrible, so predatory, like I had been a victim. I hadn't felt like a victim, not even when I'd seen the hickeys. I'd been angry and hurt, even humiliated, but not victimized.

"As to your request, for now, yes, I won't involve your parents as long as you help us," the detective said, "but I have to warn you that if this comes down to a criminal trial, you will be called as a witness whether you like it or not, and then yes, your parents will find out. I'm sorry, but it's the way these things work. I can make one promise— you'll have a lot of warning."

I bit my lip, thinking. Or I tried to think, anyway. This was… yeah. I barely remembered driving to the police station, and she wanted information. No wonder people demanded lawyers.

I eventually nodded. "Warning. I can work with that. So what do you want to know?"

"Well, I have your answers to the officer's questions, and thank you for those," she said. "I have questions of my own, and some of them will seem redundant. At this point, I'm only trying to find out if a crime was even committed. California's laws about statutory rape can be a little peculiar."

Rape? "Whoa, Josh never raped me. Let's get that out there right now."

"*Statutory* rape," the detective said. "There's a big difference, and it's because you're still a minor and by legal definitions cannot consent to certain things. As I said, the law is a little murky at times. For instance, if two minors had consensual relations, by definition, they could both be guilty of unlawful sex."

I stared at her. "That's ridiculous."

"Of course it is, but that's the way the law is written. So it's vitally important to establish your age at the time you and Mr. Brennan started your relationship. Exactly how old were you?"

"A bit past my seventeenth birthday."

She looked at me intently. "You're sure? You're not rounding up?"

"I'm quite sure. He first met me when I was sixteen, and that's when he gave me his phone number, but I didn't call him until after I'd turned seventeen."

"That's interesting and useful to know." She made notes on a pad of paper for several minutes before she looked up at me again. "You contacted him, you said?"

I nodded. "Yeah." I felt the color rise in my cheeks, and not for the first time wished I could have another—any other—physical trait. "I was too chicken to do it any sooner."

"For what it's worth, that may make the difference between a misdemeanor and a felony, along with a lifetime on the sex offender registry," she said. "Another thing, Jeremy—do you prefer Jeremy or Remy?"

"Remy's fine, but thanks for asking."

"Another thing, Remy. Listen to your gut. It'll actually save you no end of trouble in life. People train themselves out of it, but try to learn to listen to your instincts. That's what they're for. Anyway, so this was a consensual relationship?"

"It wasn't a relationship like we were boyfriends or anything. We were just using each other for sex," I said. Hearing myself say it out loud like that? It sounded sad, even pathetic.

"All right," Nakimoto said as she made more notes. "Do you think he knew you were a minor when you met? When you hooked up?"

"Actually, I highly doubt he knew," I admitted. "I certainly didn't volunteer the information." I paused. "The thing is, Detective? My brother and I, we're fraternal twins by the way, we've always looked older than our age. We were first asked what we were majoring in when we were in the ninth grade or so. So the first time Josh met me? Despite the fact that the boatyard was full of people who were obviously teenagers, I was off doing my own thing, and he probably thought I was an assistant coach or something."

She frowned at me. "Would you mind standing up for me?"

I squirmed a bit as she examined me. I was tempted to ask if she wanted to check my hooves and teeth, but managed to keep my mouth shut. I wasn't in any trouble, and I wanted it to stay that way.

"You're right. If I didn't know your age, I wouldn't peg you for a high schooler."

I wasn't lying. *Thank you very much for taking me seriously, cop lady.*

She waved for me to sit back down. "Well, Remy, this is certainly much more complicated than it first appeared."

Duh. "So what's going to happen to him?"

"Do you care about him?"

I shook my head. "No, not really. He was convenient. Do you want to know what started your involvement off?"

"Yes, as a matter of fact," Nakimoto said.

"I'll bet," I said, snorting. "He showed up at the boathouse with so many hickeys he looked like he'd been attacked by a vacuum cleaner. Mind you, we weren't dating or anything exclusive like that, but I'm not altogether out, and I'd thought we owed each other a certain amount of discretion."

"That seems reasonable," she said.

"I guess I was the only one who thought that, and I'm apparently not as good as I thought about keeping things like that off my face. Either that or my coach—"

"This would be Peter Lodestone?"

"Right, so either I'm lousy at keeping my feelings off my face or Lodestone's better at reading me than I thought, because the next thing I knew, he had figured it all out and was in the middle of a fight with Josh and then dragged Coach Sundstrom into it."

Detective Nakimoto looked at me for long moments. "You're young yet. Not being able to mask your feelings isn't necessarily a failing."

"Seemed like it this morning," I muttered.

"I know. Give it time and you'll be every bit as jaded as the rest of us," she said, sounding far more weary than she had moments before. "Anyway, this Coach Sundstrom, he would be Mr. Brennan's supervisor in adaptive rowing?"

"I guess," I said with a sigh. "Yes."

"Tell me about adaptive rowing. You assisted with it as your summer job."

I nodded. "It's a way to get people who lack full mobility into boats. You know, exercise what they've got by modifying the boats to suit them, usually in a two-person boat with an able-bodied rower. I was the able-bodied rower, obviously. It's pretty cool if you think about it."

"It is indeed." She checked over her notes like she wanted to be sure she had not missed anything important. "I know this will be uncomfortable for you, but I need more information and detail than 'hooking up'."

I stared at the detective. "You're kidding."

"No, I'm afraid not. The law is very specific. I need to know what acts you and Mr. Brennan did and how often. It'll help make the determination between misdemeanor and felony, although a lot of that depends on the age spread, frankly." It did not make me feel any better that she seemed embarrassed, too.

I felt myself heating up. "Is there any way I can write this down? Because I'm pretty sure telling you all this would make me die of mortification."

Detective Nakimoto slid another pad of paper and a pen across the table to me. "I'll be at the other end of the table with my laptop. I've got things I can work on while you write me a narrative of your summer with Mr. Brennan, starting with how you met and how you hooked up the first time. Something tells me this is important."

And that was how I passed the most excruciating thirty minutes of my life. She wanted it all, and that was what I gave her, at least so far as Josh and I were concerned. The rest of my extracurricular activities this summer were exactly that—mine. She didn't need to know about my adventures with hookup apps. However the fact that this was a criminal investigation had slowly started to pierce my standard rowing-related obliviousness. It scared me, and I had two major fears: that somehow it would keep me from competing in the Youth Nationals and that the good detective would find a reason to tell my parents. I needed to do what the police wanted.

When I finished, I coughed to get her attention. "I'm sorry to bother you, but is this all right? I'm afraid I can't remember every single thing, and honestly, it's probably not as much as you're thinking it was."

Detective Nakimoto scanned what I had written down. "I think I have what I need for now, although I will doubtlessly be in touch with you. I'll call your cell phone to protect your privacy. I won't use e-mail because that's not secure."

"So what happens next?" That was the big question and the one that scared me the most.

She looked at me with sympathy. "For you? You do your best to put this out of your mind and concentrate on that national competition coming up. The wheels of justice turn slowly, particularly with the courts being so overburdened. For me, I'll continue to interview people and gather evidence to see if there's enough to send this to the district attorney. It's up to him to make the call about whether or not there's a case here."

"Do you think there is? If you had to guess and off the record and all that?" I said.

"That's a tough question and one of the reasons I'm glad I'm not the DA." Detective Nakimoto thought about it. She looked like she gave it her honest consideration and didn't just blow me off. "I'll say this much. The law states that he could be guilty of either a misdemeanor or a felony, depending on his criminal history. The fact that you two are so close in age means he falls within the window of discretion between the two classes of criminal act. That you sought him out and hid your age could count as a mitigating factor. The ball's in his court, and I haven't interviewed him yet. I'm sorry if this sounds like a cop-out, but right now it's all I've got."

"I understand. Are there any more questions, or can I go?"

The detective looked at the time. "Will you be in trouble for being so late?"

"Only with my brother for hogging the car, but I texted him before we started, so he knew to take our shared Vespa to work," I said. "He told our parents I had to stay late for practice."

"You two are thick as thieves, aren't you?" When I started to stall, she continued, "Don't even bother. I'm a twin myself."

I nodded. "I'd be lost without him."

CHAPTER
NINE

SURE ENOUGH, when I checked my e-mail on my phone in the parking lot of the West Sacramento PD, I found a terse e-mail from Lodestone. Somehow I knew that my interrogation by the detective had been nothing compared to the one I faced at the hands of my coach.

I made it home in time to hand the car off to Goff after all, decreasing by one my list of things to feel guilty about. I also managed to beat both parents home, decreasing by one the number of things I had to lie about. Since I had dinner about halfway done by the time both parents made it home and also helped clean up, no one had any issue with me meeting Lodestone to "discuss race strategy" after dinner. I saw no point in putting this off.

I had wanted to meet in a public place, because duh, I'm not stupid and I knew that whatever Lodestone had in store for me would not be pleasant, but my coach prevailed.

"Walk with me, Remy," Lodestone said. So we picked up warm beverages at Peet's downtown to ward off the chill of a summer evening in the Sacramento Valley and then went for a walk away from the city center toward Central Park.

"So what's going on, Remy? What the hell was today about?" Lodestone said.

I squirmed in the darkness. "It's really kind of personal."

"Oh for the love of—that's not good enough, not this time. I had to call the police on the adaptive program's intern for statutory rape, Remy."

That tore it. "You know, Coach, it *is* personal, and it'll *have* to be good enough, because it's none of your business." He didn't say anything for a few moments, and I hardly knew what to make of that, but my temper kept ratcheting up.

"Remy—Jeremy—when another coach preys on one of my rowers, it actually *is* my business. I absolutely *cannot* have a sexual predator anywhere near my program." I could tell Lodestone fought manfully to keep his temper under control, but he wasn't the only one with a temper.

Why the hell did everyone see this as predatory? I totally understood that the age differences weren't necessarily cool. A twenty-year-old and someone younger than me? Yuck, and get the shotgun and the pruning shears. Or someone older than Josh going after me? Oh hell no. I would have called the cops myself. But there was nothing special about my eighteenth birthday. I would not magically discover sex that day, and there was no use pretending otherwise. I understood why those laws existed. I truly did. There were people too young to consent, and if mental age were taken into account, some people would never be old enough. I, however, could consent and had, but no one would listen to me.

"You should've asked me first, Coach. You should have fucking asked." I felt my voice thickening with rage. Then something horrible occurred to me, something that rocked my world on its axis. "Is this some kind of gay thing?"

Lodestone spun me around so fast I dropped my tea. "No, and you listen and you listen good, kiddo. Don't you dare play the homophobia card with me. This has nothing to do with homophobia and everything to do with stopping a sexual predator."

"Sexual predator?" I laughed, but my voice verged on the hysteric. "Are you kidding me? I went after him."

"That's what he said, but I don't believe it, not entirely, and it really doesn't matter."

I sputtered. "It doesn't matter? How the hell can it not matter?"

"I'm not a lawyer, but it depends on how much older than you he is." Lodestone looked at me. "Well? How much older is he?"

"I don't know, but the detective said the same thing."

Lodestone sighed. "I think you'd better find out."

"I really don't see why you're making such a big deal about this. I was upset this morning, yes, but that was between Josh and me. I'm sorry other people are involved, but it won't happen again." If only because after my talk with Detective Nakimoto, I knew that Josh would never speak to me again, not that I wanted him to. Honestly, what more did Lodestone want me to say?

Lodestone's jaw clenched. I didn't think I'd ever seen him so angry. "It's not just you and your closet on the line here, Remy. It's me and my future as a coach. It's the juniors rowing program. Hell, it's all of Cap City. Josh was working with the adaptive rowing program, so it's Coach Sundstrom, it's Coach Bedford. It's all of us and everything everyone associated with Cap City has worked for. I get that teens can be self-centered naturally, but you really need to work your way around that, because honestly? You're being a selfish asshole, and I don't like you very much right now."

"What? How?" That was just too much. I gave Lodestone and crew everything. I had no social life, my grades were lower than they would have been, people mocked me for my single-minded obsession with the sport, but it was all worth it because everything I gave crew, I received back tenfold. Or thought I did.

"If I didn't report this, I'd be in legal jeopardy as an accessory to statutory rape." Lodestone sounded like he was explaining this to a child, and a particularly stupid one at that.

He sounded just like the detective, and I told him what I told her. "Rape? He never raped me."

"Statutory rape. There's a difference, and you'd better learn the difference. It's when someone too young to give legal consent has sex with someone old enough to know better. From what the police told me, the law's a little different in California. It all depends on your relative ages. This all might blow over in a week, or you could be looking at a drawn-out legal mess. Do your parents even know?"

My mouth hung open. He wouldn't dare.

"I see I've finally gotten your attention." Lodestone shook his head. "Think, Remy. You're an intelligent young man, but you're completely self-absorbed. Until recently, I'd thought your total focus on rowing was an asset, even a gift, but now I have to question that. You need to step back and look around. There's a lot more to your life than rowing."

But there wasn't, not since Mikey had thrown me out of his bedroom. I realized that now. I had thrown myself into crew—and that other thing—to avoid thinking about Mikey. As far as realizations went, that one sucked, and I pulled away from it like it burned. *Hic sunt dracones* and all that.

"What… what about practice? The Youth Nationals are in two weeks."

Lodestone laughed, but I didn't think there was any humor in it. "You're something else, Remy. I don't know whether to tie you up and deliver you to your parents with instructions that you never set foot in my boathouse again or applaud your determination to win, I really don't. Yes, you have practice as usual."

"Then that's all that really matters." I turned and left. I wouldn't give him a chance to see me crack, not after what he had just told me. He had been my mentor, my hero, but now? I didn't know anything anymore. That was not true, strictly speaking. I still had rowing, even if Lodestone himself had broken faith. People might come and go, but my devotion to crew would never and could never waver. The water would always be there for me, the water and the ergometer. People could play me false, but those two would reward my devotion. They always had before.

"Remy!" I heard Lodestone call, but I ignored him. He was not one of my favorite people at that moment. I knew I would have to think about his words later, but just then I was homesick for anywhere but there.

I took off, running back to where I'd parked the Vespa.

I FIRED off an irate text as soon as I got home.

> R: *Men are dicks, all of them—alleged best friends, hookups, coaches, all of them are dicks.*

It didn't take long for my friend Todd to text back. He had chatted me up on Grindr one day early in the summer, apparently able to tell from my pictures that I rowed. He himself had rowed in high school and now rowed as a freshman in college and was an assistant coach for a juniors program to earn money. It had not taken very long before we'd abandoned innuendo-laden flirting for crew babble. Okay, we still flirted once in a while, but mostly we kept it under control. Todd was an interesting soul, and if we had lived closer to one another, we might have hooked up. As it was, we settled for a long-distance friendship. We were only a year apart in age—he was eighteen to my seventeen—and that made it very easy to talk to him. That said, I knew where that tall blond stud had some interesting tattoos.

> T: *Well, duh. What brought about this revelation, pray tell?*
> R: *How long have U got?*
> T: *About 8 inches.*
> R: *Don't make me kill you.*
> T: *Sorry, go ahead.*

So I did. I unloaded all over him.

> T: *So what's wrong with slowing down?*

I blinked. He was right.

> R: *Not a damn thing.*
> T: *Oh hey, guess what? I didn't tell U sooner cuz it wasn't a sure thing but guess who's coming to Youth Nat'ls?*

So I slowed down. I flat out ignored Adams2Steves.com and deleted Grindr from my phone. They were distractions, and I needed to process everything that had happened vis-à-vis Josh, although I had a sneaking suspicion that might take a good long time. You picked up a thing or two when one of your parents was a shrink, and I did not mean spare neuroses. If my gut told me I needed to process, then that was what I needed. Funny how my gut had already started to sound like Detective Nakimoto, but the thing was, she was right. We do train ourselves not to listen to our guts, which is nothing more than a crude term for instincts. Some people say humans don't have instincts, but I don't think that's true. What we have are the critical faculties to convince ourselves that there are no things that go bump in the night and that there aren't monsters in the skins of men. When I wasn't sculling, I went back over every single encounter I had ever had with Josh.

Then there was that staggering realization I had stumbled over about how I had spent my summer after Mikey's rejection. Early in the summer, Mikey told me the first time that he was waiting for the right guy and the right time, so I buried my hurt fee-fees and called Josh. After we'd done our thing, Josh and I, I ended up calling Mikey anyway because even still, he had been my best friend. Looking back, Mikey had been by turns fascinated and repelled by what I told him. And weirdly hung up on my T-shirt. He reiterated his stance on the right guy and the right time, and that twisted like a knife in my heart since it reminded me I wasn't it. Then he kicked me out. That was the moment—the exact moment—when I turned into a cockhound.

Looking back, that had clearly been the wrong thing to do, because Lodestone called the cops on Josh when things went sour. Was it weird that part of me thought Josh and I could've salvaged things if only people could've left us the hell alone? Scream and yell, make-up sex, and then it would've been fine. Or not. It still would've been ours to end. Jeez, could I even hear my own thoughts? Monsters in the skins of men? Maybe I wanted to have been the one to pull the plug?

Besides which, if there were any truth at all to my realization about Mikey's rejection and how I spent my summer, not only should I have ignored those hookup sites, I should have deleted them immediately. Oh well, better to realize it late than never. There was a saying about that, one I thought I remembered from freshman-year humanities. Minerva's owl flies at dusk? Great, more classicism from the mouths of babes. I had to get out of this town.

Oh, Mikey and my T-shirts. I automatically glanced at the one I was wearing. I'd chosen it to piss off Lodestone, actually. "I'm not gay, but $20 is $20." Goff almost choked on his cereal when he saw it at breakfast. It was a little tight, but not too much worse than the others. Whatever. Come to think of it, Mikey was at the boathouse this morning, and when he saw it, he dropped his duffel bag and stood there with his mouth open. I've gotten so used to ignoring him that it barely registered.

SINCE THE men's and women's crews combined entered fewer crews for the Nationals than the Crew Classic, de-rigging and loading the trailer struck me as lower key. I don't think I was alone.

"He won't be here, if that's who you're looking for," Lodestone said quietly when he noticed me looking around.

I hadn't realized I was, but the circumstances were much the same as they had been for the Crew Classic once I thought about it. I was de-rigging a small boat, in this case the single I planned to race. Cisco and Jack worked nearby on the pair they'd be racing.

"Good." I felt Lodestone's eyes still on me, but I didn't say anything.

"Remy… if there's anything you want to…."

I looked up. "No."

What did he want me to say? *Gosh, Coach, Josh and I have been getting it on all summer, and we still would be, but I screwed it up by overreacting to his hickeys. If he hadn't been mauled or I'd been better at hiding my disappointment, you'd never have known about this and called the cops.*

He looked like he didn't believe me. His choice. I had a boat to de-rig. I tried to smile. I'm sure it came out looking like I was about to bite him. Smiles never came naturally to me. Why did so much of my life lately consist of reassuring adults of my mental status?

I finished with my single and all its parts. "You guys need any help?"

Jack nodded. "We wouldn't turn it down."

"Can you bind up the riggers?" Cisco said.

"I'm on it." The ritual of the process calmed me in a way. We'd all done our best to prepare. The races started the day after tomorrow, and we were into our taper. Sure, we'd have short, hard rows at the venue, but the long practices were done. Now all that was left was for me to psych myself out, but the common chores like these kept me from that. I suspected Lodestone had me figured out by now, which was why he inevitably assigned me to de-rig and re-rig. Then, too, as soon as I reached the venue, I'd take my prerace walk to suss out the course, never mind how many times I'd raced on it.

After we had secured all the rowing shells to the trailer and stowed the rigging and boxes of spare parts in the base of said trailer, we were essentially done.

"All right, ladies and gentlemen, this is it. You've worked hard all year and especially all summer for this," Lodestone said. He had been the coach in charge because he had been able to take the afternoon off.

Sabrina Littlewolf was at work, as nurses were in demand and she had actually been required to work overtime. "I want you to take it easy for the rest of the afternoon and get a good night's rest. Sleep in tomorrow morning and tell your parents it's coach's orders."

We all laughed at that. Our parents knew the score and had agreed to this when they had given permission for us to participate in the Nationals.

"I'll be driving the trailer up to Lake Natoma in the morning, and I expect to see you all—rested—by noon," Lodestone continued. "Any questions?"

Someone from the girls' team raised her hand. "How much do we need to bring in the way of food or drinks or anything?"

I stifled my groan. She had been rowing with the junior crew as long as I had. Had we *ever* had to bring anything? I mean, there was a reason the juniors' program cost so much.

"Don't worry about a thing, unless there's something special you want or need. At this point, it's about race psychology. There'll be the usual parent volunteer table there," Lodestone said. "If you want a T-shirt or any other merchandise to validate the experience, you'll need money, otherwise, that's it. Anything else?"

When no one said anything, Lodestone said, "Git, y'all."

"Git, y'all?" I said as everyone left.

Lodestone smiled. "I've told you guys about how French is the international language for crew, right?"

"It's called *aviron* in French, right?"

Lodestone nodded. I used to love these times when it was just the two of us. He always seemed more relaxed, even freer somehow, but now? Would I ever recapture that? "Right, so the command to start a race used to be in French—*à vos marques, prêts, partez!* I've never actually heard that at a regatta, by the way, only during practice in college. Well, one time in college, I was at a regatta in Texas, and I swear, the starter forgot it was a US Rowing event or something and yelled, 'Git, y'all!' Funniest thing I've ever heard."

Regattas had always seemed so constipated, with an air of High Seriousness. The thought of an actual US Rowing official saying this had me doubled over in seconds. "That... oh my gawd."

"Easy there, sport," Lodestone said as I struggled to regain my breath. He still had a smile on his face, though.

"You realize that's all I'll hear tomorrow, right?"

He nudged me with his elbow. "That might've been why I said it. You tend to wind yourself up."

I longed to nudge him back, but could not bring myself to do it. "Maybe just a bit."

"I'll see you tomorrow, Remy. Have a good night."

"Good evening, Coach Lodestone."

Behind me, I knew he was frowning but couldn't bring myself to care.

CHAPTER
TEN

I WOKE up at a leisurely pace in the morning. My parents had already left for work. They had offered to come see me race, but I hadn't thought it necessary. They had seen me race before, after all, and I had plans up there that definitely did not include them. They weren't offended, and we planned to go out to dinner that evening when I intended to have hardware—medals—around my neck.

Goff was still home, however, since he had changed his work schedule after the SAT prep and summer school had ended. He knocked on my bedroom door.

"Yeah?"

He stuck his head in and was all smiles. "Hey, you're awake. I just wanted to wish you luck before I left for work. You sure you don't need anyone up there to cheer you on?"

"I'm fine." I smiled back. "It feels like a good day to race."

"Is the only race suicide pace?" he asked, the old crew joke.

I nodded. "And it's a good day to die."

"You're insane." He shook his head. This from a man who regularly let people the size of major appliances land on him?

"I'd be the last to know, I guess."

"Text me the results, okay?"

I smiled again. "Absolutely."

"Okay, I gotta go. See you tonight." Goff ducked out and left.

I didn't bother to shower. What was the point? In a few hours I'd be sweating like a thoroughbred.

Then I got a text, hopefully from Todd, my tatted Viking. I think I had a crush on him just from texting. How pitiful was that? Or maybe I was just pitiful.

I dove for my phone. Yep, pitiful.

T: *See U in a few hours, buddy*
R: *It'll B good 2 finally meet in person.*
T: *Team colors?*
R: *Here's a pic of me in my uni.*
T: *Daaaamn.*
R: *Stop it. Now my uni doesn't fit right.*
T: *Picture. Now.*

I shivered and complied, even though he had changed the terms of our relationship. Or maybe this had been there from the beginning, waiting. Regardless, I was coming to realize I liked being told what to do.

I quickly received one in return.

T: *U do this 2 me.*

He was rock hard.

R: *You'll find me?*
T: *Bet on it and not just because UR hot, Remy. I want to meet U IRL 2.*

I smiled.

R: *Me 2. Now I've gotta get busy or I'll B late.*
T: *Don't U dare :-)*

I had my orders, didn't I?

THE CAP City junior crew got lucky this year. The US Rowing Youth Nationals were held at Lake Natoma, just east of Sacramento, forty-five minutes away from our boathouse. That was as the boat-trailer drove, not as normal traffic moved. As far as regattas went, it was in our backyard. Last year it had been in Oak Ridge, TN, and talk about an expensive trip. We'd spent as much time raising money for the trip as practicing. Anyway, all the rowing clubs and programs in Northern California, if not the northern Pacific coast, lucked out in another way. The course at Lake Natoma on the American River counted as one of the best in North America. That the dam operators were willing to oblige regatta organizers by raising or lowering the water level made it all the better. Okay, the river lacked docks, which entailed wading out into the water, just like the Crew Classic. Since runoff from the Sierra snowpack fed the river, fall races with their colder weather could be an exercise in misery, but in late July? It was heaven.

As always at a regatta, re-rigging was the first order of business. We carried all the boats from the trailer to the staging area along with their rigging and the equipment boxes. Who would row what didn't matter; men and women carried each other's boats. What mattered was transporting boats from the trailer to the slings waiting in our assigned place along the beach.

I worked on my single, but I felt Mikey glaring at me the entire time. I didn't even know what I'd done this time. Probably nothing. Every time I looked up at him, he'd look away quickly, but I knew what that game looked like. What I couldn't figure out was why he was there in the first place. He wasn't rowing in the regatta and kissing the coach's ass was not a part of his makeup, particularly since Lodestone wasn't even his coach.

Another thing puzzled me, however. Where was Cisco?

I wasn't the only one who missed him.

"Where's my pair partner? I'm going to have a hard time racing if he doesn't show up," Jack said. He had a point.

"We've got time," Lodestone said.

That didn't stop our coach from checking his watch with increasing frequency. I also noticed that he called Cisco more than once. As much as being late to a regatta was not done, things happened. Maybe traffic had gotten bad after I'd arrived at Lake Natoma. It wouldn't have been the first time. Or his car had trouble. Things happened. Not calling, however? That was unusual. Cisco was a stand-up guy.

I put it out of my mind. Jack and Lodestone were worrying enough for the whole team, and ultimately it would have no impact on my race. I needed to get moving if I was going to walk the course before my practice row.

"Walking?" Jack said.

I nodded. "You know it."

"Can I come with?"

"Always." I'd hoped to go find Todd, but what could I have said?

"Hey, Mikey! You coming?" Jack called.

I flinched. Great. The whole team, even the women, were joining me. Oh well, nothing to be done about it, especially not since Goody Castelreigh, who seemed to be in a censorious mood again, decided to tag along. So much for scoping out Todd on the sly.

The Nationals course was the same length as the Crew Classic—two thousand meters—but unlike that race, I only went through the motions. I'd rowed this course so many times, and I was so distracted, but unlike the San Diego race, the weather up here was far less variable. Yet there I was, walking the two thousand meters again, pretending to look at the water levels and where in the river the regatta organizers had situated the race lanes, things like that. It struck me as so pointless. The race would be what it was, and I'd verify it empirically all too soon.

And there he was, my tatted Viking. Todd kept it strictly professional. His program—the one he coached for, not the one he rowed for—had fielded a much larger crew than Cap City, which explained why he was there as assistant coach. Funny, that. They had had to travel much farther than we did, but perhaps it was a larger club or maybe they were just better than we were this year. But that wasn't what I was thinking about right then. He stayed in coaching mode, I stayed in rower mode, just another high school rower amidst his teammates. But eye contact was established, and I saw a definite glint in his eye. He turned away as quickly as he'd made eye contact, but a short time later my phone vibrated in my pocket.

I played it cool. I didn't check the message until we were back to Cap City's boats. I had to work hard to keep my face neutral as I read his message: very precise instructions on where to meet him after my row. He even included a picture of the location. Fortunately, I knew this venue well.

I opened a sports drink, but drank only a small amount, mostly to stay hydrated rather than tank up. It was time for a practice row, anyhow. "Any instructions, Coach?"

"I want you on the water for no more than a half hour. That includes warming up and cooling for ten minutes each. That leaves you ten minutes for hard work," Lodestone said. "This is just to warm your muscles up and keep them warm, and nothing more. That goes for all of you. Ladies, you too, unless Coach Littlewolf has told you something different. These prerace practices aren't to increase your conditioning. You're in the shape you're going to be in...."

I nodded obediently. I knew all this. He said it before every race. I had other things on my mind, things like Todd. Something had shifted, maybe with this morning's texting, maybe with the knowledge that we'd be in the same general area. We weren't flirting anymore, we were circling, sniffing each other out. Now that I knew what to look for, I realized I could see Todd clearly from where we were. He could see me, too. I felt his eyes on me while I stripped down to my uni. Smiling to myself, I stretched and scratched. I couldn't hear him, but I certainly saw him stumble.

"Crap!"

I looked up. Mikey had spilled chocolate milk down his front and was now glaring at me, like somehow it was my fault. I would never understand him, but then, it wasn't my job to, either. I realized that by launching and taking a practice row I could escape Mikey and his issues.

"Mikey?" I heard Lodestone say. "There's still no sign of Cisco. If he's not here in fifteen minutes, could you go out with Jack? I'd like him to get a row in, too...."

I frowned. It really wasn't like Cisco to be so late for a regatta.

I'D TAKEN my practice row and then found some shade to rest in. Fortunately a breeze took the edge off the heat, enough to cool the place off but not so much as to count as a crosswind. Crosswinds bad, cooling off in late July good. Watching the races might have been courteous, but I launched soon as it was and I wanted to rest up and psych myself up.

I sensed rather than saw someone sit next to me. "Hi," Mikey said softly.

"Hey."

The silence thickened.

"You're not going to make this easy on me, are you?" He laughed uncomfortably.

I sighed. "I launch in less than ten minutes. It's a big race. I'm not in the mood for any drama, and Mikey? All I've gotten from you since school got out is drama."

"I know, and I'm sorry. That's… that's what I wanted to talk about," he said, his voice almost too quiet to hear.

I sat up and looked at him. That was the last thing I needed right then. "Did you hear me? This needs to wait. You've waited this long, another hour won't kill you."

"You know what? Never mind." Mikey got up. "Forget I said anything."

Fat chance. "Thanks, Mikey. Timing's everything, and yours sucks."

I tried to ignore him as he stomped off. I abandoned any hope of real rest and tried to focus on deep breathing to calm down, but it was a lost cause. I gave it up and got ready to launch. More sunscreen, oars to the water, and then Lodestone.

When I reached Lodestone, he was on his phone. "Cisco, man. Where are you? Call me."

I frowned, worried now. This was so unlike Cisco.

"Anything to say before I launch?"

Lodestone shook his head. "This is your race to lose. The competition will be stiff, but you know that. Keep your head in your boat and in your lane. When you get excited, you sometimes row at a higher rating than you need to, so don't be afraid to take your pace down a few strokes per minute."

I nodded. "Right-o. Time to get on the water."

Whatever my distractions on land—I saw Todd wink at me as I took my single to the water, but ignored him—I focused on the water and the rowing to the exclusion of all else. It irritated my friends, or so I was told, but they weren't the ones rowing in the Youth Nationals.

Carrying my boat on one shoulder, I waded out until the water lapped at the bottom of my unisuit. Flipping it up and overhead, I placed my boat in the water and held it steady while someone brought me my oars. I've seen some scullers who could do it all, but I wasn't there, yet.

By the time I had the oars secured in the oarlocks I was so deep inside my rowing headspace I didn't even know who had helped me. Then I climbed into my boat. I could have done this in my sleep, but I was wide awake and taking everything in as I paddled away from the shore.

The American River just before the Nimbus Dam was wide enough to accommodate six lanes this year. I had seen seven after particularly wet winters. It all depended on how much runoff came down from the Sierra Nevada range, or rather, on how much water the dam operators thought they could spare if they fiddled with the water levels for us. Oddly enough, regattas weren't the reason the dam existed.

I had an okay lane, not great. I was on the far side of the course but not the farthest lane. Those far lanes usually felt the crosswinds the worst, but it was a poor rower who blamed his performance on weather, at least not until the weather turned severe. Chop, strong winds, hail, lightning, sure, but this little breeze? I ignored it in favor of getting to my lane before the line refs grew cranky. So long as I wasn't the last one at the line, I was golden.

I sized up my competition. I was larger than a lot of the other scullers, save for one guy. He looked like a gorilla. On the one hand, more muscle mass meant more weight to haul down the course. On the other, the water supported a lot of that weight. Still, I pegged him as the one to watch. I could just see him out of the corner of my eyes. Sure, being on the starting line like that was always a head trip, but I also knew that they all felt the same way and at least one of the guys was no doubt thinking the same thing about me. I smiled and sat confidently in my start position. Let them sweat. I was ready.

"We have alignment," the announcer said.

"Ready all!"

The muscles of my legs bunched, coiling like powerful springs, ready to push the boat from a dead stop into motion with the first stroke.

"Row!"

Git, y'all!

I laughed as I left the line.

The thing was, even with a single, I couldn't just go from a dead stop to full speed. Doing so only courted premature exhaustion and risked injury. So I used a fairly common start sequence. A first stroke that was legs-only—no back swing and no arms—and only half of the slide, just enough to overcome the boat's inertia, and then two more quick strokes that used only three-quarters of the slide and nothing else, and then a final a legs-only stroke before lengthening a bit and taking "twenty high," twenty strokes above my planned pace for the rest of the race. That was what Lodestone had meant about rowing too fast. I had the nasty habit of lengthening my stroke out—legs, body swing, and arms—while still maintaining a high number of strokes per minute.

It drove Lodestone crazy when he was coaching me, particularly when other people were trying to follow me, but out here? I was alone. Races had been lost because some fool turned his head to look around—no joke—but I could flick my eyes back and forth. But that afternoon, I didn't need to. I counted five people behind me, which looked like in front of me. Join crew! Find happiness looking backward! That said, the gorilla and a smaller guy were gaining on me, and hell no.

The only pace was suicide pace, and today was a good day to die.

Up to this point, I'd been rowing at a fast clip, but my ratio—the speed of my leg drive down the tracks that held the seat compared to the time it took me to travel back up to get back into position for another stroke—needed improvement. That was one reason Lodestone distrusted my tendency to speed. If I kept the ratio clean, great. I flew across the top of the water. If I got sloppy, I wasted my energy and didn't let the mechanism of the boat do its job. I'd gotten sloppy, and the result was those two guys gaining on me.

With a deep breath and herculean effort, I marshaled all my focus and forced myself to slow down my recovery. "Let the boat run under you, Remy," I repeated over and over. A longer recovery meant more oxygen for my starved muscles, which in turn meant stronger leg drives.

Slowly, I pulled away from my competition, and by the fifteen-hundred-meter mark, my change had made a noticeable difference. Sure, the gorilla and the smaller guy made changes in response, but would it be enough to make a difference?

I'd wasted a lot of energy earlier in the race. I knew that, but with five hundred meters left in the race, it was time to make a move. I didn't have much choice. My two challengers were making theirs, trying to outsprint me at the end because they knew the mistake I'd made, too.

This was it. I had to empty the tank and hope I had enough left to last. Struggling to maintain that all-important ratio, I brought the stroke rating back up. At that point, technique was a fantasy. All I did was hack at the water.

By the time I saw the red buoys that marked the final one hundred meters, the gorilla and I were bow to stern. If I let up for even a second, that ape would take the race. Son of a bitch. I was pissed. My race to lose, huh? We'd just see about that.

It was personal now. The gorilla knew it and I knew it. He looked over his shoulder and his boat wobbled. That was it. My legs burned with all the fires of hell, but I stood on the foot stretchers for the last ten strokes. I didn't care how I hurt or if I broke the boat. I was going to win this if it was the last thing I did or if I popped a tendon. This race was mine, dammit.

Then the air horn blared. I had won, but it had been close, hard-fought, and only by half a boat length. I was furious and had only myself to blame.

"Good row, man," Gorilla said.

I was pretty sure I managed something polite in return, but it was time for me to be out of there. Out of my headspace, I remembered Todd. What was going on with him? I knew he wanted to meet, but beyond that? I was bereft of clue and rowing back to shore was not the time to hunt for one. Far too many boats jockeyed for position for me to space out.

I paddled back to Cap City's stretch of beach, allowing myself a small smile as I passed Todd. To my surprise, he unabashedly stared as I passed. Maybe he was telling his rowers what not to do.

When I landed, far enough from the shore that I wouldn't scratch the rowing shell's hull, no one was there to take the oars. Classy. Someone was *always* supposed to be there to take the oars.

I didn't think the current would take the boat, so I took one oar out its oarlock and anchored the other oar's handle in the sand, hoping it would hold long enough to dash up the beach and stash the first oar. I figured I could handle the boat and the other oar.

I guess Todd saw me struggling because he ran up to me. "What the hell? Where're your teammates?"

"Beats me." My mood had grown worse since I landed.

Todd looked at me. "You okay?"

"It was a shitty row, and this isn't helping."

"For what it's worth, you looked good out there," he said. Then he gave me a once-over, grinning slowly.

I laughed, I couldn't help it. "Thanks. I threw my race plan right out and then scrambled to make up for it during the second thousand meters. Then my team was apparently busy enough that a coach from another team has to come help me. Not that I'm not grateful, by the way. It's all just...."

"I get it." Todd moved in closer. "Just like I'm going to get you in about twenty. You still game?"

I shuddered, then checked my heart-rate monitor for the time. "Yes."

Todd had to hustle back to his own team, especially if he was going to disappear in twenty minutes, but he first helped me with the oars as I carried my boat back to its slings.

"Hey, thanks for the help, you guys!" I said brightly as I lowered the boat into the slings.

Some of them jumped, like they'd forgotten about me, and that felt oh so swell. At least a few looked guilty. Good. You're there when your teammates land. Period.

I sighed. What was the point? Suddenly none of it felt like it mattered. I was about to start on the de-rigging and then realized that didn't matter, either. Someone else could do it. I had just worked rather hard, and I wanted to rest and stretch.

Instead I grabbed a sports drink and a protein shake from the parent volunteer table and started to stretch. The last thing I needed was a set of cramps due to dehydration or loss of electrolytes.

A shadow fell over me, and I looked up, expecting to see Mikey. It was Lodestone.

"No one met you, did they?" he said.

I didn't trust myself to say much, particularly not to him. "No."

"I'm really sorry."

"Whatever." I turned back to my stretching, unwilling to admit to him just how it had hurt, how betrayed I had felt at that moment. Maybe I hadn't wanted to admit it myself, either. I'd always bought into the "team" bit wholeheartedly, but now.... I wasn't so sure. "It's fine."

Lodestone sat down. "It's not, is it?"

I hated how well he could read me. Hated it. I jumped up. "Not now. Not right fucking now," I yelled.

I took off down the jogging path that snaked around Lake Natoma.

"Remy!" he called.

I ignored him.

At the end of it all, he wasn't the boss of me.

CHAPTER
ELEVEN

I MADE it halfway around the lake before I remembered there was somewhere else I wanted to be. *Good going, Remy*, I thought. *You're cocking it up left and right today.*

I turned around, not at all sure I wanted to meet Todd anymore, not at all sure I *should* meet him just then. I mean, how much more of a buzzkiller could the day turn out to be? But I found my way to the place Todd had suggested, an out-of-the-way spot, secluded and neglected. Hope there weren't any rattlers....

One thing for sure, with all the dried leaves and pine needles, we'd hear anyone approaching, which was how I knew Todd had arrived.

He stepped up behind me, embracing me from behind. I relaxed into him. It was actually a relief to do so. I realized something in that moment, too. This was what I had been missing all summer, and I hadn't even known it.

Todd kissed the back of my neck, and I arched into it. "Hey, beautiful," he said.

"Hi."

"Is this okay?" he said.

I thought about it for the briefest moment because that was all it took. "Yes."

"Good, because do you have any idea how long I've been waiting to do this?"

I shook my head. "All day?"

"Since we first started getting to know each other."

I didn't know what to say to that. I pulled his arms tighter around me instead.

"Is something wrong?" he asked.

"Yes? No? Maybe?"

"Can you repeat the question?" He laughed. "What? I like They Might Be Giants, too."

"Let's go sit down," I said, pointing at a picnic table, "but watch your feet. There're snakes up here, and some are poisonous."

Todd froze. "You're kidding."

"No, but rattlesnakes almost always warn you before they strike." I tugged on his hand, finally getting him moving.

I ended up spilling my guts about Mikey, about Josh, about feeling abandoned by the team, even about Lodestone coming up to me. The entire time, Todd peppered the back of my neck with ghostly little kisses, sometimes just resting his lips against the soft skin back there, holding me close the entire time.

I'd never been held like that by someone who cared. It was… amazing. He didn't try to fix things, he just listened. Somehow that helped shrink the things that had infuriated me earlier, the things that made me run from my coach and teammates, back down to size. Maybe they were not so bad, after all. Was this what having a boyfriend would be like? Was this what I'd been missing?

Todd groaned, burying his face against my back. "Aww, Remy. You're killing me."

I scooted back against him, suddenly desperate for closer contact. "What? How?"

"You make me want things with you I can't have."

I thought I knew what he meant. I craned my head back to kiss him. "You mean like something besides a hurried encounter in an unused campsite?"

Todd's shoulders slumped. "Yeah, that."

He sounded a little sad, but I still felt something poking me. "I know what you mean, but that doesn't mean I'd turn down that encounter."

"Does this mean someone's feeling better about things?"

"I'm feeling really good about at least one thing." I reached behind me to feel him. "Whoa. You really live up to that picture."

"Yeah? Think you can take it?"

I turned around so I could kiss him properly. "I know I'm going to try. I hope you thought to bring something to get me ready, because I can't take that monster dry."

"Then it's a good thing I was a Boy Scout, isn't it?" Todd said before he captured my mouth. Funny, but his kisses weren't scary at all. He ran his hands down my chest before he pulled the top of my uni down. I wondered how much I'd be left wearing before he was done with me.

I broke the kiss. "You clean?"

"Yeah, you?" he said breathlessly.

"As a whistle."

I JOGGED back to Cap City's staging area in a melancholy mood. I knew exactly what Todd had meant by wanting things he couldn't have. He made me want to keep something going long-distance for the next year and then apply to Iowa State, just so we could be together. I hadn't said anything about that to him. I needed to think about it first, maybe talk to Goff about it, but damn. We seemed to click on a bunch of levels—

"Where've you been?" Mikey hissed. "You launch now!"

"Wait, what?" I stopped. He grabbed my arm, but I yanked it out of his grip. So much for feeling better about things. What was it about Mikey that made me angry all over again? That boy got under my skin like nothing else.

"There's no time to explain. Cisco still isn't here. You're in his boat, which you would know if you hadn't been AWOL, debasing yourself up against a tree," Mikey hissed.

"What I do or don't do, Michael Castelreigh, is none of your goddamn business, whether it involves trees or not," I snapped, "because as you may or may not recall, you rejected me. As for AWOL, I rowed my race. The last I'd heard, when I put my boat in slings, I was entered in only one race, a race which I won. Perhaps someday you'll know what a win at Nationals feels like, but until that far-off day, you can blow yourself straight to hell. And it wasn't a tree, it was a picnic table."

Mikey flinched. "Remy…. I'm… I'm sorry. You and I have unfinished business, but now's not the time. Lodestone needs you."

I was still mad at Mikey, still furious at Lodestone even. I'm not sure I'd have peed on Mikey if he were burning, but Lodestone? I knew I'd still walk through fire a hundred times over for him, even if I was angry at him, even if I'd taken off on him. I ran for Cap City's boats.

"Thank God," Lodestone said when I ran up. "I need you to jump in the pair for Cisco."

"What? I can't row a pair."

Lodestone shook his head. "Not now, Remy. Just do it. I have to go beg the race organizers to allow the substitution."

"Coach. I don't row pairs. I can't. You know that."

Suddenly Lodestone looked about a thousand years old. "Remy, you're my best rower. You can row anything, and you know it. Right now, Cisco needs you more than you'll ever know, and so do I."

Which was how I ended up in a pair, a configuration I hated, with Todd sticking to my back. Mikey knew it and gave me a look of purest disgust, but worst of all, Lodestone seemed to know it, and that cut like a thousand knives. It might've been a river launch without a dock, but no amount of water could wash away how disgusted I was with myself, by myself, just then.

I'd already downed a sports drink to recover electrolytes after my race, and that plus the run and stretches were going to have to count as my recovery. Jack and I had just enough time for some power pieces on the way to the starting line.

"Nice job, you sick fuck," Jack hissed once we were on the water. I guess he knew what I'd been up to, as well.

"Shut it." The one thing he'd overlooked when he mouthed off was that Cisco had been the stroke and now I was. I might've already raced today, and while Jack was fresh, I was furious. My revenge would take the form of a punishing stroke rating.

Then we were at the starting line and ready to go. "We're rowing this between a thirty-six and a thirty-eight, asshole," I said to Jack. "Try not to fuck it up."

"What! I can't—"

I smiled, but it lacked all humor or mirth. "You *will*. First thirty strokes at a thirty-eight, settle to a thirty-six, bitch."

"No way." He smacked the back of my head, but I didn't care.

"There's no pace but suicide pace, Jack."

"We have alignment," said the starter through her bullhorn.

Jack spat in the water. "Fuck you."

"This is for Cisco. I'll kill you if I have to."

"Ready all! Row!"—*Git, y'all!*—came the starter's call, and we were off.

My legs burned right after that start, but I would've died before I called the stroke rating down. I had something to prove, and Jack needed to back up his attitude with performance or quit rowing. Besides, my coach had said he needed me, and I'd have done almost anything for Cisco.

By seven hundred and fifty meters, I knew only pain—pain in my legs, pain in my lungs, pain in my hands as I tore them to shreds on the oar handle. I didn't care.

By a thousand meters, I heard Jack gasp, "Remy... *please.*"

I grinned. I lived for this.

"Cisco," I gasped.

By fifteen hundred meters, Jack was sobbing.

I became a death eater then, punishing Jack, punishing myself.

"Thirty-eight... lengthen in two.... One... two.... Now!"

Now I am become Death.

My vision tunneled down. I saw only the water in our lane.

"Remy!" Jack cried.

The destroyer of rowers.

"There's... line!... Empty... it!"

I saw only the red haze of blood. Then I heard the air horn that signaled we had crossed the line. Jack and I dropped our oars. I fell backward, gasping for breath, gasping for life. Our boat drifted.

"Cap City, check it down."

I couldn't have cared less. Jack vomited over the gunwales.

"Cap City, check it down now. Acknowledge."

I sat up, my lips and hands numb, my vision blurry.

"Cap City, you are heading for the dam's spillway. Check it down or forfeit."

I roused myself from my stupor enough to raise my hand. "Check it down," I mumbled to Jack.

"Huh?" he said, just as groggy as I.

"Check it down," I said sharply. "The refs are pissed."

Over the PA I heard the ref chuckle. "That, ladies and gentlemen, is giving it your all. Are you boys all right?"

I waved listlessly, then gave the commands to turn our boat and take it back to Cap City's place on the beach. As we rowed by, bystanders in the grandstands and along the beach clapped, but I was too wiped to care. The announcer said something else, something about us and our row, but it was nothing more than a buzz in the background.

"You, Remy, are an asshole," Jack said, "but a damn good rower. Dude… I think we won."

"Whatever." I was too dead to care.

"Remy… is something wrong?" Jack said.

I turned to look at him. "Like you even care."

"Asshole."

"If it's not rowing, it's not my concern," I said as we climbed into the water.

He sighed behind me. "You really do operate on a different plane from the rest of us, don't you?"

This time our team actually met us. I regarded them like a sovereign does his subjects because I had nothing left to give anyone. "Deal with it."

"Dude…," Mikey breathed as I brushed by.

"Don't even." There was only one person I would talk to right then. "Where is he?"

"Who?" Mikey said.

I looked at him like he was stupid. At least he was smart enough to figure it out. "Oh. At the judges' tent."

I grabbed another sports drink and some flip-flops. I hoped they were mine. I was in no mood to deal with anyone I didn't have to, and right then I was stalking my coach.

I caught up to Lodestone, and yes, he was right where Mikey had indicated.

One of the US Rowing referees spotted me before Lodestone did. "Congratulations, young man. That was quite a performance," she said, shaking my hand.

"Thank you, ma'am."

The referee, an older woman, looked grave. "A tragic situation, very unfortunate."

I'd only ever heard the phrase "blood ran cold." Just then I lived it. "Then you know more than I do, ma'am. This was the hottest hot seating I've ever done. All my coach told me was that he and Cisco needed me more than they ever have before."

"I'd better let your coach fill you in, Mr. Babcock. Under the circumstances, we allowed the substitution, but your performance made them both proud. We awarded three medals in this case."

"Thank you again, Maryanne," Lodestone said. "I've got some news to deliver."

The referee nodded. "I understand."

"Coach? What's going on?" I felt my fury drain away, leaving only fear.

He wiped a tear away. "Let's find somewhere private, okay?"

As we walked, he put an arm around my shoulder. "Sometimes I really hate being an adult."

We ended up sitting in the shade of a tree far away from the tumult of the regatta. "Please, Coach, can you tell me what's happening? You and that ref, you're kind of scaring me."

"I'm sorry, Remy. That was never the intention." Lodestone sighed. "First of all, your race was amazing. I get that you were pretty angry—"

"I was furious. Jack mouthed off once we were out of range—"

Lodestone snorted. "You weren't out of range, and I'll deal with him. Let's just say sound carries on the water."

"Yeah? Well, we raced at a thirty-eight for most of that piece."

"I know. I counted. You looked good. He looked miserable." Lodestone grinned and held up a stopwatch. "Anyway, it was a good race, and if you haven't figured it out, you won. Two golds today, Remy. I told you, you can row anything. Next year, you're rowing small boats for any race that has them, but that's not the point. I owe you an explanation."

"Cisco," I whispered.

He nodded. "Cisco. After your race in the single, I got a call from a member of Cisco's family, one of his older brothers. His parents were running late, speeding to get here. They were in an accident."

I gasped. "No."

"His parents didn't make it. Died at the scene. Cisco was airlifted to the Med Center and was in surgery." Lodestone choked up. I could tell he was fighting not to cry. "His... his brother knew how important this was to him and called me. His little brother was on the table and fighting for his life, and he called me to tell me that Cisco was in surgery."

We both lost it at that point. After Lodestone recovered enough to talk, he said, "He didn't make it, Remy. He's gone."

We didn't return to the boats for a long time. Mikey stomped up to me when Lodestone and I trudged back, but one look at our red eyes and he backed off, a question on his face. All I could do was shake my head and clutch my gold medals, which meant nothing that afternoon. Maybe later they would. I sat numbly on a bench. I thought I heard someone yell something about getting off my ass, but Lodestone bit his head off. Then the poor man took Jack aside and got to repeat the bad news all over again.

The referees made an announcement about Cisco, however, and the regatta observed a moment of silence. A rower had died on the way to the races, and that lightning-fast pair? That had been a race in his honor. It hadn't been in Cisco's honor at the time, but it helped Cap City's legend and made a fitting memorial for my friend. Rowing had no tradition to honor our dead, so it wasn't like people saluted or anything, but Cap City—juniors and masters—would honor Cisco later.

Mikey pried my phone away from me and called Goff. Goff and my dad drove up to get me. Todd came and held me as long as he could, but ultimately he had responsibilities of his own. Then Mikey took over. I remember Goff driving me home in our car while Dad drove home in his. I felt safe letting go in front of him and telling him about the accident, because he knew Cisco, too. Mom was waiting for us when we pulled up, and I was never so glad to be around my family as I was that afternoon. My family circled the wagons around me and allowed me to let go in a way I hadn't since I was little. I remembered the phones ringing too much, my cell phone as well as the home line, but Mom unplugged the landlines and Goff took control of my cell phone. Goff also undressed me and made me shower. He dried me off and made me go to bed, too. Mom cancelled everything, and surprisingly, she stayed home from work for a few days to take care of me. I'd never lost a friend like that before, and I didn't know what to do. Dad did, however. He was a shrink, after all.

CHAPTER
TWELVE

AFTER GIVING me a few days to recover physically and emotionally, days in which Cisco's funeral had been scheduled and Dad had dragged me and Goff out to buy new suits since ours no longer fit, Goff moved in for the kill. I was sure he didn't see it that way, but that was how it felt.

We lazed around the pool in the backyard. It wasn't much of a pool, but then, the yard wasn't that big, either. Land cost too much for huge lots in California, or at least in Davis. Smallish yards meant small pools. We could get wet, but it wasn't good for swimming laps or anything.

"So," Goff said, paddling his inflatable raft over to where I rested in the shade, "who was that guy holding you before Mikey took over?"

Aww, jeez, so much for dodging that bullet. "What guy?"

"Don't play dumb." Goff splashed me. It actually felt pretty good.

I started thinking about Todd. We had continued to text and had even added Skype after the regatta. I missed him. A lot.

"Oh. My. God."

I looked up at Goff. He sported the biggest shit-eating grin I had ever seen in my life. "What?"

"My brother's got a crush on a guy. The great ice prince falls."

I made a face. "Your obscene gloating is very unbecoming."

"Oh no, you don't," Goff said. He cackled with glee. "You're not going to wriggle out of this that easily."

"I could roll off this and swim for a while. You'd never believe how long I can hold my breath," I said hopefully.

Goff rolled his eyes. "You'd have to surface sooner or later, and if you're down there too long, I'll get the skimmer and fish you out. Now talk."

"His name's Todd Nelson, and he's an assistant coach for another team. Before you get too excited, he's only eighteen, so it's not creepy or anything." I let myself smile at the thought of him. "He's the closest I've had to a boyfriend, I guess."

"That's great, Remy. I'm happy for you. So where'd you meet him?"

It was a logical question, but somehow I felt defensive. "Um... online?"

"Is that a question or a statement?" Goff said.

Maybe I could pretend my embarrassment was an impending sunburn. "A statement," I said with a sigh. "We met online, Grindr, actually. We're just friends, really, but by the time the Nationals rolled around, we both realized it could be so much more."

"That's great, Remy. So what's the problem?"

"He lives in Iowa."

"Oh."

"Yeah, 'oh' is right. It totally sucks, too. I meet someone I really like, and he lives half a continent away." I threw an arm over my eyes, like I could block out the truth along with the sunlight or something.

"Very nice," Goff said. He sounded far too content for what was basically a sucky situation for me, and I said as much. "Okay, no, the fact that this Todd person lives so far away isn't good, but the fact that you found someone who—ahem—floats your boat, that's good, right? I've been worried about you, Germy. You've always been so aloof, and that's not what I want for you. A crush is better than nothing."

I sat up. "It is not a crush. Is Laurel a crush?"

"No, she's not."

I chucked an empty soda can at him. I missed by miles. I should've put water in it. "Damn straight."

"As it were." Goff snorted. "But long-distance. That's rough."

"I know. Do... do you think I'm crazy for considering applying to the school he goes to?"

Goff tilted his head like he always did when he thought about something. "Not necessarily. How long did you two get to know each other before the race? Two weeks?"

I shook my head. "Most of the summer, but it was all online."

"By itself, that's not enough, but if you can keep the flame going all next year? I don't see why you shouldn't head out there," Goff said. "I mean, one school's pretty much the same as another for undergrad education, isn't it?"

"I guess so." The fact that Goff didn't think I was totally insane made me happy.

"Wait, Germy, did you say Grindr?" I knew it had been too good to last.

"Yeah, but that shouldn't matter, should it?" I really didn't want to talk about that anymore.

Goff shook his head. "Jeez, that's basically a germ farm, right? A Petri dish?"

"How do you know all this?" I asked with a sinking feeling. Because he was right.

"My brother's gay. I'm educating myself."

I thought about it. For some reason, I felt the need to tell him everything. Maybe after the regatta and Lodestone's look when I came back from meeting Todd, it was time to come clean.

"Let's go inside. This isn't something that needs to be broadcast to the neighborhood."

"All right," Goff said, looking at me closely, like he could see the dirt on me, which was absurd. I wasn't dirty. I wasn't morally unclean. I wasn't even germ-ridden. So why did I feel like I had to confess?

After we had dried ourselves off, we flopped out in my room. "So… my summer activities."

"I assume this is beyond work, school, and rowing?" Goff said, raising an eyebrow.

I nodded. "You assume correctly. I've been a busy boy."

And with that, I told my brother how I'd learned my way around men's bodies. I spared him some details, but I made my point.

To Goff's credit and my surprise, all he said was, "Were you safe? What about condoms? Our stash didn't go down that fast. Were you using them?"

"I made sure the guys were clean."

Goff narrowed his eyes. "How?"

"I asked them." Funny how I'd felt that was enough all summer, but I was suddenly afraid of talking to my brother. "Besides, even if they had it, if they were on meds, they couldn't pass it on."

Christopher Koehler

Goff shook his head. "Dude, I don't think that's how it works," Goff whispered. "I'm going to check with Laurel. And Remy? I think you should get tested."

I didn't need to ask him for what.

"HOW'RE YOU holding up?" Todd said. We were on Skype again. He wanted a lot more of my time after Nationals, or so it seemed.

I smiled, or tried to. "I'm okay. Cisco's funeral's tomorrow. That's going to be rough."

"I wish I could be there to support you." He looked worried.

"I'll be okay." What choice did I have? "I'm more worried about what's left of his family, you know? Both parents, plus Cisco? He has—had—a younger sister. What's going to happen to her?"

Todd frowned. "That's rough. Any relatives close by?"

"A couple of older siblings, including the one who called my coach while I was racing my single. It's not like she'll be at the mercy of the system or anything, but still. That's a lot of loss for one family."

"It is indeed."

We deliberately moved the conversation into safer waters after that, or at least less emotionally fraught waters. You can only talk about death for so long, even the death of a friend. But I soon realized rowing and that one hookup were really all we had in common, and even I got tired of talking about rowing.

Then Todd grew still. "Who's that?"

"What? Who's who?" I looked around. The only person in the room was Goff, and all he was doing was reading on my bed.

"That guy in your room." Todd looked pissed, like crazy jealous pissed.

I felt rather than saw Goff sit up behind me. I think he snickered.

"That's my brother," I said, laughing.

Todd's eyes narrowed, like he didn't believe me. "You never said you had a brother."

"No, but I never said I didn't either. Jeez, calm down. Geoff, meet Todd. Todd, this is Geoff, my twin brother."

"You two look nothing alike." Todd was turning redder by the minute, and I was suddenly glad he lived halfway across the country.

"Did I say identical twin? No, I did not. You really need to calm down. Even if I weren't—"

"Pardon me, Germy," Goff said. He held his iPhone up to the camera on my computer. "Excuse the small print, but check it out. It's the wiki entry for 'fraternal twins.' Read it. Absorb it. Become one with it. Then have a little more respect for my brother, asshole."

"Germy?" Todd's eyes had gone flat.

"My full name is Jeremy, and believe it or not, brothers sometimes have nicknames for each other." I realized I was speaking very slowly, as if Todd's comprehension was in question. It might sound patronizing, but right then I didn't care. "It really doesn't matter if you believe Geoff and I are fraternal twins or not. Even if he were just a friend, I get to have those, too. It's not like we're boyfriends, so I'm not sure where you're getting this jealousy bullshit? But it needs to go back there."

"I have to go," Todd said.

I nodded. "I think that's a good idea."

"I've got a boyfriend," he blurted suddenly.

Goff appeared back over my shoulder. "What?"

"Get him out of here," Todd snapped.

"No, he's fine where he is," I said. "So about this boyfriend...."

Todd laughed. "Dude, I thought you—"

"Don't 'dude' me. I've got all our texts. You never said a damn thing about a boyfriend." I had a feeling this was more about Todd's jealousy and less about a boyfriend, real or imagined.

"It's not like it matters."

I thought about it for a short while. "It would've to me. We wouldn't have hooked up, for starters."

Todd didn't say anything, but I suddenly didn't like the whole vibe of our interaction since the Youth Nationals. I reached for the keyboard to disconnect the conversation. "Lose my number."

Todd looked panic-stricken. "Remy, wait! I'm sorry, I didn't mean—"

I cut him off and deleted the app from my desktop.

Goff, still standing behind me, said, "I know that must've hurt, but I think you did the right thing."

"I don't really know what just happened, but I'm younger than Todd, so why am I older than he is?"

"Remy," Goff said, putting his hand on my shoulder, "you've never been young, not once in your whole life."

THE DAY after Cisco's funeral, Cap City honored his passing with a ceremony on the dock. Lodestone had already hung his portrait and a framed copy of his obituary along with his honorary medal in the pairs at the back of the boathouse. That made me sad. Within a few years, no one would know who he had been, the chemicals in his picture would turn and the portrait fade, the obituary's cheap newsprint would yellow, and then it would all end up in a drawer.

With those depressing thoughts on my mind, I sat on the dock watching the setting sun and waiting for Lodestone, who'd said he wanted to speak to me. I was probably ruining my suit, but whatever. Maybe if I looked hard enough into the setting sun....

Lodestone sat down beside me, rubbing his hand over his face, like he was tired or something. Then again, the Nationals were over, and it occurred to me he'd put at least as much energy into this as we rowers had. Everyone was all tired.

"Remy...." He paused, and I realized he was red under his tan and not from the August heat. "I nominated myself for this because I'm your coach, but I'm also hoping in a way I'm still your friend and because I doubt very much you've spoken to your parents about this."

I cringed. I knew where this was going. "Coach, please... don't."

"Remy... Jeremy, I think I have to. After a certain conversation with Josh Brennan, as well as my own observations, I have an idea what some of your leisure-time activities might've been—might be—this summer."

"This isn't any of your business." I stood up, or tried. Lodestone put his hand on my arm. Damn, he was strong.

"Sit down, Remy. Please. This isn't an inquisition or anything, and I'm not going to run to your parents. I'm worried about you." Lodestone sighed. "Your sexual orientation isn't a secret around the boathouse, and wasn't before the Crew Classic in April. I know you're gay, and hopefully you know by now that I don't care, but you're doing some risky things, and I need—as your friend—to make sure you're taking care of yourself."

I swallowed the lump in my throat. "What do you mean, risky?"

"That you can say that tells me I'm way too late." He closed his eyes for a moment. "Sabrina would be far better suited for this. She's a nurse, you know. I'm glad I asked her—"

I jumped to my feet. "That's it. I'm out of here—"

"Sit!" That time he didn't place his hand on my arm, he clamped on to me and forced me back down. "I didn't name names, I just told her I needed information. You should know by now that you're not the only gay rower. Neither you nor Mikey, for that matter. Remy, there's nothing intrinsically wrong with what you're doing, but you've got to take care of yourself. Has anyone ever talked to you about safer sex?" Lodestone said.

"I've heard the term, but that's like, from the eighties or something, right?" Suddenly this whole conversation made me very uncomfortable.

"That's when it started, yes," Lodestone said, "but it's still very real. How about negotiated risk?"

I shook my head. Something told me I might've made a lot of mistakes this summer.

"Okay, Remy, what do the words 'safer sex' mean to you?"

I thought about it for a few moments. "Condoms, mostly. But that's for older guys, like older than you. AIDS is practically curable now, and if you don't play with older guys, there's almost no chance of getting it."

"Oh, Remy." Lodestone looked sad, like someone just kicked his dog. "Nothing could be further from the truth. So what does negotiated risk mean?"

"I know what the words mean, but apparently not what they mean in terms of this conversation." Honestly, what was he getting at?

"It means you and your partner decide together before—got that, *before*—you're intimate what level of risk of exposure to HIV you'll accept." Lodestone looked me in the eyes, and his were bright, like maybe he was trying not to cry. "Some acts are inherently riskier than others, and strangers generally accept less risk than committed partners. This isn't just a gay thing, Remy. My girlfriend and I went through all of this too, and— get this through your head—HIV isn't the only sexual transmitted disease out there."

I didn't know what to say. I wanted to deny all of it. "I'm all right. Everyone said they were clean, Coach."

"You'd better hope they were telling you the truth. You'd better hope they knew the truth themselves, because according to the CDC, most people don't." Lodestone stood up. "Think about what I've said, okay, Remy?"

Like I would've been able to do anything else. "Thanks, Coach. I… yeah. I'll be thinking about it."

CHAPTER
THIRTEEN

TODD TRIED to text me a few more times, but I ignored him. Then Goff showed me how to block his number. I suppose I could have tried to reason with him, but after talking it over with my brother, I decided I didn't need to deal with that kind of bone-deep crazy. Anyone who freaked out because my *brother* was in my room when I spoke to him was not someone I needed in my life. I felt nothing but relief that I had never brought up applying to Todd's school or trying to keep something going long-distance to anyone but Goff.

The last few weeks before my senior year looked to be slow ones, just sculling to stay in shape and light weights at the gym, nothing exciting. Crew resumed regular practices that consisted only of easy, steady-state rowing to ease those who hadn't rowed at Nationals back into the groove. That was most of the team, and true to his word, Lodestone kept me in the single. I enjoyed rowing circles—literal circles—around the big boats. I think Lodestone enjoyed watching it, too.

I caught up on pleasure reading, a relief to read for fun instead of necessity. Goff had also cut back on his activities, although football started to ramp up and much more intensely than crew. So while seeing Goff and spending time at home with him was great, he was dog-tired most of the time.

Seeing Mikey at practice raised specters I thought had been laid to rest. Naïve of me, I suppose. He always looked like he had something he wanted to say to me, too. Since I rowed in a single, I usually managed to be off the water and out of there before he could corner me. The last time he'd cornered me, he'd given me an earful about my mating habits right before what had literally been the biggest race of the year. Since his timing and choice of subject sucked, I didn't see the point to a repeat performance.

Then he cornered me. "You're a slippery one."

"Well, you know, Astroglide." Damnation. I knew I'd gone too far down the river during practice, but the water had been perfect. As a result, I found Mikey sitting on the hood of my car after practice. Sure, it had been a cheap comment, but his consternation made it worthwhile.

Mikey shook his head. "Why do you always make things so difficult?"

"Me? That shoe fits you, Cinderella," I said, jerking the car door open. "Now please, get off my car."

"Actually, you have to give me a ride home. My ride already left." He didn't even look apologetic. In fact, he looked pretty damn smug.

"I should make you walk."

"But you won't, will you?"

I smirked at him and drove off. The sight of him standing there, mouth agape, in my rearview mirror was one I'd treasure forever.

Oh, I knew I would give him a ride home, but there was no way I'd reward that kind of behavior without making him sweat for it. Actually all I did was drive until I was out of view and then text him.

R: *Get up here, you fucker.*

Then I opened the passenger door so there could be no mistaking my intent.

"You're an asshole, you know that?"

"But I notice you're not turning down the ride."

Mikey slammed the door and fastened his seat belt. "I was going to ask if we could talk, but maybe not."

"Is there anything to talk about, Mikey? Really? You've made your feelings about me pretty clear since San Diego," I said. "I have to be honest. It's sucked."

"That's what I want to talk about," he whispered.

We drove back to Davis in silence. I didn't look at him, no side-eye action or anything, but my mind raced about a million miles an hour.

"Can we go to your house?" Mikey said.

"Why?"

He sighed. "Because I need to talk to you and my dad's working from home today."

"Very well. My parents are at work and Goff's at football practice."

"I know." Mikey gloated. "I already cleared it with him."

I shook my head. "Do I even want to know?"

"Probably not."

I parked the car in front of the house. My parents didn't ask for a whole lot from me and Goff, but they were pretty insistent that the driveway and garage belonged to their cars. It was hard to argue with that.

I sat on the hood of my car. "So… here we are. Start talking."

"You're not going to invite me in?" Mikey didn't sound all that serious, like he knew he had already pushed me further than was wise.

"Fine. We can go sit in the backyard," I said, dragging him around back through the side gate. I motioned to one of the loungers on the deck as I took one myself. "Start talking."

Mikey sat down and took a few minutes to gather his thoughts. "First, I'm sorry for the way I've been acting all summer."

I blinked. "Okay, that's not what I expected to hear."

"I know." He smiled sadly. "I've been doing a lot of thinking, and I'm sorry for overreacting. Do you have any idea how much it hurt to see you whoring yourself out to that guy—what was his name, Josh?—all summer? I wish it had been me, but it seemed like you hated me."

I saw red, and before I knew what I was doing, I had surged up and out of the lounger. I loomed over him, my hands on either armrest.

"Hey, I get that you're angry, but step off," he said.

I backed up, but I was still livid. "I am not," I hissed through clenched teeth, "a whore. If you ever call me that again, I will kick your nose in. And in case you've forgotten a few key facts, *Mikey*, let me remind you that I all but threw myself at you earlier this summer. You had your goddamn chance. 'Right guy at the right time,' remember? You turned me down, and it burned like the heart of the sun. I've spent the summer running from that."

Mikey jumped to his feet. "I was scared, okay? Is that all right with the emotionally invulnerable Über-rower who scares the crap out of the rest of us on the water? The guy I've wanted since I met him? Then you threw yourself at me, and it scared the hell out of me. Then I had to watch you all summer being with everyone but me, and how do you think that made me feel?" As he yelled at me, he moved closer and closer, backing me into the wall of my house until we were nose to nose, chest to chest. "I never got another chance, and my name is Michael," he all but screamed. "If you don't stop calling me Mikey, I will end you."

Mikey liked me? "I... I never knew."

He laughed bitterly. "Of course you didn't. You never gave me a chance to explain, and I was as much of a mess emotionally as you were, especially knowing I'm the one who encouraged you to call Josh."

His hands were on either side of my head, and his chest pressed mine back into the wall, and it was impossible to process what he said. "Um, Mikey—Michael—I can't really think when you're doing that," I said, my voice rough.

"Oh. Oh! You like this, do you?" Michael growled in my ear. "You like it like this?"

"Uh... yes?" I squeaked. I had barely figured it out over the summer, but somehow, suddenly, Michael was hitting every button I had, and I thought my mind would never function again.

He smirked. "Rough, but not roughed up?"

I nodded slowly.

"I can work with that. Now open the door."

Then Michael frog-marched me upstairs to my bedroom. When the hell had he hit puberty, because damn, was he strong. On the way, he grabbed a few rubbers from the stash, just in case. "How'd you know about those?"

"Geoff."

I shook my head, trying to clear it of the Michael-induced buzz. I guess I had always suspected he had a crush on me but figured he had managed to cure himself after the Crew Classic. But there was nothing like a guy pinning you to a wall and growling in your ear to confirm he still had a thing for you. And yeah, he had grown at least an inch, and his shoulders had gotten broader. No wonder he had been cranky lately. Growing would do that. You could never eat or sleep enough, your joints always hurt, and your coordination was shot to hell.

The best part of all was that Michael liked to cuddle. So that time Goff had walked in on us, he hadn't been wrong, just premature. While he held me, I leveled with him about my summer, not the gory details, just the highlights.

I shrugged, suddenly shy about it. "I think I was about at the end of it. Todd had helped me figure that much out."

"How so?" Michael looked down at me while stroking my hair.

I looked up at him. "It feels good physically, but it's lonely. Tricks don't hold you afterward."

Michael kissed the top of my head. "I'm sorry."

"Don't be." I reached up and pulled him down so I could kiss him.

I didn't know about older or wiser, but I felt like I'd learned a lesson or two over the past couple of months, and I spent the rest of the summer happily exploring this new version of Michael Castelreigh. He seemed just as enamored of me. Let Goff exhaust himself with football practice. Michael and I spent our fast-dwindling summer on leisurely rows and each other.

WE RECHRISTENED the car the "Love Boat" on the first day of school because its occupants were two couples and two of us were rowers. That it was white didn't hurt, either. Goff helpfully pointed out that I was a princess.

I was shy about it at first, but Michael dragged my arm around his shoulder, and as I was quickly learning, Michael was very assertive and toppy. As I was also learning, I liked it that way. We earned a few raised eyebrows, but Michael acted like he was impervious, and I learned to ignore them. Eventually. A few people made rude comments, and even though I wanted to hide, I didn't. We got a few wolf whistles, generally from other Cap City rowers who'd watched us last spring, along with "About time, you two!" Those felt good.

"I told you it'd be fine," Michael said, giving me a quick peck on my cheek.

I blushed. I didn't know I still could.

Michael chuckled. "You're so adorkable."

The first week of school was borderline useless as far as academics went, and clubs and other application fluffers didn't really crank up until the third week.

"Do I have to be out at school?" I complained.

Michael gave me a very convincing facsimile of the evil eye. "Yes." I still must've looked rebellious, because he leaned over and whispered in my ear. "I'll reward you as soon as we get back to your place after practice."

I swallowed. I didn't know where Michael got his ideas. Either he had a lurid imagination or he watched a lot of porn. I wasn't sure which one intrigued me more.

So that was how Michael dragged me into the GSA meeting. Much to my surprise, Goff and Laurel were already there. I would've said something about irony, but Goff had already made it clear to me that he was educating himself about all things gay because of me, and Laurel was obviously an advocate, too. I wondered if she had someone in her family who was LGBT. I also wondered why I had never asked her. Was I really that absorbed by rowing? I would've asked Michael, but he'd just tousle my hair or kiss me or something and then laugh.

Similarly, while on-the-water practices at Cap City increased in intensity after school started, the real testing for who would row where started only during the third week.

"Okay, as you know, it's erg testing today," Lodestone called, trying with only limited success to overcome the noise of chatting teenagers in a boathouse with a concrete floor. "This is preliminary, and nothing today is set in stone, so even if you crater, you'll have plenty of time to bring your time down. But we need a place to start, and today's it."

I hated erg testing, and based on the look Michael shot me, he felt the same way. In fact, no one on either the boys' varsity or junior varsity liked erg tests. This one was a 6k test, six thousand meters in purgatory but not true hell. The strategy behind an early-season test was to give it your almost-all, to be tapped out but not riding the vomit comet, if only because reality entailed beating the resulting score in a few weeks, or so it seemed to me. Part of my game for each season was to show steady improvement with each test. I refused to accept a plateau, and a slower score on a test sparked endless self-loathing. I hadn't done that since my novice year.

Someone put Outbreak Monkey on the sound system, and then we all sat on our ergs at the catch positions, just like in the boats.

"Ready all!" Lodestone called. "Row!"

I set out at a few seconds per five hundred meters slower than my usual 6k pace, my standard practice for this sort of test early in the season.

By two thousand meters into the test, I knew I was in trouble. I felt like I hadn't rowed all summer, like I had done nothing to stay in shape since San Diego. What the hell?

I tried to maintain my pace, but within another five hundred meters, I knew I had to back off or stop rowing, and not even my fury at the thought of slowing provided enough fuel for me to keep going. Worse, I kept having to slow down. By the time I slumped over at the end, I had pulled a time almost as slow as that one my novice year.

Lodestone leaned over to look at the monitor. "Remy? Are you all right?"

"No, not really." I sighed and then looked up at my coach. "I can't rest up. No matter what I do, I'm always tired."

Lodestone nodded. "Talk to me after practice."

I grabbed some water and texted Goff to let him know I'd be a few minutes late.

"What happened?" Michael said as people filtered out of the boathouse.

I shrugged. "I was too tired to pull anything resembling a reasonable erg score."

"That's not like you. Lodestone wants to talk to you?"

"Of course."

"I'll wait out of the way."

"That's okay," I said. "There's no reason you can't hear this, I don't think."

Finally Lodestone was ready for me. "So talk to me, Remy. What happened?"

"Beats me." I sighed. "I'm tired all the time. It was a hellacious summer in terms of physical activity—"

Michael snorted, but Lodestone rolled his eyes.

"You know, it's entirely possible you're depressed," Lodestone said. "A good friend and teammate died during the Nationals, and you had to jump in to take his place without warning. Sure, you pulled off a virtuoso performance, but that doesn't change the fact that he died."

I opened my mouth, then closed it. I'd never considered the possibility. Cisco and I were friends, good friends even, but I'd never thought of us as besties. It was something to talk over with Michael and Goff, maybe even my dad. He was a psychotherapist, after all.

"That had never occurred to me."

"Give it some thought," Lodestone said. "Or you might just be exhausted. You set a punishing schedule for yourself this summer, and the month or so between Nationals and school weren't really much of a break, not with the demands you placed on your body." He thought for a moment. "Oh! Something else to consider. You could have your iron checked. Athletes have different iron demands that nonathletes, so what counts as anemic for us is different. Be sure to include your ferritin levels. No one ever tests for it, but it's important. In fact, right after the blood test, go ahead and start supplementing your iron. Don't wait for the labs. You're active and growing. It won't hurt."

I nodded. "Got it. Rest up, be depressed, have my iron checked, take pills for it."

"I'm not sure that's how I put it," Lodestone said, looking pained, "but yes."

Michael put his arm around me as we headed out to the car. He liked to do that, I'd noticed, and I realized I liked him to, but just before I left the boathouse, I looked over my shoulder and caught Lodestone's eye. He looked thoughtful, thoughtful and worried. I didn't need to ask why.

CHAPTER
FOURTEEN

SOME THINGS never changed in the Babcock household, like my mother and her nearly single-minded determination that her sons make the world a better place for those who might never otherwise go to the prom. What Goff and I could never figure out was why she fixated on the *junior* prom. We didn't mind, we just couldn't figure it out.

Goff, Laurel, Michael, and I had taken over the living room one evening in early September to study. The Davis High grind was well under way, and we figured if we ever wanted to see each other, parallel play while studying was the only way.

Mom brought us dinner, which should have been my first clue that she was building up to something. Goff shot me several significant looks, but as usual I missed them, since they had nothing to do with rowing.

Michael nudged me. "I think Goff's trying to get your attention."

"What?" I blinked, looking up from my O-chem text.

Goff nodded. "Don't you think it's odd she's catering our study session? School's starting, and you know what that means, don't you?"

"Um… homework? Tests?" I said, floundering.

Proms, you fool, Goff texted.

Suffering Christ, I fired back.

I looked up to see Laurel and Michael snickering at each other.

As if Goff had summoned her, Mom came back into the living room. "Geoffrey, Jeremy, I'd like to talk to you about something important."

"Yeah, Mom?" I said, looking up, joined shortly by Goff.

"I know it's just September, but it's never too soon to start thinking about the junior prom," our mother said. "Now I'm sorry, Laurel. I know you and Geoff are going steady...."

Mom burbled on, but I mouthed "going steady" to Goff as Michael elbowed me in a pointless attempt to force me to behave. He should've known better by then.

"...but I think you'll agree that something like this, that strikes a blow for all womankind, is so much more important. Besides, Jeremy, you're not currently seeing anyone that I know of, so it shouldn't be too great a hardship for you."

By this time, Goff and Laurel were biting their lips to keep from exploding into hysterical laughter, because they knew full well who I was seeing and that he was rolling his eyes at my mother's spiel. The outrageousness of it all was enough to keep them from puking at Mom's nonsense about splitting them up in the name of social engineering.

Meanwhile, Michael, who was sitting close enough that not even the holy spirit could've fit between us, texted me: *Strike a blow, Remy.*

As the apparently unattached member of the Babcock family present for this farce, it fell to me to disabuse Mom of her delusions. I finally pushed Michael, who was shaking so hard it annoyed me, away.

"The problem with that, Mom, is that it's the *junior* prom, as in organized by and for the junior class. As seniors, if Geoff and I go, it'll be because we're invited by juniors. Since he's dating a fellow senior, I'm thinking that's not going to happen," I said.

Mom pouted, a surprisingly unattractive look. "You could...."

Michael growled, softly but still a growl.

I smiled. "I have a reasonable expectation of being asked, I think."

That was enough for my brother and his girlfriend. They broke and ran for the stairs, howling the entire way.

"I wonder what got into them?" Mom said. "Keep your door open!" she called after them.

"Probably the fact that you keep harping on this. Honestly, Mom, it's not healthy." Mom crossed her arms in a way I knew meant trouble a-brewing. "Please, Mom. You need to let this go. Geoff and Laurel are *dating*, and you just tried to make it sound rational for him to take someone else to a formal dance."

"But—"

I shook my head. "Mom, you've told me what your high school years were like, and while I sympathize, my brother and I can't rewrite the past."

"It's just a dance." Mom sounded petulant.

Aaand my sympathy ran out as she insisted on being a clownish caricature about this. She was the most rational woman I knew about almost everything else, but this? Whatever, crazy lady. Oh well, they say even the most intelligent, rational of people believe at least one insane thing....

Michael and I managed—somehow—to keep absolutely straight faces. "We might as well go up to my room," I said. "Laurel's in my O-chem class, and if I'm going to study with her, it'll be easier if I'm at least somewhere near her."

So we gathered up our things while Mom took the dishes to the sink, shaking her head the entire way. Michael and I made it to my bedroom and shut the door before we fell to my bed choking with laughter.

"Bad rower! Bad!" Michael said, kissing my nose and not coincidentally pinning me to my bed. I liked that. A lot.

Goff coughed from the bathroom door, but it's not like he'd interrupted anything, at least not yet.

"Thanks for trying, Remy," Laurel said. She wore a broad grin.

"Shame on you, taking advantage of our mother's weird obsession." Goff wagged his finger at me.

I looked up at him from where Michael had me trapped under him. "Oh, like you wouldn't."

"We're not talking about me," Geoff said like he had some sort of moral ground to stand on. He smiled. "Behave, you two."

"Yeah, right," Michael whispered, diving in for more kisses. I wasted no time in allowing my hands to roam. I liked his geography and took every chance I could to explore it. For all my adventures this summer, I felt strangely reluctant about going certain places, like Michael mattered where those other guys hadn't. When Michael and I were intimate, I wanted it to mean something.

When we were kissed out, at least for the time being, Michael looked down at me with a look in his eyes I hadn't seen before. But I liked it. It made me feel wanted and not just physically.

I smiled up at him. "So... am I officially invited?"

He rolled over next to me and pulled me close. "You are indeed."

"Hmmm, you in a tuxedo," I said. "The thought of that excites me. I don't know if I'll be able to keep my hands off you."

"That works both ways, you know. I get to look at you wrapped up like a present all night, and then you know what I'll get to do?" he said.

"No." I liked where this was going, however.

Michael sat up a little to look at me. "Well, since the prom is less than a month before Christmas, I think I'll unwrap you like the best Christmas present ever."

I swear I choked at the thought. Two hot guys in tuxes teasing each other all night? Okay, one hot guy and me, but still. That image alone would get me through many a lonely night.

"You think...," I started to say, but stopped.

"Go on." Michael started to play with my hair, and that usually short-circuited about half of my synapses.

"You think that would be a good time to come out to my parents? That night or sometime around then?"

He nodded slowly. "Seems like as good a time as any." He hesitated. "I know the GSA annoys you, but they'll have some good advice for coming out."

I thought about it for a while. Then something else occurred to me. "Are you out to your parents?"

"Not officially, no, but I've never made a secret of it, either." Michael laughed. "I'm not sure what they thought this summer with me alternating between moping around because I'd run you off and then swearing at you because you'd rejected me."

I thought about that for a while. "Depends on how insightful they are. We spent a lot of time together. If they had a clue, they might've figured it out. If they're like mine, they just chalked it up to a busy summer."

"So maybe this would be a good time for us both to come out, then," Michael said softly, looking into my eyes. I smiled back. It was a while before we returned to our homework.

MY IRON panel came back normal, and as near as I could tell, the supplements did nothing. Still, I did my best to eat right and get enough rest, but it was never enough. Fatigue was my constant companion, and even my parents noticed. The only reason they didn't say anything was because Lodestone and I were already taking steps. On my coach's advice, I dropped my weight section. I didn't need the units, it wasn't a requirement to graduate, and it only wore me down further.

There were more pressing issues, like college applications. Lodestone had already been in contact with the crew coaches at the schools that interested me—UCSD, UCLA, UCSB, the University of Washington, and Boston U—so I knew they were interested in me, particularly after my performance at the Nationals. I would've loved to apply to small private schools in New England, but the reality was my parents had two people to put through college at the same time, so the three UCs constituted my practical schools, UW was my crew powerhouse fantasy, and BU was my East Coast dream. I knew CalPac's coach wanted me and had even offered early admission, but I wanted out of the Sacramento area. All college applications meant were more essays to write on frankly bizarre subjects on top of my schoolwork.

Goff had been forced to pare his list down, too, although he knew he wouldn't be playing football in college. He cheerfully admitted he wasn't that good and wasn't nearly big enough and in any case preferred not to risk traumatic brain injury. Sensible one, that Goff. But Goff too had his three practical schools and his pie-in-the-sky schools. If only the University of California gave bulk discounts, because odds were my brother and I would both end up at one or more of the system's campuses.

Of course, my dreams of collegiate crew depended on figuring out why I was so tired. Neither Lodestone nor I could find any good reason, and I finally broke down and asked my parents if I could have a doctor's appointment for a complete physical. My doctor didn't ask about sexual health, even though that seemed kind of obvious to me. I didn't have the nerve to say anything. I knew Goff and Lodestone wanted me to get tested, but I just couldn't. What if I did, and it came back positive? Everything covered on the physical came back normal.

When it came to rowing, since Lodestone had me in small boats, I had some leeway. I rowed in the single to stay in what condition I could, and it was not as if I were exhausted constantly. Some days, even many, were fantastic, but I was fatigued enough to worry me, my parents, and Lodestone. Michael, too. It went on long enough that I refused to accept my intense summer as an excuse, as October was well underway and college applications were starting to come due. Only Michael and Goff knew how badly this rattled me.

Then I got sick two weeks before Halloween. I didn't think much of it at first. I felt like I had a cold.

Michael felt my forehead. "You're not going to practice."

"It's just a cold," I said, knocking his hand away. "You know as well as I do that if it's upper respiratory and you feel like it, light exercise is all right."

"That's cute. Look me in the eye and tell me you feel like doing anything besides sleeping."

I sighed and looked him in the eye. I felt like death warmed over, and we both knew it. Light exercise? The only exercise I felt like right then was pulling my comforter back and crawling under it.

"Oh, Remy." Michael drew me into his arms. "I'm taking you home right after school. Then I'll bring the car back here for Geoff and catch a ride with someone else."

I nodded, and even that hurt. "I've got some Tylenol in my backpack. Maybe that plus a Rock Star will hold me together until school gets out."

Michael pulled out his phone and started texting.

"Geoff?" I said.

He nodded. "Just updating him. If you get worse, text me and I'll take you home right away."

"You'll miss class." I knew I should have protested more, but that would have taken more than I had in me right then.

"I'll take you by the office first. They'll take one look at you and I'll be excused."

I thought for a moment. Even that was sluggish. "Actually, Michael? Will you take me home now?"

"That's the first sensible thing you've said in weeks," Michael said.

We stopped by the office, and then I handed my boyfriend the keys. Michael probably didn't have a full driver's license, but I was in no shape to get myself home. I guess I fell asleep on the way, because the next thing I remembered was Michael gently shaking me awake. "We're here, sleeping beauty," he said, kissing my forehead. "Damn, you're burning up. Should I take you to the doctor, instead?"

"I'll see if I can get an appointment an' text you," I mumbled.

Michael shook his head. "Can you make it into the house and upstairs by yourself?"

Now that I'd given up, I didn't have to pretend. "Probably not."

Michael jumped out of the car and came around to open my door. After helping me out, he grabbed my bag and supported me as we went inside and up to my room.

He held me steady while I stripped out of my jeans and sweatshirt, admiring the view. "Ordinarily I'd love to take advantage of you in nothing but a T-shirt and your boxer briefs, but I don't think you're up for it."

"I could just lie there and let you have your way with me," I said, my voice muffled by my pillow as I all but collapsed into bed.

"I—damn, Remy. How much weight have you lost this fall?" I pried my eyes open to see concern all over my boyfriend's face.

"S'not weight, it's just bulk from not lifting."

"If you say so." Michael didn't look convinced, or even sound it. "I mean it. If you get a doctor's appointment, call or text me. Or Geoff. I'll let him know what's happening."

"Okay," I said, but I felt sleep closing in.

WHEN I woke up, it was to my mother's gentle shaking. "Wake up, Jeremy. We need to change your sheets."

"Whaa—"

"You've got a fever, and you've soaked them clear through. Your T-shirt too, sweetheart."

I sat up and immediately fell back down. "Dizzy, Mom."

"Take it more slowly this time," she said gently.

This time she helped me to sit up, holding me steady until I caught my bearings. Then she helped me out of bed and over to my desk chair. I slumped over onto my desk, resting. "I feel horrible."

"I don't doubt it for a moment, Jeremy, not with a fever like this one," she said, pulling my apparently soaked sheets off the bed.

Then Goff padded in, squinting against the light. "What's going on?"

"Geoffrey, your brother's sick. Would you go get him one of those sports drinks, but cut it in half with water?"

"Sure, Mom." He left, scratching his belly on the way out.

When Goff returned a short time later, Mom mostly had my bed remade. She handed me some Tylenol. "Take these, dear, and then drink as much of that sports drink as you can. You need to replace fluids and electrolytes in the worst way."

I sat at my desk, sipping watered-down sports drink and generally feeling miserable. "How'd you know?"

"Know what?" Mom said, sitting down on my bed, waiting for me to finish.

"To check on me."

She smiled. "You've caused quite a stir. Michael texted Geoffrey, who skipped practice to look in on you. A good thing, too, because this isn't the first set of sheets you've been through. You looked horrible, and he called me. This is the first time we've been able to rouse you. You've got a doctor's appointment in the morning. Urgent care's closed or I'd take you in right now. If you hadn't woken up or your fever hadn't broken, you'd probably be in the back of an ambulance at some point in time."

"Oh," I said, still listless. The fluids helped.

"Can you tell me what's wrong?" Mom said. She looked worried.

I sighed. I had no energy. "Uh... fever. Fatigue, but you knew that. My throat's sore. I ache all over, and if I don't stop drinking this stuff, I'm going to puke it all back up." I shuddered, suddenly unable to stand the taste.

"Any bit you keep down will help, I'm sure. It sounds like flu to me, but I'm not a doctor," she said. "Geoffrey, can you bring the bathroom trashcan in here in case your brother throws up? It's bigger than the one in here."

"Sure, Mom."

Mom got up. "Why don't you try getting back in bed? Sleep can only help at this point. Then the rest of us can get back to sleep, as well."

"Sorry to get everyone up," I whispered, barely awake.

"Oh, sweetheart, you've nothing to apologize for," she said, kissing my forehead.

"Goodnight, Germy, I hope you feel better soon," I heard Goff say. It sounded like he was far, far away.

When I woke up again, it was morning. I lay still, taking stock. I felt only marginally better, but at least my fever was gone. Mostly. I felt wretched, but had stopped sweating. So... progress?

I checked the time and obviously wasn't going to school since it was well past 10:00 a.m. Then I looked at my phone. Three texts from Michael, all of which were variations on "How are you? I'm really worried."

I texted him back. *Rough night. Still feel horrible. MD later 2day?*

When I sat up, I still felt dizzy but nothing as bad as last night. I rested in place before trying to stand. After that, I hoisted myself up using my desk chair for support. I didn't even bother with clothing, wrapping myself in my robe.

"Jeremy, is that you?" Mom called.

Who else would it be? Goff was at school and Dad at work. "Yes, Mom."

"I was just about to get you up," she said, coming up the stairs. "You have a doctor's appointment in forty-five minutes. Are you hungry?"

I shuddered at the thought of eating anything. "No, but I'm going to shower."

"Are you sure that's wise? What if you fall down?"

"I feel gross. What if I sit on that plastic step stool from the kitchen?"

Mom nodded. "That'll work. I'll be right back."

I shuffled into the bathroom I shared with Goff and sat on the toilet to wait. Mom came back soon enough, and I turned on the recirculating pump to heat the water without running it all down the drain. California and its droughts. What can you do? I undressed myself while the water warmed up and then turned on the shower and its now-hot water.

It felt wonderful to sit under the water and let it run down me. I knew I didn't have a lot of time, but I needed to be clean. While I was in there, Mom set out fresh clothes for me, nothing fancy, just jeans, a tee, and a hoodie.

I checked myself out in the mirror. I really had lost weight. I could see ribs that had not been visible this summer. I knew I'd told Michael that it was loss of bulk from not lifting, but I was worried. Maybe I was just dehydrated, I told myself, but deep down I knew that wasn't it.

I pocketed my phone and left my room. Mom waited outside. "Ready? We have just enough time to get to the doctor's. Your regular doctor was booked up, so you'll be seeing the nurse practitioner. I hope that's all right."

"It's fine." Like I had the energy to argue even if I actually objected.

Mom looked worried. "We can reschedule—"

"No, Mom, it's really fine. I'm just bushed."

Neither of us said much on the drive over, but I pulled out my phone and stared at the browser's search field. It was the last thing I wanted to do, but I made myself do it. I typed "HIV symptoms" and hit Enter.

CHAPTER
FIFTEEN

"WELL, JEREMY," the NP said. "You present a bit of a puzzle."

"Yay, me." I'd been out of bed for an hour, and it had been about forty minutes too long. I sagged against the exam table.

He smiled. "Most of your symptoms sound like the flu. That the fatigue has gone on so long concerns me, and that rash you say has just developed in the last twenty-four hours isn't a typical sign of the flu. Otherwise, everything else sounds like classic flu symptoms. It's a bit early for the flu, but it's not unheard of."

The NP pulled a tube with a swab sealed in it out of a drawer. "I'm going to swab you for the flu to see if indeed you have it, but in the meantime, we'll go ahead and treat you as if you've got it." He broke the seal. "What I need you to do now is tip your head back and try not to sneeze. This isn't going to be particularly comfortable."

With that, the NP stuck the biggest cotton swab I'd ever seen all the way up my nose. I swore I felt it against the back of my eyes. "What the hell?"

"I'm sorry," he said, quickly resealing the swab in its test tube. "There's no way to warn anyone. As I said, we'll treat this as if it were the flu, and that means plenty of rest, fluids, and Tylenol to help keep the fever and aches under control. You can gargle with saltwater for your throat or use cough drops. Some people recommend a teaspoon of honey in a cup of warm water, so you might try that, as well. Since we've caught this within a day, there'll be a prescription for Tamiflu at the pharmacy within fifteen minutes for you. Stomach upset, even vomiting, can be associated with the flu, so if that continues to be a problem, call, because there are antiemetics that can be prescribed. As for the rash, it may just be contact dermatitis due to your fever sweats. If it gets worse, try some cortisone cream, one of the ones with colloidal oatmeal in it since that's good for the skin. It's over the counter, so you won't need a prescription."

I felt his eyes linger on me as I noticed a discreet red ribbon pin on his name badge. His name was Heath Nichols. "Jeremy... I'm concerned about the long-lasting fatigue, the weight loss, and the rash. Combined with your other symptoms, they point to other illnesses."

I looked at the floor. Thanks to my reading on the way there, I knew exactly what he meant, and I couldn't cope with it, not right then.

But he plowed on. "I noticed in your chart that no one seems to have talked to you about your sexual health. That's a major oversight for a man your age."

"My coach has," I mumbled.

"That's good," the nurse practitioner said, "very good, but is there a chance, no matter how small, that this could be something else? Maybe you've had some encounters, even just one, where you might not have been careful?"

I couldn't say anything, like my mouth had been welded shut. I knew the answer, and by my silence, I was pretty sure he did, too.

He helped me sit back up on the exam table, then put his arm around my shoulder. I didn't feel like he was a creeper or anything. "The other thing this looks like to me is acute retroviral syndrome, or ARS, the first, early stages of infection with HIV."

I only stared at the floor. "I know," I whispered. "I looked up the symptoms."

"Have you been tested?"

I shook my head.

"Can I order a test for you?"

"I can't... not right now. I mean, my parents...." I trailed off.

"Under the law, there is strict confidentiality in matters of sexual health to protect people over the age of fourteen," the NP said. "Your parents have no right to see the results or even know what you're being tested for."

"If I start seeing an AIDS specialist, that'll pretty much let the cat out of the bag," I said. My eyes welled up with tears. "I just can't face this right now."

He nodded. "I'll be right back."

When he returned, the NP handed me his card. "This has my e-mail address and direct line. Enter this in your phone so you don't have to worry about anyone finding it or asking you questions you're not ready to answer. I want you to think about this, and when you're ready, contact me and I'll give you resources outside the HMO about free and low-cost testing. At least you'll know."

I sniffled. "Okay."

"Just promise me one thing."

I looked up.

"Don't go alone. Bring someone with you, both when you go the first time and when you get your results."

I nodded. "I can do that."

"I'm going to put in one last pitch for a test today," he said. "If I'm right and this is ARS, the sooner you're on medication, the easier it will be to control and the sooner you'll go back to leading a perfectly normal life. Did you catch that last bit? A normal life—sports, dating, and everything else."

I only shook my head.

"I understand—"

"How can you? My life is over, and I'm not even eighteen," I said thickly. "Two months of crappy decisions, and I'll pay for it forever."

"Because I've been poz for eight years."

My mouth fell open.

"I do triathlons. I'm active in the community. My husband and I have been together for six years, married for four," Heath said. "I think I get it."

Something did not add up. "Wait… you've had it for eight years, but you met your husband after that?"

"Life doesn't end with a diagnosis, Jeremy." Heath almost looked amused, and that didn't make sense, either. "In my case it started. I knew I had to get my act together and get healthy."

My head spun from too much information and input. "Can I… I just need to get through this, and then I'll get tested, I promise."

"Can I hold you to that?" Heath smiled when he said it.

"I'll tell my boyfriend what you said. He'll never let me wriggle out of it," I said.

"He'll need to know, too, you know."

I smiled, or tried. "We got together after my slutty phase."

"See? You know what I'm talking about, but can we not use the term 'slutty'? You'll experience enough criticism without attaching moral terms to sex," Heath said.

I nodded. "As soon as I kick this, I'll e-mail you for information."

"I hope so," Heath said. "Don't forget to stop by the pharmacy."

I SHOOK off the flu or the ARS or whatever it was but never felt back to my normal self. I still had applications to submit and schoolwork to attend to, so a prolonged convalescence was not a luxury I allowed myself. Crew, however, continued to suffer from whatever was wrong with me.

"Whatever." I knew. I didn't want to say it aloud, but I knew.

The Saturday after I had gotten so sick, Michael and I were hanging out in the backyard. He had already endured practice. I'd ridden in the launch since rowing required more energy than I had to give it at that point. School, I managed, but rowing, no. Fortunately, October was basically summer lite in the Sacramento Valley, beautiful weather without hideous temperatures.

I still wore jeans and a hoodie. I never seemed to warm up.

"I'm glad you're doing better," he said softly. He took my hand. "You scared the hell out of me."

"I scared me, too."

"So what'd the doctor say?"

I smiled, thinking about Heath. "I saw a nurse practitioner. He said he'd treat it like the flu, although the culture came back negative." I said nothing for a moment. I looked around to make sure neither parent was in earshot. I think Dad was watching Goff's football practice or something manly like that. I couldn't see Mom, but that didn't mean anything. "He said the other possibility was something called ARS—acute retrovirus syndrome."

Michael looked at me blankly. "Which is...?"

"HIV is a retrovirus."

His mouth formed a silent O of surprise. Then, "Did you get tested?"

I shook my head. "I couldn't face it right then."

"You need to."

"Of course I do," I said, rolling my eyes. "I just... not then."

He opened his mouth, presumably to launch into an impassioned argument about why. I knew why, but that did not mean I was prepared for the test results.

"Michael, stop. I never said I wasn't going to get tested. I said I couldn't face it right then. I could barely stand upright. Getting tested for a life-changing disease? Give me a break."

He looked at me strangely. "You didn't say life-threatening."

"Huh. You're right." I thought about that. "I talked about it with the nurse practitioner. He must've reached me more than I thought. He's poz. From what he said, his life actually improved after he found out."

"That's bizarre."

I shrugged. I was the last one to judge. "I guess it made him take charge and clean up his act or something. He's into triathlons, and get this: he met his husband years after the diagnosis."

"Wow. That's kind of cool if you think about it," Michael said.

"It certainly gave me something to think about, like maybe it's not the life-ending disaster I'd been building up for."

"Maybe not, but it's still not what I would've chosen for you," he said quietly.

"Me, neither." I sighed. However, it was the life I had ended up choosing for myself anyway, and didn't that just suck?

"So what're you going to do?"

"Get tested, obviously." I thought for minute. "Will you go with me?"

"Of course I will. Like you even have to ask?" Michael looked hurt.

I wrapped my arms around myself, telling myself I was cold and not scared. "I didn't want to assume…."

Michael launched himself at me. "Start assuming." He moved me around until we were both on the same lounger, kind of like on that roof that night in San Diego. So much had happened since last April. "So when do we do this?"

"I'll e-mail Heath and get some info—"

"Who," Michael said, "is Heath?"

"The nurse practitioner," I said. "This new jealous streak of yours is kind of cute, yet disturbing."

"I'm not jealous."

I smiled. "Of course you're not."

"I'm not," Michael protested, pulling me onto his lap. It was not so much his lap as it was me leaning back against him, like spooning, only we were sitting up. "I just want to know who this guy is who's somehow managed to give you even a little bit of hope."

"I told you. He was the nurse practitioner I saw. Anyway, he told me when I was ready, he'd send me info about testing at the free clinic so I don't have to tell my doctor right away."

"You'll have to tell her sooner or later, won't you?" Michael said softly. "Preferably sooner."

"Yes, but baby steps. This is a lot for me to wrap my mind around." I relaxed back into Michael. He felt good. I felt moderately horrible. I knew I should have been worried about my mom finding us like that, but it struck me as one more thing I didn't have the energy for.

"So how will we explain your absence from school?" Michael asked a few minutes later.

"Or yours." I thought for a minute. "It'll be a medical office. I'll get a note."

"Or," Michael said, "I'll tell Lodestone what's going on and take you after school. He's not going to mind if I miss one practice."

The thought of telling Lodestone.... "You can't miss practice. I'll go by myself."

"The hell you will." Michael sounded fierce. "I'm not letting you face this alone, and I wouldn't even if you weren't my boyfriend."

"Am I?" I said. "Your boyfriend, I mean?"

Michael kissed the back of my neck in a way that made my skin crawl in an entirely good way. I shuddered. He had to know what it did to me. "I am absolutely, positively, one hundred percent your boyfriend. I thought you knew that."

"I'm not really very secure these days, and we've never actually talked about it," I mumbled.

I felt him nod behind me. "True enough, but we've done a lot about it."

"I told Heath you were my boyfriend."

Michael growled. "Good."

I laughed. "He's too old for me. I like my men younger."

"I'll keep that in mind."

I pulled his arms around me. "I'll get the information on where to go, and then...."

"Yes?"

The entire idea terrified me, but if indeed I had it, Lodestone would know soon enough. "Are you sure you don't mind skipping practice?"

"I wouldn't have brought it up if I hadn't meant it," Michael said.

I could get used to someone who said exactly what he meant. "Who knows, maybe there'll be Saturday hours, and we won't have to miss practice or school."

WAITING FOR the results was the most nerve-wracking thing I have ever done, harder even than walking up the steps to the clinic in the first place. Fortunately the clinic indeed had Saturday hours, and there was one not too far from the port in West Sacramento, so I avoided Davis entirely. Michael stood by me the entire time. Unfortunately, he couldn't graft himself to my side, so I endured the waiting alone. Well, not entirely alone. Goff knew I'd gotten tested, but if our parents knew anything was up, they remained oddly silent.

"Germy, you've got to tell them." He sat at the end of my bed where I had curled up under the comforter because I—as usual—couldn't stay warm.

"Tell them what? That I spent my summer as a manwhore?" I said. "There's nothing to tell them yet."

Goff made a disgusted noise. "That's bullshit, and you know it. You're sick. Just look at yourself. This isn't a cold or the flu, this is serious. They're not the enemy."

I sighed. "You keep telling me that, but as I keep telling you, we've had different experiences with them."

"And you won't tell me what that means. I hate that."

"I don't want to ruin your view of Mom and Dad." I didn't, but it was true. I'd overheard them on more than one occasion, and it didn't make me feel good. I knew when it came out in the open that it would be ugly. Why couldn't they have just kept their mouths shut, or at least made sure they were alone in the house? "I don't want to argue about this anymore. I have my reasons, and you're just going to have to accept that."

"Yeah, whatever." Neither of us said anything for a while. "So when do you find out?"

"I'm supposed to call in and a recording will tell me if my results are ready."

Goff looked surprised. "They don't tell you on the phone?"

"Nope." I shook my head. "They don't want anyone doing anything stupid if the results are positive."

"You'd think they'd at least tell you if you were negative."

I had to laugh. "Yeah, but if they did that and you got a recording, then you'd know you were positive and still might do something stupid, right? They've been doing this since the eighties, so they've figured out all the tricks."

"I guess. I just hate waiting. It's like I'm nervous for you or something," Goff said.

"Of all of us, I think I want to know the least," I muttered.

Goff gave me a knowing look. "Is that because you know the answer?"

"Probably. Anyway, to answer your question, I call in tomorrow." I sounded calm, but the reality was that my stomach had wrapped itself around my spine, I was so wrecked about it. Thinking I knew the answer and receiving confirmation were two entirely different things. So spending the day at school tomorrow while waiting to call in would probably have me puking up breakfast or something. I also knew I'd skip the rest of the day when the clinic told me to come in.

"You'd tell me, right?" Goff said. "If you were poz?"

"Of course," I said. I gave him a pained look, even though I knew full well that if the results went the way I thought they would, I would have to take the time to process it. "You're my brother. Besides, I'd need your help to break it to Mom and Dad."

Goff looked relieved, and I let him steer the conversation in other directions. There was only so long I could contemplate my mortality anyway.

While we talked, I texted Michael. *I call in tomorrow.*

M: *Like I could forget? Let me know ASAP?*
R: *All they tell me is whether or not 2 come in.*
M: *Yeah, but I know U. U'll drive there ASAP.*
R: *Guilty and yes.*
M: *I'll go with.*
R: *xoxo*

"Mikey?" Goff said.

"He goes by Michael now, but yes."

Goff snorted. "We've known him since what? Fourth grade?"

"About that, yes. Let's just say he was very persuasive when he told me to call him Michael." I smiled at the memory.

"Is there a story there?"

I felt myself turn red. "Not that I'm going to tell you."

Then I yawned.

Goff looked at his watch. "Okay, time for bed."

"It's eight thirty."

"So? I didn't say it was time for me to go to bed," Goff said.

I replied in the appropriate manner. I threw a pillow at him. "I'm not an invalid."

"No, but you're not at full strength, either," he said.

There wasn't anything I could say to that, so I got out of bed and immediately started shivering. Goff looked at me as if to say, *See?*

"All right, all right, I'll go to bed."

I SAT in my car with my head against the headrest, eyes closed.

"Talk to me, Remy. Don't shut me out."

I had called in as soon as lunch started. The recording told me my results were ready. I guess it wasn't technically a recording, more like a computer-generated response, since no one had used actual recorders during my lifetime so far as I knew. If they had used a recorder, I wonder how the clinic would have updated it for each client's results—

It took a conscious effort to halt the mental freefall.

"What do you want me to say?" I said, not opening my eyes.

"I don't know, just tell me what's going on in that complicated mind of yours," Michael said. "Silence can't be good."

I sighed. "I don't know which is worse, suspecting or knowing for sure." I opened my eyes and looked at him. "Actually, I do. It was the look of pity in the counselor's eyes."

"I think she was just sorry to deliver news like that to someone still in high school," Michael said.

"Yeah, but I don't look like I'm in high school." I thought for a moment. "It occurs to me that's part of what landed me in trouble in the first place."

Michael put his hand on my knee. "So what do you want to do now?"

"I have no idea. Saying 'Go to Disneyland' is so trite, don't you think?"

"At least your sense of humor—such as it is—is intact." He shook his head.

"Gallows humor may be the only thing that gets me through this," I snapped.

"Easy there, tiger, I'm on your side," he said. "And honestly, antiretrovirals are the only things that will get you through this, so suck this up and listen. You need to tell your parents and get on medication. Now."

"Don't you think I know that?"

Michael gave me a bland look. "I know you do, but that doesn't mean you're going to do it. You need careful management, Remy. I've learned that much about you."

"Don't patronize me!"

Goddamn, where did he get off saying shit like that? I'd just been dealt a diagnosis of death, and he's telling me I need to be led about like a child?

"I'm not patronizing you, Remy. I'm stating a fact. If you know you need to do one thing, you're just as likely to do its opposite." He reached over and took my chin in his hand, turning my face toward his. He kissed me lightly. I didn't kiss him back. "I want you around for a long, long time. You need to talk to your doctor. I don't know anything about treating HIV, but I'm willing to bet your doctor does, just as I'm willing to bet it involves medication."

I didn't say anything, but I'd noticed we had not kissed on the lips as much since I'd gotten so sick with what we both knew was ARS.

"I know I need to, okay? That doesn't make it any easier."

"I know," he said softly.

I refrained from screaming "how" or anything like that. He meant well, and he had cut class—again—to help me.

"Besides," Michael continued, "You can't row, not at the levels you want to, if you keep losing muscle mass and strength."

Of course he chose that line of reasoning. "You fight dirty."

"Is there some other way to fight?"

I laughed. I had to. "Asshole."

He smiled. "But hopefully I'm your asshole."

"For as long as you'll have me," I said. I might have been temporarily upset, but I knew when I had it good.

"Then that's all that matters. But you know," Michael said. "You don't have to do this alone. Geoff and I will be with you when you tell your parents."

I made a face. "Ugh, that means coming out to them at the same time."

"Well, yes, unless you want to tell them you use IV drugs, which I don't think you do," he said. "Keep in mind, this likely means coming out to my parents sooner than I'm ready to as well, and before you say anything, I do realize it will be far less traumatic for me."

"At least you admit that much," I grumbled, but far more good-naturedly than before.

"I'm younger than you are," he said dryly, "but that doesn't make me dumber. So how do you want to spend the rest of the afternoon?"

"Oh, I don't know. Cutting class is only a thrill if you're having fun, and this? This ain't it. Take me home, I guess? I don't think I feel like going to practice. I may just veg out and watch television."

"That sounds fine." Michael got out of the car.

"What're you doing? You make no sense."

Then he stood at my door. "I'm driving. You're distracted, and I want to live."

"Yeah, okay. That works." Then I thought of something. "Let's hit the store. I want ice cream."

"Sure, why not?" Michael laughed. "You could use the calories, and one day won't destroy my training."

"You're staying with me?" For some reason that made me feel more hopeful than I had for a while.

Michael smiled. "I'm not leaving you alone."

"I'm paying, but get your own flavors. I'm not sharing."

"That's my Remy."

CHAPTER
SIXTEEN

M: *What the hell's going on?*
G: *Laurel says he collapsed in the middle of O-chem lab.*
M: *Shit.*
G: *Yep. She said he looked bad, real pale but kind of red. Cold 2 & confused about lab. Next thing she knew he was on the floor.*
M: *Where R U now?*
G: *Ambulance. EMTs giving him fluids. Say his pulse&breathing R really rapid.*
M: *See U at....*
G: *Sutter Davis* [sends contacts] *Can you keep trying my parents? Dad's seeing patients and who knows where Mom is? She's on the road a lot.*
M: *Will do.*

"YOUNG MAN!" someone called after him, but Michael ignored her. He had to find Geoff and the critical-care ICU. He caught an elevator going up just before the doors closed. When the doors opened, he took off again. He skidded to a halt in front of a nurses' station.

"Where's the fire?" an older woman asked.

He looked at her tag. Nurse supervisor. "I'm sorry, ma'am. I'm here to see Remy Babcock. He was brought in earlier this afternoon. I was told he was in this ICU."

She flipped through the inventory of who was on the ward. "Do you mean Jeremy Babcock? He's in room 8A, but I have to warn you.

He's not conscious right now. He's also scheduled for tests and might not even be there."

"That's all right. I'll take my chances. Besides, his brother's here, and I'll talk to him if Remy's not there," Michael said.

"I'll buzz you in," the nurse supervisor said.

Once inside, Michael quickly found 8A. He knocked on the glass door.

"Hey, Michael. Come in," Geoff said.

Michael claimed the other seat in the bay, a stool. "Sorry I couldn't get here sooner. If I cut class any more, I'll be on probation for crew. Lodestone's been really patient, but he said enough's enough. How is he?"

Geoff gestured to Remy. He lay on a typical hospital bed, his trunk elevated, hooked into supportive apparatuses, not just an oxygen feed but an actual mask, as well as more of the IV fluids Geoff had mentioned and another bag that could only be the antibiotics. Vancomycin, the label read. None of it made much sense, but it all looked frightening.

"Wow."

"Yep. Any luck reaching my parents?"

Michael nodded. "I actually spoke to your mom. After she chewed me out for interrupting her, she thanked me for calling. She was in the South Bay, but she said she'd be here as soon as she could. But your dad's receptionist? I don't like him."

"No kidding," Geoff said. "I don't know why 'My brother's on the way to the hospital by ambulance' doesn't count as an emergency, but Dad needs to talk to that jerk."

"Unless those're your dad's orders," Michael said.

"Remy's always had a different relationship with them than I have," Geoff said, looking troubled. "I'll worry about that later."

"Right, we've got bigger issues."

Geoff met Michael's eyes. "Like, what are we going to tell my parents?"

"Did he ever tell your parents about his test results?" Michael ran a hand through his hair.

"No."

"That's just great." Michael shook his head. "I know he was having a lot of problems facing it himself, not that I blame him, but he's just dumped it in our laps."

"'Our'?" Geoff said.

"Yes, 'our.' I'm not leaving this all to you, even if it scares the hell out of me. I'm still his boyfriend." Michael thought for a moment. "Unless you're kicking me out."

"Oh god no. No way, Michael. You don't know what you mean to Remy," Geoff said. "Or what it's meant to me not to be the only one who knows about any of this."

"Knows what, boys?" said Dina Babcock.

"Crap," Michael said, turning to face the curtain-covered glass wall.

Geoff stood up. "Hi, Mom."

"Hello, Geoffrey. Michael. Now someone needs to start explaining, because one of my children is lying in the ICU and I'm about sixty seconds away from hysteria." She looked around. "Where's your father?"

"I'm sorry, Mrs. Babcock. I left him a message, but I couldn't get through to him," Michael said.

"Same here, Mom." Geoff sighed.

"Let me guess. His receptionist. I'm so sick of that man," Dina said. "Now. Start. Talking."

Michael and Geoff looked at each other. "So far it's looking like sepsis, some kind of blood poisoning?" Geoff said. "The doctors are running tests—"

"How does a healthy seventeen-year-old boy get sepsis?" Dina demanded.

"We'll get to that in a moment," Michael said. "Geoff's telling you what he knows, which is all I know. Other than tests, he's on fluids to keep him hydrated, plus antibiotics."

Dina looked at the IVs. "Vancomycin? Damn. That's one of the most powerful antibiotics around. They must be scared." She looked to Geoff and Michael. "There's still something you're not telling me, isn't there?"

"Mom, this isn't really the time—"

"Oh no, this is exactly the time—"

"The time for what? And why am I always the last to know?"

Geoff sighed. "Hi, Dad."

"Thanks for joining us, Steven," Dina said. "You'd know more if that creep who answers your phones listened to your son and his friend when they called you with emergencies."

"Dina, that's not fair. Just because you're in sales and can dash off from lunch with doctors at some high-priced club doesn't mean I can. I was in the middle of a patient—"

"Yes, well, it looks like your son's a patient, too, and you're the last to know because there's no way to reach you," Dina said flatly.

"Why don't I see if I can find a doctor who can tell you what's going on?" Michael said, slipping out of the bay before anyone could say anything.

He returned momentarily with one of the ICU's physicians. "I was just coming to talk to you. I'm glad you're all here."

"Why's he here?" Steven said, indicating Michael. "I get that you're a friend of Remy's—"

"Dad," Geoff said.

Dina sighed. "He's here because Remy would want him here, and because he knows more than he and Geoff are letting on right now."

"It's rather crowded, and there are more of you than there should be," the physician said. "There's an unused bay down the hall. We'll talk there."

She led them to the empty patient room and then shoved the bed over. When everyone was seated, she started talking. "First the good news: your son has sepsis—"

"That's good news?" Steven said.

"It's better than septic shock," the physician said coolly. "It means a massive infection has triggered a body-wide immune response but that Jeremy has not yet suffered any organ failure. So while there is systemic inflammation, which is not a good thing, he won't be facing the more extreme complications. We caught it before the inflammation got too far out of hand, which means that his body didn't have enough time to form little blood clots that might've blocked the flow of blood to his extremities or his brain. So no gangrene in his fingers and toes or loss of cognitive functions.

"All of that said, this is a very serious condition, and he's nowhere near out of the woods. What concerns me is that he appears to have a very compromised immune system. Is your son HIV-positive? Because that makes a difference in terms of treatment. Ordinarily, he'd already be on Prednisone to knock out the inflammation, but Pred is a powerful immunosuppressive drug. For obvious reasons I don't want to give it to someone whose immune system is already failing."

"Boys?" Dina said.

Michael and Geoff looked at each other hopelessly. "He was going to tell them," Michael said. He hated to break Remy's confidence, but damn, his life was on the line.

"He was also stalling," Geoff said.

"Because he didn't feel comfortable, and you know it," Michael said.

"Damn it, didn't feel comfortable telling us *what?*" Steven yelled. "This is his life you're dithering over."

Geoff took a deep breath. "Okay, you're not going to like it, and don't you dare yell at me or Michael because we had nothing to do with it, but yes, he's poz."

"What?" Steven screamed. "How the hell could you keep something like this secret?"

"Because of this," Michael said, looking around the room, "and it was Remy's job to tell you because it's his life. I'm out of here. Good luck with your family melodrama. I'll talk to you later, Geoff."

"Thank you," Remy's doctor said. "That makes a huge difference in his treatment. I'll bring an HIV specialist in immediately."

Dina followed him out into the hall. "Michael, wait. I'm sorry for my husband's behavior. Obviously we're shocked, and just as obviously there's more to this story. Are… are you okay?"

"Thank you, Mrs. Babcock." Michael took a steadying breath. "I'm fine, perfectly healthy, and yes, there's a whole lot you don't know that will be coming out soon. As it were. This happened… before Remy and I got together."

"So you and Remy…."

"Yes, he's my boyfriend. I'm sorry you had to find out this way, but he really did intend to tell you. I hope you can understand how hard this has been for him to deal with, and I think I understand why. Now maybe Geoff will understand, too."

"I'll deal with Remy's father, and Remy's right. He and the boys' father have always had a more difficult relationship. Geoff's never wanted to see it, but…." Dina trailed off. "Well, no sense in airing dirty linens in a public hallway. You'll find it all out eventually. Thank you for being there for my son. If you're in any trouble for missing school or practice, I'll talk to your parents."

"Thanks, Mrs. Babcock, that would be great. I've missed a bit of school, yeah. Coach Lodestone's been great about all of this, but I'm at the end of line with him, too," Michael said.

Dina nodded. "Go ahead and send your parents' contacts to my cell phone. I'll be here for a while, but it's not looking like Jeremy will be waking up anytime soon."

"I'll do that before I bike home, but right now I think I need not to be here."

"Yes, sometimes Steven has that effect on people, but don't let him run you off," Dina said. "Jeremy needs you, and so does Geoff. Do you know how to reach Geoff's girlfriend?"

Michael nodded. "I'll call her once I'm outside of the hospital."

"I CAN'T believe my son did that," Steven said, disbelief as plain in his voice as the nose on his face. "Not Remy."

Dina met Michael's eyes and shook her head.

"Well, Dad, he's got the HIV status to prove it, so I'm not sure where you're coming from," Geoff said.

They met in the Babcocks' living room. Michael's parents had offered to come with, but he had assured them that he'd be fine, that Remy's mother would watch out for him. Dina had spoken to them, assuring Michael's parents that her husband was stunned but not hostile. Dina had ended up speaking to Michael's mother in particular about having a gay son. As Michael had predicted, his parents had not known, per se, that he was gay, but were not surprised, either.

"I still think this conversation needs to wait until Remy's well enough to participate in it," Michael said. Despite Mrs. Babcock's assurances, he would put nothing past Mr. Babcock. Between what Remy had told him, plus his own observations, the man struck him as the sort to use bluster to make up for being parentally AWOL.

"I'm not sure Remy has that much time," Steven said. "He needs to start treatment."

"But how does invading his privacy help that?" Dina said.

"His privacy is what allowed this to flourish under our noses, Dina. I don't think he gets to have any privacy for a while."

Michael coughed. "If I may, Mr. Babcock, what allowed this to happen was being closeted and not feeling like he could be open. The stress of the closet cuts you off from the support of friends and family, your whole life, really. I was lucky I was never really in the closet. Remy wasn't so fortunate."

"I'm sure it's not that bad," Steven said, justifying in Michael's mind everything Remy had ever told him.

"Dad!" Geoff said.

"Are you gay, Mr. Babcock? Do you have many gay or lesbian patients?" Michael knew he had to be strong for Remy, so he stared Mr. Babcock right in the eyes. When Steven didn't reply, he said, "Are you? Do you?"

"I don't like your attitude, young man."

"I can live with that," Michael said. "Can Remy?"

Geoff snickered.

"I don't see what that has to do with anything. This isn't about me," Steven said. "I'm a therapist, so I can set my personal feelings aside."

"Just answer his question, Steven," Dina said. "You're being deliberately obtuse, and you know it. In any event, this is your personal life and not your practice, so don't pull that 'I'm a mental health professional' garbage."

Michael and Steven continued their stare for dominance, and it was not Michael who backed down. "All right, fine. It's different when it's your son. Are you happy, now?"

"No, I'm not. My boyfriend is in the ICU because he made a lot of risky decisions this summer. Those are on him, but part of that was because he didn't feel safe coming out," Michael said. "So not only am I not happy, I don't really like you a whole lot if this is what Remy faced."

"You don't have to like me, you just have to respect me as your 'boyfriend's' father."

"Respect is earned, Mr. Babcock," Michael said, his pulse racing, understanding Remy more and more if this was what his father was like. "Now, as far as what happened, what I do know is that he met someone at the boathouse—"

"The boathouse! I'll sue those bastards into the ground. I'll make sure Lodestone never coaches anywhere again—"

"This had nothing to do with the junior crew, and when Coach Lodestone found out about it, he went nuclear. I watched the fight, and it almost turned physical," Michael said tightly. "It was someone involved in one of the masters programs. I think Lodestone turned the guy into US Rowing, so his coaching career is over. As I understand it, the police investigation is ongoing, but from what Remy's told me, the laws in this state covering statutory rape are complicated by 'Romeo and Juliet' clauses and made even murkier when the people involved are the same gender. So go right ahead and sue, but Cap City's followed the letter of the law and the rules of US Rowing."

"Sounds to me like you're still trying to dodge any responsibility for letting Remy down, Dad," Geoff said. Michael looked at him gratefully.

"Go to your room," Steven said. All Michael could do was shake his head.

"That'll make it hard for him to tell you what he knows, Steven," Dina said.

Steven swore. "I wish I'd never heard any of this."

"How'll that help Remy?" Michael said. "Anyway, he branched out and started meeting people online, and before you ask, I don't know. He never gave me the details beyond Grindr."

When Steven and Dina made noises of disgust, Michael said, "For what it's worth, I felt the same way."

"I… uh, encouraged him to delete all that after Nationals," Geoff said.

"That's something, at least," Dina said.

"Why?" Steven demanded. "That could be evidence."

Geoff rolled his eyes. "He lied about his age, Dad, which is how minors get around those things. And he deleted it because one of the guys he met went nuts with jealousy because I happened to be in the same room when they were talking on Skype—just talking, before you get any sick ideas. He didn't believe we were twins."

"That's about when Remy and I started dating," Michael said.

"Yeah?" Geoff said. "I was wondering how you wore him down."

Michael smiled. "Pretty much that was it, although we started at the Crew Classic."

"What the hell is going on with that crew? Boys hooking up? I'm taking this to the board," Steven said angrily.

"Why, because they're boys? That's a little homophobic," Geoff said. "Boys and girls hook up all the time, and nobody has a problem with that."

"And we're not the only gay kids on the crew," Michael said. "After all, other guys on the team were jealous, or so we were told. Take it to the board, and you'll sound like the raging homophobe you look like from here."

"What!" Steven roared. "I think it's time you went home, young man."

Michael stood up. "I've told you what I know. I'm not sure what good it did."

"I'll see you out." Geoff jumped up to follow him. On the front porch, he said, "Please don't judge him too harshly. He's just shocked."

"Whatever, man. He's your father. Hopefully he gets over it before Remy comes home." Michael was pissed.

Geoff sighed. "Mom'll manage him. She always does."

"If this is what he's like, I think I understand why Remy was so reluctant to say anything. Anyway, keep me posted?"

"I will," Geoff said, "and thanks."

CHAPTER
SEVENTEEN

"GOOD, YOU'RE awake," said an affable voice.

I frowned, blinking against the bright light. "I… am, yes. Where am I?"

"You're in the intensive care unit at Sutter Hospital," an older man in a doctor's white coat said. "I'm Dr. Kravitz, your HIV specialist. I took over your care from the intensivist once your status came to light."

I closed my eyes again. Maybe all this would prove to be an elaborate nightmare. "Can you tell me what happened? Last thing I remember…. I don't remember the last thing."

Dr. Kravitz snorted. "I'm not surprised. You were a very sick young man when you arrived. Your brother was terrified, and the other young man wasn't far behind. Is he your boyfriend?"

Oh crap. Had I been babbling or something? "No, he's just—"

"You don't need to hide anything from me, Mr. Babcock," Dr. Kravitz said with a low chuckle. "I've seen it all where this disease is concerned, believe me."

"What disease?" HIV was the last thing I wanted to discuss with a doctor or anyone else.

Dr. Kravitz set his chart down and gave me a look that made me squirm. "Don't play stupid with me. I've been with this disease since the beginning, and I've seen more young men die than anyone should. I was in residency at UC San Francisco in the early eighties when gay men started dying from some mysterious plague that no one could name. They called it GRID—gay-related immune deficiency. In 1984, we discovered it was caused by a retrovirus. It wasn't called HIV until

1986, long after I'd lost too many patients." He gave me a piercing look, like he was angry, even furious. Not at me, but at the disease. "Some people gave up hope, so I decided to specialize in the treatment of men like you. I still do. You're HIV positive. Your brother and your boyfriend told my colleagues when you were brought in with blood poisoning. They saved your life."

I frowned. "What do you mean?"

"What do I mean? It made a big difference in the drugs we used to treat you, to say nothing of getting you started on treatment for HIV itself, that's what I mean."

Son of a bitch. They told. I hardly knew what to think. That meant…. "My parents know, don't they?"

He nodded. "They'd have found out eventually."

I fell back against my bed, my mind awhirl. My parents were going to freak, had already freaked. But they would have kittens all over again the next time I saw them.

"I can't deal with this, any of this."

"And why not? This is a good thing," Dr. Kravitz said, looking up from his charting again.

I made a face. "I don't want to deal with a daily cocktail of drugs, for one thing."

"You already are." Dr. Kravitz laughed. "Why do you think you're doing so well? Seriously, Jeremy, refusing to do this basic thing to take care of yourself is cutting off your nose to spite your face. The drugs available now, they can reduce your viral load—the detectable level of the virus in your body—essentially to zero. You'll still have to be careful if you bleed in public, you'll have to be safe with your sexual partners and inform them, but you'll lead a normal life. You'll learn to take care of yourself, to follow the schedule you'll need for your meds, but this will quickly become second nature."

"I don't want to do this." I crossed my arms. I knew I was being childish, but I couldn't stop the words from tumbling out.

"You already are. We're pumping them into your IV. Before you're released you'll learn to take care of it yourself." Dr. Kravitz patted my hand. "Let me put it this way. Learning to do it yourself is a condition of your release. Now, as far as what else you can expect, you're still sick from the septicemia and you'll be on the antibiotics for a while longer. You'll be shaking that off faster and faster, however. Now that you're awake, you'll find your energy coming back quickly."

As much as I couldn't cope with the idea of HIV, I wanted out of the hospital. "Good. I can't really afford to miss more school. Or more crew."

"It'll take a little longer to build your strength for sports back up, but it'll come back fast. Taking care of the HIV will help with that, too."

"I really am going to have to deal with this, aren't I?" I said.

"Only if you want to live." He looked at me over his glasses.

"That was blunt."

Dr. Kravitz shrugged. "I don't have time to hold your hand. Neither do you. You have a life to live. One of the HIV educators will be by later today or tomorrow to get started with you and tell you about the classes we have about managing a chronic disease. You'll talk about the condition itself, taking care of yourself, sexual health, notifying past partners, all kinds of things."

I nodded, suddenly exhausted by it all. I had a lot to learn and maybe not much time to learn it.

THE HIV education specialist assigned to me turned out to be majorly cool and helped set my mind at ease. It did not hurt that he wasn't more than ten years older than I was. He hadn't been a manwhore like I'd been, but he understood the need, the sexual drive, and didn't judge. I would receive enough of that from my family, and he understood that, too. They were holding back until I was stronger, but I knew it was only a matter of time.

In the meantime, I was moved from the ICU to a regular room and started working on missed assignments brought to me by Goff, Michael, and Laurel. My parents visited every day. Dad struggled with me and what happened, I could tell. Mom did, too, but not nearly as much. Then again, Mom and I always had gotten on better than Dad and I. Eventually I was cleared to go home. I still did not feel entirely normal, but my doctors told me I wouldn't, not with the septicemia, not for quite a while. I would have weekly appointments with Dr. Kravitz and the HIV educator for some time to come, but I was okay with that.

I went home in early November, so yeah, this year the Babcock and Castelreigh households had something to be thankful for. I, however, was just thankful that the two families decided not to share the holiday meal, because all hell broke loose at my house. So much for circling the wagons. I mean, when Cisco died, they were right there for me, but now, when I had a manageable disease? There was a circle, all right, a circular firing squad, and I was right in the middle.

"Remy," Dad said, sighing, "I still don't understand how you could do something like this."

And with that, my appetite, a sometime thing at the best of times, vanished. "Do we have to talk about this right now?"

"Yes, I think we do. Was this some kind of a suicide attempt? Gay kids are far more likely to attempt suicide, something on the order of two or three times more likely," Dad said.

I could only stare at my dad and blink. That was... unbelievable.

"Well?" Dad said. "I think it's a legitimate question. Was this some kind of slo-mo suicide attempt?"

"Yes, Dad. You got me. That's how I decided to kill myself to escape the existential agony and irony of suburban life—by banging as many men as possible," I said flatly. Suffering Christ, where the hell did he dig this garbage up? "In this case, it was in the neighborhood of eight or ten. You can just call me the he-whore of Babylon."

"Damn it, Jeremy, I'm just trying to understand—you, what you did, all of it. You don't have to be so sarcastic," Dad yelled.

Mom looked like she was about to toss the gravy boat at him. "Steven, please lower your voice. I get that you have questions—so do I—but you'll get nowhere with your grand inquisitor act."

"I'm sorry, Dina, but coming out this early can mean lacking the maturity to deal with the emotions and issues involved, and based on what's happened, Jeremy definitely lacks a certain maturity," Dad said, further endearing himself to me.

"Dad—" I said.

Dad shushed me with a gesture. "It's true, Jeremy. This was a very immature thing to do."

"Steven, I'm not sure I'd call it immature," Mom started to say.

Dad rolled his eyes. "Then what would you call it?"

"Since it's my life," I said, "I'd call it 'exploration that ended poorly,' but maybe if even one of those riveting sex-ed talks had actually covered sexually transmitted diseases, perhaps I wouldn't be in this predicament—"

"Be quiet, Jeremy, this doesn't concern you," Dad said.

Goff, quiet until this time, let out a bark of cynical laughter. "Excuse me!"

Dad flushed, realizing what he'd just said. "Geoff, if you can't say anything relevant—"

"No, Steven, you can't blame that on anyone but yourself," Mom said. "What I wonder, Jeremy, is why you didn't look around at school, maybe join the GSA? That has to be full of gay kids."

Was she even for real? How would she know? "Mom, it's full of drama fags and girls looking for projects. Look at me. I'm just a normal guy. I'm not a jock. I'm not a geek. I'm not a brain. I get decent grades, and I row boats. Or did, anyway. Why do I have to fit into someone's notion of what a gay kid is?"

"Jeez, Remy, could you be more homophobic? You know I'm in the GSA. About half of those girls have brothers or sisters or aunts or uncles who're gay, bi, lesbian, or trans. And the theater crowd's kind of fun." Goff shook his head.

"Then there's the fact that most of them are straight," I said.

Goff sighed. "Okay, I have to give you that one."

"Obviously we made some mistakes, I see that," Dad said, "and at some point you locked us out, and that was your mistake. We're not the enemy here, and when you started to see us that way, you went off the rails."

I didn't say anything right away. I wasn't sure I could, because I did not want to admit that I'd made a mistake, even though I had. I had the T-cell count to prove it. Mom and Dad not the enemy? Goff had been saying that for a while, and maybe to him they weren't. What none of them understood was that I had locked them out for a reason. Our parents did not understand me like they did Goff, Dad especially.

"You may not be the enemy, Dad, but you're not exactly on my side, are you?" I said, looking Dad straight in the eye. "After all, I was the changeling left in the cradle in place of your other, normal baby, right? The extraterrestrial dropped in your midst? Does that sound familiar, Dad?"

"I never said those words, Jeremy." The fact that Dad turned white and then dark red gave Dad's game away.

Mom looked at Dad like she had never seen him before. "You didn't."

"I didn't think he could hear me." At least he sounded defensive. He looked anywhere but at her.

I met Goff's eyes. His mouth hung open. I had told him he and I had a different relationship with our parents—our father in particular—more times than were worth counting, but he had never believed me. I thought Goff was surprised I would say this to our parents, but then I realized that was not quite it. He was shocked I was right.

I wished I could say I felt some sense of triumph from all of this, but it just made me sad. All it really did was prove their ultimate failure as parents. Since I no longer felt like eating dry turkey or any of the sides that traditionally accompany it, let alone giving thanks for anything but a steadfast Michael or loyal brother, I left the table.

"Where do you think you're going, young man?" Dad demanded.

"I'd say to hell, but it looks like I'm already there," I called over my shoulder on my way up to my room to lie down. Maybe Michael would have his phone on him.

AFTER I had woken up from a restless nap and started working on more make-up work, my parents joined me in my bedroom. This did not bode well, not if they once again presented a united face. I could deal with it. I had a few more weapons left in the arsenal, but I needed to see where this landed.

"Can we come in?" Mom said.

I put my book down. I was so far behind in AP English that it hardly mattered. "Do I have a choice?"

Dad shook his head, but Mom just put a hand on his arm. "While your father and I clearly have many things to discuss, we still need to talk to you."

Dad coughed. "Right. We're still very angry that you engaged in such dangerous activities, even if we're slowly coming to understand the reasons why you might've done so. We're also very hurt that you couldn't talk to us about something so important."

Oh that was it, that was absolutely it. "You want to talk about that? Okay, we'll start with your compulsory heterosexuality, Mom."

"My... what?"

"Yeah, you heard me. Compulsory heterosexuality. Every time you brought up proms and told me I had to take some girl, you sent me the message loud and clear: the only thing I could be was a good little straight boy making the world better, one desperate and dateless chick at a time."

Mom looked surprised, I'll give her that much. "Remy, that's not what I meant—"

"Well, that's the message that came through." I was done, done justifying myself, done explaining the impact of their words to clueless heterosexuals. Goddamn, if you couldn't have figured out what you were saying, then have a big bowl of shut the fuck up.

"Jeremy, that's just not fair," Dad said. "You never told us—"

"Dad, the fair happens once a year. It's in Woodland and features rides and deep-fried 'I ate *what* on a stick' and unicorns crapping glitter. We're talking about my *life*." I was breathing heavily by this time. I was pissed. "Then there was your obliviousness. I tried to bring it up. I tried to tell you your stupid sex-ed talks were wrong, that I needed more, and you never *listened*."

"Rem, I'm sorry, you have no idea, but you should've been more persistent—"

"Dad, stop!" I screamed, so angry that tears ran down my cheeks. "I'm seventeen. Who's the adult? It's not my job to make you smarter."

While Dad stood there, looking on helplessly as usual, Mom braved the storm and held me, letting me cry myself out. I cried not just for their stupidity and blindness, but for myself. At last, I cried for myself.

By the time I was cried out, Dad had seated himself at my desk chair. "There's no good time to tell you this, so I'm going to get it out in the open… we—your mother and I, but mostly me—think that given everything that's going on, it's not a good idea to have you too far from home for college, at least not for the first year, maybe the first two."

That sounded bad…. I lifted my head from Mom's shoulder. "You what?"

"I'm not even talking about the summer. I'm talking about how sick you've been, and the HIV you're learning to control." Dad took a deep breath. "We want you to stay locally for at least your freshman year of college, meaning either UC Davis or California Pacific."

"No." I said. "What about UC San Diego? Or BU? You can't do this to me."

Dad closed his eyes. "Please don't make this a matter of whether we can or can't, because the reality is that we can. This is something we think we have to do for your health. With your grades and test scores, plus Coach Lodestone's input, you've already been accepted on early admission to California Pacific with a crew scholarship. It was a slam dunk."

I looked at my parents stupidly, like my ears were lying to me or something. "I... what?"

Mom nodded. "We know it's not what you want, and we'll talk about transferring at the end of your freshman year. For the first year, while you're learning to keep your HIV under control, you need to stay where your doctors are."

"We didn't mention your medical issues to the coach," Dad said. "We want you to know that. We only told the men's novice coach that we had personal reasons for keeping you home. We didn't say anything to her about the potential for you transferring, either. That's family business."

"In essence, you'd be starting with a blank slate at California Pacific. All they know is that you've been sick and your parents want you home," Mom said.

They looked so hopeful, and I was so tired that I couldn't explode, even though that was what they deserved. I narrowed my eyes. They would pay for this one way or another. "Transfer, you say? Even to Boston University if I can get in?"

Dad flinched. "Yes, even to BU. It's the least we can do after this. I want to reiterate that this is not a punishment, although it may seem like it. Our only concern is your health at this point. We'll even write up a contract between the three of us and have it notarized."

"We're also not ignorant of the fact that your boyfriend has one more year in high school," Mom said. "This way you and Michael will still be together."

I had to hand it to them. They might have been bastards, but they were good at it. "I guess there's nothing to think about, but I need to sleep on it. I'm exhausted."

"We understand," Dad said. "Everyone in this family has a lot to process these days. I know I've been a less than ideal father, but that doesn't mean I don't love you, Jeremy, or that I'm not trying to understand."

"You've had time to get used to things, Jeremy. We've had a lot dumped on us," Mom said.

"Believe me," I said dryly. "HIV's pretty new to me, too."

"Maybe this is something we can all learn about together, because, Jeremy? We want you around a long time," Dad said.

"And when the time comes, we want to welcome a son-in-law to the family," Mom said.

And then Dad shocked the hell out of me. He hugged me. "Your mother's right, Jeremy. If I play my cards right, I'll come out of this with another son. If I screw this up any further, I'll lose one of the ones I have, maybe both, knowing how close you and Geoff are."

I sagged against him. Turned out, all I'd been waiting for was for Dad to say something like that.

"We'll get through this, Jeremy. I promise. I'll still say stupid things, you'll still fly off the handle, but I'll still be your father and you'll still be my son."

"And so will I," Goff said from the doorway. "Group hug?"

Which was how all four of us ended up squeezed on my bed and how my brother and I ended up sleeping there, curled up together just like when we were little kids.

RIGHT AFTER the holiday, I had another checkup with Dr. Kravitz, and my goodness was it ever embarrassing.

"You're recovered enough, and you have a boyfriend, Remy. It's time to talk about sex," Dr. Kravitz said.

I felt my cheeks heat right up. "Um… really? Can't I just read about it?"

"How'd that work with your father's chats?" he said, peering over his glasses in that way of his.

"Uh… not so well."

"Right, then. First, we'll clear up some common misapprehensions. So, you may have heard that if you're poz, it's fine to throw condoms out and have unprotected sex with other poz men. It's called serosorting, and it's notoriously unreliable. There are multiple strains of HIV, and being infected with one doesn't protect you from infection with others."

And that was news to me. "Lovely."

Dr. Kravitz nodded. "Not only that, the new strain could be resistant to your drug regimen."

"So you can't win for losing." I sighed.

"Please don't think of it as losing. You didn't lose. You contracted a retrovirus that can be managed through medication and lifestyle decisions," Dr. Kravitz said. "No, it can't be cured yet, this is true, but you didn't lose, at life or anything else."

I snorted. "What do you call it when you end up in the hospital with blood poisoning because your immune system's taken a nosedive?"

"I call it ending up in the hospital because your immune system's taken a nosedive." Before I knew it, Dr. Kravitz took my hands between his. "I intensely hate assigning moral terms to medical issues. I saw enough of that in the eighties. It's a disease, Jeremy, not divine judgment. You're not a loser. You didn't lose. You lived, and once we figure out the right drug combination, not only will you live, you will thrive."

"It doesn't feel like it." I looked down. I still struggled with depression over this, maybe because of the crap I got at school. *What does GAY stand for? Got AIDS Yet?"* I'd heard that more than once. So much for living in an ostensibly liberal community.

"I know it doesn't, not right now, but trust me. I've seen a lot of men in your position. We'll find the right combination of drugs for you, and your viral load will drop to undetectable. Do you understand what that means?"

I shook my head.

"It means that on testing, your blood and other bodily fluids will look just like everyone else's. This isn't the cure we've all been waiting for, but let me tell you, it has this old AIDS warrior's heart dancing for joy."

Dr. Kravitz squeezed my hands. He did that a lot, but I didn't mind, because right then I could see the tears in his eyes. I wondered how many patients he had lost to get to this moment. I realized it didn't matter because I knew right then that I'd been very ungrateful. I had been given the golden ticket that they had never lived to see. I would never know their names, but I had to live because they had never had the chance.

"Then HIV will feel more like a chronic condition than the death sentence it may seem right now." Dr. Kravitz pulled some flyers out of a folder. "The HIV educator was just the beginning. These are for classes about living with HIV as well as about managing your condition and the importance of your drug regimen."

I looked at them. They were a lot to take in. "These... wow."

"Yeah, wow is right. Educating yourself is critical, because eventually you'll have to educate your boyfriends, and hopefully one day a husband."

A boyfriend. "Will I be able to date? Marry? Live a normal life?"

"That's the whole point, Jeremy. This isn't the death sentence it was back in the day, but you have to believe that in here"—Dr. Kravitz pointed to his heart—"and here"—he pointed to his head. "That's what these classes are for, and what therapy is for."

"Okay, then." So much to learn. I just wanted to be with Michael, not to sign up for more classes, but here it was, the ultimate AP class. If you passed the test, you got to live. When had my life become *The Hunger Games*?

Right after that first infected load hit my ass.

Something caught my eye. "What's PrEP?"

"PrEP stands for Pre-Exposure Prophylaxis," Dr. Kravitz said, "the ongoing administration of low-dose antiretrovirals to prevent infection in the sexual partners of men with HIV. It's one of the things you might need to educate your future sexual partners about. Given the ongoing nature of PrEP, it would be more appropriate for a long-term partner, as opposed to PEP, Post-Exposure Prophylaxis."

"Is that like Plan B or something?"

Dr. Kravitz chuckled. "Something like that. PEP was originally developed for medical professionals who were exposed to HIV through accidental needle sticks. An antiretroviral course started as soon as possible after exposure—"

That made sense. "That needle stick?"

"Or a condom break in your case, and it can be very effective in preventing infection. After seventy-two hours, it's worthless, however. Something to keep in mind."

More information, more overload. Dr. Kravitz wasn't exaggerating at all when he told me I had a lot to learn. I needed to learn all this before the junior prom.... Michael meant everything to me, and I'd do anything to protect him. "So if Michael and I are intimate—"

"Condoms for oral and anal," Dr. Kravitz said, handing me a card. "If a condom breaks, contact me immediately, and I mean twenty-four seven. I'll phone a prescription to a twenty-four-hour pharmacy to start PEP immediately. I won't tell you not to have sex, because we both know that's futile, but I will tell you to take all precautions necessary."

Then something occurred to me. "What about kissing?"

I wiped my hands on my pants, suddenly nervous. Before I was tested, after I got so sick, I had noticed that we hardly kissed. I missed it.

"If your boyfriend has cuts in his mouth, say from braces that tend to slice things up, or open sores, you should keep it to on the lips, but otherwise?" Dr. Kravitz shrugged. "It shouldn't be a problem."

Before, Michael and I had obliquely decided that after the junior prom we might do the deed. Now? I had no idea. Negotiated risk was one thing Michael and I had not discussed since my recovery.

"Dr. Kravitz?" I hesitated. "Can you tell me about some of them?"

"About who, Jeremy?"

"Some of the ones who didn't make it?"

CHAPTER
EIGHTEEN

I SIGNED back up for weight training, hoping to speed the recovery of at least some of my previous strength. Fortunately, Dr. Kravitz and I homed in on the right drugs reasonably quickly, and the fact that I was young helped, too. I still despaired of getting back in a boat for the simple reason that casual cuts and ruptured blisters meant bodily fluids everywhere. I was terrified of risking my teammates' health, but even more than that, I was embarrassed that I would be called out for it by those teammates. Crew meant so much to me that being sent away in shame would be more than I could ever handle. I thought it better to fade away in shame than face rejection at the hands of the sport I had devoted my life to until this point.

Besides, the weight room was proving to be difficult enough to cope with. Stephens, my old nemesis, was in my section, or maybe I was in his? Regardless, he was back and had learned some new words.

"Fuck off, leper. We don't want your kind in our weight room," he growled at me.

I groaned. "Go to hell, will you?"

"Seriously, get out of here. No one wants you or your diseases. What if you get a cut and bleed everywhere? We could get your plague."

I stood up and looked him in the eye. "The way I see it, Neanderthal, is that you'd better stay away from me. I mean, I could accidentally cut myself open like this," I said, biting my wrist. "Then what would happen to you?"

The panic on his face was hilarious, but the sentiment was not.

"All right, what's going on?"

"Coach, he's threatening to bleed on us!" Stephens said. He actually sounded scared. I had no idea ignorance still ran that rampant, and in Davis, no less. Maybe it was bussed in under affirmative action.

"Can I see you in my office, Babcock?" Coach Robertson said. I swore I heard "Badcock" as I followed him.

"Remy," Robertson said. Then he sighed. "Couldn't you just... you know, not?"

"Not what?" I said. I had an idea where this was going, but I wanted him to say it. For legal reasons. My parents had warned me about this. I think Dad had already called lawyers, just in case.

Robertson stared at me long and hard. "Do you really need to be in the weight room? You know, with your condition? Go join a gym or something."

"I don't understand what you're talking about. I've been sick and my doctor recommended weights. This section fits in my schedule." I shrugged. "I don't see what's wrong."

"That's just it. You're sick. No one wants to catch your disease." He sighed. "Maybe you could come in after hours? That's an accommodation, isn't it? We've already added bleach to the wipe-down spray bottles."

And he had just said the magic words, the words that would put the school district's collective chestnuts in a vise. I stared at him for a few minutes, and then left without saying anything. There was no point.

I cleaned up in the locker room and then sent a group text to my parents, finishing up with: *Was this what you were waiting for?*

My dad replied with a terse *Yes.*

And within forty-eight hours, my family filed an ADA lawsuit against the school district and the city. Furthermore, our lawyer notified every major media outlet across the state, along with Lambda Legal and the ACLU. I guess it didn't matter whether or not my parents had told the crew coach at California Pacific about my HIV anymore....

"YOU KNOW Lodestone thinks you're being silly, right?" Michael said to me one Saturday afternoon in early December. He had come to make plans for the junior prom, and it had quickly turned into making out.

"I know I'm glad you're not afraid to kiss me." I combed my fingers through his hair.

Michael looked a little shamefaced. "I'll admit I was at first, but I've done some reading. My doctor helped put my mind at ease, too."

"I guess we both have things to learn about my disease," I said softly. This gave me hope for other possibilities. He *had* promised to unwrap me like a Christmas present, after all.

"Disease," Michael said, wrinkling his nose. "I've come to think of it as a condition. Anyway, Lodestone basically told me to tell you to stop kvetching and haul yourself back to practice. Time's wasting."

"He doesn't get it." I hid in the comfort of Michael's side. His summer growth spurt had clearly not finished with him. He was almost as tall as I was and definitely broader. If his joints weren't killing him, I'd be shocked, but he never complained.

"Dude, you just whined."

I sighed. "I know, but seriously. I could cut myself, and there'd be plague blood all over the place."

I couldn't see it from where I was snuggled up, but I would've bet money Michael had just rolled his eyes.

"'Plague blood,' Remy? Did you get that from *The Decameron* or *The Plague*? And I'm going to tell Lodestone you said that."

"Mean."

"No, practical. We've all discussed the matter, and we've agreed. It's time for you to get back in a boat."

We? Suddenly all my spidey senses went into full alarm, or maybe it was simple paranoia, and I sat up. "What do you mean by 'we'? Who's 'we,' Michael?"

"I knew that'd get your attention." Michael cackled. "Interested Parties, and that's all I'm going to say. Seriously, Remy. You're recovering physically very well," he said, glancing up and down in a way that gave me hope for that unwrapping, "but mentally? Psychologically? I'm really worried. Rowing's always been central to your world, and you've bailed on it. That can't be healthy."

I knew what he meant, I truly did. I was depressed and I knew it. I had chalked it up to a life-changing diagnosis, but what if he were right? I knew that if I pulled this kind of moping where Lodestone could see me, he'd have had me on the ergs so fast I'd have gotten whiplash, if only to shut me up. The ergs did that to a body.

"Think about it, okay?" Michael said, sitting up. "In the meantime, we've got tuxes to shop for."

I tilted my head. "How much shopping is there to do, really? Tuxes are black and white. If they fit, we're golden."

"Remy, Remy, Remy." Michael sighed. He stood up. "You call yourself gay? It's a winter prom. Why should we settle for black and white when we have things like red or midnight blue or forest green to choose from?"

He yanked on my hand until I stood up.

"Let's get this over with," I said.

"'Over with'?"

I flinched. "Poor choice of words."

"I should think so," Michael said, leading me by the hand downstairs.

"Where are you boys headed?" Mom called.

"Shopping for tuxes!" Michael called. "Your son's hopeless."

My brother snickered from where he and Laurel were ensconced on the sofa watching a movie.

"Hopeless, huh?" I said as I got in the car. Michael might have been the alpha male, but I was the one who could drive with others in the car under California law. Legally, at any rate.

He grinned at me. "Totally."

I snorted. "We'll see about that. So where are we going, anyway? I don't think there's any place in town that rents tuxes that isn't a dry cleaner."

"And what's wrong with dry cleaning? It's made my family fairly well-off," he replied.

"Guess I stepped in that, didn't I?"

"You guess? You're in it up to your hips and sinking fast." He grinned like his meds had just kicked in.

"So which one of your parents' shops are we going to?" I said, trying to salvage some shred of my tattered dignity.

"We're not. We're going to Nordstrom," he replied cheerfully.

I sighed. "Remind me why I put up with you, again?"

He turned in his seat and batted his eyelashes. "Because I'm cute, clever, and loyal."

"I knew there was a reason."

When I stopped at a red light, I leaned over and gave him a quick kiss.

"I'm also hung like a donkey," he said when the light turned green.

I slammed on the brakes again and almost got rear-ended—and not in the good way—for my troubles. "Don't do that while I'm driving."

His only response was wicked laughter. I was in so much trouble with him.

THERE MUST have been more Interested Parties than Michael let on, because when we returned to my house after looking at what was on offer, I found not only Coach Lodestone but the ladies' coach, Sabrina Littlewolf, in my living room.

I must have looked shocked, because Goff laughed. "Relax, Remy. It's not an intervention."

"Actually, it is. Of a sort," Lodestone said. "I'm tired of your excuses and want you to come back to crew before you throw your entire senior year away."

I turned on Michael, all but shooting lasers from my eyes. "You knew about this."

"Kind of." Instead of backing away, which was what most sane people would've done, he pulled me closer. "If you think back to earlier, you'd realize why. Not rowing is killing you."

When, I wondered, had I lost control of my life? Seriously, up until Nationals, I thought I was in firm control of my destiny, or at least as much as any seventeen-year-old could be, but now? I was lucky if I got to choose my own breakfast.

"Don't be too mad at him, Remy, your parents asked me here," Lodestone said. "All Michael did was tell me your reasons, which I have to admit sounded legit to me, at least at first."

"But at least he was smart enough to talk to me," Coach Littlewolf said. She was on the short side, but I knew she had come to coaching as a former cox'n rather than as a rower. "Hello, Remy. I know we've seen each other in passing, but I don't believe we've been formally introduced. You probably already know that I'm a nurse, but what you may not know about me is that I'm in patient education for chronic diseases, and yes, that includes HIV, kiddo."

"So have a seat," Lodestone said. "I think you might be interested in what Sabrina has to say."

Littlewolf nodded and then pushed a strand of dark brown hair behind her ear. "First of all, kudos to you for taking charge. HIV can be frightening, and it takes many people a lot longer to wake up to reality."

"It's not like I had a choice," I muttered.

"And that's where you're wrong," Littlewolf said. "A choice is exactly what you had, and you made the right one, but maybe not where crew was concerned. That's what I want to talk to you about."

I looked around and noticed that the living room had emptied of all but the rowers, no Goff or Laurel, no Mom or Dad. "Okay," I said, taking a seat, albeit somewhat hesitantly.

"How much do you know about the retrovirus?" Littlewolf said.

I took my time thinking about it and realized I didn't know all that much about HIV's natural history. Sure, I had a vague idea about how it reproduced, but mostly I'd been learning what it did to me. I said as much.

Littlewolf nodded. "I thought so. It's actually very fragile. So if you were to cut yourself and bleed all over the place—say the tracks for the seat cut into your calves—the virus wouldn't survive very long outside of your body. That's not to say we wouldn't clean it up with a bleach solution, but that would be a simple precaution and not a public health necessity."

"But what about the oar handles? They're made of wood, and that's a porous surface," I said. "What if I develop and pop a blister? That's a body fluid, and that's what scares me."

"I can understand that, and to be honest, I hadn't thought of that possibility since the women's teams use composite handles. Again, HIV is very fragile, and while I'd have to research this to say for sure, I don't think the concentration of the virus in blister fluid—retrovirus, really—would be all that high."

But I could tell that one had stumped her.

"Those are good points, Remy," Lodestone said. "I agree that it's a concern. One solution might be to soak the handle of whatever oar you use in a bleach solution for twenty minutes or so after practice and to make sure you always use an erg with a composite grip. Another might be to buy a set of composite handles for the varsity boys' oars. They could be wiped down after every practice."

"You can buy wipes with bleach at Costco." All eyes turned to Michael, who blushed. "You can. My parents use them *everywhere*."

"So what do you think, Remy? Would you come back if we made sure oar handles were easily washable?" Lodestone said

I thought about it. The tracks had never been a real concern. I couldn't remember a single instance in my entire time with the Capital City junior crew that tracks had ever so much as poked at my calves, let alone dug in so deeply as to draw blood. I had only wanted to come up with any scenario I could that might involve putting other people in danger.

"I'll help you make a safety kit, Remy. It won't be too hard," Littlewolf said.

I was wavering, and they knew it. Michael had certainly read me right. Rowing definitely constituted the missing piece of my puzzle. If there was a way to row safely....

"Why don't you come back and work on your conditioning on the ergs?" Lodestone said. "That, more than anything, will tell you where you are in terms of recovery... and in terms of your teammates." When he saw my shocked look, he nodded. "Don't ever think I don't know everything that goes on with my crew. I know you've been hassled."

I looked at Michael, who looked right back at me, a hard, accusing look. "Don't you try to pin this on me. This is the first I've heard about this."

"It's only been a couple of guys," I said, suddenly tired.

"That's a few too many," Lodestone replied.

"Knock, knock," Mom said, rapping on the doorjamb. "Is this a private conversation?"

"No, not at all, Mrs. Babcock," Lodestone said. "We're just trying to talk some sense into your son."

"Good luck with that," Mom said, sitting down across the room.

Dad came in carrying a very long, thin box. "Maybe this will help."

I glanced at the box and then did a double take. The label "Concept2" was displayed prominently. It was too small to contain an ergometer, which meant....

Dad set the box at my feet like a retriever and handed me a box cutter. "Open it."

I looked at Michael, but he shrugged, as in the dark as I. Then I glanced at Lodestone and noticed a very definite twinkle in his eye. Yep, a conspiracy. I must have been a bear to manage if it took this many people.

So I opened the box. "Sculls?"

"With composite handles," Dad said. "Obviously your mother and I had help."

Mom nodded. "You need to row, dear."

"And we're not taking no for an answer," Lodestone said.

My brother nodded. "It's not your own single, but with your own oars you won't have to worry about blisters."

"Brat," Michael muttered. "I don't have my own oars."

"So what do you say?" Littlewolf wheedled. "Have we convinced you?"

I nodded, suddenly overwhelmed. "I'll be at practice on Monday."

"You'll start on the ergs," Lodestone said. "I'll help you set your new sculls to your measurements so you can get back in a boat over the winter break. So what do you say?"

"Thanks, you guys." I tried not to choke up.

Lodestone nodded. "Good boy."

CHAPTER
NINETEEN

"WHY'RE WE doing this again?" I hissed at Michael without moving my lips. My cheeks hurt from faking a smile.

We stood on the stairs in my house as my parents snapped pic after pic of us dressed to the nines in our tuxedos. Technically, they were dinner jackets, but no one in these latter days knew the difference, and neither Michael nor I felt like wearing full eveningwear for the junior prom. Perhaps we would for the senior ball.

"Because your parents have been super cool about everything."

When I thought about it, I realized he was right. Mom and Dad had been troupers, at least once they got over the initial shocks to their systems. The ADA lawsuit, the ongoing issues surrounding Josh Brennan, and the elephant in the corner that was my HIV status, all of it. My smile turned more genuine.

"That's what we're looking for!" Dad exclaimed.

"Now the boutonnieres," Mom called.

We had gone through all of this at Michael's house so the Castelreighs could play paparazzi, too.

"Is this why your mom insisted we buy two sets of boutonnieres?" Michael said, unpinning his from the lapels of his dinner jacket, and then waiting while I fumbled with mine. I had to be careful with the pin and all that.

I nodded as we traded boutonnieres. "By the time we're done with all this, these poor gardenias will be trashed."

"Does this count as conspicuous consumption?" he said as I pinned his to his lapel. The cameras flashed.

"Probably not."

Goff chortled. "We'll save that for the senior ball."

"Do you need to be here?" I said, glaring at him.

"Yes." Then Goff snapped some more pictures.

"Seriously, shouldn't you be at Laurel's house helping her parents hang Christmas lights?" I said. I thought that's what he was supposed to be doing.

"They'll wait for him. I had to do some fast talking to keep them from coming over," Laurel said, winking at us.

Michael and I groaned at the same time. All that produced was a chorus of "Aww, how cute."

It was so time to get out of here. I made a production of checking my cell phone. "Wow, just look at the time. We'd better jet if we're going to make our dinner reservations."

"You're not even trying to be subtle, are you?" Michael whispered.

I leaned into him to speak into his ear. I might've nibbled while I was there. "Do you want to do this anymore?"

He shuddered. "Damn, don't do that in public, and no."

"Wait there, boys. I'll be right back with the fresh flowers," Dad called as he went to the kitchen.

Michael leaned over and planted one on my cheek. Unfortunately he damn near speared me with his hair.

"How much gel is in your hair?" I asked him.

Michael made a face. "Carcinogenic quantities. You?"

"The same."

Dad dashed up the stairs to where we stood, waiting like mannequins. He made quick work of the old boutonnieres and then handed Michael a fresh one. "Okay, Michael, first we'll take pictures of you pinning Jeremy."

I met Michael's eyes, and sure enough, the devil mouthed, "Later."

My oblivious parents took picture after picture while my smirking boyfriend attached a fresh gardenia to the lapel of my dinner jacket. I was sure people on the International Space Station could see my face, I blushed so hard. After this summer, I honestly thought I had lost the ability, but apparently I only waited for the right man to bring it out again.

"Now it's your turn, Jeremy," Mom said.

Goff snickered. "Oh, he'll get his turn, I'm sure."

Laurel smacked his arm. I was just glad no one had said anything like "Total bottom city" or anything, regardless of whether or not it was true. Hmmm, maybe I could get a T-shirt with that on it....

Mom handed me the other boutonniere, and instead of making an off-color remark, I let my feelings for Michael shine through with my expression. I might have been bad at saying what I felt, but I could show him.

I took a certain satisfaction in Michael's reaction, because for once I'd made him speechless. Maybe he didn't blush like I tended to, but he looked... softer around the edges or something, and I knew he had understood.

Goff and Laurel look at each with eyes aglow with a gimlet light. "Wait, black and white. It would capture the moment so nicely," Goff said.

Michael rolled his eyes. "How many times have they seen *Sixteen Candles*?"

"About a million. We've already worn out one DVD."

Michael's look said everything. "We can't even pay them back at the senior ball, can we?"

"No, because my parents will subject us to it all again, too."

"Mine, too, if tonight was anything to go by." Michael thought about it. "Maybe we can split a limo with them."

Always practical, my Michael.

"We're leaving now," I announced to the room at large. I grabbed Michael's hand and headed for the door.

"I know you won't drink, but if you do, call. You won't get in trouble because you'll have made a smart decision," Dad called after us.

"Yes, sir!" Michael replied.

I grabbed our overcoats from the coatrack by the front door. I'd planned ahead. I knew my family, and I knew I had to be ready to make a quick getaway. I heard Goff laughing as I slammed the door behind us.

Michael slid his wool topcoat on. "Your brother laughs a lot, have you noticed?"

"He does, yes. It's a good quality to possess, isn't it?" I put my coat on, as well. December in northern California could be cold, and the stars in the clear night sky glittered like diamonds.

"I just wish it weren't always at us."

"We can't have everything." I looked at him. Damn, he was handsome. "Are you ready?"

He tucked his arm in mine and smiled at me. "Yes."

"Then your pumpkin awaits, Cinderfella."

"Why do I have to be Cinderella?"

"Cinder*fella*, and because I'm the one with a pumpkin and a license to drive it."

Michael made a frowny face. "If you're going to take that attitude—"

"When you pout like that... it's not a good look." That didn't stop me from turning him around before we got to my car and then pulling him in close. We were forehead to forehead.

"What are you going to do to make me stop frowning?" Michael said. As handsome as he was, I could have done without the baby-talk voice.

"Kiss him already!" my brother called from the dining room window.

I started to sigh, but it turned into a laugh. What else could I have done? I kissed him and made it count. Besides, I knew how to deal with straight boys. I held Michael's face between my hands and kissed him, long and hard and deep. When I felt my boyfriend's knees shake, I moved my arms, wrapping him securely, and dipped him down like that famous picture of a sailor and what was apparently a total stranger after the Second World War.

"Aww, crap," Goff said before making gagging noises.

Laurel's peal of laughter echoed across the neighborhood. "What did you expect?"

Then I heard the dining room window close. I stood Michael up, but it took a moment or two to steady him. "How was that?"

He looked a little dazed. "A very effective ploy."

"Come along, then. We have dinner reservations."

I pretended I didn't see him adjust himself.

THE PROM was fun, special because of the company rather than the clichéd "winter wonderland" theme in a high school multipurpose room. We were not the only same-sex couple there, and I'm proud to say we didn't spend the entire evening dancing in a group with the girlfriends. I was there with my boyfriend, and hiding in a group with other same-sex couples was not on the agenda. Michael and I were not there to prove anything to anyone, but we were there to dance with each other, not other people. Given that my parents were already suing the school, I doubted any of the chaperones would say anything, and in any event, Michael and I weren't the type to make any public displays, our demonstration in front my house notwithstanding.

As much fun as we had, the dance eventually ended, and I drove us back to his house. The night was still and cold around as we stood outside.

"Well?" he said.

I smiled. "Well what?"

"Don't be goofy. I've been looking forward to this for weeks. With that bow tie of yours, you look like a package—"

I snorted. "The bow's not around the package."

"You," he said, "are horrible."

"What? I didn't say you couldn't unwrap it, I just said that's not where the bow was."

Michael dragged me to the ladder. "Just for fun."

Smothering our giggles, we climbed the ladder up to his room. Form-fitting tuxes made that surprisingly difficult, but I had a feeling we wouldn't be wearing them very much longer.

He shut the window behind us and drew the blinds. Music played softly in the background: my favorite, alt rock from the eighties on. Then he turned to me. "Well?"

"Well what?" I said again.

Michael shook his head. "You. Come here."

Then he grabbed me by the lapels of my topcoat and pulled me close. "Are you really determined to make this as difficult as possible?"

"No. Help me with my coat?"

"Turn around." I wondered if he knew just how much I liked following orders, especially his.

Divested of my coat, I helped him with his and then with his dinner jacket. Michael looked at me with his hazel eyes, and it looked to me like they held his heart. People say teens don't know anything about love, but I don't understand how they could say that. We knew what we knew with the experiences that we had had. If we did not know as much as adults, it was because we had not lived as long. That did not mean we didn't feel as strongly.

"Here I am," I whispered.

He caressed my jaw and captured my lips with his, and I melted into him. He untied my bow tie and unbuttoned my shirt, one button at a time, so slowly I didn't notice until my shirt fell open and I felt his hands on my chest. Then he unbuckled my belt, and still kissing me like he owned me, he unfastened the scratchy synthetic of my rented tux pants with hands that shook just a little.

I felt him guide me back to his bed. When my knees hit the mattress, I crawled backward on it. Tall guys meant making room. "Where'd you get these moves?"

Michael grinned. "Here and there."

"I like a man of mystery." Then I noticed something. "You're wearing too much."

"I can take care of that."

I watched with hungry eyes as he slowly undressed. His eyes never left mine. For all my imagined experience, this had to be the hottest thing I'd ever seen for the simple reason that we were into each other.

Michael stood there in his underwear. "Like what you see?"

His voice dripped bravado, but we were still teenagers, and I could tell he was nervous. I swallowed the lump in my throat, suddenly full of trepidation. All I could do was nod.

He smiled and then climbed on the bed, looming over me on his knees. I pulled on his hands, bringing him down onto me, and ZOMG that felt incredible. It was the closest we had ever been and with the least amount of fabric in the way.

We both shuddered at the contact, responding immediately. My hands started roaming, but Michael growled in my ear. I shook under him, vulnerable and wanting and desperate.

"No," he said, his voice raspy. He grabbed my hands and pulled them over my head. Transferring them to one hand, he reached out and turned off the light by his bed. "Tonight, you're mine and you'll do what I say."

"How did you know?" I whispered.

It was moments before he spoke. "You've told me in a hundred little ways."

"Is that okay?" I had never felt more exposed in my entire life. It scared me. It thrilled me.

"Listen to me, Remy… Jeremy," he said roughly, taking my jaw in his free hand. He had never called me by my full name, and I stilled at his touch. "I need it, too. You taught me that."

And then he claimed me. We claimed each other.

I woke up later, early in the morning. Music still played in the background. Irony of ironies, LaTour's "People Are Still Having Sex." Interestingly enough, the lyrics were different from the CD I had at home, instead of "this AIDS thing's not working," it was "this safe thing's not working." The thing of it was, safe would have worked, at least for me. If I had received the information in time. If my partners had said something. If I had thought with the big head.

Curious, indeed. The lyrics let me know that on some level, despite all the mistakes I had made, my need for sexual contact was a natural one. People needed to be touched, and no matter what kind of message society sent, people would always seek out the touch they needed. So no, this AIDS thing wouldn't and didn't stop it, not in the West among gay men and not in Africa among heterosexuals.

Last spring, I had wanted that touch from Michael. He had wanted to give me that touch. We had both been confused and hadn't known how to do it. Maybe I should have tried harder to make him see. No maybe about it, actually, but I hadn't, and that oar's puddle had passed the stern deck and disappeared. It was time to worry about the next stroke. We were here now, and that was what mattered.

That was what I loved about crew. Every stroke was another chance to do it right, an entire sport devoted to do-overs. That thing you had just done wrong? That was old news. Lesson learned, forget it, and move on.

So yeah, I had sought out the touch of others, and it hadn't gone so well. That didn't mean I had been wrong to have done so. It meant I had gone about it the wrong way. I had flown the nest a little sooner than I should have. It meant I had thought I was a little more grown-up than I really was. That was all. I flew back, wings singed, lesson learned.

Michael and I had ended up together, after all. Who knew what the future would bring us? I started college next year. Michael had one more year of high school. For now, we were together. I hoped we would stay that way, but we both faced a lot more growing up. I knew one thing: he would always be my friend.

EPILOGUE

April, my senior year

THIS WAS it, the last race of my high school rowing career. In seven minutes or so, I would finish my time with the Capital City Rowing Club junior crew and hand it all over to Michael. I couldn't think of better hands. They'd certainly handled me well. Damn, so not the thought to have when I wore nothing but form-fitting Spandex and a tight jockstrap. Then it would all be over but the post mortem and the good-byes. I was proud of my time with Cap City, for all its ups and downs. I had grown up on the crew, and I had made some lifelong friends. Some I had already said good-bye to, some I hoped would accompany me through life. But right then was not the time to dwell on my sorrows and my joys. We had finished our warm-up row on the ass end of Mission Bay, and it was time to get my head in the boat.

"Good luck," I said, reaching a fist back to seven. Right then, he was no more than my seven seat, even if on shore he was my smoking-hot boyfriend.

"Good luck," Michael said, bumping his fist into mine before he turned around and repeated the ritual with six seat, and so on down the boat.

I was in my zone, sensory input flowing in and out of my consciousness but not lingering. I responded but didn't react.

Howie, the cox'n, called low-voiced commands to bow and two to correct the boat's trajectory in our lane. Not my problem. That responsibility lay with Howie and the kid in the stake boat holding our stern. If they needed me to do anything, they would tell me.

"We have alignment."

"Ready all," Howie said softly.

We were already at our catch position, the blades of the oar buried in the water. I wiggled my fingers on the oar's composite handle to avoid a death grip. Those led to blisters and were indicative of sloppy technique.

The starter's horn shattered the silence of the starting line.

"Row!" Howie barked into his microphone. *Git, y'all!*

Eight rowers moved as one through the starting sequence to break inertia's hold on the *Helena Sundstrom*.

Half!

Three-quarters!

Half! Half!

Full! Full!

"Twenty high!" bellowed Howie.

By that time, the *Helena* flew across the calm water of Mission Bay.

So did the hulls of the other crews, and we were not the fastest.

I knew only the world before my eyes, the steely-eyed glare that was the determination of Howie Chen.

"Three boat lengths to the Little Knights," Howie barked. "How badly do you want this? Show me!"

A short man on dry land, he spoke with the voice of a titan in the boat.

"Five hundred meters in. Big legs, this stroke." He would be all but voiceless by the end of the race, but right now, his voice was our world.

"Focus thirty. Now."

So we focused. Our bodies burned. But I knew I lacked that essential fire I had summoned at the Nationals, that fury that had made me consume myself. Where had it gone?

"We've barely moved on the Little Knights. Halfway through the race and they're holding us off. What are you waiting for?" Howie yelled. "Bring your focus into the boat. Not what you're going to do at the end of the race, fuck that. Right here, right now. Ratio shift, in two."

That was me. I was stroke. They were rushing me, and I would slow them down. Me and Michael.

"Let's do… this," I huffed to Michael.

Howie smiled. "That was one... and two."

And we did it, Michael and I. We stood on our foot stretchers and pulled our blades through the water faster and took just a bit longer on our recovery.

"That's it, men. That's what I want to see... and we just took a seat on the Little Knights. Do it again. Then gimme that focus thirty."

Slowly but surely we started to walk up on them as Howie counted off the strokes.

"Less than a boat length," Howie said tersely. "Show them how we row at Cap City."

We didn't have that much time left. I couldn't look, but I knew Howie's expressions—he looked super intent. That meant we were close, damn close.

His eyes lit up. "*Bow ball!*"

That wasn't for us. That was for them, just to psych them out.

"Up two in two," he all but whispered, his voice caressing us. "One... and two."

So Michael and I took the pace up, the six behind us backing us every breath and stroke.

The *Helena* flew once again.

So focused had we been on the Little Knights that we had never seen the other boats, and that was probably Howie's strategy. By the time I saw the buoy indicating the final five hundred meters, it was only Cap City and the Little Knights.

"We're half a boat length ahead of them. Are we going to make a move or not?" Howie said tightly. He looked straight through me and the rest of us to the finish line. He carefully glanced to the side and behind. "They're starting. They know they have to if they're going to pull this out. This is the finals. Bring it up now. Empty the fucking tank or lose. You choose."

To our credit, we kept it smooth, no panicked flailing, just a measured increase, step by step, beat by beat. I had found that fire at long last, and it was a pleasure to burn.

I heard screaming on the shore, but I didn't care. Step by step, stroke by stroke. I could almost—but not quite—sense another boat out of the corner of my eye. "Now!"

"You heard him! All of it!" Howie screamed. "You can puke when we're done."

Cap City! Cap City! Cap City!

Then an air horn's wail, and again almost immediately.

"Way enough! Oars down," Howie rasped, his voice barely above a whisper. "All eight, check it down."

With a flick of our wrists, we turned the blades of our oars from parallel to the water's surface to perpendicular and stabbed them into Mission Bay, halting the momentum of our boat.

And it was over.

CHRISTOPHER KOEHLER learned to read late (or so his teachers thought) but never looked back. It was not, however, until he was nearly done with grad school in the history of science that he realized that he needed to spend his life writing and not on the publish-or-perish treadmill. At risk of being thought frivolous, he found that academic writing sucked all the fun out of putting pen to paper.

Christopher is also something of a hothouse flower. Inside of almost unreal conditions he thrives to set the results of his imagination free, and for most of his life he has been lucky enough to be surrounded by people who encouraged both that tendency and the writing. Chief among them is his long-suffering husband of twenty-two years and counting.

When it comes to writing, Christopher follows Anne Lamott's advice: "You own everything that happened to you. Tell your stories. If people wanted you to write warmly about them, they should have behaved better." So while he writes fiction, at times he ruthlessly mines his past for character traits and situations. Reality is far stranger than fiction.

Christopher loves many genres of fiction and nonfiction, but he's especially fond of romances, because it is in them that human emotions and relations, at least most of the ones fit to be discussed publicly, are laid bare.

Writing is his passion and his life, but when Christopher is not doing that, he's an at-home dad and oarsman with a slightly disturbing interest in manners and other ways people behave badly.

Visit him at http://christopherkoehler.net/blog or follow him on Twitter @christopherink.

Nail Polish and Feathers

Jo Ramsey

http://www.harmonyinkpress.com

Pukawiss the Outcast

By Jay Jordan Hawke

When family complications take Joshua away from his fundamentalist Christian mother and leave him with his grandfather, he finds himself immersed in a mysterious and magical world. Joshua's grandfather is a Wisconsin Ojibwe Indian who, along with an array of quirky characters, runs a recreated sixteenth-century village for the tourists who visit the reservation. Joshua's mother kept him from his Ojibwe heritage, so living on the reservation is liberating for him. The more he learns about Ojibwe traditions, the more he feels at home.

One Ojibwe legend in particular captivates him. Pukawiss was a powerful manitou known for introducing dance to his people, and his nontraditional lifestyle inspires Joshua to embrace both his burgeoning sexuality and his status as an outcast. Ultimately, Joshua summons the courage necessary to reject his strict upbringing and to accept the mysterious path set before him.

http://www.harmonyinkpress.com

Ben Raphael's All-Star Virgins

By K.Z. Snow

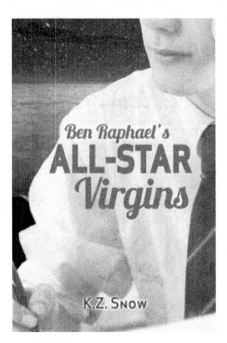

Sixteen-year-old Jake McCullough and his friends Rider, Brody, Carlton, and Tim are the invisible boys of Ben Raphael Academy, an exclusive coed prep school. Brody decides they need "mystique" to garner attention. "Nobody has more mystique than a desirable virgin," he declares. Thus is born Ben Raphael's All-Star Virgin Order or BRAVO.

The boys polish their appearances. Brody launches a subtle but canny publicity campaign. Soon, the boys are being noticed. But they're emotionally fragile. Two have succumbed to a seductive female teacher. Jake and Rider, roommates and best friends who are attracted to one another, fear the stigma of being gay.

It takes an unspeakable tragedy to make the BRAVO boys realize what's important in life and that "virginity" has more than one meaning.

http://www.harmonyinkpress.com

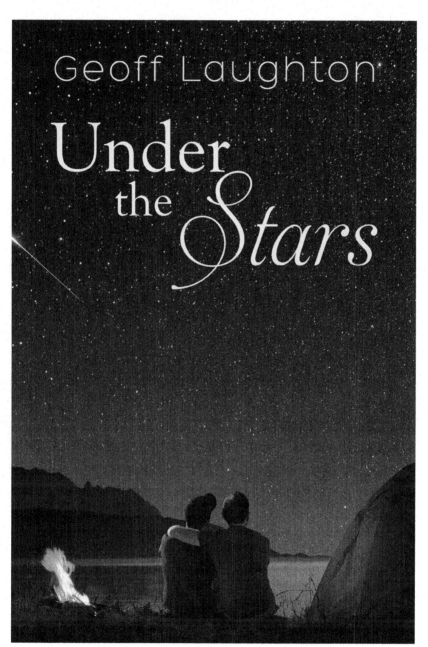

Geoff Laughton

Under the *Stars*

http://www.harmonyinkpress.com

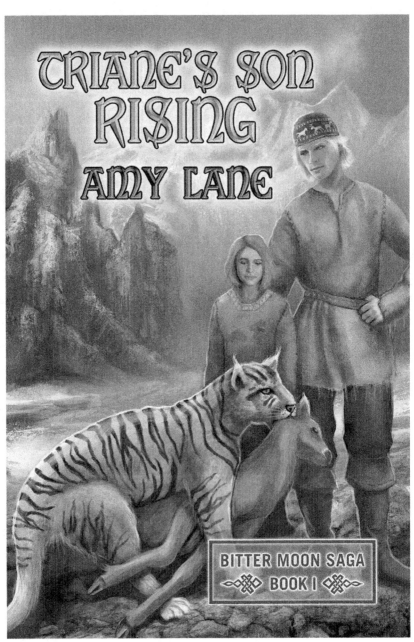

TRIANE'S SON
RISING
AMY LANE

BITTER MOON SAGA
BOOK I

http://www.harmonyinkpress.com

BLOOD MOON

M.J. O'Shea

http://www.harmonyinkpress.com

JOHN GOODE

Straight   GAY   Gay ish   STRAIGHT

TALES FROM
FOSTER
HIGH

http://www.harmonyinkpress.com

BINARY BOY

RJ Astruc

http://www.harmonyinkpress.com

CPSIA information can be obtained
at www.ICGtesting.com
Printed in the USA
BVOW09s0212070518

515408BV00007B/95/P

3 1901 06143 1385

A GUIDE FOR CO-OPS, INTERNS AND FULL-TIME JOB SEEKERS

FIND YOUR FIRST PROFESSIONAL JOB

Scott Weighart

This textbook is dedicated to Tim Hall and Jan Wohlberg, the two mentors who were the most helpful and influential in beginning my career in academia.

Third Edition
Copyright © 2007 by Scott Weighart

ISBN-10: 0-9621264-5-4
ISBN-13: 978-0-9621264-5-1

Mosaic Eye Publishing has the exclusive rights to reproduce this work,
to prepare derivative works from this work, to publicly distribute this work,
to publicly perform this work, and to publicly display this work.

Printed in the United States of America

CONTENTS

ACKNOWLEDGEMENTS

Given that this book has been a work-in-progress since 1995, many people have played important roles in its ongoing development. At Northeastern University, I owe thanks to Donna Smith, Mel Simms, Betsey Blackmer, Charlie Bognanni, William Sloane, Mary Kane, and Elizabeth Chilvers for their materials and perspectives over the life of this book.

Thanks also to Rose Dimarco, Ronnie Porter, and Bob Tillman for contributing their sidebar boxes, which pushed the 2003 edition of this book to a higher level. Likewise, I am very grateful to Marie Sacino of LaGuardia Community College for giving us perspectives regarding students and employers from her institution. Many of our Northeastern University alums and employers deserve thanks. In particular, thanks to our alums Ted Schneider, Mark Moccia, Gabriel Glasscock, and Keith Laughman for expansively and passionately including their ideas here. As for co-op employers, Myretta Robens of Harvard Business School Publishing, Steve Sim of Microsoft, and Mike Naclerio of the workplace HELPline were kind enough to offer their thoughts for publication. Thanks to Sarah Burrows for suggesting several great internship websites to add to Chapter One of the 2005 edition. This edition also benefits from the inclusion of behavioral-based interviewing stories by Alexandra Ciccariello, Aimee Stupak, Nat Stevens, Jared Yee, Rebecca Harkess, Cheyenne Olinde, and Jake Thaler, who were in my co-op prep class over the last three years.

With every edition, it seems like someone new comes out of the blue to make a crucial contribution. For this third edition, that person was Linnea Basu. Linnea wasn't shy about critiquing old and new material, and we have a much better end product as a result. Some of her suggestions confirmed my own belief that changes needed to be made, and others were completely fresh ideas that had never crossed my mind. Thanks and hats off to Linnea. Additionally, Kate Fiefer and Bonnie Brock provided me with a great new sample resume, and Robin Friedman of Visual Velocity updated the cover design on short notice. Mary Rose Tichar of Case Western Reserve also has been a most encouraging colleague.

Thanks also to those who have brought this book a long way in terms of its appearance. Victoria Arico greatly enhanced the professionalism of the book with her cover design. Marjorie Apel from Manhattan College gave me valuable feedback on the book's style, and Alison Molumby gave us great ideas for redesigning the text for the previous edition. Lastly, my wife Ellie and my mother-in-law Lorraine Boynton have contributed significantly with editing and proofreading. Thanks to everyone.

Scott Weighart
July 2007

INTRODUCTION

Being successful in your first professional job is not magic: It requires a positive attitude and the willingness to keep taking small steps toward self-improvement in your career. Whether you are planning for your first co-op job, internship, or first full-time job out of college, this guidebook was written to show you exactly what separates the extraordinary new professional from those who are ordinary or mediocre. Follow these steps carefully, and you can transform yourself into a great job candidate and performer... a little at a time.

Find Your First Professional Job was initially written to be a key resource for business students at Northeastern University, which has one of the largest co-op programs in the world. Yet although a Northeastern-specific version of this guidebook has been used with thousands of students, the last few editions have been geared to offering much of the same reliable and time-tested information to students in other programs. Although Northeastern's students use this information as a resource on everything from sprucing up their resume to dealing with multiple job offers in our business co-op program, I have broadened the aim of this guidebook to provide more useful support to co-ops, interns, and full-time job seekers in all majors and at colleges and universities anywhere.

Universities across the country are embracing multiple forms of practice-oriented education, including co-op, internships, practicum assignments, volunteer work/community service learning, work abroad, and clinical rotations to name a few. Basically, the rising cost of higher education has resulted in students and parents asking, "What return will I get on my investment in higher education?" As a direct result, schools ranging from small community colleges to big-name Ivy League institutions have found it necessary to give their students more opportunities to get real-world experience.

This is a terrific development for the 21ˢᵗ-century student: Working in your field gives you a chance to test a career, build a resume and reference, make connections between the classroom and the real world, create connections with post-graduation employers, and—often but not always—earn money.

While this represents a great opportunity, it also creates challenges for students. Some of these challenges relate to planning your co-op or internship: Will professional organizations want to hire you when your job experience is limited to retail, restaurant work, and childcare? What can you do right now to increase your chances of getting the best possible job—even if you don't intend to look for your first job for a year or more? How will the job market affect your search? What are your job search options? The first chapter of this guidebook, "Planning For Your First Professional Job," tackles these questions.

Other challenges arise during the preparation stage—the weeks and months immediately preceding your co-op job, internship, or other work-related endeavor. How can you write an effective resume when your best job was working as a Burger King cashier or as a babysitter for families in your neighborhood? What should you include and emphasize on your resume, and what is best to leave off? How can you overcome your jitters about interviewing and present yourself positively but honestly? How can you deal with fuzzy open-ended questions, tough interviewers, and the fact that you can't possibly anticipate all questions that may be asked. What do you do if you get an offer from Company A when you're waiting for Company B to get back to you? Chapter 2 ("Writing An Effective Resume") and Chapter 3 ("Strategic Interviewing") of the guidebook cover this terrain and much more.

Once you have lined up your work experience, the real work begins. What is at stake when you are working as a co-op? How can you live up to your interview and make the most of your co-op opportunity? How can you balance a part-time internship with full-time classes? What should you do if problems arise? How can you get the best possible evaluation and reference? Chapter 4 reviews "Keys To On-The-Job Success" in handling these concerns among others. For the first time, this edition features comprehensive information on e-mail and IM etiquette, as these forms of communication have become much more critical in today's workplaces.

You also may wonder about how to make sense out of what happened during your co-op or internship when you return to campus for classes. What steps might be required of you when you return to school? What might you need to do to get credit for your work experience? What are some options to consider as you process the experience? Chapter 5 goes over "Making Sense Of Your Experience" and considers the reflection steps that are required at NU and many other institutions.

The appendices include many other materials that co-op professionals may or may not want to incorporate into their courses, time permitting. Appendix A details job search logistics and NU's Co-op Learning Model. This is a great section for understanding the job search process as well as the steps involved in learning from practical experience. Appendix B features our Skills Identification Worksheet. This is a useful confidence builder for many first-time job seekers who have a hard time believing that they actually already have many soft skills that are attractive to employers. Appendix C covers how to write effective cover letters, whether you are looking for a co-op job or pursuing your first full-time job after graduation.

Appendix D is a brief "bridging" exercise, geared to helping students make connections between their resumes and actual job descriptions. Appendix E covers behavioral-based interviewing, which is an increasingly common feature of employer interviews. In this appendix, I explain how to develop great stories for behavioral-based interviews and also how to use these stories in a conventional interview. For this edition, I have more than doubled the length of this appendix, as students love mastering this form of interviewing, while employers utilize this approach more and more. Appendix F includes various other resources that may prove handy in the classroom or as homework assignments. The Job Search Scenarios are a new addition and are useful for small-group discussion in the classroom.

This book has been through numerous editions and has been used by thousands of Northeastern University students and hundreds of students at LaGuardia Community College in New York. As such, the material here is tested by experience—just as you will be as you go through your first professional job experiences. While this is certainly serious business, I have tried to write the book in a light and conversational way, including many real-life anecdotes and quotes to make the book as fun to read as it is informative. It's really exciting for me to have the voices of some of our best co-op students included in the guidebook. You'll find these thoughtful perspectives in sidebar boxes.

Here's an example.

> **A Student's Perspective On This Guidebook**
> *by Keith Laughman*
> The co-op guidebook is a student's Bible to landing that great job during co-op semesters and even upon graduation. It's the only book that I've used for all five years of college! The information contained in this guidebook may be overwhelming at first, but believe me when I say that it will greatly influence your resume skills, interview skills, and job searching skills.
> *Keith Laughman was an MIS/Marketing student at Northeastern University, Class of 2002.*

This guidebook also includes the perspectives of other co-op faculty from outside the College of Business Administration and even from outside Northeastern University. At NU, I interviewed three of our most experienced co-op faculty: Bob Tillman in the College of Engineering; Ronnie Porter in the College of Arts and Sciences; and Rose Dimarco from the Bouvé College of Health Sciences. I also have been fortunate to include the perspectives of Marie Sacino at LaGuardia Community College in the form of sidebar boxes and sample resumes from her students. You might be surprised at how much a student in ANY major can learn by reading and reflecting on advice from these various perspectives. There is a considerable amount of wisdom in this field that proves to be universal.

Like most aspects of being a first-time professional in the workplace, what you get out of this guidebook will depend heavily on the amount of effort you spend in truly understanding the material that we present to you here. If you just skim through the chapters, you will find that this text is no more useful than giving a menu to a starving man.

If, however, you really put some energy into thinking about how this material applies to you and incorporating these concepts into how you approach resume-writing, interviewing, and your actual co-op job, you will find that these principles will help you in your career long after you have graduated.

I hope that this book helps you gain confidence as you approach your first co-op job, internship, clinical experience, practicum, or full-time job after graduation. Good luck in your preparation activities and in all of your efforts to professionalize yourself in the weeks and months to come. You might just amaze yourself with the results!

Scott Weighart
July 2007

CHAPTER ONE
Planning For Your First Professional Job

Whether you opt for a co-op or internship, a clinical assignment or simply your first full-time job after graduation, you have a great deal at stake. Yet even though many students now realize how important some form of practical job experience is these days, not all students really understand everything that they're going to get out of the experience. Additionally, many students fail to realize that there is a great deal that can be done to get ready for a co-op or internship—even if their first professional job is months and months away.

This chapter is intended to get you thinking about your next professional job now so you will have a better understanding of the benefits of getting practical job experience and what you can do to give yourself a head start on the process.

BENEFITS OF PROFESSIONAL EXPERIENCE

For all undergraduates getting real-world experience, there are still many common themes when we consider the benefits of doing a co-op job, internship, clinical assignment, or practicum before graduation.

Career Testing
In any form of what we at Northeastern University call "practice-oriented education," getting practical work experience as an undergrad helps you test out different careers. This will help you determine whether you are on the right career path. It's one thing to be in a finance class for three or four hours per week: It's a whole different ballgame working in a finance job 40 hours per week for a summer or six months. You really wouldn't want to spend $100,000 or more on your education over four or five years, only to find out six months into your first "real job" that you actually dislike working in that field as a full-time professional. What do you do then? Go back to school?

It's not at all uncommon to see the following scenario with our students at Northeastern University: John Schlobotnik goes to see his co-op coordinator right after completing his first co-op job experience in accounting (or psychology or physical therapy or any other major). The co-op coordinator welcomes John back and asks how the job went. "What did you learn on your job, John?" John blushes, looks at the ground, and sheepishly says, "Uhhh, I think I learned that I don't want to be in accounting."

It's almost as if John thinks that his co-op coordinator will criticize or condemn him for such rebellious thinking! Hardly. We remind the student that this is a primary purpose of internships and co-op, and then we can begin a dialogue about what other concentration or major may be more appropriate.

Career Testing – A Co-op Professional's Perspective
by Bob Tillman
Most of the students I have coming in want fieldwork. And then when they do it, they don't want it anymore. Okay, well, tell me what that means: What changed? How hard was it? What does it feel like when people scream and yell at you? You know, you're only as good as your last mistake—and that's big in engineering, especially civil. And when you're the engineer or the super some day, how are you going to handle it differently? Remember what it felt like to be a beginner.

Bob Tillman is a cooperative education faculty coordinator in
Civil Engineering at Northeastern University

I have known more than a few physical therapy students at Northeastern who absolutely loved the subject in the classroom. During their first field experience, however, a few found out that they felt amazingly uncomfortable having to touch people in their role as a physical therapist in training. For most, this was a startling and upsetting realization—but also an absolutely critical discovery that led them to make a necessary change very early in their college careers.

See another example in the sidebar box on the next page.

Experience Building

You may not begin your first internship or co-op with much directly relevant job experience on your resume, but you can change that fact dramatically over the course of a few real-world experiences. How this happens will vary depending on a few different factors.

If you begin your undergraduate years with a very clear sense of your career goals—and if your real-world experience merely confirms those goals for you—you will graduate with great depth of experience. For example, I primarily work with Management Information Systems (MIS) students at Northeastern University. Student A may know before she even meets with me that she wants to be a Network Administrator. Even if she has no direct experience, we can ensure that she ends up with in-depth knowledge of the field after completing

Confirming Career Plans At LaGuardia Community College
by Marie Sacino

An internship can provide an opportunity to discover your passion, to make a solid contribution to your employer, and to grow. Zoe Cornielle, a liberal arts student in our social science and humanities curriculum, explored her interest in the field of social work during her first internship at the Hospital for Special Surgery. Zoe was assigned to work in the Department of Patient Care and Quality Management. Under the supervision of a program coordinator and a managed care associate, Zoe worked as part of a health care team to provide education, advocacy, and assistance to outpatients in both rheumatology and orthopedic clinics.

With training, support and supervision from social work professionals, Zoe began to provide outreach services to patients in various patient waiting areas. Zoe listened to patients' concerns and questions, provided information on education and support groups, made referrals to community based agencies, and kept records of patient activity.

On my visit to HSS, I got a first-hand opportunity to see Zoe at work. I was so impressed by her professionalism, her ability to engage patients, her understanding and sensitivity of the impact of barriers to health care as well as her dedication to the patients with whom she worked. HSS was also quite impressed: Zoe was invited back for her second full-time internship this past summer. She discovered her passion—helping people—and confirmed her career plans: social work. Zoe expanded her role greatly as she took on the new role of "first" lead volunteer. She had an opportunity to participate in developing training materials and in leading group discussions. Zoe also provided support and supervision to new interns and trainees as they began to work with patients. She now plans to transfer to Hunter College to pursue a degree in social work.

Marie Sacino is an Associate Professor of
Cooperative Education at LaGuardia Community College.

three six-month co-op jobs. Maybe her first job is a rather light Help Desk job. With that on her resume, she is able to get a substantial PC/LAN position next time around, complete with opportunities to troubleshoot problems, upgrade software on the network, and perform fundamentals of networking such as adding new users. On her third co-op, she might be doing substantial computer room work, handling tricky interface issues between Novell NetWare and TCP/IP, maybe even setting up the hubs and routers that form the "guts" of the network. She graduates with a rich and deep understanding of one part of MIS.

Meanwhile, Student B doesn't really know what he wants to do with MIS—he just knows that he likes doing stuff with computers. Maybe he starts out with that same Help Desk job but finds it frustrating to deal with impatient end users and to juggle competing priorities and requests amidst numerous interruptions. Next time around, he tries a database development position and likes it more but finds it too much on the opposite extreme—too much time sitting at his computer, not enough variety. Finally, he gets a Systems Analyst job on his third co-op and acts as a go-between for programmers and financial planners who need software. This student graduates with greater breadth of experience. He may not command as much money in his first full-time job, but he may have more options available to him now and more doors open to him later. So there are positives either way.

Additionally, any professional experience that you obtain as an undergrad will do more than improve your technical skills in a given field—the experience will provide you with great opportunities to professionalize yourself. While most students come into internships and co-ops focusing on what technical skills they may be able to acquire, many come away from their first job rather surprised at how much they learn about working that has nothing to do with learning technical skills and responsibilities. Every workplace has its own written and unwritten rules about performance and behavior. Organizational politics can have a dramatic impact on your ability to function effectively in a position. Supervisors can vary dramatically in terms of their managerial skills, expectations, and pet peeves. Developing the adaptability to handle different work environments and to obtain great evaluations in situations that require radically different behavior can be a big challenge. Learning the changing rules of the game and making sure that you succeed regardless of varying expectations is a characteristic of the best future professionals.

Most students—especially those working full-time hours in their work experience—find that they feel more confident about their professionalism after each job experience. The discipline required to get to work on time every day and to get your work done well and on time seems to develop good habits that become more automatic over time in most cases. It's often exciting for a co-op or internship coordinator to see a student after one job experience: I often am amazed to see big changes in professional etiquette when these students return to my office and interact with me. Frequently, going to work in a professional setting helps you develop a greater sense of purpose both in the classroom and in your professional relationships.

Building a Great Resume and Getting Valuable References
If you're building your experience, then you obviously are also building an impressive resume detailing all of that experience. Just as importantly, if you perform well, you can end up with a long list of respected professionals who will recommend you to future employers. Developing a network of people who are able and willing to assist your future job searches can make a big difference— many jobs are filled through personal connections rather than simply pulling in a bunch of anonymous candidates through newspaper ads.

Enjoying a Trial Period with Potential Full-Time Employers
Many organizations who hire students for co-op jobs, internships, and other

4

forms of practice-oriented learning are looking for more than a person to do a job for six months—they are using the co-op period to "test out" someone that they may or may not wish to make a job offer to upon graduation.

As one large co-op employer told me: "If we hire ten co-op students, we figure that at least nine of them will work out well and get productive work done in a cost-effective manner. If three of those nine are such stars that we want to hire them after graduation, then that's really the ultimate goal for us. After all, at our company, we can't just fire someone—we have to coach them to death!"

Indeed, this organization doesn't allow managers to fire employees who are clearly poor performers. Instead, the manager must hold regular "coaching meetings" and document them heavily. In the end, the employee still ends up being terminated. As you might imagine, this employer really doesn't want to hire the wrong people—that's a mistake that costs thousands of dollars in addition to causing numerous headaches! Hiring co-ops helps them know what they're getting and makes it less likely that they will have to go down that costly and time-consuming path with a wayward employee.

Integrating Classroom Learning with Workplace Learning
Certainly one of the greatest payoffs for students who immerse themselves in a relevant real-world setting is the opportunity to make meaningful connections between theory and practice. Better still, it's a two-way street: Concepts that are hard to really understand in the classroom can come alive for you when you see how they apply to real-world situations. At other times, you will learn how to do something while on co-op but perhaps not really understand the underlying concepts until you learn about them in a class after completing your work experience.

Better still, co-op, clinicals, and internships can bring home the importance of classroom concepts, sometimes in dramatic and unexpected ways. Students who don't get meaningful, career-related job experiences during their undergraduate years sometimes have a harder time believing that some required courses are all that important. Even if you have a gifted professor, it may be hard for a student to believe that coursework in finance or accounting has any relevance to them if they "know" that their future is in MIS or Human Resources.

Getting that professional experience as an undergrad can reveal that this way of thinking is an illusion. One of my students who completed an MIS position in senior management support at The Gillette Company had to provide computer and audiovisual assistance to some of the most powerful people in the organization. His coursework in accounting took on a newfound urgency for him as he ended up assisting during several heavy number-crunching meetings, in which the executives spoke with great passion about balance sheets, income statements, and other concepts that the student had found only mildly interesting before the job began.

Another student felt rather lukewarm about taking his Organizational Behavior requirement, mainly because our NU offering is an eight-credit course meeting twice a week for over three hours at a time. Before long, he found that his class with Professor Brendan Bannister was "almost like therapy." It helped him process and understand many elements of motivation, leadership, and group dynamics that had absolutely baffled and confounded him on his previous co-op job.

Coursework outside of your major also can have a dramatic impact on your career, and vice-versa. One of the biggest mistakes students make when picking electives is to just pick something that sounds relatively painless without considering the possible benefits of liberal arts electives. A marketing student might be well-advised to take a communications course that helps build public speaking skills; a civil engineering student with lofty aspirations might be wise to take classes in corporate finance. I knew a student who felt that her self-confidence and interpersonal skills improved dramatically by taking a class in acting. Likewise, there can be good synergy for computer science students and modern languages majors who take some electives in each other's disciplines.

One of the funniest stories along these lines came from one of my students who absolutely had to add a social science course to meet a liberal arts requirement for business students. He signed up for Introduction to Psychological Counseling, basically because the class hadn't filled up yet and it fit the requirement. When his next co-op ended up being a PC support job, he couldn't believe his dumb luck: He was shocked to find himself using techniques he had learned in class—such as active listening—when trying to calm down and help computer users who were frequently angry, embittered, and impatient due to their PC problems.

Earning Money (including Part-Time Work)

While co-op earnings will not pay all the costs of education for most students, they can make a nice dent in your expenses. Many internships are unpaid, but some offer stipends or at least modest salaries. Many students also have the opportunity to stay with their employer to work part-time hours after returning to classes. How much money you make will depend mainly on your field and your experience. For example, even an outstanding co-op student in early childhood education will make much less than the average student in accounting, engineering, or computer science. Also, it makes sense that a finance concentrator with no job experience and no coursework in the field will have much less earning power than an upperclassman with classroom knowledge and co-op experience. As for part-time internships, it makes sense that someone doing a computer-related job is more likely to get a paid position than someone who wants to work in an aquarium or at a TV station or record company.

Your earnings as a co-op or intern also can be affected heavily by your flexibility. Having a car obviously will open up numerous opportunities for you versus the student who is stuck on public transportation. While this is true in all fields, it can be especially dramatic for some majors depending on where they are seeking a job. For marketing students at Northeastern, most of the good quality jobs are not incredibly far away with a car—but they are completely inaccessible by public transportation. Additionally, being open to the possibility of relocating to work out of state and/or being willing to work in a variety of areas also will increase your earning—and learning—potential. When you're competing against dozens of students who cannot or will not consider working out of state, you may find numerous terrific jobs and surprisingly little competition beyond the immediate reach of your university.

Other factors affecting earnings may include grades, the time of year that you choose to work, your effort in the job search (including effort in teaching yourself relevant skills), and soft skills such as communication skills, interpersonal skills, and attitude.

Return on your Investment in Education
Above all, real-world experience gives you a chance to get a nice return on the investment of time, money, and energy that you have put into your collegiate career. Studies have shown that full-time co-op students get a nice head start in terms of post-graduate earnings and quality of job opportunities. The more you strive to accomplish, the bigger the payoff at the end.

GETTING READY FOR A FUTURE REAL-WORLD EXPERIENCE

Maybe your first professional job experience is still a long way off. For some people reading this book, their first clinical or co-op or internship may be more than a year away. That's a long time, and there's no point in beginning a job search when your availability is in the distant future. Still, there are plenty of things that you can do right now to improve your chances of getting a better job when the time comes. But first, it's important to understand a critical question: What do employers want when they are looking to hire an intern, co-op candidate, or even a full-time hire coming right of college?

Common Fears
As stated earlier, about 90 percent of NU students who are admitted into our College of Business Administration cite co-op as their number-one reason for picking the program. However, many students still experience a good degree of fear and anxiety about beginning their co-op careers. This is natural: Most students recognize the value and importance of practical job experience but begin the program with limited knowledge about the job market and the co-op process as well as significant concerns about their lack of professional jobs in the past.

Very frequently, students meeting with their co-op coordinator for the first time express concerns about what their first co-op may hold: "No one will ever want to hire me—I have absolutely no corporate experience!" Believe me, we hear that one a lot. In fact, I would guess that probably two-thirds of our students begin the program without anything more than unskilled-labor positions on their resumes. Students also worry about the negative impact of poor grades, lack of a car, a sagging economy, and competition from other (presumably better) candidates.

The first thing to remember is that we want you to limit your fears and concerns to the things that you can control. You can worry about the economy, the job market, and how good other job candidates are—but in the end, worrying about these things won't change them at all.

Fortunately, there are quite a few things that you can control. You also may have more going for you than you realize, as you'll soon see.

What Are Employers Seeking When Hiring Co-ops and Interns?
When I first took over the MIS program in March 1995, my colleagues Bill Sloane and Charlie Bognanni suggested that I get out on the road to meet as many employers as possible in order to understand the needs of my program. It was great advice, and it yielded surprising information. I thought I already knew what MIS employers were seeking when they hired co-op students: computer skills, naturally! I expected employers to list applications: "Well, we want someone who can use Novell NetWare and who knows Visual Basic or another programming language...."

I did hear some employers say those kinds of things—but only about one-third of the time. Two times out of three, the manager would say something like this: "Computer skills are great—the more the better. But more than anything, we want someone who wants to be here every day, someone who thinks it's fun to learn new things, a hard worker who communicates well and gets along with people.... Someone who can work independently and show initiative but also work in a team... Someone who doesn't complain and moan and whine when something has to be done that's a little less fun. We'd much rather have a student who is weak on technical skills and strong in terms of these other qualities than to have it the other way around."

After hearing this several times, I asked a few managers to explain why they felt this way. "In six months, I can teach someone a lot about UNIX or Windows NT, assuming that they're smart and motivated," a manager said. "But I can't teach a person to want to come in to work every day."

Another manager flipped it around the other way. "If you haven't learned how to take pride in what you do, how to respect other people, and have a positive attitude in the first 18 years of your life," she mused, "then how am I going to change all of that in just six months!"

Even Microsoft—an employer that obviously features an extremely technical environment—basically follows this rule. On the next page, look at the sidebar box, and consider the emphasis.

Hiring Co-ops and Interns – An Employer's Perspective
by Steve Sim
From a Microsoft perspective, it's difficult to specify anything in particular, but we look for the core competencies we wish all MS employees to possess:
  ♦ Passion for Technology
  ♦ Big Bold Goal Mentality
  ♦ Honest and Self-Critical
  ♦ Accountability
  ♦ Intelligence
  ♦ Team & Individual Achievement
Steve Sim is a Technical Recruiter at the Microsoft Corporation.

For most co-op students, this is extremely encouraging news: Students who want to be in a practice-oriented program requiring work generally have a strong work ethic. Most students I've met have at least some of those desirable soft skills. I have found—just as those managers had told me—that it is indeed very hard to change who a person is as opposed to changing their skill set. This attitude is not unique to MIS employers. Consider what one of our marketing employers has to say in the following sidebar box:

Hiring Co-op Students – An Employer's Perspective
by Mike Naclerio
Energy and passion: You can teach a student or an employee the skills that are necessary for a position, but you cannot teach someone dedication and enthusiasm. If you build an organization based on quality people, you will get quality results.
Mike Naclerio is the Director of Relationship Management
at the workplace HELPLINE.

This is not just true in business environments. Consider what one of our physical therapy co-op faculty told me when I asked her what her employers wanted in first-time professional hires:

What Employers Want – A Co-op Professional's Perspective
by Rose Dimarco
They're looking for someone who wants to learn, who's dependable, reliable, and who has some experience in a team environment—whether an athletic team or a debate team. Those are the things that they really are buying when you start school. When you graduate, they'll look more at technical skills, but they'll always be hiring professional behaviors. Always. That consists of how you perform in a "professional" environment.
Rose Dimarco is a cooperative education faculty coordinator
in Physical Therapy at Northeastern University.

Even for students in highly technical disciplines, this holds true. Employers do want to see basic technical skills, but they are not the primary concern when hiring:

What Employers Want – A Co-op Professional's Perspective
by Bob Tillman
Does it look like you have the skills and abilities? Does it look like you have your head on straight, and does it look like you'll show up at work on time every day? Because we're going to teach you everything else. So the question is, does it look like you'll fit in? Does it look like you have the entry-level skills so you know how to turn a computer on, you know how to plot in AutoCAD already, you know how to bring drawings up. We'll teach you everything else, but you need to look like you can learn. So you need to talk about being able to learn, being responsible, showing up, and doing the job.

Bob Tillman is a cooperative education faculty coordinator
in Civil Engineering at Northeastern University.

Of course, there are a few catches here. If possible, most typical managers would prefer to hire someone who has the soft skills AND some relevant technical skills—especially in a tough economy in which jobs are less plentiful. An inexperienced student who is a great person will not get a position if they're competing with great people who also have experience. Additionally, can't any snake oil salesman walk into an interview and claim to have a great attitude, excellent ability to work independently, and a terrific work ethic?? Absolutely. But there are steps you can take to change your skill set NOW and to help prove that you really have those soft skills, so let's consider those next.

Ways to Improve Your Marketability Before You Start Your Job Search

This has to be one of the most underutilized steps that you can take, and there's nothing to keep you from starting to do this right away—even if your next job search is not on the immediate horizon. Here's the key: start devoting some time toward improving your knowledge of your field. A criminal justice student could go out and do informational interviews with professionals in law enforcement and security. A veterinary science student would gain valuable experience and demonstrate a great deal about her interest in her field by volunteering at an animal shelter. For a finance student, this could mean reading The Wall Street Journal or Smart Money or any number of other periodicals or books that will help you understand stocks and bonds, mutual funds, investment philosophy, and concepts such as risk versus reward and the present value versus the future value of money. Just about any Information Technology student (whether majoring in computer science, engineering, or business) would benefit by picking up computer skills on their own—whether through using online tutorials, reading books such as HTML for Dummies, attending on-campus workshops on specific computer skills. Last year I worked with a student who had earned about five computer certifications on her own. This absolutely raised the eyebrows of potential employers. Likewise, taking meaningful courses in other majors such as Computer Science or English Composition instead of some bunny course to get an easy grade also can boost your technical skills and soft skills.

Improving Your Marketability – A Co-op Professional's Perspective
by Rose Dimarco

I'll tell you what you can do: Get the best possible understanding of yourself. When you're president of your class, or when you go and work in a camp job or as a waitress, start looking at what energizes you in that job and what doesn't. Once you know that, you can better assess what a better job is for you at co-op time. It's getting beyond 'I only want to work with children,' 'I only want to work with chronically ill people.' It has to do with understanding the role you play at that site: Does that site value what you bring to that role naturally? You're not going to have all the academically critical skills to do the job; everyone knows that. You're bringing *you*, and you have to be able to articulate who you are and what you can offer that environment. There's no such thing as a lousy job; there are just jobs that are incompatible with who you know you are.

Try to be around people who need health-care assistance. That can be an elderly grandmom; that could be a neighbor who has a child with some form of disability. That could be volunteering in a nursing home part-time, even working in a hospital gift shop: You're seeing families going through your gift shop on their way to see someone who is ill. Seeing how all that fits will take time, but there is a connection between the healing process that's underway on that floor and that conversation in the gift shop when that mom and dad were heading up to see their child, and what they did to try and make things better. I would say that any experience involving some sort of service can go on your resume, and employers will value students who have volunteered and have exposure to different areas.

Rose Dimarco is a cooperative education faculty coordinator in Physical Therapy at Northeastern University.

Making Connections with Professional Associations

Joining a professional association in your field is another way to make yourself more marketable... but that's not the only reason to do so. If you attend professional association meetings and events, you'll have an opportunity to rub shoulders with professionals in your field. This is a great way to do some networking that eventually could lead to an interview, a co-op job, an internship, or even a full-time job after graduation. Also, your conversation with these professionals can be informal informational interviews: What do professionals in your field actually do? What do they like most and least about their jobs? This may help you figure out if you're in the right field or not.

Another great thing to know is that while some professional associations can be expensive to join, they may offer substantially discounted student membership rates. For example, as of summer 2005, the Council of Supply Chain Management Professionals (SCSMP) charged professionals $250 for an annual membership, but students only had to pay $20 to join and have the opportunity to receive career-related newsletters, attend conferences at reduced rates, and many other benefits. Ask your co-op, internship, or career services coordinator—or an academic faculty member—for information about professional associations in your field and whether they would be worthwhile for you.

Making the Most of All On-Campus Resources

Most universities have tons of resources that you pay for with your tuition, whether or not you take advantage of them. Most universities and colleges have Departments of Career Services—featuring numerous resources that you may find valuable. You can research jobs in different fields, take tests that help you build self-awareness about how you might match up with different careers, and perhaps even have a practice interview videotaped and critiqued. In particular, you may want to look into whether a campus professional can administer the Myers-Briggs Type Indicator, Myers-Briggs Career Report, the Campbell Interest and Skill Survey, or the Strong Interest Inventory. The Myers-Briggs tests are often useful in understanding your personality, which can translate into a better sense of what elements you should seek in a job. The various interest inventories are great for seeing how your preferences and dislikes match up with professionals who are happy and successful in a great variety of fields.

Your university library is a good source for periodicals relating to different fields, careers, and organizations. Most universities also have counseling centers—good places to go if personal problems are causing you difficulties, whether job-related or otherwise. Another little-known fact is that some counseling centers—such as the one at Northeastern—also can help with issues such as time management and test-taking anxiety.

Utilizing On-Campus Resources – A Co-op Professional's Perspective
by Ronnie Porter

We now encourage students to obtain part-time positions or internships over the summer to prepare themselves for getting their first co-op job. It would really depend on the field they're interested in. We might direct them to Career Services. There might be other resources on campus: we might direct them to the departments to check with faculty. We encourage them to really take advantage of their work-study positions, maybe working with a faculty member on research or some capacity like that to further develop their skills. We would really ask them to think about making the best use of any opportunities like that to develop their transferable skills.

Ronnie Porter is a cooperative education faculty coordinator
in Biology at Northeastern University.

Taking Advantage of Online Resources

Even if you aren't able or willing to get assistance from professionals on campus, there are some online options that may prove helpful. If you Google terms such as "Myers-Briggs" or "Campbell Interest Inventory," you'll get links to sites that offer online testing for a fee. Some sites offer free testing as well—try Googling

"Free Myers-Briggs test," for example—but you may be surprised to fill out a 70-item test and then be told very little... unless you THEN shell out some amount of money.

Taking Career-Related Courses

Increasingly, many universities are offering and even requiring career-related courses. Some—such as the excellent Gateway To The Workplace course at LaGuardia Community College in New York—are mandatory prerequisites to obtaining an internship or co-op job through the program. Given that these courses are often one-credit, pass-fail courses, some students might be tempted to go through the motions in these courses, doing just enough to get by. However, that would be a missed opportunity. These classes give you a chance to get questions answered, undergo some career counseling, learn the fundamentals of resume writing and interviewing, and start to understand the logistics of how the co-op process works for you. It also can help you develop a good relationship with a co-op coordinator who can be a resource for you during all of your undergraduate years.

Start Owning the Responsibility for Your Success

One characteristic of interns and co-op students who are highly successful is that they own the responsibility for their success. In other words, a great co-op student is one who doesn't wait for things to happen but instead makes things happen for themselves. Just recently, a student came to see me ONE FULL MONTH after the official start date for his first co-op. Why did he blow off working with the co-op department? Well, a couple of friends had told him that the job market was tough and that he probably wouldn't be able to get a professional job. In talking to him, I quickly learned that he had good communication skills and a car. I had to tell him that basically 100 percent of our students with cars had been able to find related jobs in their majors—even in the bad economy. What a shame that he listened to people who knew little about the situation: Based on gossip and speculation from uninformed classmates, he went out on his own and got a job as a cashier in a restaurant. He looked absolutely sick when I told him that people with less going for them than him were making as much as $16/hour doing work directly related to their major!

Show some initiative as you plan ahead for your future co-op. When you interview for a psychology job and are asked about some aspect of the field, you don't want to say "I don't know anything about that because we haven't covered it in class yet." Maybe you can talk about reading Irvin Yalom's excellent book *Love's Executioner,* which features remarkable tales of psychotherapy. Likewise, journalism students should be able to cite *New York Times* articles that they thought to be excellent; political science students should be able to speak—very diplomatically, of course—about pressing political issues in their city, state, or in the nation. Hiring managers look for results-oriented self-starters who don't sit back and wait for someone to force them to learn a new skill set or about relevant developments in the field.

Co-op Success Factors – A Student's Perspective
by Mark Moccia
A student should be active as soon as the college career begins. The key to landing the job you want is not throwing pennies into a fountain, hoping for the Gods of Co-op to "bestow the perfect job upon thee." A student must work hard to improve grades, add skills, participate in clubs, and take on other activities to show they are hard working and potential leaders.

Equally as important, students must first decide their priorities before looking for a job. Some students might be looking to make good money, gain valuable experience, work for a large company, small company, etc. Once this is decided, the student then can begin to search for particular jobs.
Mark Moccia was an Accounting/MIS student at Northeastern University, Class of 2002.

A great deal will depend on your outlook. If you have negative expectations about your co-op or internship, you are more likely to focus on the negatives in your job. If you take the attitude that hard work, good performance, and a cheerful tone can overcome the negatives in most jobs, you probably will find that to be true. The key is to start taking small steps toward success.

UNDERSTANDING THE JOB MARKET

As stated in the last section, you cannot control the nature of the economy, the job market, or cyclical factors that affect the quantity and quality of jobs available in your field. Yet although it does little good to fret about what you can't control, you still need to be aware of these elements and the impact they may have on your job search.

The Economy
The United States economy is large, complex, hard to understand, and certainly impossible to change. Yet you should realize how this can affect you as an individual. Throughout the lives of most college students today, there have been very few economic crises in this country—especially during the last decade or so. However, it's naïve to think that the stock market and job market will always work in your favor.

Some students seeking jobs in 2001 and 2002 found out the hard way that this is the case. While there has not been rampant co-op unemployment, there certainly were fewer jobs available in many fields due to the sagging economy. A few co-op employers went bankrupt or laid off the majority of their workers; some co-op employers cut back their co-op headcount to some degree due to economic uncertainty.

The upshot has been that many students struggled to get jobs during these years, especially if they a) started their job search late, b) were inflexible about what type of job they were able and/or willing to do and where, geographically, they would or could work, or c) were inconsistent in their job-search efforts. Doing everything on time and to the best of your ability is no guarantee of getting a job in a challenging economy, but expending energy on the controllable part of your job search will help you fare better when grappling with something as uncontrollable as the US economy. The amount of effort expended on the job search is the single biggest factor in determining whether or not an individual student is meaningfully employed or not—a much bigger factor than skills and job experience! Most co-op and internship programs are NOT placement agencies—they don't simply assign you to a job; you have to earn it.

Even in a tough economy, it's also important to remember that there can be opportunities if you know where to look. According to Paul Harrington at the Center for Labor Market Studies at Northeastern University, full-time job seekers coming out of school in May 2005 may have fared best if they were willing to look at Portland, Oregon, Washington, DC, and the Rocky Mountain region— especially given that New England had been losing quite a few jobs. Each year, the hot place for new hires after graduation may be the southwest, northwest— who knows? Again, the more you lock yourself into thinking that you MUST work in your local region, the more you are going to limit your options.

The Job Market in Your Field

Your chosen field will have a big impact on the quality and quantity of job options available to you. Although the economy also affects job markets—for example, computer science students had incredible options in the mid-nineties but struggled when the technology sector cooled off in 2001 and 2002—you will always be affected by the simple laws of supply and demand. 2002 and 2003 were great years for health science students in the Northeast—even though they were lean years for many other fields. If the demand in the job market for professionals in your field is greater than the supply of workers available, you may have some amazing options, even as an entry-level co-op student. But if you're in a field that is very popular with college students who are competing for a limited number of jobs, then it's a very different story.

In the previous section, I mentioned Paul Harrington and the Northeastern's Center for Labor Market Studies. Along with Neeta Fogg and Thomas Harrington, Paul Harrington wrote a book called *The College Majors Handbook, With Real Career Paths And Payoffs* (Jist Publishing). This 2004 publication is a great resource for understanding how your choice of major affects your future earnings potential as a full-time professional.

In the co-op realm, though, let's consider a few specific examples. Recently, it became more difficult for students to complete all of the requirements necessary to become Certified Public Accountants (CPAs). As a result, a significant number of students have drifted away from this concentration. Yet companies still need people to do accounting work, and accounting firms are still hiring at a healthy rate. The result is that accounting students now enjoy one of the best job markets amongst business students, as the supply of jobs is greater than the number of co-op students who are able and willing to fill them.

On the other side of the coin, there are always students who want to get into what I often call "sexy" jobs. A "sexy" job involves working in a field that individuals between the ages of 18 and 25 find to be glamorous. Imagine how many people in your age range want to work in the music industry, fashion, television, professional sports management, publishing, and advertising. Likewise, how many co-op students would want to work for organizations such as Reebok or the FBI or in the White House?

Given that so many students want to work in these fields or with these organizations, the result is that these employers often opt for students who will work for free as interns instead of hiring paid co-ops. If you really, really want to work in a "sexy" field, be prepared to work for little or nothing.... Or be creative about how you break into the field.

When I worked with NU's entrepreneurship students who wanted to get into sports management and who fantasized about working with the Boston Red Sox, I would tell them about my friend Tom Ford. Tom got his MBA and wanted to get into professional baseball, so he got the best job he could get to gain experience: He became a jack-of-all-trades for the Idaho Falls Braves—a very low-level minor league baseball team. Tom did everything from groundskeeping to taking tickets to picking out goofy sound effects to play over the loudspeaker when a foul ball went into the press box. He often worked 12+ hours a day for pitifully low wages. But within a few years he landed a dream position: general manager for a team in the high minor leagues in Tom's home state of Tennessee.

So you can break into glamorous fields if you're willing to pay the price in terms of time and money. The other way to do it is to acquire hot skills and use those skills as a way to differentiate yourself from other candidates. A few years ago I did a presentation on interviewing at a national co-op conference. Afterwards, two gentlemen from the CIA introduced themselves. Without any prompting from me, they said "Tell your students that if they want to work for the FBI and CIA, the way to do it is to major in computer science, MIS, or computer engineering. You have no idea how many criminal justice students contact us, and we're not interested in them!"

You always have to think about whom you're competing with for jobs and how you're going to be able to say, "I'm different!" We'll talk about that more in the interviewing chapter.

Time of Year

Your ability to get the job of your choice also can be influenced by the time of year during which you hope to land that job. For students at Northeastern, the two most common choices are to work for six months starting in early January or to work six months starting in mid-June. Our first-time students trying to pick one of the options always ask, "Which is a better choice?"

Basically, if your program lets you choose what time of year you do your co-op or internship, there are tradeoffs either way. There are more job opportunities available in early January because fewer students are available to work during that time of year—yet this also means that there is more competition from other students in the same program, and you also may need to be in school during the summer—which some students think is great but others don't like.

If you start work during the late spring or early summer, you're competing with everyone else in the collegiate world who is seeking a summer job. Thus, there are fewer jobs available, but there are also might be fewer students from your program seeking a job at that time. If your program allows you to work more than the three months that a typical summer-only worker can promise, this also gives you an edge over students from conventional programs.

As we saw when considering "sexy" jobs, what you want to avoid is doing what everyone else does. Again, how can you differentiate yourself from other candidates? For example, the worst thing you can do as an NU student is look for a summer-only job: Then you're competing with every other college student PLUS all of the NU students who can work for six months. Not recommended.

Your chosen field also may have a different supply of jobs at different times of the year. About two-thirds of our accounting students choose to be on co-op for the first six months of the year due to tax season. This is a win-win situation because organizations can get help for their busy season and not have to pay for year-round people who won't be necessary during the summer and fall. Meanwhile, students get to work in action-packed jobs, which are always preferable to slow-paced work environments.

Having Realistic Expectations
This is especially true for first-time co-op students. We sometimes meet with nursing students who think that their first job as a nursing co-op will entail providing direct care for patients—even though their background is limited to prerequisite courses in anatomy and physiology. Then there is the entrepreneurship student who wants to own a restaurant some day and thus gets a job in a restaurant, believing that she will be making decisions about the menu. Or the computer science student who believes he will be a key member of a software development team, taking the lead in designing a new software application for the company. Wrong, wrong, and wrong!

No company in their right mind is going to hand major decision-making power to a business intern or co-op student who has not even taken a single course in finance or marketing! Legally, health care providers have to be very careful about what they allow co-ops, interns, and clinical students to do. For American Sign Language students, most job opportunities require fully trained professionals with degrees. As a result, the best that an ASL co-op or intern may be able to hope for is a position that provides them with informal opportunities to practice their ASL skills with deaf people, rather than a role in which he or she is an "official translator."

More than anything, your first co-op is a great opportunity to gain initial exposure to the professional world in the field of your choice—just "being around" in that kind of environment can be a good learning experience, even if your job duties entail monotonous Quality Assurance software testing to find and document programming bugs or chopping vegetables up at a restaurant or being a "sitter" in hospital: basically sitting by a patient in an Intensive Care Unit for hours to make sure that they don't pull any of their tubes out (all possible duties for the students mentioned in the previous paragraphs).

Co-op students need to work their way up the ladder by proving themselves in whatever role they are given. Repeatedly in this book, you will hear about how co-op success—versus mere survival or outright failure—is all about momentum. Co-ops and interns are often given low-level tasks when starting a new position. Why? Employers want to see what you can do, and they often want to give you tasks that you can handle to build confidence and start off successfully.

If you take on these low-level tasks cheerfully and efficiently, you may find that you are suddenly being asked to take on more and better projects. Fail to do them with the right attitude or without success, and you are less likely to get more advanced work to do. Having realistic expectations about your first job will enable you to approach the job with a good attitude—an understanding that you may need to work your way up in the organizational world.

JOB SEARCH OPTIONS

At a large institution, it is very unlikely that a co-op, internship, or career services coordinator will hold your hand throughout the job search process. At NU, we do a great deal for some of our students—generally the ones who are planning ahead, putting considerable energy into their co-op careers, and actively seeking our guidance and direction. However—given the size of our student loads—we just don't have enough hours in the day to call you up regularly during placement season to ask why you haven't come in with your resume. It's really up to you to be on top of what you need to get done and when you have to do it in terms of the placement process.

Working with a Co-op or Internship Coordinator and/or Career Services Department
If your university has a co-op/internship coordinator or career services department, by all means take advantage of these resources. At schools with established programs, these career professionals are the liaison to hundreds, even thousands, of jobs. The co-op/internship or career services coordinator

should have a good understanding of the specifics of the job market in your field and region. Plus, he or she talks to hundreds of employers about their employment needs. If you don't work with a coordinator, you won't have access to all kinds of information!

The best advice I can give you regarding working successfully with your co-op or career services coordinator is to treat this individual in the same way that you would treat your supervisor in the workplace. Use your interactions with co-op coordinators as opportunities to hone your professionalism.

What does this mean in practical terms?

- When meeting a coordinator for the first time, introduce yourself, shake hands, and clearly state your reasons for the office visit.

- Be on time to appointments with these professionals. If you absolutely cannot make an appointment, call in advance to cancel instead of just being a no-show.

- Be sensitive to the coordinator's need to juggle multiple priorities on a tight time schedule.

- When faced with uncertainty, assume the best: For example, if your coordinator asks you to change your resume, assume that it's with your best interests in mind, not to inconvenience you!

- If you need to state concerns or air conflicts, try to do so in an upbeat, solution-oriented way rather than simply blowing off steam or complaining.

- When in doubt about what you should do in any situation—before, during, or after you obtain your job—ask your coordinator.

It's definitely in your best interest to develop a good working relationship with your coordinator. Inevitably, when great new jobs come in, we think first about the students whom we know well and who are in touch with us regularly. With large student loads, students can easily fall off our radar screens. Stay in touch regularly to make sure that doesn't happen, and you likely will be the beneficiary of a wealth of good advice and assistance in the job search process. "I just haven't had time" or "You're not available at times that are convenient to me" just don't cut it as excuses—it only takes a minute or two to write an e-mail or leave a voice mail with an update. More often than not, your coordinator also can make accommodations to meet with you if the posted appointment times or walk-in hours don't correspond well with your availability.

Finding a Job on Your Own
Some students may find it useful or even absolutely necessary to find a job without much help from their college or university. Some schools don't have formal co-op or internship coordinators or programs. Even if you go to a big

co-op school, you may want to look for your own job for various reasons. A Northeastern student seeking a job in his home state may need to find her own job—especially if the desired job is outside of New England, southern New York, or New Jersey. You also may need to or want to find your own job if you are seeking work in a field that your co-op department typically doesn't work with. Examples might be some of those "sexy" fields that were mentioned earlier in this chapter: music industry, fashion, sports management, and advertising come to mind.

Although your job search falls outside of the conventional paths available through your school, you still have options. However, there are a few things to bear in mind before striking out on your own:

1. *Always check with your co-op or internship coordinator before approaching any companies.* If you have a connection with IBM, for example—even one through a classmate, friend, or family member—it would be a mistake to approach the company without getting clearance from your co-op coordinator first. The reason is that your school may have already established a co-op relationship with them, and both IBM and the co-op department may perceive you as trying to "beat the system" or do an "end run" instead of legitimately following the process as other students do. In some cases, you may need to discuss your job lead with the appropriate co-op coordinator before making contact to avoid any misunderstandings.

2. *You must get your co-op coordinator's approval before accepting any job found on your own, and you must get that approval BEFORE the beginning of the work experience.* Not all jobs qualify as co-op positions. For many students at Northeastern, the jobs must be full-time positions (Minimum 35 hours/week) and they must be appropriate to your career; other programs may be more flexible and less strict about what qualifies as a co-op, but you need to be sure. Also, your coordinator is responsible for knowing your whereabouts on co-op and for submitting data on your salary to the university administration. In most programs, coordinators simply will not give a student credit for a work experience if they fail to discuss the position with her or him beforehand—even if the student obtained a fantastic position on his own.

3. *Even though you are pursuing your own job, don't forget that your co-op coordinator can be very helpful to you in your job search.* Sometimes coordinators can give students job leads depending on their circumstances, and most coordinators can help with resumes, cover letters, networking tips, and advice on how to sell the idea of co-op to an organization. Take advantage of this resource. Also note that Appendix C in the back of this book has information on how to write a cover letter. You would be amazed at how many long-time professionals really have no idea how to write cover letters effectively. Learn now!

4. *Be sure to complete the appropriate paperwork with your co-op coordinator.* Have a copy of an agreement form (or any other paperwork required by your school) ready to fill out and give it to your coordinator upon locating a suitable position.

Coming Up with Job Options on Your Own

For most students, one of the most challenging parts of finding their own co-op job is managing to get in the door for interviews. After all, co-op employers don't usually put co-op job listings in the newspaper or on a job board. The trick is becoming more creative about how you come up with options. Here are some suggestions:

1. *Network through family and friends.* As stated earlier, don't use family and friends to get to employers that already work with your school's co-op or internship program—discuss this step with your co-op coordinator first. After clearing that hurdle, you'll find that networking is the single most effective way of finding your own job.

    An entrepreneurship/small business management student of mine a few years ago came to see me and announced that she wanted to find a job in Denver. She had a cousin who lived there but otherwise knew no one in Colorado. Together, we worked hard on how to network. Armed with that knowledge, she began grilling her cousin: Whom do you know who works in a small business? Where do they work? What's their phone number? When she found people who worked in small businesses, she tried to get them thinking about her situation: Could your company use someone to work on marketing projects? Someone to help with computers? An individual who could crunch numbers, work as a good team player, and serve as a Jill-of-all-trades?

    Even though she experienced a lot of rejection, the student stayed positive, upbeat, and persistent—to the point where people really wanted to help her find a job. Plus she tried to avoid any dead ends: Anyone she talked to was an opportunity to get more names and phone numbers. Finally, she got a fantastic job, working for a small business that helped other businesses put together IPOs and go public. How many people did she have to go through to make this happen? The job was obtained through her cousin's boyfriend's father's friend's friend!!! It just shows what you can do if you are willing to expend some energy in an intelligent, directed search for your own job.

2. *Check out job boards and newspaper listings.* Many Northeastern undergraduates could benefit by using HuskyCareerLink, which you can access by going to www.northeastern.erecruiting.com on the Web. Hundreds of employers list jobs through HuskyCareerLink. Find out if your school has a similar site that is worth checking. Some employers are purely interested in hiring full-time employees who have completed their degrees (or who will do so very soon), while others can be approached about co-ops

or internships and are interested in forging bonds with the university. Some even list temporary or hourly positions that are appropriate for a student seeking a co-op job.

Beyond that, there are numerous job boards out there. A few include www.monster.com, www.vault.com, www.brainbuzz.com, and www.USJobBoard.com. Another fast-growing site is www.careers.msn.com. More recently, my graduating seniors tell me that they've done best through going to www.craigslist.com to review job possibilities. Many of these sites also have timely career advice and industry updates. Some sites are extremely national and general, while others focus more on specific fields and regions: For example, www.dice.com features high tech jobs. The Princeton Review's website (www.review.com) lists numerous internships around the country. Just go the bottom of the home page and click on "Internship Search" under Academic Programs. Another intriguing site is idealist.org, which lists over 46,000 nonprofit and community organizations in 165 countries. They list paid internships and volunteer opportunities spanning the globe for those interested in civic-minded ways to gain experience and broaden your exposure to the world. Journalism students can go to asne.org (American Society of Newspaper Editors) to see dozens of paid internships with newspapers. There are dozens of other possibilities broken out by region or field—ask your co-op, internship, or career services professional for other ideas.

Bear in mind that most employers list full-time jobs on some of these boards—not co-op jobs or internships. Therefore, undergrads may not be successful at targeting specific listed jobs. Instead, the job boards will give you some indication of who is looking to hire in your field. Chances are that an employer hiring significant numbers of full-time employees may view a co-op program as another good (if longer-term) recruiting option.

Of course, sometimes organizations listing multiple jobs on the boards are actually employment agencies, which generally are not interested in placing co-op students. While these may be useful for those of you seeking your first full-time job after graduation, co-op and internship seekers probably should steer clear of them at this point in their careers.

Most of the same rules apply for newspaper listings. One good thing to know, though, is that many newspapers also have their classified jobs online. You can save a lot of time by searching for key words in online listings as opposed to reading thousands of ads in the Sunday paper!

3. *Making Cold Calls.* Telephoning, e-mailing, or stopping in at an employer is a last resort because you will put in a lot of energy without much return in many cases. You can improve your chances by targeting larger employers, checking whether there is information about co-op jobs on their website, and then getting in touch to express your interest.

Selling a Company on the Value of a Co-op Employee

One of the best things about finding your own job is that it is a great way to test your ability to be entrepreneurial. You have to not only sell yourself in the interview as you ordinarily would: Often you will need to be able to articulate how cooperative education works and why it benefits potential employers. Here are some key points to hit:

1. *Co-op employees and interns represent cost-effective labor.* In many cases—especially with corporate jobs—these employees are a less expensive resource than the alternatives, such as contractors or temps.

2. *Co-ops/interns do not need to receive benefits.* Health care benefits and paid vacation time are expensive to employers; many companies are under pressure to keep their "headcount" (full-time employees who are eligible for benefits) at a minimum. Co-ops and interns are one way to help achieve this goal. Note that co-ops are NOT contractors: state and federal taxes DO need to be withdrawn from your pay.

3. *Co-ops/interns can provide long-term help but are not a permanent commitment.* If you can make yourself available for at least six months, that's a long time—long enough for you to provide a return on the investment the company may need to make in training you. However, the company need not make any commitment beyond the six months to you or other co-op students or interns. This may be important to start-up companies, which may need help now but are unsure about what their future needs may be. Likewise, even large employers may be reluctant to commit to a permanent hire during times of economic uncertainty. Hiring a co-op or intern for three to six months is far preferable to hiring a full-time employee without knowing if they will need to lay off the person in the next year. Better still, when the economy turns around, these programs mean that the organization has been able to maintain a recruiting pipeline.

4. *Interns and co-op students have much at stake and are therefore more motivated than other temporary workers usually are.* People who work as temps usually do so simply to make money. Co-op student workers usually focus on learning as much as they can and securing a good reference for future employment. As a result, co-ops often show more interest and effort in their jobs.

Your coordinator may be able to provide you with an introductory brochure about co-ops and interns for potential employers and other materials that may be useful to you in marketing yourself as a temporary student/employee.

Now that you have a good understanding of how to plan ahead for your first professional job, you are ready to tackle the nuts and bolts of the preparation stage: writing a resume, learning how to interview, and generally ramping up for your job search.

CHAPTER 1 REVIEW QUESTIONS

1. Name at least four of the benefits of working as a co-op or intern.

2. List three things that you could do now to make yourself more marketable for a future position in your field.

3. Why do many hiring managers consider soft skills more important than technical skills when hiring co-ops, interns, or graduating seniors?

4. What are two specific things that you could do to prove to a future interviewer that you are willing and able to learn quickly?

5. What does the text describe as the single biggest factor in determining whether or not an individual student is meaningfully employed or not?
   A. The economy
   B. The job market in your field
   C. Skills and Experience
   D. Amount of effort expended in the job search
   E. Flexibility, including willingness to relocate

6. Name at least three ways in which co-ops and internships are beneficial to employers.

CHAPTER TWO
Writing An Effective Resume

INTRODUCTION

Your resume is a vital component of an effective job search. It is a personal statement and advertisement of who you are. You may have more talent, knowledge, and skills than any other applicant for a particular job. However, if you don't get an opportunity to communicate those qualities to an employer, you may never get the chance to demonstrate your abilities. A good resume will provide you with that opportunity. It WILL NOT get you a job but it CAN get you an interview.

As you will see in this chapter, there are different schools of thought on how resumes should be written. This creates some degree of confusion, as you may come across contradictory advice when you talk to employers, look at resume tips online, or consult your professors. Some co-op and internship coordinators or career services professionals believe that resume writers should go beyond describing simply what they did to weave in soft skills demonstrated in previous work experience. Alternatively, your co-op coordinator may encourage you to put some "spin" on your job descriptions—encouraging you to describe *how* you did a given job or what made you a good or great employee in a given position. That will help a potential employer *infer* what soft skills you have. However, other co-op coordinators believe that it's best to emphasize what you did and not force the potential employer to wade through a long-winded job description— especially given that a prospective employer may only look at your resume for 60 to 90 seconds! From this perspective, the idea is to use the interview to convey your soft skills and anything more qualitative that the interviewer may want to know about your previous positions. Some employers believe that resumes are somewhat overrated (see box).

> **Resume Writing – An Employer's Perspective**
> *by Mike Naclerio*
> Not much impresses me on resumes. I don't spend much time reviewing them
> and view them as a mere formality. The personal interview is what counts, and
> where you can truly determine whether an individual will fit into your unique
> working environment.
> *Mike Naclerio is the Director of Relationship Management at the workplace HELPLINE.*

Conversely, some employers believe resumes are *critically* important. This type
of employer may not call a student in because of a careless typo or a poorly
organized resume. There is definitely no one "right" way to prepare resumes. For
example, some people believe that an Interests section is completely meaningless.
Yet I also have had more than one employer tell me that they can't imagine why
anyone would be foolish enough to exclude this element from his or her resume.

Your best bet is to find out what your co-op or career services professional
believes would work best for you, given your work history as well as your field.
After all, this individual has direct communication with the employers who will
receive your resume, so they generally have the best idea of what will resonate
with interviewers. You also need to think about what feels right and comfortable
for YOU. Maybe your brother's girlfriend thinks you should do your resume a
different way—the approach that *she* used in getting some fantastic job—or your
mom is an HR manager who sees hundreds of resumes per year and believes
she knows what is best for you. In the end, though, your co-op coordinator is
the one who has dozens of co-op jobs available, whereas your brother's girlfriend
probably doesn't have any! Make sure your coordinator understands your goals
and values: Are you comfortable, for example, with a resume that really sells
your skills? Once your coordinator knows you, trusting that person's judgment
is usually the best move. Of course, you also need to feel comfortable that your
resume truly reflects the real you. Even if you urged to have a resume that
features a "hard sell" of your skills, you shouldn't do so unless you're comfortable
with that.

Just about any professional would agree on many factors that differentiate a
strong resume from a poor one. An effective, competitive resume is one that
highlights your best achievements, accomplishments, and contributions at work,
at school, and in the community. It also can reflect your hobbies, interests, and
background, making you into a three-dimensional person instead of a name on
a page. A strong resume also must be *flawless* in terms of typos or errors—after
all, if you can't get things right on your resume, why would anyone expect you to
have excellent attention to detail as an employee?

In contrast, a mediocre resume will provide minimal work and academic history
plus extremely basic job descriptions. Also, a poor resume is unattractive to look
at—maybe it's hard to read due to small type or poor alignment, perhaps it is
just very inconsistent in terms of formatting. A weak resume also will have poor

grammar or outright errors on it: failure to abbreviate properly, misspelled or misused words, or significant omissions. Employers often go through dozens of resumes in search of a handful of interview candidates. If you want your resume to stand out positively from the rest of the pile, you need to invest considerable time and thought. Therefore, to learn how to write a winning, professional resume, read on!

Resume Writing – A Student's Perspective
by Mark Moccia
It has been said by many that your first impression is a lasting one. The resume is the first impression a student leaves on an employer and is critical in determining their chances of receiving an interview/position. A student with a bad resume is similar to a house with a faulty foundation; without the proper strength and support in the early phases, the final product will be less appealing. The resume is a perfect opportunity for the students to capture themselves and "wow" the employers with one sheet of paper. Simply put, a resume of poor quality will make the job search extremely difficult for the student.
Mark Moccia was an Accounting/MIS student at Northeastern University, Class of 2002.

WRITING YOUR RESUME

The first step in writing your resume is easy. It has to do with the way your resume will look when it is finished. Remember, appearance does create a strong first impression. Just as you would not go to an interview dressed in a t-shirt and shorts, your resume also needs to look professional. The following five tips will help you to have a "good-looking" resume.

FIVE RESUME TIPS

- As a co-op student, your resume generally should be only ONE page in length on 8 1/2 X 11 inch bond paper.

- Use neutral colors when selecting bond paper (white, ivory, off-white, gray).

- It is recommended that you type your own resume on a word processor and save it on disk. This will enable you to make changes and corrections at any time. Also, most students will need to upload their resume onto the school's computer system and/or give an electronic copy of their resume to their coordinator.

- Almost everyone uses Microsoft Word when writing their resume, and 90 percent of resumes seem to use Word's default font—Times New Roman—as a result. Dare to be different! Experiment with other fonts. Arial is one reliable alternative... and there are many others such as Garamond and Helvetica. Just don't go too wild—unusual fonts may cause you problems when submitting a resume online or converting it to a PDF format.

27

- Your resume should reflect you as a professional and as an individual—do not directly copy from the sample resumes in this chapter. Employers have commented on how too many resumes look exactly alike. Write your own!

Resume Writing – A Student's Perspective
by Keith Laughman

One of the greatest attributes of this book is its coverage on resume building. The first time someone writes a resume he or she might be too humble to beef themselves up. A resume is a marketable representation of who you are; it's the first and sometimes only impression that employers see of you. You want to create a sharp image in their eye and leave an imprint on their mind when they are done looking at your resume. This is what sets you apart from everybody else and this is why Northeastern is number one with its co-op program.

Throughout your lifetime, you will be revising your resume constantly. It's important to put a lot of energy into developing it for the future. Students should understand that a good resume takes time and thought. The process of building a resume is also a great opportunity for the student to learn more about themselves and how they have dealt with certain people and situations in the past, thus preparing them for the next big step, the interview.

Creating a resume was actually a fun experience for me. It helped me realize that I did much more at work than I thought and that although I had few skills relevant to my major, I had many interpersonal skills. These skills are just as effective as technical skills. Technical skills can be learned; you may have interpersonal skills, but they need to be developed! Four years later and I am still using the co-op guidebook as a resource to improve and refine my skills.

Keith Laughman was an MIS/Marketing student at Northeastern University, Class of 2002.

SECTIONS

Your resume will be broken down into a number of separate sections, which will be used to describe aspects of your life and qualifications. Every co-op resume should include sections on:

- Education

- Experience

- Skills

Depending on your background, you also might include several other possible sections, such as Interests, Military Experience, Volunteer Experience, Memberships, Major Accomplishments, and Professional Certificates or Licenses.

HOW TO START

Every resume should start with an introduction. When you meet someone for the first time, you always tell them your name. Your resume is the same. Your name should be at the top, either centered, left, or right—whichever you think fits best. Address, telephone numbers, and e-mail address are critical. Employers need to reach you should they want to interview you or make you an offer! Therefore, include a permanent (family) and temporary (local) address if they are different. Remember, your resume may stay on file for over a year with an employer while you move in the meantime. Your permanent address and telephone number will ensure that you can always be reached for a job offer. Likewise, you always want to include a reliable e-mail address that you check regularly. If you're always having trouble with your Hotmail or Yahoo account because you exceed the storage limit for messages, you need to do something to make sure that that won't make it difficult for a potential employer to reach you.

It's advisable to make sure that the number and address you want employers to call first is on the left-hand side, as they are most likely to use that one.

For example:

JANE SMITH
Janesmith89@hotmail.com

CURRENT ADDRESS	PERMANENT ADDRESS
7 Speare Hall, Box 10	89 Fifth Avenue
Boston, MA 02115	Natick, MA 01760
(617) 377-0000	(508) 555-0001

International students who use an Americanized nickname can include that on their resume. It could look like this:

WAI MAN "ANDY" LAM

What if you have an extremely difficult to pronounce name and are afraid that an employer may be reluctant to call you as a result? Recently, we heard of one enterprising student who included the pronunciation of his name right below it. You could do that like so:

OLUMIDE NGUNDIRI
(first name pronounced "oh-LOO-mee-day")
olumide@yahoo.com

EDUCATION

While you are still a college student, the education section is usually listed first. Upon graduation, this section often moves below the EXPERIENCE section. When writing the education section, you should use the following guidelines:

- Format: reverse chronological order (current university listed first, other universities and colleges second, high school last)

- Include anticipated degree (i.e., Bachelor of Science Degree in Business Administration; Bachelor of Arts Degree in English) and expected month and year of graduation (e.g., May 2010)

- Include concentrations and dual concentrations or minors, if applicable

- Honors: include GPA if 3.0 or above and any scholarships received (Compute your GPA to no more than two decimal places: 3.45 is fine; 3.4495 does not indicate greater honesty or make any significant difference to an employer)

- Include activities related to the University, especially leadership roles

- Include the above information for transfer schools

- If you are financing a significant portion of your education yourself, you could opt to include that fact. For example:

   Financing 80% of college tuition and expenses through cooperative education and part-time job earnings.

Here's how the section might look:

EDUCATION
NORTHEASTERN UNIVERSITY   Boston, MA
Bachelor of Science Degree in Business Administration   May 2011
Dual Concentration: Marketing and Finance
Minor: Communications
Grade Point Average: 3.2
Activities and Honors: University Honors Program, Joe Smith Memorial Scholarship, Intramural Basketball, Residential Life Representative, Outing Club
Financing 75% of tuition and living expenses through cooperative education earnings and part-time job income.

Many students who have not yet had significant work experience will find it helpful to include their high school education in this section. Since your resume is written in reverse chronological order, the recording of your high school experience would come AFTER your university or college notation.

EXPERIENCE

This is the most vital section of your resume. This is the time not only to list where you worked and what you did, but to list your accomplishments and achievements! Take time to think about what you want to say—it's worth doing right! Here are some key points:

- *Include company name (the official name), location, job title, and dates of employment.* Employers want to see this information in order to determine exactly what you have done and how long you spent doing it. They might use this information to contact your present or previous employer in order to find out more about the relevance of your experience and the accuracy of your statements. Note that you probably shouldn't bother listing a job if you only did it for a month or two: Fairly or unfairly, it may raise questions about your ability and willingness to keep a job.

- *Jobs should be listed chronologically from present position, then backwards.* List your present or most recent position first, then your second most recent and so on. As you go through your university years, you probably will be getting more and more advanced jobs. If you have already had two internships jobs related to your major, for example, you certainly wouldn't want it to look like your retail job in high school was your most important experience to date. One exception to this rule: If your most recent job experience was not related to your major—for example, a part-time restaurant job that you did while attending classes—you might want to have a section called "Relevant Job Experience" or "Internship Experience" *first*, followed by another section called "Other Job Experience" or "Part-time Job Experience," etc.

- *Sentences should always begin with an action verb.* Avoid starting sentences with weak linking verbs such as had, got, did, etc. Use verbs that convey confidence, such as handled, improved, managed, designed, etc. There is a long list of great action verbs toward the end of this chapter. An alternative is to start with a compelling adverb: "*Effectively* handled," "*Successfully* managed," etc. There is a helpful list of action verbs on page 50.

- *Do not underestimate the power of word choice: Use power words, not passive words.* For example, don't say "Got information on orders for people who asked for it." Instead, say "Responded effectively to customer and colleague requests by tracking order status on computer and over the telephone."

- *Do not use personal pronouns such as "I," "me," "we," or "them."* On a resume, this amounts to stating the obvious. If your name is on the top of the resume, the reader knows that the statements refer to you unless you state otherwise.

- *If possible, include accomplishments as opposed to just listing responsibilities.* Never begin a sentence with "Responsibilities included..." or "Duties include...". This type of beginning may capture *what* you did, but you need to go further than that. Starting with action verbs helps you capture what you did and *how* you did it. Were you good at your job? If so, tell us why. If not, well, then stick with your responsibilities, simply stated.

- *Quantify and qualify whenever possible.* For example: "Increased sales by 15%," or "Increased sales significantly by using suggestive-selling techniques." Either of these statements tells the reader much more about precisely how well you did or how you went about accomplishing this task. This is far preferable to simply writing "Sold products." Notice how much more powerful the following descriptions are when the large, bold-type descriptive part of the sentence is added:

  ▫ Owned and operated snowplowing business **grossing $3,500 a winter**

  ▫ Hired and supervised **five** employees

  ▫ **Using Harvard Graphics**, created a **750-page color** presentation for the annual sales meeting

Highlight transferable skills. As stated earlier, professionals disagree as to whether so-called "soft skills" or transferable skills—such as interpersonal skills or attention to detail—should be included in a resume. However, most professionals agree that job seekers who have NO experience in their chosen field should consider including at least one or two specific soft skills in each job description. Think of it this way: Let's say you're a human resource management concentrator who has never worked in a corporate environment. Perhaps the only jobs on your resume are working as a waiter and as a house painter. In all probability, you will not want to wait on tables or paint houses as a co-op employee. Therefore, most co-op coordinators—but not all—believe that it's helpful for inexperienced candidates to include some transferable skills on your resume.

How can you identify what your transferable skills are? Ask yourself two questions: Were you good at the job you did? If so, why? Was it because you managed to figure out how to do the job well in a short time (**ability to learn quickly**)? Your ability to keep customers happy (**customer-service skills** or maybe **interpersonal skills**)? Was it that you never missed work or showed up late (**dependability** or **strong work ethic** or **positive attitude**)?

The transferable skills that you choose to highlight will depend heavily on your concentration and the type of co-op job that is being sought. As my co-op colleague Rose Dimarco points out in the following sidebar box, it also depends very much on what purpose the resume needs to serve. If you're in a co-op or internship program in which the coordinator arranges

32

the interview schedule for the employer, this calls for a very different resume compared to a situation in which the resume alone must get you in the door! She also emphasizes that sometimes it's enough to *imply* that you have a specific transferable skills. For example, why bother saying "demonstrated ability to multi-task" when you could have a bullet as follows: "Simultaneously handled telephone calls, in-person customer service, data entry, and invoice processing." I think that the reader will figure out that you are a bona fide multi-tasker!

Tailoring Your Resume – A Co-op Professional's Perspective
by Rose Dimarco
A resume initially gives you a script. When you think about what you're willing to put on paper about yourself, it typically reflects how you're going to explain yourself. So are we talking about a resume that's going to *introduce* you, or is it going to be a *leave-behind* that is going to help an employer remember you and differentiate you from someone else? It might introduce you and that may be the only decision-maker that they have to determine whether they call you for an interview, and that might adjust your resume somewhat. I'm just concerned that you're not boastful; that it's factual, but you also give yourself credit for what you've done.

If transferable skills are things that you feel are of value, that's what I would help you put on a resume in such a way that the interviewer reading it would conclude those things that you know about yourself: That you're a hard worker; that you're flexible—you don't necessarily want to use those terms on a resume, but you want them to conclude that from reading it. That's the art of resume writing in general, but in health care those are the things that we want to bring to the surface.

*Rose Dimarco is a cooperative education faculty coordinator
in Physical Therapy at Northeastern University.*

Look at the list at the end of this chapter for a more complete list of transferable skills for the various majors and concentrations.

Certain verbs are very helpful to know when capturing transferable skills. Some good examples are displayed, demonstrated, utilized, exhibited, showed, and used. Often you can start out a job description sentence using one of these verbs and an appropriate adjective in front of a transferable skill. For example:

▫ Demonstrated excellent interpersonal skills when....

▫ Utilized solid communication skills when....

▫ Displayed outstanding ability to learn quickly while....

A "transferable skill cheat sheet" toward the end of this chapter has lists of these verbs and a summary of this transferable skill formula.

Note that you need to be a little careful about throwing transferable skills around. The worst thing you can do is to just mention these skills and leave out anything about what you actually did on the job. Employers need to know what you actually did—even if it was simply mopping floors or washing dishes! Also, be careful not to overuse the transferable skills—working one or two them into each job description may be adequate. Above all, NEVER claim that you have a certain transferable skill unless you are confident that you really have that skill—and that your former employer would agree. At worst, overemphasizing the transferable skills may come off as "BS" to some employers—especially if they believe that you're using them as smokescreen to hide the low level of what you really did. Calling a garbage collector a "sanitation engineer" doesn't change the nature of that smelly job. Likewise, it can come off as insincere overkill if you say "Demonstrated outstanding ability to learn quickly when maintaining lawns." How hard is it, really, to learn how to mow a lawn? In that case, it might be better to keep it simple: "Efficiently mowed lawns for neighborhood customers."

Resumes – An Employer's Perspective
by Myretta Robens
In a co-op resume, we mostly just look to see that it is neat and grammatically correct. Experience is not essential. In fact, one of my favorite resumes included the line, "Demonstrated a positive attitude while cleaning out horse stalls." I figured that if Sara could do that, she could handle anything our users threw at her. And that turned out to be the case.
Myretta Robens was the Director of Technology Operations at Harvard Business School Publishing. She is now the published author of two romance novels.

• *Take time to think about how your job/contribution fits into the "big picture."* When capturing your job experience on a resume, don't just think about what tasks you did each day. Instead, consider the importance of these tasks with relation to what helped the organization accomplish its goals. For example: Don't just say, "Created window displays." Instead, show how your work made a small but important difference for your employer: "Generated customer interest by creating innovative window displays."

• *Either the bullet/outline format or the paragraph format is acceptable.* When writing up your job description, use which works best for you. If your job experience is complex and relatively hard to explain, the paragraph format may work best. If you had numerous and highly varied job responsibilities, you might find the bulleted format easier to use. It's up to you.

• *Volunteer experience can be included under EXPERIENCE or in a separate section.* Although you can be flexible about where to include volunteer experience, just make sure that you don't fail to include it somewhere on your resume. Working as a volunteer can show concern for others as well as a desire to learn through unpaid experience.

- *In most cases, write out numbers below 11.* Unless you're writing about percentages (e.g., 5%), you generally should write out numbers from one through ten (e.g., "Utilized two database programs"); higher numbers are written numerically (e.g., "Generated 75 leads for potential sales").

Remember, the Experience section usually is what a potential employer studies to make a preliminary decision about whether you can do the job. An ordinary description means you are an ordinary person. Now is the time to show an employer that you are extraordinary. The following are some helpful hints on how to do that.

A STEP-BY-STEP APPROACH TO WRITING UP YOUR JOB EXPERIENCE

Writing job descriptions takes time, effort, and practice. But once you learn how to do this effectively, you will have mastered a skill that will help you for the rest of your career. Let's look at a step-by-step formula to writing effective job descriptions. Note that the changes in each step are indicated by having the text underlined: You would not underline any job description text on a real resume.

In the interest of giving equal time to two different perspectives, the first example will incorporate transferable skill phrases; the second will show how to write a job description without touting your soft skills.

Step 1
Write down the organization's name and location, then the job title and dates of employment on the second line:

SANTA'S TREE FARM Kent, CT
Laborer November 2004 - Present

Step 2
Write down in simple terms the various duties you have or had in a given job:

SANTA'S TREE FARM Kent, CT
Laborer November 2004 - Present
- Plant trees and help them grow.
- Mow property.
- Cut down trees for customers, accept payment, and tie trees to customers' cars.

Step 3
Unless you worked for an organization that almost everyone knows (such as Pizza Hut), consider adding details about the nature of the employer and the purpose of the job:

35

SANTA'S TREE FARM   Kent, CT
Laborer   November 2004 - Present

♦ <u>Working as only hired employee for small family-owned business,</u> plant trees and help them grow <u>to ensure that adequate supply of Christmas trees is available each winter.</u>

♦ Mow property <u>regularly to make sure that trees have adequate exposure to sunlight and room to grow.</u>

♦ Cut down trees for customers, accept payment, and tie trees to their cars.

Step 4

Add quantitative details and professional terms when possible to bring the experience to life:

SANTA'S TREE FARM   Kent, CT
Laborer   November 2004 - Present

♦ Working as only hired employee for small family-owned business, plant <u>over 300 trees annually</u> and help them grow to ensure that adequate supply of Christmas trees is available each winter.

♦ Mow property regularly to make sure that <u>all four varieties of evergreen</u> trees have adequate exposure to sunlight and room to grow.

♦ Cut down <u>approximately 200 trees per year</u> for customers, accept payment, and tie trees to their cars.

Step 5 (Optional)

Add a phrase or two containing transferable skills in order to capture how well you did the job and what you might be able to provide to a co-op employer in a more professional setting:

SANTA'S TREE FARM   Kent, CT
Laborer   November 2004 - Present

♦ Working as only hired employee for small family-owned business, <u>exhibited an outstanding work ethic</u> when planting over 300 trees annually and helping them grow to ensure that adequate supply of Christmas trees is available each winter.

♦ <u>Demonstrated strong attention to detail</u> when mowing property regularly to make sure that all four varieties of evergreen trees have adequate exposure to sunlight and room to grow.

♦ Cut down approximately 200 trees per year for customers, accepting payment, and tying trees to their cars.

By crafting this type of job description, a student shows a potential employer that they have many qualities that might be desirable in an employee. Again, note that the inclusion of transferable skills is generally considered to be a good idea if you lack experience in your field of choice. As you advance in your career and obtain jobs that are directly related to your field, the explicit use of transferable skills becomes less important. But if you fail to include them when you do not have highly relevant job experience, you are asking an employer to make a mental leap in terms of figuring out whether you have any qualities that might be useful to her or him.

ANOTHER EXAMPLE OF THIS STEP-BY-STEP APPROACH

One of the great advantages of using this step-by-step approach is that it will make your interview easier. If you take the time to nail down an excellent description of your job and employer, then that becomes one less thing that you will need to worry about accomplishing during the interview itself... when you won't have much time to think about what to say! Instead of having to explain the basics of your previous experience, you can build on the resume by diving into specific examples of the points made on your resume.

Let's consider another step-by-step example, leaving out the transferable skill formula this time around:

Step 1
Write down the organization's name and location, then the job title and dates of employment on the second line:

FENWAY PROJECT ADMINISTRATIVE OFFICE   Boston, MA
Office Assistant   April 2003-Present

Step 2
Write down in simple terms the various duties you had in a given job, like this:

FENWAY PROJECT ADMINISTRATIVE OFFICE   Boston, MA
Office Assistant   April 2003-Present
◆ Schedule and organize events.
◆ Perform research and administrative tasks.
◆ Recruit and train student interns.

Step 3
Add details describing the nature of the employer in question and the purpose of the job:

FENWAY PROJECT ADMINISTRATIVE OFFICE   Boston, MA
Office Assistant   April 2003-Present
◆ Schedule and organize events <u>and community services for needy socioeconomic groups in inner-city Boston.</u>
◆ Perform research on <u>corporate and nonprofit organizations to identify strategic methods for getting donations of resources.</u>
◆ Recruit and <u>motivate college students to participate as volunteers.</u>

Step 4

Add quantitative details and professional terms when possible to bring the experience to life:

FENWAY PROJECT ADMINISTRATIVE OFFICE   Boston, MA
Office Assistant   April 2003-Present
- In a timely manner, schedule and organize events and community services for over 50 inner-city Boston teenagers in needy socioeconomic groups.
- Research roughly 250 corporate and non-profit organizations to identify strategic methods for soliciting donations of resources.
- Successfully recruited and motivated ten college students to participate as volunteers.

From this job description, we get a much better sense of who this student really is. We get a sense of her research experience, altruistic motives, and ability to juggle tasks—without directly mentioning these soft skills. A hiring employer could infer that the student was responsible and motivated. As you will see when you read the chapter on interviewing, these qualities are probably the most important that any potential supervisor wants to see in a new hire.

PASSIVE VERSUS ACTIVE VERBS

If, after all this, your resume is still lacking something, try to review your use of verbs. Remember: never use passive verbs where you can use active verbs instead. The following is a list of POWER words for inclusion in your resume.

PASSIVE VERBS	**ACTIVE/POWER VERBS**
Maintained	Enhanced
Assisted	Contributed (to)
Answered	Directed
Spoke to...	Resolved problems
Sold	Increased sales by...
Taught	Instructed
Processed	Expedited
Received	Earned
Coordinated	Negotiated

As mentioned earlier, a more comprehensive list of action verbs in various categories is available toward the back of this chapter.

COMPUTER SKILLS (OR SPECIAL SKILLS)

This is a very important section and should be included on your resume. Every college student will have at least some basic computer skills. This is the place to state what they are. Do not overstate your abilities, but don't be modest either.

You need to state your abilities clearly. Are you proficient with, familiar with, or do you just have exposure to a particular software program? Can you work with IBM PCs, Macs, or both? In this technological age, stating your computer skills can be the edge you need to get an interview—even when pursuing jobs in supposedly non-technical fields such as the humanities and social sciences!

With this in mind, let's take a closer look at how to capture your computer skills on this section of a resume. Sometimes people either will forget about what PC skills they have or—incredibly—feel that they can't put a given skill down because they learned it on their own, outside of the classroom or workplace. Did you know that some employers are actually *more* impressed with candidates who taught themselves how to use software applications? Even if you taught yourself "just for fun," that says a great deal about your ability and enthusiasm to learn on the computer. With this in mind, here's a quick checklist you can use to determine whether you have included *all* of your relevant computer experience.

Do you have experience with:

- **Word processing** (Microsoft Word, WordPerfect, etc.)

- **Spreadsheets** (Microsoft Excel, Lotus 1-2-3)

- **Databases** (Microsoft Access, dBase, Oracle, SAP, Lotus Notes, etc.)

- **Operating systems** (Windows NT/2000/XP/Vista, UNIX, MacOS, etc.)

- **Programming languages** (C, C++, Pascal, Visual Basic)

- **Network administration** (Novell NetWare, Windows NT, TCP/IP, etc.)

- **Web design** (HTML, FrontPage, DreamWeaver, Java, ASP, Perl, etc.)

- **Presentation graphics** (PowerPoint, Harvard Graphics)

- **Desktop publishing/graphic design** (PageMaker, Corel Draw, Adobe PhotoShop, etc.)

Many students are unsure about whether their skills with a given application are good enough to put on their resumes. Obviously, you want to be honest, but you also want to give yourself credit for what you do know. One suggestion for dealing with this dilemma is to break down your knowledge of applications under the categories of "Proficient with," "Familiar with," and "Exposure to." If you have tons of experiences with Excel, say that you proficient with it. If you know how to do formulas, alter columns and rows, and create charts and graphs but not much more, you might say that you are familiar with it. While if you have only used it a few times or your experience is in the distant past, play it safe and say that you just have exposure to Excel. This way you can be honest without selling yourself short.

You also should take care to ensure that you correctly spell the names of any computer applications that you list under the heading of "Computer Skills" or "Special Skills." Use the following list as a quick reference when proofreading your resume. Although this is particularly important if you are applying for an MIS job, everyone should try to make their resume as perfectly accurate as possible... never an easy task when it comes to the bizarre spellings of many software applications.

Correct spellings of typical MIS terms
(and acceptable alternatives)

WordPerfect	Microsoft Word (MS-Word, Word)
Microsoft Excel (MS-Excel, Excel)	Microsoft Access (MS-Access, Access)
Microsoft PowerPoint (PowerPoint)	MS-DOS (DOS)
MacOS	FoxPro
TCP/IP	HTML
Lotus Notes	Dreamweaver
Windows XP	Windows 95
Windows 2000	UNIX
C++	Novell NetWare
PageMaker	AutoCAD

Note that it's also acceptable to include what version of a program you have worked with (i.e., Novell NetWare 3.x, etc.). This is especially true with operating systems such as Windows, as there is a big difference between, say, Windows NT and Windows Vista.

Also note that Microsoft Office is a family of Microsoft applications (Word, Excel, Access, PowerPoint, and Outlook) that some employers may buy as one complete package. If you have experience with Microsoft Office, though, we still suggest writing out all of the applications, as some employers may not be familiar with the term. Also, there are different versions of Office, so it may not be clear from that term if you know Access, for example, as that is not included in all versions of Office.

Now that you know how to capture your computer skills, let's consider other skills that you want to make sure to mention. In addition, you should include skills you have in the following areas:

•   Language Skills: Fluent in..., Conversational ability in..., etc.)

•   Laboratory Skills (see sidebar box)

•   Licenses and Training (Real Estate, CPR, First Aid)

Capturing Skills On Your Resume – A Co-op Professional's Perspective
by Ronnie Porter
I really started noticing a few years back that students who did not have much experience and who were not explicit about their skills were not getting jobs. There may be technical skills that they've not really thought about it because they haven't practiced them on a job, but they've learned them in a laboratory setting. So I created a skills list with a set of things that they might have learned in lab that they could replicate in a work setting. I had them start communicating that to employers, and it made a huge difference. On their resume, they would have a section called Laboratory Skills. I found that that made a big difference in being successful. Employers weren't making the leap from Bio I and Bio II to the skill sets, so students had to break it out for them. The interviewer might be an HR person who might not be able to communicate effectively to the supervisor what the candidate is capable of doing.

Ronnie Porter is a cooperative education faculty
coordinator in Biology at Northeastern University.

Here's an example of what your skills section might look like:

SKILLS
Proficient with Microsoft Word, Excel, and PowerPoint
Familiar with Windows XP/Vista and Access
Exposure to HTML and Dreamweaver
Conversational in Spanish

If you have a very strong background in computers—meaning that your knowledge goes well beyond applications such as Microsoft Office—the recent industry standard is to break out your computer skills by category. This is fairly standard for students in MIS, Computer Science, Computer Engineering, and similar majors. Here's an example:

COMPUTER SKILLS
Operating Systems: DOS, Windows 95/98/2000, MacOS
Languages: Visual Basic, HTML
Networking: Windows NT, Novell NetWare 6.5, TCP/IP
Applications: Microsoft Word 6.0, Excel, Access, PowerPoint, Lotus 1-2-3, Adobe PhotoShop, Minitab
Exposure to: C++, Perl, SQL, Peachtree Accounting

INTERESTS

How you spend your free time reveals another dimension of your personality, as well as important skills such as communication skills, leadership, motivation and initiative, time management, resourcefulness, organization, and energy. It is a chance to include activities, hobbies, and interests—to show you're well-rounded. Interests humanize you—and anything that makes you seem more like a real person than just a name on a page will make an employer more inclined to give you an interview.

Resumes – An Employer's Perspective
by Mike Naclerio
An "Interests" section is a good icebreaker for interviews. It gives the resume a personal/unique touch and is an area I always seek out to open conversations with students in an interview.
Mike Naclerio is the Director of Relationship Management at the workplace HELPLINE.

As before, try to be specific. Listing "dancing, reading, sports, and movies" is much less interesting than, say, "ballet, contemporary short fiction, ice hockey, and foreign films." A specific and unique list is much more likely to catch the eye of a potential employer. It also shows that you are serious about your interests and have some depth of character. This makes you come off as a three-dimensional person, and it also can make an employer want to get to know you a little better in the interview. As an ice-breaker question, interviewers may ask you about one of your interests...which is a MUCH easier first question than, say, "Why should we hire you for this job?" Better still, a potential employer may share one of your interests and believe (rightly or wrongly) that the two of you share a connection as a result. That can't hurt!

If you include political or religious organizations or affiliations, be aware that this could work for you or against you. Choosing not to hire you for these reasons would be illegal, of course, but you still run a risk in including certain kinds of information. Imagine writing about your volunteer work for the Republican Party on your resume, then going into your interviewer's office and seeing an autographed photo of former President Clinton! In other words, try to be sensitive to the fact that others may not share your enthusiasms and may even be turned off by them.

Avoid anything that might be controversial or that may raise a potential concern. This includes such common college student interests as nightclubs, partying, girls, hanging out with friends, or shopping. You want to show interests that require some intelligence or at least energy.

As a part of your resume, some consider the Interests section to be optional or irrelevant. However, make every effort to include it. It can't hurt you, and it might help you. If you don't think you have the space, take a close look at the rest of the resume and ask yourself why you can't *make* room for this section. If I have students who are skeptical about including this section, I always ask them: "What would you prefer as the first question of your interview: "Why should we hire YOU for this job?" or "I noticed that you're interested in contemporary fiction. Who are your favorite authors?"

Here is a sample Interests section:

<u>INTERESTS</u>
Russian literature, skiing, chess, current events, triathlons, and camping

REFERENCES

And, lastly, don't forget your references and reference page. On your resume, simply write either "References Furnished Upon Request" or "References Available Upon Request" on the bottom. But don't stop there. Create a reference page on the same bond paper that you use for your resume. Be sure to contact your references first to ask their permission to be used as a reference. This will help your reference person to be more prepared and thus able to give you a better reference when called upon by an employer.

You should have at least three references and ideally around five. Try to include two or three professional/work references, one or two academic references, and one or two character references. A character reference is a coach, a religious leader, or a family friend who has known you since you were more or less in diapers, while a work reference is usually a direct supervisor. Include name, title, company, company address, telephone number, and, if you know it, an e-mail address. As long as you include these items, the format isn't critical: some people center their references on the page, while others have them flush left. *Just make sure that whatever format you use is consistent with your resume.*

You should always bring a few copies of your reference page to an interview, so you can give them to the interviewer immediately, if asked. If you're asked to supply references, you don't want to reply "Um, uh.... Can I get it to you in a few days?" A sample of a basic but good reference page is included at the end of this chapter following the sample resumes.

SAMPLE RESUMES

At the end of this chapter, we have included a few sample resumes that you can review to see how other students have captured themselves on resumes. These resumes reflect varying degrees of education and job experience as well as many different business majors, but they all are unique and effective.

Check out Hannah Snow's resume on page 54. This is the resume of a young woman with no real professional experience, yet it's packed with plenty of attractive attributes. With a variety of extracurricular activities complementing thorough documentation of various jobs and her high school background, Hannah comes across as a substantial individual despite her inexperience. Consistent with what we've covered in this chapter, note the use of powerful active verbs, strong qualititative details, and a determination to include *accomplishments* as opposed to simply listing *responsibilities*. Also note that Hannah has shunned the use of transferable skills in this resume in favor of a more concise approach. As I've indicated, this is a judgment call: Hannah shows here why they are not an absolute necessity if the resume finds a way to convey the individual's strengths.

Look at Lana Schillman's resume on page 55. This is an example of the bulleted list form of resume, as opposed to the paragraphing format. One nice thing about this resume is that she has used the font Arial. As mentioned earlier, employers see many resumes in Times New Roman, which looks fine but doesn't stand out. Elsewhere, this resume has consistent and strong verbs throughout the job descriptions, and it is easy to read.

Of course, this is the resume of a senior: someone looking for one last co-op job. But what if you're looking for your *first* co-op job? Consider the next resume at the end of this chapter. Gabrielle Bueno has an effective approach. She uses the bullet format, which works nicely. Bullets tend to work well in jobs involving a variety of duties and/or jobs that are relatively uncomplicated. This student does use transferable skills effectively but sparingly. Regardless, she is able to imply that she possesses those soft skills. Her job descriptions are thorough but concise. They reflect accomplishments but don't overhype her unskilled jobs. Another point here is the power of extracurricular activities. Although Gabrielle obviously hasn't had a real professional job yet, her school activities are definitely eyebrow-raising.

The third sample resume is a great example for international students. Look how much background information LaGuardia Community College student Eva Mendez has been able to pack on one page, all without overcrowding. By conserving space with her heading, she has managed to explain a great deal about her educational history, including relevant courses. She breaks out two different jobs with the same employer effectively. This resume will save her considerable time when it comes to the interview. While some students with international backgrounds are compelled to explain their personal history in the interview, Eva should be able to move right into why the employer should hire her. After all, they already know a good deal about who she is before she walks in the door.

Next we have another promising student from LaGuardia Community College. Like the first individual we sampled, here is a student whose job experience is longer and stronger than that of many college students. As a result, Pui Sze Ng opts against using the transferable skills within the job description: Her experience doesn't need as much selling as someone who has never had a professional job. Appropriately, she chooses to push her computer skills higher up on the resume, just after the education section. This is her top selling point, and she wants it to be noticed right away. The skills section breaks out her computer skills in a way that will be useful to her prospective employers: It's easy to follow both aesthetically and conceptually. Lastly, the resume is in a font called Verdana—always a good idea for an aspiring computer professional to show that she can get beyond the default font in Word!

As for the fifth and last sample, the first thing that catches your eye with Meghan Brooke's resume is that it is neat and eye-pleasing, with nice use of boldface and italics. She has opted for a different font called Arial Narrow, which is a nice change from the usual Times New Roman rut. This resume also shows how to display both a local and permanent address if you feel inclined to both. As her job experience lacks work related to her concentration, she has chosen to use transferable skills throughout all of her job descriptions in order to highlight skills that an MIS employer might want to see. Meghan chose the paragraphing format, too, probably because it saves a little space, but she could have used bullets just as easily. This resume attracted multiple interviews and a great entry-level co-op job for her.

As you can see, each of these three resumes differs significantly in terms of how to use font, boldface type, italics, centering, headings, and underlining. Some of the resume writers' choices may appeal to you more than others. There really is a great deal of flexibility in how you make your resume look, as long as you capture each of the required sections on a one-page resume, and as long as your resume is completely free of spelling mistakes or typographical errors.

Is it easy to write an effective resume? Not necessarily. As you hopefully know by now, you may have to be creative to show how some of your past job experience relates to the jobs you plan to pursue. But with considerable effort and a little assistance from your co-op coordinator and/or Career Services, you can write a resume that will help get you in the door for an interview.

MULTIPLE RESUMES

What if you are applying for jobs in more than one concentration? Perhaps you plan to apply for both finance jobs and MIS jobs, for example. One option for those who are more ambitious is to create TWO resumes: one emphasizing your desire to get a finance job, and another focusing on your strong interest and aptitude in MIS. In fact, our software application at Northeastern actually lets students upload multiple resumes and then designate which employer should receive which resume.

Is it "okay" to do this? Of course it is! In fact, trying to capture both of these interests in one resume is extremely difficult; you run the risk of coming across as someone who lacks focus or who is "jack of all trades, master of none." This should give you some incentive to consider writing more than one resume. One cautionary note, however: *It is crucial that YOU keep track of which resume has been faxed or e-mailed to each employer. If the same employer receives one of your resumes from your coordinator and another when you arrive for an interview, this will definitely work against you! This is especially true given that many coordinators now use a computerized system for e-mailing resumes—make sure to discuss using multiple resumes with your coordinator before trying to do this.*

Much of the information on each of your resumes will be identical: Obviously, this won't affect your Education section much, and you still list your places of employment. But how you describe your job experience could vary quite a bit. On a finance resume, you would emphasize work experience that relates to financial experience: budgeting, calculating, analyzing, assessing, etc. On an MIS resume, though, you might describe the same job in terms of what computer skills were required to perform these financial duties. Or, if some of your previous job related to computers but some of it didn't, then move your computer-related duties to the *top* of the job description for the MIS resume. On the finance resume, put the computer-related duties lower and don't emphasize them as strongly in your description. In your skills section, the MIS resume should be more all-inclusive, featuring the version number of each software application if possible. Even your interests might be reflected differently on each resume: You might take "investments" off of your MIS resume and add interests pertaining to learning new computer applications, Web design, foreign languages, and the Internet: all of which may be perceived more favorably by an MIS employer. Keep in mind that we're not suggesting that you *lie* about your interests and your job experiences. Just remember to emphasize those things which will be relevant to an employer in that field.

THINGS TO AVOID: OBJECTIVES AND TEMPLATES

Now that you are almost through with this chapter, you may be wondering why you have not read about starting off your resume with an objective—especially when many word-processing resume templates prompt you to include one.

First off, *don't use a word-processing template!* They may appeal to those who are lazy and/or fear that they don't know enough about word processing to make the format look good. Believe me, templates are not the answer. Templates make it extremely difficult for you to revise and update a resume, and they may force you into including or emphasizing items that are not appropriate for an aspiring co-op, intern, or senior seeking his or her first full-time job. A few times a year, someone shows me a resume that was thrown together in a few minutes using the resume template in Microsoft Word. The typical Word resume template is not that attractive—the student's address is small and hard to read, and the experience section's format is rather odd in its emphasis. We have plenty of options here that will work better for you.

As for objectives, they occasionally can be useful but usually are problematic or unhelpful. The problem is that they either tend to say too much or to not say anything at all. Think about it: if you write that your objective is "To find a cost-accounting position with a growing financial services firm," then what happens if you want to or need to apply for something even slightly different? In other words, you end up pigeonholing yourself. The flip side is the objective that really doesn't say anything that we don't already know: "To find a cooperative education position that will help me grow as an aspiring health care professional." Well, I hope so!

The only exception to this rule might be if your true objective is to find something that is very different from what one might infer from your previous experience. Someone who has worked in the psychology field but now wants to pursue a career in marketing could make this crystal-clear with a good objective. Generally, though, you should avoid bothering with an objective on your resume.

After you have written your resume use the following checklist to make sure your resume meets the successful resume standard.

Resumes – An Employer's Perspective
by Steve Sim
What impresses me on a resume? First of all, honesty impresses me. If you haven't done a whole lot of HTML development work, and you put that down as a skill set, be sure you can answer specific questions about HTML.
Second, clarity impresses me. If you are clear enough on a resume where someone who doesn't know anything about you (or potentially even positions you're interested in) can read your resume and say you're qualified, then it's going to get to my desk.
Third, effective use of space impresses me. Fonts and margins can change to fit your info. One should feel comfortable using them freely.
Steve Sim is a Technical Recruiter at the Microsoft Corporation.

RESUME CHECKLIST

☐   The resume is one page in length.

☐   The resume has been carefully checked for spelling and punctuation errors as well as double-checked to make sure that all addresses and phone numbers are current.

☐   Job descriptions are grammatically correct.

☐   There are no personal pronouns (I/me).

☐   Job descriptions do not begin with: "Responsibilities included" or "Duties consisted of" or anything similar to those constructions.

☐   Abbreviations of states are correct (i.e., MA not MA. or Mass.)

☐   The format is neat and attractive to the eye.

☐   The format is easily readable.

☐   All major components of a resume are included.

☐   Job titles are listed for each job description.

☐   Dates and place of employment are included for each work experience, and they are written in the same format each time.

☐   Telephone number(s) is(are) correct. (A common error because students tend to move frequently.)

☐   Resume will be copied on 8 1/2 X 11 inch bond paper in white or some other neutral color. Note that plain white paper should be used on resumes given to your coordinator: Nice paper sometimes looks awful when run through a fax machine!

YOUR RESUME IS A REFLECTION AND PERSONAL STATEMENT OF YOU!

Please note that these are suggestions, not requirements. Your resume is a reflection of you, and as such, you should feel comfortable and proud of its contents. While writing your resume, you will be presenting your experience and achievements in the best way possible. However, there is no room for deceit or lies on a resume. Lying on a resume is akin to plagiarism and is not acceptable at any university or in any professional workplace. Grade point averages, dates, computer skills, and achievements must be accurate and honest. You are building a professional reputation and should strive for a reputation known for its integrity.

While writing your resume, feel free to consult with friends, advisors, teachers, employers, and others whose opinions you respect. However, bear in mind that this guidebook and your co-op/internship or career services coordinator should be your number one resources. Again, be wary of your cousin's boyfriend who claims to be good at writing resumes—a person outside of your co-op program generally has no experience working with co-op students and employers and therefore may be not be a credible source of assistance. That said, *do* have several people proofread for grammatical and spelling errors. "I have employers that will teach you many things that you don't know," says Bob Tillman, co-op faculty coordinator for the civil engineering program at Northeastern University. "So on your resume, I have other concerns: let's get rid of all of the dumb mistakes." Many employers will discard your resume as soon as a typo is discovered, the theory being that if you cannot take the time to submit an error-free resume (which should reflect your best effort), then the quality of your work may reflect the same low standards. To put it more simply, an employer might think "If this is the best, I'd hate to see the rest!"

So invest your time wisely and do a superb job! There is no exact formula for a perfect resume, but these suggestions are based on experience, employer recommendations, and research. Learn to do your resume well now, and you will find that this skill will be helpful to you throughout your career.

GOOD LUCK!

ACTION VERB LIST

COMMUNICATIONS

acted as liaison	demonstrated	lectured	publicized
advised	displayed	marketed	published
advocated	edited	mediated	recommended
authored	guided	moderated	referred
commented	informed	negotiated	sold
consulted	instructed	notified	trained
corresponded	interpreted	presented	translated

ADMINISTRATION

administered	distributed	managed	recruited
appointed	eliminated	motivated	referred
arranged	executed	obtained	represented
completed	governed	opened	reviewed
controlled	implemented	organized	selected
coordinated	instituted	overhauled	supervised
delegated	issued	presided	supplied
directed	launched	provided	terminated

PLANNING & DEVELOPMENT

broadened	devised	improved	prepared
created	discovered	invented	produced
designed	drafted	modified	proposed
developed	estimated	planned	

ANALYSIS

amplified	detected	forecasted	researched
analyzed	diagnosed	formulated	solved
calculated	disapproved	identified	studied
compiled	evaluated	investigated	systematized
computed	examined	programmed	tested

FINANCIAL/RECORDS MANAGEMENT

allocated	collected	logged	purchased
audited	documented	maximized	recorded
balanced	expedited	minimized	scheduled
catalogued	invested	monitored	traced
classified	inventoried	processed	updated

MANUAL LABOR

assembled	installed	operated	replaced
constructed	maintained	repaired	rewired

GENERAL TERMS

accomplished	delivered	originated	serviced
achieved	expanded	performed	strengthened
assisted	handled	provided	transformed
completed	increased	served	utilized

TRANSFERABLE SKILLS IN BUSINESS CONCENTRATIONS

MIS/COMPUTER SCIENCE

Ability to learn quickly

Positive attitude/Strong work ethic

Interpersonal skills

Computer skills (be specific)

Communication skills

Dependability/Reliability

Customer-service skills

Willingness to do whatever asked

Patience

Organizational skills

Good judgment

Attention to detail

Ability to juggle multiple duties

ACCOUNTING/FINANCE

Positive attitude/Strong work ethic

Quantitative skills

Responsibility

Computer skills (be specific)

Dependability/reliability

Organizational skills

Communication skills

Ability to learn quickly

Interpersonal skills

Ability to juggle multiple duties

Willingness to do whatever asked

Attention to detail

Ability to work in teams

MARKETING

Verbal communication skills

Writing skills

Positive attitude/Strong work ethic

Ability to do research

Persistence/Drive

Results-oriented personality

Customer-service skills

Selling skills/Persuasiveness

Interpersonal skills

Computer skills (be specific)

Organizational skills

Outgoing personality

Ability to juggle responsibilities

Willingness to do whatever asked

Attention to detail

Ability to work in teams

ENTREPRENEURSHIP

Initiative/Self-starter

Creativity

Ability to work independently

Willingness to take risks

Ability to identify opportunities

Openness to new ideas

Willingness to play any role

Ambitiousness

Eagerness to learn

Ability to do research

Flexibility

Enthusiasm

Commitment

Willingness to work long hours

Persistence/Drive

Ability to juggle multiple duties

TRANSFERABLE SKILLS IN OTHER MAJORS

HEALTH SCIENCES/SOCIAL SCIENCES

Interpersonal skills

Positive attitude/strong work ethic

Sensitivity/Caring

Communication skills

Judgment/Responsibility

Organizational skills

Attention to detail

Willingness to do whatever asked

Ability to juggle responsibilities

Reliability/Dependability

Discretion and integrity

Ability to work in teams

Eagerness to learn

ENGINEERING/NATURAL SCIENCES

Analytical skills

Ability to lay out and solve problems

Communication skills

Computer skills (be specific)

Positive attitude/Strong work ethic

Attention to detail

Ability to work independently

Ability to work in teams

Ability to prioritize

Interpersonal skills

Reliability/Dependability

Laboratory skills

Willingness to do whatever asked

HUMANITIES

Communication skills

Ability to research

Presentation skills

Analytical skills

Positive attitude/strong work ethic

Reliability/Dependability

Organizational skills

Interpersonal skills

Ability to work independently

Ability to work in teams

Willingness to do whatever asked

CRIMINAL JUSTICE/LAW

Integrity

Judgment/Responsibility

Analytical skills

Attention to detail

Communication skills

Positive attitude/stong work ethic

Interpersonal skills

Reliability/dependability

Ability to work independently

Ability to work in teams

TRANSFERABLE SKILL PHRASE CHEAT SHEET

If you would like to try building transferable skill phrases into your resume, try using this formula: Pick an accurate word from each column below in order to figure out how to graft a transferable skill phrase onto a bullet point or sentence in your Experience section.

VERB	ADJECTIVE	TRANSFERABLE SKILL	LINKING WORD
Demonstrated	effective	ability to learn quickly	when
Displayed	excellent	communication skills	while
Showed	outstanding	interpersonal skills	
Exhibited	strong	attention to detail	
Proved to have	solid	dependability	
Utilized	very good	attitude	
Exercised	consistent	organizational skills	
Used	exceptional	patience	
Possessed	positive	customer-service orientation	
		willingness to do whatever asked	
		ability to work in a team	
		ability to work independently	
		initiative	

Step 1: *Capture what you did in simple, straightforward way:*

♦ Cleaned out stalls at a horse farm.

Step 2: *Add quantifiable and quantitative details to make the job come alive:*

♦ Working in a busy, family-oriented horse farm, cleaned out 23 horse stalls daily.

Step 3: *If you were GOOD at the job, identify the transferable skills you used in the job and use them to create a phrase using the above formula:*

♦ Working in a busy, family-oriented horse farm, demonstrated positive attitude and willingness to do whatever asked while cleaning out 23 horse stalls daily.

You don't need a transferable skill phrase with every single sentence or bullet, but students without any directly relevant job experience probably should make sure to use at least two per job.... assuming you were GOOD at that job! One way or another, find ways to make your resume do more than list WHAT you did. Capture HOW you did it and WHY you did it well.

Hannah Snow

1234 Singha Street, #42 Boston, MA 02115
(617) 555-6543   E-Mail: hannh103196@hotmail.com

EDUCATION

Northeastern University   Boston, MA
Candidate for Bachelor of Science Degree in Business Administration   May 2010
Concentration: Marketing   G.P.A. 3.6
Awards and Activities: Dean's List, University Honors Program, Vice President Membership for the
Northeastern University Marketing Club, Chamber Singers

Truman High School   Portland, OR
High School Diploma   June 2005
Awards and Activities: National Honor Society, Student Government Association, Varsity Soccer Captain

EXPERIENCE

Applebee's Restaurant   Boston, MA
Waitress   January 2006-Present
- Advise customers on menu selections based upon their likes and dislikes.
- Resolve all issues in designated section including opening and closings, table setup, and assured food storage at appropriate temperatures.
- Utilize suggestive selling for specialty alcohol and food promotions.
- Process cash and credit transactions, calculating customer receipts to analyze percent allocation to restaurant, hostesses, and bartenders.

Gap Incorporated   Boston, MA
Sales Associate   May 2004-August 2005
- Worked on selling floor as a part of sales team to meet daily sales goal.
- Consistently increased customer sales through add-ons.
- Directed customer complaints to appropriate department for satisfactory resolution.

M&M Steam Bar   Portland, OR
Steam Cook/Cashier   June 2003 – September 2004
- Steamed all lobster and shellfish dishes in a popular seasonal take out restaurant and fish market.
- Stocked fish case, wrapped fish, and operated cash register.
- Precooked 100-200 lobsters every night for the next day.

VOLUNTEER EXPERIENCE

Junior Achievement Academy   Boston, MA
Volunteer Mentor   January 2005-April 2005
- Taught high school students business and leadership skills.
- Recognized at Financial Executives International annual banquet for participating with the program.

SKILLS/INTERESTS

Computer Skills: Knowledgeable in Windows 95/98/ME, MS Word, MS PowerPoint
Languages: Conversational French, beginning Spanish
Certifications: American Red Cross CPR, First Aid
Interests: Traveling, baseball, piano, photography

Lana Schillman

99 Tovar Road, Apt. #6   Chestnut Hill, MA 02167
(617) 490-9999   e-mail: lanas@aol.com

EDUCATION

NORTHEASTERN UNIVERSITY   Boston, MA
Candidate for Bachelor of Science Degree in Business Administration   May 2008
Concentration: Management Information Systems
Honors: Dean's List   **GPA:** 3.73
Activities: Lacrosse Club, MIS Club

EXPERIENCE

ROCOCO INVESTMENTS   Boston, MA
Architecture Assistant   June 2007 – Present
- As a member of the system architecture group, take part in the design and development of a database application system.   Repository will be internally used as a decision support component required for impact analyses.
- Understand the systems, their interfaces, the databases, and the overall architecture of the information system.
- Understand the logical model and model representation of the repository.
- Formulate the application's business requirements.
- Design and develop the application user interface utilizing PowerBuilder 5.0.

INTEGRITY FINANCIAL SERVICES   Boston, MA
Systems Specialist   June 2005 – April 2006
- As a Member of LAN restructuring task force, effectively worked toward simplifying file naming conventions on network, and combining drives.
- Created queries and reports for management evaluation, utilizing Crystal Reports.
- Created and updated Excel spreadsheets for Actuarial purposes.

HYANNISPORT CRANBERRIES INC.   Lakeville, MA
Human Resources Intern   Jan. 2004 – May 2005
- Modified organization charts by utilizing Lotus Freelance Graphics software application.
- Performed queries to determine if there were suitable internal or external candidates for specific job requisitions.
- Used Resumix database to ensure that resumes were on the computer system.

SKILLS AND INTERESTS

Computer Skills: Knowledgeable in MS Access 2.0, MS Excel 5.0, MS Word 6.0, PowerBuilder 5.0, Lotus Freelance Graphics 2.0, Crystal Reports 5.0, Windows 3.1, Windows 95, Windows NT 4.0, UNIX, Mac. Familiar with C++, SQL, and Visual Basic.

Languages: Conversational in Hebrew; Exposure to Spanish.

Interests: Aerobics, cross-country skiing, contemporary fiction, and Web page design.

References furnished upon request

55

GABRIELLE BUENO

750 Parker Street, Palo Alto, CA 94563 • 510.499.0000 • bueno.g@ggu.edu

EDUCATION

Golden Gate University   San Francisco, CA
Candidate for Bachelor of Science in Business Administration   June 2010
Concentration: Supply Chain Management and Marketing
Honors: GPA: 3.9; Dean's List; Sigma Alpha Lambda (Honors Fraternity)
Activities: Vice President of Programming and Community Service; Committee Chair, College of Business 2010 Class Council (2006-present); Vice President of Finance, GGUMA (2006)

Balamonte High School   Portola Valley, CA
College Preparatory Curriculum   June 2005
Activities: Editor-in-Chief, Balamonte Yearbook (2004-2005); President, YMCA Youth and Government local chapter (2004-2005); Founder and President, CARE Community Service Club (2003-2005)

WORK EXPERIENCE

Golden Gate University Department of Residential Life   San Francisco, CA
Office Assistant   Sept. 2006 – Present
- Provide administrative support to Resident Director including: answering phones, filing, data entry, auditing residents, assisting with move in/out procedures
- Effectively resolve problems for students and staff
- Market dorm events to 526 residents
- Handle confidential student files and work with a high degree of autonomy

GAP Inc.   Walnut Creek, CA
Sales Associate   May – August 2006
- Consistently provided customer service and greeting every customer
- Used suggestive-selling techniques to market GAP credit card and promotional add-on items
- Worked efficiently when processing shipments containing thousands of units for inventory and display
- Assisted with implementation of corporate marketing programs by assembling visual merchandising campaign materials in store

Ablove-Sloane Yearbooks   Walnut Creek, CA
Event Planner, Administrative Assistant   March – August 2005
- Efficently organized computer workshops, client parties, and a week-long camp for 300 students
- Handled a wide range of office duties, creating PowerPoint presentations and organizing travel for company employees servicing over 80 schools
- Utilized strong attention to detail when processing payments and creating invoices

VOLUNTEER EXPERIENCE

Horizons for Homeless Children   Sept. 2006 – Present
Spend two hours a week working with underprivileged infants to aid early childhood development

SKILLS AND INTERESTS

Proficient in Microsoft Word and PowerPoint; Familiar with Microsoft Excel; Exposure to FileMaker Pro and Adobe InDesign
Interests include: event planning, community service, scrapbooking, working with children, exercising

References provided upon request

Eva Mendez   11 23rd Place, Apt. 3D   Sunnyside, NY 11012
                              646-555-3333   e-mail: evamendez84@gmail.com

Education

LaGuardia Community College/CUNY   Long Island City, NY
Associate's Degree   May 2009
<u>Major: Education: The Bilingual Child</u>
GPA 3.91 – Phi Theta Kappa Honor Society
Completed 48 credits toward an Associate of Arts degree
<u>Relevant Coursework</u>
Introduction to Bilingualism   Early Concepts of Math for Children
General Psychology   Sociology of Education
Advanced Spanish Composition   Children's Literature

LaGuardia Community College/CUNY   Long Island City, NY
English as a Second Language – Level 6   September 2005 – May 2006

Universidad Central del Colombia   Cali, Colombia
Bachelor of Arts, Communications;   Sept. 1999 – Sept. 2002
specialization in Public Relations

Experience

LaGuardia Community College   Long Island City, NY
<u>English Language Center Lab Assistant</u>   August 2004 – June 2005
- Familiarized ESL faculty and students in the use of the language lab's computerized listening/ recording equipment.
- Conducted student orientations to the language lab and participated in special teaching and learning projects.
- Supervised open lab hours for students' independent study.

<u>Office Assistant</u>   September 2003 – June 2004
- Assisted the Center in helping students from Latin America adjust to living and studying in the United States.
- Guided students with information related to TELC programs and international student regulations.

Banco Popular del Colombia   Bogota, Colombia
<u>Consumer Banker/Financial Consultant</u>   June 2001 – May 2003
- Performed administrative and financial tasks for the Human Resources Director.
- Managed various financial operations including opening new accounts and providing information on loans and investments.
- Prepared banking instruments and completed monetary transactions for corporate and personal clients.

Skills and Interests

Proficient in MS-Word, Adobe Photoshop, QuarkExpress, and Netscape. Familiar with MS-PowerPoint and Excel.
Strong marketing and organizational skills.
Fluent in Spanish; Proficient in Portuguese.
Interests: Latina writers, performing arts, black and white photography, basketball.

References Furnished Upon Request

Pui Sze Ng

57 Durutti Avenue, Staten Island, NY 10201
Phone 718-222-0000, Fax 718-222-9990, e-mail: puisze@yahoo.com

Education
LaGuardia Community College/CUNY, Long Island City, NY
Associate of Applied Science Degree – January 2005
Programming and Systems Major, Business Minor
Honors: Dean's List

Skills

Software	Programming Languages	Operating Systems
Word 97/00	Visual Basic 6.0	Windows 9.x/NT/00
Excel 97/00	Visual FoxPro 6.0	Dos 5.x/6.x
FrontPage 97/00	C++	Novell Netware 4.x/5.x
Adobe Photoshop	HTML	Macintosh OS 8.5

- o Customizing computers, constructing PC systems, troubleshooting and implementing software applications
- o Strong analytical skills
- o Detail-oriented and dedicated to problem-solving
- o Excellent interpersonal and organization skills

Work Experience
Manhattan University   New York, NY
Network Technician and End-User Support Specialist   August 2005 – Present
- Work with relative independence to meet CIS project deadlines, including the setup of computers and printers for the registration department, faculty, and student labs.
- Install and configure Windows Workstations, TCP/IP, and applications.
- Run RJ-45 CAT 5 wires and terminate into Keystone jack preparing workstations for LAN services and internetworking.
- Use a variety of equipment, such as wire scope and port scanner, and applications, such as IP browser, FTP, and IRC software to complete projects.

Robins USA   Long Island City, NY
Accounting Office Assistant   June 2004 – July 2005
- Used Excel to create accounting spreadsheets.
- Posted financial entries to journal and ledger utilizing customized software.
- Organized, sorted, and maintained financial records and profiles.

Interests
Technological trends via hands-on experience, online technology resources, computer technology magazines, gourmet cooking, jazz, outdoor activities.

References
Business and personal references available upon request.

MEGHAN C. BROOKE
e-mail: brooke.m@neu.edu

Local Address	Home Address
145 Gallatin Street	6856 Camera Circle
Bozeman, MT 02115	Ocala, FL 22454
(907) 465-8822	(255) 788-8642

EDUCATION

BIG SKY UNIVERSITY   Bozeman, MT
Bachelor of Science Degree in Nursing   May 2011
Cumulative GPA: 3.6 (4.0 scale)
Honors: University Honors Program, Dean's List
Activities: Health Sciences Club (Treasurer), Big Sky Student Ambassadors, Ultimate Frisbee Club
Planning to finance 60% of tuition and living expenses through cooperative education earnings

MANATEE HIGH SCHOOL   Ocala, FL
College Preparatory Curriculum   June 2006
Honors: Who's Who Among American High School Students, National Honor Roll,
               National Honor Society
Activities: Varsity Tennis, Ocala Packers Hiking Club, Students Against Driving Drunk

EXPERIENCE

KOHL'S DEPARTMENT STORE   Ocala, FL
Point of Sale Representative   June 2003-August 2006
Increased customer participation in Kohl's credit program by persuading customers to enroll. Exhibited close attention to detail while performing cash and credit transactions and calculating customer receipts. Demonstrated ability to learn quickly while using the credit computer and cash register. Greeted customers.

GOLDEN YEARS SENIOR CENTER   Ocala, FL
Volunteer   June 2002-Sept. 2003
Demonstrated warmth and caring when working with over 75 geriatric residents. Consistently exhibited patience while dealing with demanding population on a daily basis. Effectively juggled multiple duties by answering phones, delivering food and mail, and engaging in personal conversations with residents. Taught interested residents how to use Internet. Stocked supplies.

COMPUTER SKILLS

Knowledgeable in Microsoft Word, Microsoft Excel, Windows XP/Vista.
Familiar with Microsoft Access, Microsoft PowerPoint, and HTML.

INTERESTS

Skiing, ice hockey, camping, Scandanavian literature, drawing, and theater.

References will be furnished upon request

MEGHAN C. BROOKE
e-mail: brooke.m@neu.edu

<u>Local Address</u>
145 Gallatin Street
Bozeman, MT 02115
(907) 465-8822

<u>Home Address</u>
6856 Camera Circle
Ocala, FL 22454
(255) 788-8642

<u>REFERENCES</u>

Mr. John Shumbata, Store Manager
Kohl's Department Store
777 South Garfield Drive
Ocala, FL 22454
(255) 555-3388
e-mail: j.shumbata@kohls.com

Mr. Anthony Zamboni, Facility Manager
Golden Years Senior Center
5544 Manatee Highway
Ocala, FL 22455
(255) 555-3000
e-mail: azamboni@goldenyears.com

Ms. Susan Bacher, Family Friend
43 Locklear Cove
Kissimmee, FL 22103
(313) 555-1111
e-mail: krisdelmhorst@hotmail.com

Dr. Joseph Pepitone, Professor
Timothy Paul School of Nursing
Big Sky University
24 Lone Mountain Avenue
Bozeman, MT 90601
(906) 373-0001
e-mail: j.pepitone@bigsky.edu

Dr. Singha Piqaboue, Associate Professor
Timothy Paul School of Nursing
Big Sky University
24 Lone Mountain Avenue
Bozeman, MT 90601
(906) 373-0003
e-mail: s.piqaboue@bigsky.edu

CHAPTER 2 REVIEW QUESTIONS

1. Name at least four transferable skills that you have to offer a potential employer, and identify where you developed each skill.

2. Does it always make sense to list job experience in reverse chronological order, starting with the most recent job? Why, or why not?

3. What are the pros and cons of specifically listing your transferable skills on a resume?

4. What is the best way to indicate your varying degrees of knowledge of a computer skill or a language?

5. Name five specific interests that you have, choosing only ones that would add value to your resume. Also, list three interests that should NOT be included on any resume.

CHAPTER THREE
Strategic Interviewing

INTRODUCTION

When I am helping a student prepare for an interview, sometimes I am asked the following question: "Should I try to make it sound like I would be a great candidate for this job, or should I be honest?"

My answer is, simply, "Yes." Many future co-ops, interns, and full-time job seekers don't realize that this is not an either/or question: There is no reason why you can't be honest while effectively selling yourself as an outstanding job candidate. Learning to do so is a two-step process: You need to identify which of your skills, experiences, or personal characteristics might be attractive to a particular employer. Then you need to learn how to articulate these qualities to the interviewer in the process of answering questions... and asking questions!

By the end of this chapter, you should have a better idea of how to strategize for interviews: How to show the employer that there is a strong connection between your unique characteristics as a job candidate and the job itself, as it is described in the job description.

Mastering this art will boost your chances of obtaining the best jobs. Depending on your major, the job market, the interviewer's approach, and your school's way of doing business with employers, your interview could be anything from a brief "sanity check" to a grueling interrogation. Talk to the professional at your school about what to expect, but—when in doubt—always assume that the interview will be a challenging test of your ability to research, prepare, and execute strategically.

BASICS OF INTERVIEWING

Before your resume has been transmitted to a potential employer, there are several basics that you should know about interviewing. While many may seem like common sense, sometimes we find that sense is less common than we would like to believe. Accordingly, see how you rate in terms of the following:

Voice Mail Messages

Making sure you have an appropriate voice mail message is an important start. Then you need to check it regularly during your job search. The best employers know that they need to act quickly if they hope to hire the best co-op candidates. If they have trouble contacting you, they may move ahead and hire someone else. At the very least, they may experience frustration in attempting to contact you. Obviously, this is not the kind of first impression you want to make. So check your voice mail and e-mail at least twice each day once you start the referrals process.

There is a definite dilemma with cellphones for many students in this day and age. Even if you have a land line, it's sometimes reasonable to fear putting your home number on a resume due to unreliable or obnoxious roommates. Yet if you put your cellphone number on the resume, then you run the risk of having an employer call you while you're on a noisy subway or some other awkward situation. With a cellphone, you also have to worry about annoying delays, echoes, and garbled speech depending on the quality of your service.

There is no easy solution to this dilemma. Most students these days do use a cellphone. If you do, though, be careful about when and where you pick up the phone when you are in the thick of a job search. If in doubt about whether you should pick up the phone, just let it go to your voice mail—and then call back promptly from a quiet place with good reception.

Another point on this topic: Your voice mail message and initial conversation will give the potential employer their first opportunity to hear how you present yourself. As such, you want to leave a highly professional message, one that is clear and concise. For example: *"Hi, you've reached Tom Olafsson at 718-555-1234. I cannot answer your call right now, but please leave a message, and I will call you back as soon as possible."* There have been many horror stories about students leaving messages with loud music and obnoxious roommates saying ridiculous things: "Yo, we're down at the pub with a bunch of pitchers—Later!" We had one student whose *girlfriend* left a provocative message on his machine—not the best introduction to a potential employer! Sometimes it's not even clear whether the caller has dialed the right number. On a more subtle note, many students simply mumble, sound half-asleep, or fail to express themselves in an upbeat, professional manner.

Basically, an answering machine message won't determine whether or not you get a job. At best, it may be completely neutral. At worst, it can create the beginnings of doubt about whether you have the basic professionalism to communicate in a corporate environment. And if life without a humorous answering machine message seems unbearable, you can always change your message back after you have started your co-op job.

Phone Etiquette

When speaking to a potential employer on the phone, make sure to be professional in your speech. Try to avoid "yeahs" and "uh-huhs." Speak with energy and enthusiasm—even if you're not sure if you want this particular job. You want your first conversation with a potential employer to be very positive and effective. If you're called to arrange an interview, make sure that you have your calendar on hand. Try to be flexible about what days and times you can meet. If you have another commitment, say so politely and suggest what days would be best for you. Tell the caller that you're looking forward to the interview and eager to find out whether this job would be a good match for your skills. Make sure to ask for directions to the interview, ask for the individual's phone number in case you must reschedule the interview due to an emergency, and confirm the date and time before you hang up.

Attire

Make sure that your professional wardrobe is in good shape *before* beginning the interview process. Many students have wound up buying a new suit or outfit right before going on an interview: In fact, one student forgot to take the price and size tags off of his new suit and was nicknamed "Tags" for his whole six-month co-op job! You don't want to be shopping before an interview when you could be researching the organization, so plan ahead.

Men should wear dress shoes, a suit, a shirt, and tie. Your shoes should be polished. Your shirt should be a light color, usually white, light blue, pink, light green, etc. Your suit preferably should be some shade of gray, blue, or black... NOT some unusual color like green, flamingo pink, etc. Go light on cologne. As for ties, it is generally best to be conservative: Wear something that doesn't stand out too much. To our knowledge, no one has ever failed to get a job because they wore a boring tie. This rule is especially true of jobs in conservative fields, such as finance and criminal justice. If in doubt, check with your co-op coordinator.

Women should wear dress shoes, nylons, a dress or a skirt and blouse, or a suit. Make-up should not be excessive; wear little or no perfume as well. If you're applying for finance and accounting jobs, a very conservative suit would be appropriate. Although some women balk at wearing nylons—and there are co-op jobs where they may not be considered necessary—you should always wear them for interviews... even on hot summer days.

Some students object to these guidelines, feeling that their individuality is being compromised. Well, that's true. Basically, if having a pierced tongue or nose ring, a mohawk haircut, or wearing funky clothes is more important to you than getting a job, go right ahead but be prepared to accept the consequences. Fairly or unfairly, potential employers *will* judge you based on how you present yourself at an interview. Are you really interested in "fitting in" and "being one of the team," or is it more important to make a statement about your individuality with your appearance? The choice is yours.

Hygiene

You shouldn't have to receive a gift-wrapped bar of soap from a friend, roommate, or co-op coordinator to know that hygiene is an important consideration. In an interview, hygiene is either neutral or a negative; it goes unnoticed or it distracts the interviewer from the task at hand.

You should shower or bathe before any interview. Make sure your hair is neat and clean. Use deodorant, and make a habit of having a breath mint on the way to an interview. It can be a real distraction, and no one wants to work next to someone who has a hygiene problem!

Punctuality

Short of death—your own or that of an immediate family member—or severe illness, there is never really an acceptable reason to be late for an interview or to fail to show up altogether. Even arriving with a few minutes to spare can only increase any anxiety you feel about being interviewed. With this in mind, there are a few things you can do to avoid being late to interviews:

*   Set your watch ten minutes ahead.

*   Go to the office the day before to make sure that you can find it, and so you know how long it takes to get there. Frequently, the interviewer will meet you in the lobby and ask you if you had trouble finding the office. Imagine what he or she will think of you if you respond by saying, "Oh, no... I drove out here yesterday to make sure that I could find the building, so I had no trouble being on time today." This is far preferable to beginning the interview with some excuse about why you're ten minutes late.

*   Assume that the trip will take you 30 minutes longer than you expect it will. If you allow a great deal of extra time, the worst-case scenario is that you will arrive 30 to 60 minutes early. If you do arrive early, use the extra time to review the job description, review your research, and go over questions you would like to ask the interviewer. If you're completely prepared, take a brisk walk around the block to put any excess nervous energy to use. Don't go into the reception area an hour early—that can be awkward for the interviewer, who may feel obliged to see you sooner than the scheduled time. At most, arriving 15 or 20 minutes early is reasonable.

PREPARING FOR A SPECIFIC INTERVIEW

Working with a co-op/internship coordinator or career services professional, you will look at job descriptions and choose several jobs that you wish to target. So what do you do after an employer calls you and arranges an interview? For any employer, be sure to bring extra copies of your resume and the names, addresses, and phone numbers of your references on nice paper. But how do you prepare for an interview for one *specific* employer? Let's consider several steps in the preparation process:

Knowing the Job Description

First, make sure that you have a copy of the job description. Take it home with you, and memorize all the specific skills that the employer is looking for in a job candidate. Start thinking about how the employer would think of you as a job candidate in terms of the skills needed for the job. What would the employer perceive to be your strengths? Your weaknesses? Try to understand what it was about your resume that attracted your employer as well as what concerns you may need to overcome to get the job.

One of the most underrated aspects of interview preparation is to research the job description. Many job candidates think of "interview research" as purely looking up facts and figures about the company. As mentioned below, this is important... but it also can be misguided. Think about this example: Let's say a job description mentions that you will be using a Crystal Reports database to do research on market segmentation for an athletic shoe company. Would it really be the best use of your time to memorize the company's total revenues, stock price, international offices, and so forth? Not really: If you aren't familiar with Crystal Reports or Symantec Ghost and/or with the concept of marketing segmentation, get on the Internet and use word searches until you come up with something. Anybody can say that they are a quick learner when they are being interviewed, but few people *demonstrate* their ability to learn quickly by doing appropriate research for an interview. Obviously, you can't learn a software application overnight, but with a little effort you can learn enough to have an intelligent conversation with the interviewer. That will help your cause much more than annual report data.

Researching the Organization

Doing strong research on potential employers is one thing that separates excellent job seekers from average ones. Start by asking your co-op or career services professional. They may have student job descriptions that they can share with you; they may have visited the site. Best of all, they might be able to give you contact information for someone who has worked in that exact position! Imagine what you could ask that person to prepare yourself. This takes a little initiative, but this step can give you eye-popping information to use in the interview: "I spoke to Ben Birkbeck about his experience as a co-op, and I was excited to hear that there are opportunities to work closely with patients at your site." You may want to ask about the supervisor's style, the nature of the work, the organization's culture, the possibility for employment after graduation or in future co-op periods, etc. You can even ask what the interview will be like!

For general company information, the Internet or your school library can be a valuable resource. Talk to a reference librarian if necessary about how to find company news. For publicly-traded companies, you can find recent news at websites such as www.nasdaq.com or at any number of financial services websites. Once you have assembled several sources, look them up and take notes on what you read. Companies will be impressed if you do this homework before the interview.

Here are some other tips for searching via the Web.

Learn how to use more than one search engine: The Internet contains a vast amount of information, and it's easy to get lost in the Web. Obviously, www. google.com is a great place to start for looking up a company website. You also could go to the News menu on Google in order to find any recent developments with that organization. That can be a great way to come up with some topical questions to ask at the end of your interview.

When you do a search, watch out for companies that have similar names or various branches in different locations: Make sure you're researching the right one.

With some of the most powerful search engines—like Google—a few little tricks will greatly enhance the effectiveness of your search. For example, don't just type in John Hancock, because it will pull up every website that has the name "John" or "Hancock" in it... which is NOT very helpful. Instead, put quotes around the word: "John Hancock". This tells the search engine that you ONLY want URLs with that word combination.

Leave no stone unturned in your research: In my experience, students give up far too easily when doing research for an interview. Here's an example: A small company interviewed six of my students one time. Five looked in the files, looked in the library, looked on the Internet, and found NOTHING. They gave up. The sixth student did all of the same things and also found nothing. But he kept trying. He looked at the job description again, and saw this phrase: "We provide software solutions for the vending industry." He decided to go back to the library and back onto the Internet, learning as much as he could about the vending industry and how software was utilized in it. He learned a LOT about the industry, the competition, and key issues that probably were facing his potential employer. Then he walked around campus with a notebook, looking at the vending machines: Who made them? Who serviced them? How sophisticated were they in terms of software? Armed with this information, he was able to have a sophisticated conversation with the interviewer about vending. And, of course, he got the job. So remember, you can use the Internet to research the *industry* and the *competition* as well as the company itself.

In similar ways, you need to think creatively about your research: If the product/ service is consumer-oriented, go see it in action or how it is displayed and sold. Talk to people who might use the product or service, and ask them their opinions of it. Get a *real* understanding of the company.

Strategic Interviewing – A Co-op Student's Perspective
by Ted Schneider
RESEARCH, RESEARCH, RESEARCH! It is extremely embarrassing to show an interviewer that you have not prepared by researching the company or its clients. During my Microsoft interview, the interviewer asked me to "describe an issue facing Microsoft currently - besides the unfair business practices/monopolization issue." As you may have guessed, I had nothing to say.
Ted Schneider was an Accounting/MIS student at Northeastern University, Class of 2002.

Any information that you can dig up may prove useful in the interview. Later in this chapter, we will show specific ways that you can impress an interviewer with the fruits of your research.

STRATEGIZING

Matching Your Skills to the Employer's Needs
The most crucial aspect of a great interview is demonstrating that your skills and personal qualities are a great match for what the employer needs in a co-op worker. You may have excellent grades, terrific skills, and a great attitude, but if you can't explain why YOU are a great MATCH for THIS JOB, you may be out of luck. You need to have concrete reasons that reflect specific information on the job description. If a co-op candidate fails to strategize in this way, the employer may tell the co-op coordinator something like this: "Mary seemed like a great person with good skills, and I really liked her attitude. But I'm not convinced that she meets our needs."

How can you avoid being "close but not quite" when going after a job? Consider the following example. The Littlefield Rehabilitation Center has a nursing co-op job available for a student with "great empathy and patience, some experience working with the elderly or disabled, a basic understanding of nursing, and a willingness to work long shifts."

Student 1 and Student 2 have identical skills: Both are solid "B+" students who have only limited experience with the elderly. Both have taken only prerequisite coursework in nursing, but they do have volunteer experience working in hospitals during school vacations.

In the interview, both students are asked the following question: "Why should we hire you for this position?"

Student 1 says: "I'm a hard worker, and I've always wanted to work for an rehabilitation center. I think this job would give me a lot of good experience, especially the exposure to the geriatric population. So I look at this as a great opportunity."

Student 2 says: "I know you're looking for someone who is extremely patient and empathic. Here are my references—please call my supervisor at the hospital and ask her specifically about those qualities. As for working with the elderly, my experience is limited—but in preparing for the interview today, I talked to some students who worked at your Center; it sounds like you are doing some amazing things with treatment! Looking on the Internet, I was surprised to find that a third of your beds are utilized by younger patients recovering from head injuries, so I've already started reading up on subarachnoid hemorrhages and their clinical manifestations—I want to be ready to hit the ground running in this job! As you can see on my resume, my real strength is working with people, whether I've worked as a hospital volunteer or as a waitress. So I think I bring a strong background to this position."

Who would you be more inclined to hire? Neither student has excellent skills, but Student 2 did a much better job of showing the employer the connections between her skills and the job description. Student 1 answered the questions more in terms of why she or he would like to have the job instead of focusing on why the employer would want to hire her. As such, the employer might see this student as a far better match for the job... even though the two students have identical skills!

By tying your answers to the job description, you show the potential employer that:

- you are industrious enough to prepare effectively for an interview.

- you are persuasive, self-confident, and sensitive to the employer's needs.

- you have an awareness of what your skills are and how ready you will be to do the job well—right from the start.

One good tip is to go into any job interview with a solid strategy featuring three or four compelling reasons why the interviewer should hire you to do that specific job. Being focused like this will make a big difference.

We will consider more examples when we look more closely at interview questions.

VERBAL AND NONVERBAL INTERVIEWING SKILLS

Obviously, interviewers are very interested in what you have to say. However—especially in some fields—employers are interested in *how* you say it. Many interviewers may not consciously notice what you're doing right or wrong in this sense, but these behaviors still may have a critical impact on whether or not you get a job offer.

Verbal Skills
Keep in mind the following when interviewing.

Speak at a reasonably loud volume. Make sure the interviewer can hear and understand you. If you're not sure, ask.

Don't speak too fast. If you speak quickly, the interviewer may miss the strong points that you are making, or simply fail to remember. Slow down: especially when making an important selling point about yourself. When asked a question, don't be afraid to pause before answering or between giving each of two or three points about yourself. Don't be afraid of pauses: Brief silences can be effective in allowing points to sink in or to emphasize something strongly.

It's easy to overlook just how *hard* it is to be an interviewer: All at once, the interviewer has to listen to your answer while trying to assess your answer and think about the next question to ask. If you never come up for air or give time for your points to be digested, the interviewer won't remember much of what you've said. One interviewer told me that I "use silence effectively" as an interviewee. I thought that was a strange compliment at first—aren't interviews all about what you say? Really, though, she was just saying that I was giving her enough time to juggle all her various thoughts as an interviewer.

Watch out for "verbal tics." We all have verbal tics, y'know? Um.... you should, like, try to not use them during an interview, y'know? Yeah, they like make you seem totally immature and unprofessional, right?

Seriously: Almost everyone has a tendency to fill the empty seconds between phrases and sentences with little bits of meaningless slang. Doing this occasionally will go unnoticed, but doing it repeatedly can become a major distraction. In practice interviews, I have heard students use the word "like" as many as 12 times in one lengthy sentence! Many people don't even believe they use these phrases constantly until they see themselves on videotape. Slowing down your speech will help reduce these annoying, meaningless phrases. If you fail to reduce these phrases, you may come off as very young, inarticulate, immature, or unprepared. It takes practice to get out of these habits, but it's worth it, y'know?

It's also especially easy to lapse or relapse into these habits when being interviewed by someone who is younger. Even if you feel like you connect with an interviewer who is of comparable age, don't slip into unprofessional, informal speech habits.

Speak with a professional tone. Save your slang expressions for conversations with friends and significant others. When describing your job experience, for example, avoid terms like "stuff" and "things." Be precise; use a broader range of vocabulary.

Vary your tone. Avoid speaking in a monotone. Make your voice sound excited when talking about things that interest you. This will keep the listener interested.

If English is not your primary language: Make sure that you know how to answer typical interview questions in English. Speak loudly and slowly, and cheerfully offer to repeat something or rephrase something if the interviewer doesn't seem to understand you. If asked about your understanding and use of English, discuss what you have done and will do in order to improve your communication skills in English. If appropriate, you also might mention previous job experiences in which employers were concerned about your English skills but eventually found that this was not a problem for you or your co-workers.

Nonverbal Skills

People can often say a great deal in an interview without even opening their mouths. Therefore, pay attention to the following guidelines:

Handshakes: Shake hands firmly when meeting the interviewer or anyone he or she introduces you to. Keep your thumb up as you extend your hand to shake. If you tend to get sweaty palms when you're nervous, try to wipe off your hand frequently (and subtly) while waiting for the interviewer to arrive in the lobby.

Eye Contact: As much as possible, make eye contact with the interviewer. Don't stare, but don't let your eyes wander around the room at any time; you may be perceived as having a short attention span or as being uninterested in the job.

Body Language: Sit up straight, and lean forward a little when being interviewed. Don't slouch, lean way back, or fold your arms: This comes off as being defensive, laid-back, or unfriendly. When you're not using your hands or arms to help express a point, keep them on your lap. Don't put them in your pockets, as you may distract the interviewer by jangling change. Avoid drumming your fingers, fiddling with your hair, pen, jewelry, or clothes, and never chew gum. Try to *smile!*

Using notes/Taking notes: There is no simple answer to this question. In some fields, job interviews are comparable to making a formal sales presentation. In this case, failing to use notes may indicate that you have done little preparation for your interview/presentation. You will give the impression that you are "winging it," which—even if you're good at it—may not send the message you want to send. Conversely, other business employers might feel that relying on notes indicates that you are *not* adequately prepared.

When moderating a co-op employer discussion panel recently, I was intrigued to hear that some employers are very impressed when an interviewee takes notes during the interview. These employers felt that the note takers were showing sincere interest and good attention to detail. They cautioned, however, that you need to be judicious in exactly what you write down. Otherwise, note-taking can be very distracting and also may keep you from making adequate eye contact.

In most cases, using notes or taking notes will not be necessary in business interviews. But if you are afraid of "blanking out" or failing to cover several points, you might try using them... as long as you are not reading directly from them or looking at them constantly. If you are unsure about what is most appropriate for your field, ask your coordinator. We will talk specifically about how to use notes later in this chapter.

TURNING NERVOUS ENERGY INTO AN ALLY

Some people enjoy interviews, but most people experience at least some nervousness about them. Feeling nervous is a completely normal and rational reaction to going on an interview. After all, you want to make a good impression, and you want to make sure you get the best possible job for each co-op period. You care! That's a good thing.

One big mistake that many individuals make is believing that their goal should be to eliminate any nervousness that they feel. The more you try to order yourself to be relaxed, the harder it becomes to do so.

Here is a more helpful strategy: Remember that nervousness is nothing more than energy. The last thing you want to do is go into an interview without any energy! The trick is to *use* your nervous energy in positive ways. If you begin to feel nervous during an interview, put that excess energy to use by:

• speaking louder and with more enthusiasm

• using your hands to be more expressive instead of keeping your arms folded

• focusing harder on the interviewer, listening closely to what he or she is saying

• pushing yourself to come up with excellent questions and answers

Perhaps most importantly, remember another important fact about nervousness: *People can never tell exactly how nervous you are if you don't tell them.* In mock interviews, many of my students will openly admit that they're nervous. This is a mistake. The interviewer can rarely tell if a student is nervous, and admitting nervousness sometimes makes the interviewer focus on trying to determine how nervous the person is instead of really listening to his or her answers. In some cases, admitting nervousness may make the interviewer feel awkward or nervous too.   Regardless, discussing nervousness only moves you both further away from determining whether you are a good match for the job.

Interviewing – A Student's Perspective
by Mark Moccia

I fit the "sweaty palms" prototype perfectly on my first interview. I previously worked in an office environment, although I did not have a formal interview because my mother hired me! I thought I would not be as nervous because of the ease with which I handled my practice interviews. Despite my glowing confidence from the day before, I was nervous from the moment I woke up that morning. When I arrived at the office, I was sweating as if it were 100 degrees outside; the only problem with this is that it was only 75 degrees and cloudy! I experienced all the nightmares that come with nervous first interviews; I stumbled over words, dropped things on the floor, and apologized 50 times, along with many other little, embarrassing moments.

The most important lesson I learned from this interview is to relax and be yourself. I was trying too hard to impress the interviewer (who was the president of the company, which did not help matters) when I should have been selling myself more. It is important to impress the interviewer but you have to earn this right through hard work. You simply cannot impress the interviewer with your "uncanny multi-tasking ability" if you have never experienced multi-tasking.

It is important to figure out your strengths and sell those to the interviewer. It is also important to figure out your weaknesses and what you are doing to improve on them because interviewers will ask that question frequently. Finally, as mentioned earlier, the more research you perform on the company before the interview, the more questions you will have for them at the end of the interview when you hear the dreaded, "Do you have any questions for me?" This was pretty ugly for my first interview; I believe my response was, "Uh, uh, no. I do not believe I can learn anything else from this interview." BIG MISTAKE!

Mark Moccia was an Accounting/MIS student at Northeastern University, Class of 2002.

Here are a few other ideas about how to keep nervous energy from becoming a negative force for you in interviews:

- Formulate a specific strategy for each interview: Come up with at least three specific reasons why YOU should be hired for THAT specific job description.

- Prepare yourself thoroughly by considering how you would answer typical questions and by doing extensive research about the company.

- Allow yourself plenty of time to travel to the interview location.

- Practice your interviewing skills by working with your co-op/internship coordinator or with the Career Services Department.

- Practice answering questions with a friend, roommate, or family member. Remember that these individuals generally aren't experts. Practice with them to get used to saying your answers out loud rather than to seek useful criticism.

It's hard to overemphasize the importance of thorough preparation. In the classroom, when you are most nervous before taking an exam? It's when you really haven't studied and aren't prepared. The same is true for interviews: When you know your stuff, you'll be much more at ease.

People who learn to use their nervous energy effectively come off as energetic, enthusiastic, motivated, and focused in interviews... even though they have butterflies and knots in their stomach the whole time!

ORDINARY QUESTIONS, EXTRAORDINARY ANSWERS

Although it is impossible to anticipate every question that an employer will ask you in an interview, you should be prepared to answer the typical questions that arise in many interviews. Preparation makes an enormous difference in being able to deliver extraordinary answers to ordinary questions.

Individuals with little interviewing experience seldom give "bad" answers to questions. However, many people fail to understand the difference between a pretty good answer and an extraordinary one. In this section, we will dissect the most common interview questions and show you specific examples of mediocre, ordinary, and outstanding answers to these questions.

1. *"Tell me about yourself."*
In one form or another, this is a fairly common opening question. You may be asked about your background, or about what kind of person you are. Many people—particularly those who have failed to prepare—dislike these questions and struggle to answer them. The question seems incredibly broad and general: There are a thousand things you could talk about. However, those who are well prepared look forward to this kind of question. Basically, the interviewer is giving you a very open-ended question: You could choose to talk about almost anything in your response.

Why do interviewers ask this question? For one thing, it's an ice-breaker, a way of easing into the interview before asking tough questions about your skills. Another reason employers ask this is because it's a quick way to test your judgment. What you choose to say about yourself says a great deal about your personality and character.

There are many possible ways to answer this question effectively. Here are some guidelines to bear in mind:

1. *Don't waste time telling interviewers what they already know.* Many students answer this question too literally, telling the interviewer that they go to Northeastern, that they're a finance major, etc. Your resume or cover letter and the fact that it was e-mailed by a given co-op coordinator makes this kind of response very obvious.

2. *If you're not given a specific question, focus on why YOU are a good candidate for THIS specific job.* An open-ended question is always a good opportunity to sell yourself. Talk about what the job description requires and why you represent a good match for these requirements.

3. *If you are an unconventional candidate for a job, discuss why you are interested in this job and why you are a strong candidate.* For example, if you're a finance major who is interviewing for an accounting or MIS job, you should explain why you are excited about an opportunity in one of these fields and how this job relates to your career goals. In other words, anticipate an employer's concern and deal with it enthusiastically.

Let's look at some possible answers to "*Tell me about yourself.*"

Mediocre answer:	*"I live in Brookfield; I'm an accounting major; I like sports, reading, and rollerblading, and I'm a sophomore."*
Ordinary answer:	*"I'm a hard worker, and I've got solid grades and good co-op experience. I think this job would be really interesting, and I'm eager to learn from this experience. I'm persistent, and I expect a lot of myself."*
Extraordinary answer:	*"Working in public accounting is my objective. I have excellent grades in my accounting classes, and I did a great deal of bookkeeping in my first co-op job. I have a strong combination of classroom and professional skills, and I'm dedicated to proving myself in a public accounting environment."*

Can you see how different these responses are? The first tells the interviewer almost nothing that couldn't be inferred from reading the resume. The second conveys a positive attitude but tells the interviewer nothing about why the person would be good for THIS job as opposed to any other position. The third response shows that the job candidate read the job description carefully and has thought a great deal about why the position is a good match for his or her skills and traits. It also shows initiative by referring to research that the candidate did to prepare for the interview (provided the candidate really DID do that research). With this kind of response, you can go a long way toward showing an employer how your skills connect with a given job opportunity.

But what if the employer really was asking the question to find out more about your interests outside of work? Well, he or she can always ask a more specific follow-up question, which you can answer accordingly.

2. "I see on your resume that you're interested in _____. Tell me more about that."

This is another common ice-breaker question. Some employers may ask about your interest in books or skiing or whatever in order to help you relax and have a less artificial conversation with them.

This type of question also illustrates why you should always list some of your hobbies and interests on your resume. Basically, an employer is hiring an individual: not just a list of skills and qualifications. Talking about your hobbies and interests gives you an opportunity to make yourself a real person in the employer's eyes: hopefully, a person they would enjoy working with for a lengthy period of time. Believe it or not, this type of question can also help you sell yourself for the job, sometimes in subtle ways.

For example, one of the first questions that *I* get asked in most interviews is about my interest in writing fiction. When I get asked about it, I'm delighted: For one thing, it gives me a chance to speak about something with great enthusiasm. More importantly, though, this type of question allows me to convey personal qualities that may be very useful in the job at hand. If a job requires creativity, communication skills, persistence, patience, listening skills, etc., I can mention these qualities as aspects of fiction writing that have proven valuable to me.

Let's look at some examples relating to a fictional student named Pete Moss, a marketing student who lists his interests as follows: Photography, camping, skiing, and volunteer work. Check out some possible options for Pete if he's asked about his interests during a marketing interview:

"I see on your resume that you're interested in camping. Why does that interest you?"

Mediocre answer:	*"Yeah, I like to go up to Vermont once in a while. I guess that just being outdoors is what appeals to me. It's relaxing."*
Ordinary answer:	*"Yes, I try to go as often as I can in the summer. I find that it's a good way to clear my mind on the weekend, so I can return to work on Monday with a good focus."*
Extraordinary answer:	*"Besides being a relaxing way to recharge my batteries, camping is enjoyable to me because it requires a combination of characteristics: resourcefulness, good judgment, planning, stamina, and thinking on your feet. Some trips can be quite challenging, and I like to challenge myself."*

An employer who hears the first answer might wonder whether Pete can handle being indoors for six months! At best, this answer won't hurt you. The "Ordinary answer" is better: It shows that Pete values a balance between work and other interests, and that he sees his weekend time as a way to be more energized in the workplace. However, the "Extraordinary Answer" reflects a job candidate who really "thinks marketing" and is able to make some subtle but creative connections between his career interests and his personal interests. With this answer, he never says anything directly about being a good candidate for the job, but the employer may start thinking that Pete's individual traits fit nicely with a marketing position.

But what if Pete had been asked about one of his other interests? Let's consider some options:

Photography: *"Photography appeals to my creative side, which is a very strong aspect of my personality. I also enjoy photography because I like the challenge of trying to capture something in a picture. It's like marketing, where you're trying to capture the nature of a product or service with one simple slogan or image. I like that."*

Skiing: *"I haven't skied for very long—only three or four years—but I really enjoy everything about it. I like researching different ski mountains, finding out which appeals to me, and trying to sell my friends on which one I think is the best. On the mountain, I like taking on challenging terrain without sacrificing technique. I've improved very quickly."*

Here we see two different approaches. In the photography example, Pete ties his interest in photography directly to its relevance in the field of marketing. In the skiing example, though, Pete is more subtle. He describes many aspects of skiing that are appealing to him, but the interviewer also can see that he's demonstrating many traits that are useful in a marketing job: researching, salesmanship, reasonable risk-taking, an outgoing personality, and a focus on results. The interviewer may be more likely to think of this student as a job candidate without even realizing why he or she feels that way!

Whatever your interests are, think about how you would talk about them if they come up in an interview. Are there connections you can make between your interests and a co-op position? If you can learn to do this well, an interviewer may be pleasantly surprised at your ability to turn a simple ice-breaker question into another showcase of your abilities.

3.   *"Why should we hire you for this job?"*
If the interviewer has a more aggressive personality, you may hear this exact question in an interview. If not, you may find it in a more polite form (i.e., "What is it that makes you a good candidate for this job?"). In either case, the question an employer is *really* asking can be broken into many possible questions:

- How much self-confidence do you have?

- Are you a good match for this job?

- Do you *know* if you are a good match for this job?

- We expect you to sell our products or services, so how well can you sell yourself?

- Can you articulate your strengths clearly, confidently, and realistically?

Answer this question directly, focusing on your experiences, attitude, and aptitude in relationship to the job requirements as explained in the job description. In other words, don't just tell the employer why you're a good person, or a good candidate for *any* co-op job. Focus closely on why you are a good match for *this* co-op job. And if you don't have everything they're looking for in terms of skills, present a strategy for overcoming this obstacle.

Mediocre answer:	*"I've always wanted to work in this field, and I'm kind of intelligent. I think I could probably do a pretty good job."*
Ordinary answer:	*"I'm hard working; I have good grades; I'm eager to learn more, and I learn quickly. I also have good job experience that relates well to this position."*
Extraordinary answer:	*"According to the job description, you want someone who knows AutoCAD, and who has strong communication skills. In my class, I was the AutoCAD expert, and I help most of my friends with that and other software at school. As for communication skills, I encourage you to contact any of my previous employers. They'll tell you that I not only have excellent communication skills: I also was well respected by my colleagues on a personal and professional level. I also noticed that you prefer someone who has used Oracle. Since reading the job description, I've familiarized myself the basics of this program and am confident I could hit the ground running by the time this work period starts."*

The first answer gives the employer absolutely no incentive to hire the job candidate. Even worse, the candidate comes across as someone who has little or no confidence in himself/herself. The "Ordinary answer" is more positive, but it's rather generic: If an interviewer talks to ten students, this kind of answer will turn up three or more times. To stand out, you have to push your skills. In the "Extraordinary answer," the job candidate talks with confidence about past job experiences and shows a keen awareness of what the prospective job demands. If the employer didn't see these connections when looking at the resume, he or she will be clear on them now.

4. *"Why did you choose Physical Therapy (or Communications, etc.) as your major?"*

An employer who asks this kind of question hopes to learn more about how focused, enthusiastic, serious, and mature you are. There are many good ways to answer this question, but there are also several bad ways. Thus, some helpful hints:

- *Show that you have a career plan.* You don't want it to sound like someone imposed the major on you, or that you're only majoring in it because some advisor or relative suggested it. Don't be vague when presenting your reasons. Relate the career plan to the job. If you have notions of going to law school, for example, don't talk about that option when you're dealing with a public accounting firm looking to recruit interns and co-ops after graduation.

- *Show some excitement.* One option is to tell the interviewer a short anecdote about what first excited you about economics, history, etc. You might mention a high-school job experience, a previous internship, a classroom experience, or some extracurricular activity that inspired you to major in your given concentration.

- *Make sure to connect your response to the interviewer's job description.* If you're seeking a job within your concentration, this should not be difficult. However, if you're pursuing a job in a different concentration or major, you are very likely to be asked about this discrepancy. Basically, if you're a psychology major, why are you interviewing for a job as a webmaster, for example? There may be plenty of good reasons, but you will need to make the connection. Otherwise, the employer may perceive a mismatch between you and the job.

Here are some sample answers for a student who is asked why he or she chose physical therapy as a major.

Mediocre answer:	*"I dunno; I think it's kind of interesting. My dad says that the economy stinks for just about everything except the health sciences these days, so I figured it would be the best way to make a lot of money."*
Ordinary answer:	*"I've always seemed to do well in my science courses, and I've enjoyed working with people in various jobs over the years. I think it's just a nice fit for my abilities."*
Extraordinary answer:	*"I think I've always been a natural for the physical therapy field: Heck, I had to undergo physical therapy at the age of five, when I broke my arm falling off my bike. I'm great with people; I'm caring, and I really want to be in a healing profession that can help others in the way that I was helped*

as a child. I can't imagine another major that would fit so nicely with these qualities."

What if someone is interviewing for a marketing job but actually majors in, say, communication studies? The interviewer may ask: *"Given that your major is communications, why are you interested in a marketing position?"*

Mediocre answer: *"Well, no one wanted to hire me for a communications job... ."*

Ordinary answer: *"I think it would be interesting, and it would give me broader experience in business in general."*

Extraordinary answer: *"I am majoring in communication studies because there are many skills associated with it that I need to master to become a successful businessperson. I have the same interest in marketing, but I feel that many aspects of it—understanding the mentality of customers, knowing how to pitch to a specific market niche, and having a good mind for numbers and business—come naturally to me through my experiences in a family business. I decided I should use my college classes to improve on my weaknesses... not to build on what are already my strengths."*

5. "I see on your resume that you worked for Organization X last summer. What was that like?"
Employers have much to gain by bringing up one or more of your previous job experiences. They want to:

- determine whether your experience at *that* job makes you a better candidate for *this* job.

- see how well you can articulate what another organization does and what your role was for that organization.

- see whether you have a positive attitude about previous work experience.

Keep these things in mind when working on an effective response to this question. Most interviewers will ask you about prior job experience, and you want to be ready for it. Follow these guidelines:

- *Describe what the organization does.* Unless the organization is very large or well known in its field, you may have to use a sentence or two to explain the nature of the work done by the organization. Show the interviewer you can capture the big picture of what a company does.

- *Describe what you did at the organization.* You probably did numerous things in your job at Organization X. Focus primarily on what you did well, what you enjoyed, and—most importantly—how it relates to the job for which you are currently interviewing.

- *Go beyond what is stated on your resume.* The interviewer can read, so you have to say more than what is written on your resume. This is why it is so important to tie your work experience to the description of the job for which you're applying.

- *ALWAYS focus exclusively on what was positive about the work experience.* Even if you hated your boss and found the job boring or unsatisfying, focus on the positives about the experience. Nobody likes a complainer or whiner, and the interviewer may start wondering if you might have significantly contributed to the problem and therefore would be a "risky hire."

Here are some responses interviewers might hear in response to *"Tell me about your job at Organization X."*

Mediocre answer:	*"Well, I did some pretty tedious office work: You know, answering phones, sending faxes, things like that. It wasn't much fun, and my boss was a pain, so I definitely want something different this time."*
Ordinary answer:	*"I worked for Organization X in Anytown for my last co-op job. I worked in an office and did a lot of administrative support work: xeroxing, answering phones, basically doing anything to help out the team."*
Extraordinary answer:	*"Organization X makes galvinators, which are electronic parts used in the automotive industry. I was an Administrative Assistant, responsible for handling many clerical jobs in the Finance Department at Organization X. The job was a good entry-level experience; the best thing about it was just having a chance to work alongside finance people and getting to pick their brains about the company's financial operations. That's why I'm interested in the position at your company: I'll get more exposure to the world of finance and get a chance to use some of the skills I've picked up in my finance classes over the last six months."*

Strategic Interviewing – An Employer's Perspective
by Steve Sim
If I can add any perspective on interviews, I'd have to say one thing: each and every experience you listed on your resume or talked about in an interview should have taught you something. Whether that lesson is how to do something right every time or how to do something right the next time, it's a lesson learned. Be prepared to talk about it.

Steve Sim is a Technical Recruiter at the Microsoft Corporation.

Obviously, all three responses reflected a job that was not too demanding or exciting. The extraordinary answer, though, shows that you can be honest about this kind of job while still focusing on the positives of the experience.

6. *"What would you say are your strengths?"*

This question makes some interviewees uncomfortable: People often don't like feeling that they are bragging about themselves, fearing that they will come across as egotistical. But remember: if you don't sell yourself in an interview, who will? Interviewers ask this question to assess your self-confidence, maturity, and self-awareness in addition to how well your strengths match up with the requirements of a job.

Here are a few guidelines to bear in mind when answering this question:

Be honest. On the one hand, don't exaggerate about your abilities. If you say you have a given technical skill, many employers will follow up with a question to assess how well your knowledge matches up with your claim. Or—if you do get hired by saying you have a skill when you actually don't—the truth will come out shortly after you start the job. Lying about your credentials is grounds for immediate dismissal with most employers.

On the other hand, be honest about what you *can* do. Many co-op candidates sell themselves short when asked about their strengths. If asked about their experience with computers, for example, many candidates will say they don't have any... overlooking the fact that they have taught themselves many software applications and, sometimes, even programming languages. Yes, self-taught skills count when you are asked about your strengths, skills, or experience in a given area.

Describe your strengths in terms of the employer's needs. One common mistake in answering this question is failing to tailor your reply to the employer's needs. Sure, your strengths may include fluency in speaking Swahili and Swedish, great speed in using a slide rule, and the ability to program in Pascal, but how are these skills going to help yourself as a candidate for a marketing position?

Before the interview, decide which of your strengths should be emphasized. If a telemarketing position primarily requires persuasiveness, excellent communication skills, and the ability to do straightforward mathematical calculations, you should strategize accordingly. In addition to citing examples of experience you've had that required persuasiveness, for example, you should plan on presenting yourself in an extremely persuasive manner. You also might cite a strong grade in a business statistics class. In contrast, you might not focus on your PC skills or your marketing research experience. However, you might cite these skills heavily if interviewing for a position requiring these talents.

Let's consider some possible responses to the strengths question. Let's say that the job in question is a finance job requiring good experience with numbers, an ability to work as part of a team, and knowing how to calculate present values.

Mediocre answer:	*"I guess I'm a good worker, and I've done pretty well in most of my classes. I'm really good with computers too, especially spreadsheets and stuff."*
Ordinary answer:	*"I'm a real self-starter; I'm motivated and eager to learn. I got an A- in my finance class last semester, and I have strong writing and presentation skills."*
Extraordinary answer:	*"I consider myself a real team player: I have no problem in doing any task that will help my team achieve our goals. I've always been a natural with numbers, although I do find a calculator is most effective for calculating present values. I learned about present values in my first finance class, and my ability to calculate them probably helped me earn an A- in the course."*

Although the second answer discusses many bona fide strengths which may help the candidate land a job somewhere, it goes into little detail regarding strengths that will prove beneficial to *this* employer. The extraordinary answer covers all of the areas mentioned in our mini-job description. Of course, this answer is only effective if the candidate is prepared to "walk the talk." A shrewd interviewer may follow up this question by giving the candidate a simple problem that requires the calculation of a present value. Be prepared to back up any claims that you make in an interview.

7. *"What are your weaknesses?"*
Less experienced interviewees dislike this question, probably because they're afraid of exposing a legitimate weakness that the interviewer will use against them in making a hiring decision. Or the interviewee may worry about giving an answer that really isn't an honest weakness, which may come off as an insincere response.

The good news is that this is not a difficult question to answer *as long as you are prepared to answer it.* You'll need to think it through beforehand because coming up with a good answer on the spot is quite challenging. Here are some basic guidelines in answering this question:

Start off your answer by acknowledging your strengths. You don't want to dwell on negatives more than necessary when answering this question, and you want to reinforce your strengths to make sure the interviewer understands them. One way to make sure you acknowledge your strengths is by starting your answer with "although" or "despite": "Although I have solid skill and experience in areas X, Y, and Z...."

Avoid cliché responses. Frequently, interviewees will cite "working too hard" or "being too focused on the job to the detriment of having a social life," etc. This kind of answer comes off as a cliché, at best, and insincere and defensive, at worst. In a way, you're telling the interviewer that you feel a need to dodge the question, as if you have something to hide.

Choose a legitimate weakness, but not one that would keep you from getting a job that you want. There are many ways to do this. If you are opposed to a job that would require 12 hours of work each day, you can describe your weakness as "I burn out if I have to work 60 hours a week on a regular basis." You can go on to explain that you get your work done efficiently, that your strength is in prioritizing, and that you have no objection to working long hours when necessary as long as it isn't every week. This kind of answer may keep you from getting a job... but it might be a job that you wouldn't have wanted anyway.

Keeping the job description in mind is also helpful when thinking up good weaknesses. If you're applying for a nursing job that requires good interpersonal skills, strong communication skills, and great attention to detail, your weakness could be the fact that your computer skills are limited to word processing and doing research on the Internet. Sure, you don't know databases, but you may not need to for this particular job. If you're a computer science student looking for a software development position, you probably wouldn't have a weakness such as shyness held against you. If a job description mentions the need for someone who is able to work independently with little supervision, you could discuss your inexperience in working with groups. If a job description mentions a hectic, unstructured work environment with unpredictable demands, you could state your weakness as follows: "I find that I tend to get bored easily if I'm forced to do the same job day in, day out. I don't deal with a steady routine and a rigid structure, which I find stifling and monotonous. So I think that would be a real weakness for me in some work settings." Of course, your weakness also needs to be an *honest* weakness.

Computer skills are almost always a great choice when looking for a weakness that is sincere without being fatal. No matter how much you know about technology, there is *always* going to be a long list of computer skills that you lack. Even better, many will be completely irrelevant to the prospective employer. If you're an arts and sciences major, you could tout your MS-Office skills but acknowledge that you have never done any Web design or programming. If you're a computer science major applying for a programming job, you could talk up your C++ background while admitting that you know little or nothing about network administration. As long as you aren't dwelling on a skill that might be valuable to the employer, this is a safe option.

Remember that you aren't expected to know everything. Perhaps the easiest way to deal with a question about your weaknesses is to acknowledge what the employer already knows about you: that is, admit that while you have a strong foundation of knowledge in your field of study, you still have a great deal to learn before you could be considered an expert in finance or computers or accounting or whatever. As long as you are enthusiastic and can convince the interviewer that you have aptitude for learning new skills, this kind of answer will work for you with most jobs. After all, you're applying for a job as a student or graduating senior who is in the process of learning a given field. As such, employers would expect that your learning is incomplete.

Emphasize what you have done or what you will do to improve your area of weakness. Who would you rather hire? A person who doesn't admit to having any weaknesses, or a person who tells you about a weakness and how he or she has worked to overcome it? This is a good strategy for anyone, but especially for students who struggle with the English language. Just saying that you're weak in English won't help you. However, if you explain that you have only been in this country for two years, and that you have been taking courses and practicing regularly to improve, and that you enjoy working on your English skills, you will impress some interviewers: most of whom know only one language!

Try to anticipate any concerns or perceptions employers have about your weaknesses as a job candidate. This ties in with the previous example about problems with speaking English. Most likely, an interviewer can tell if English is challenging for you, and he or she may wonder whether this will hurt your ability to do the job. You don't want the employer to be distracted with thoughts like this. So what you can do is bring up the concern yourself—maybe even in responding to a first question such as "Tell me about yourself." If you can anticipate the interviewer's concerns and eliminate them early in the interview, the interviewer is more likely to focus on your strengths.

One undergraduate business student does this very effectively in interviews. Due to a physical disability, this student needs metal crutches to help himself walk. The student knows that interviewers are probably curious about his disability but feel it would be impolite to ask him questions about it. And maybe they're wondering what's wrong with him: Would he be able to get around the workplace, for example?

The student figures that if the interviewer is thinking about his crutches, he or she is *not* giving him the attention he deserves as an individual. Maybe the interviewer isn't really listening to his carefully-prepared questions and answers. So right when the interview starts, the student says, "You're probably wondering why I'm on these crutches." He explains what happened (a motorbike accident), and he assures the employer that the disability doesn't keep him from being able to take a computer apart and put it back together again. Now the interviewer can focus on the student as a job candidate, not as a medical curiosity.

Let's consider some possible answers to *"What are your weaknesses?"*

Mediocre answer: *"I don't really know anything about [sociology, journalism, etc.], and I don't really have any kind of real job experience."*

Ordinary answer: *"I guess it would be that I work too hard. I forget to go to lunch, and the security guard has to ask me to leave at 10:00 each night, then I just sleep in my car so I can start working when the doors open at 6."*

Extraordinary answer: *"Although I have done extremely well in my sociology coursework, I would say my weakness is that I haven't yet had an opportunity to work directly in the field. Of course, that's hard to do without an advanced degree. But I hope to build on what I've learned in the classroom by honing my research and analytical skills and by getting some practical job experience in a human services position such as the one at your organization. There's always more to learn, and I can do so quickly."*

8. *"How are your grades?"*

If your grades are good, you probably won't be asked this question because your grade point average will be right on your resume. Obviously, the best solution to this question is to have good grades to begin with! If your grades are not good enough to put your GPA on your resume, though, you'd better be ready to answer this question.

Do employers care about your grades? Generally, yes. Admittedly, some don't care if your grades are mediocre as long as you can do the work. Others, however, may *require* a GPA of 3.0 or better, and others believe that grades are a good predictor of job performance. Therefore, you have to be ready to address this question.

Once again, preparation will help you handle this type of question more effectively. Here are a few strategies that may prove helpful:

- *If your grades are good in the field for which you are applying, discuss those grades explicitly.* In other words, if you have a 2.4 GPA, but your grades in marketing classes are all Bs or better, then focus on those grades if you're applying for a marketing job.

- *If your GPA reflects one or two very low grades in a class outside of your major or concentration and/or in a class that may not relate to your success in this job, then say so.* Just be sure that the class *really* isn't relevant to the job at hand.

- If your GPA reflects the fact that you need to work a significant number of hours during school to help pay tuition, then say so.

- If your grades have improved significantly over the last few quarters or semesters, acknowledge that you got off to a slow start but have improved significantly.

Obviously, the best way to handle this question is to get good grades in the first place. Even though the statistical evidence shows that there is almost no relationship between grades and job success, employers don't necessarily know or believe that.

Anyway, here is the range of responses to *"How are your grades?"*

Mediocre answer: *"Not too good. I have a 2.4."*

Ordinary answer: *"Well, they're okay; they could be better. I've done pretty well in classes in my major."*

Extraordinary answer: *"Given that I've been working part-time while taking classes to help pay tuition, I think my grades are okay. When I take classes outside of my major, it's hard for me to put enough time into them. But my average in my psychology classes is a 3.2, so I think you'll find my academic background is strong in areas that will really count in this job."*

9. "Tell me what you liked LEAST about your job at Organization X."
This request is basically a check of your attitude and your tact. Don't be tempted to bash your former boss, your co-workers, your lousy job, etc. Doing so will make you come off as a complainer or as someone who dislikes work.

For example, I interviewed a young woman for a medical writing job a few years ago. When I asked her about her previous job, she was only too happy to go on for a full 15 minutes about her horrible employer. Since this horrendous job was also in medical publishing, I finally put on a very concerned face and asked her "Do you think your previous experience has made you too bitter to continue to work in this industry?" She immediately realized her mistake, but it was too late. She had already been interviewed by our company president, who afterwards dismissed her with a simple sentence: "She's a whiner." We never did discuss her qualifications, which, actually, were quite good.

Instead of harping on the negatives, your best bet is to acknowledge that the job had many good aspects, but that you felt you wanted to broaden your experience and move on to something that would provide you with a bigger challenge.

Here are some sample responses for this request:

Mediocre answer: *"They made me do all kinds of busywork that any idiot could do. Also, the pay was bad, my boss was totally clueless about how to manage me, and my co-workers were pretty useless, too."*

Ordinary answer: *"It was an okay place to work, but it got kind of dull after awhile. And since I was just a co-op student, I had to do a lot of jobs that other people didn't want to do. Basically, it was just a way to make money for school."*

Extraordinary answer: *"The job was definitely a good entry-level experience for me; I learned a great deal about _____, which I think will prove useful in my next job. I just believe that I could only learn so much in that job, so I decided it would be in my best interest to pursue something more challenging and interesting. That's why your job description caught my eye."*

10. *"What are your long-term career goals?"*

A variation on this one would be, *"What do you see yourself doing in ___ years?"* When employers ask this type of question, what they really want to know is many different things:

• *How focused or goal-oriented is the job candidate? Is she or he someone who plans ahead? Is she or he ambitious?* After all, you wouldn't want to hire someone who's just looking to make some quick cash, or someone who isn't achievement-oriented.

• *Does the job at hand really make sense as a match, given the job candidate's long-term goals?* If you're applying for a psychology position in an after-school program, but your long-term career goal is to become an entrepreneur, you had better be ready to explain why you're interested in the psychology job now. "I just really, really need a job" is not the best reason! It is entirely possible to explain the apparent disconnect, of course, but you have to give some thought as to how a job would fit into your career plan *before* you go out for that interview.

• *How mature and realistic is the candidate?* Your answer can reveal a great deal about your maturity and perception of yourself. If you don't have much of an answer, you may come off as someone who lacks focus and maturity. If you say that your goal is to someday be an administrative assistant, you may come off as lacking confidence or ambition. If you say that your goal is to be CEO of Microsoft, you may be seen as a dreamer, or as hopelessly naive... particularly if you have shown no initiative in acquiring computer skills.

That said, let's look at the range of replies an interviewer might hear to a question about long-term career goals. We'll assume that the student is interviewing for an entry-level bookkeeping job for a small company that manufactures furniture.

Mediocre answer: *"Well, I'm kind of undecided about that right now... I guess it would be to just pursue a job in my major after I graduate, then see what comes along."*

Ordinary answer: *"I hope to gain some valuable experience in accounting during my co-op jobs, then I'll pursue my CPA and see if I can get a job with a Big Five firm."*

Extraordinary answer: *"Down the road, I plan to get my CPA and work for a Big Five firm. I feel that the experience that I would gain from this opportunity would be very valuable, because an accountant needs to build good relationships with companies of all types and sizes. Working here would give me an understanding and appreciation from that perspective, which is essential to success in public accounting."*

But what if you don't *know* what your long-term goals are? Don't lie about that. But do give some general sense of your priorities and why the job for which you're interviewing is a good step with that in mind:

"Right now I know that I want to have a career in the corporate world, but I think a number of possibilities are plausible in the long run. Regardless of where I land, though, I know that any management professional has to be able to understand financial statements. So I'm excited about this job, as it would be a great first step toward any number of future management careers."

11. *"What kind of hourly rate are you looking for in this position?"*
The issue of pay can be an awkward matter in an interview. It's natural for you to be wondering about the pay rate or hoping for a specific figure, but your best bet is to not bring it up unless the employer does. Even then, you have to be careful about what you say. You don't want to get ruled out of a job for being greedy, but you don't want to accept $11.50 an hour when they would have been delighted to give you $14.

So how should you handle this question? First of all, always check the job description or ask a co-op coordinator what the pay rate is before you go in for an interview. If the job pays $11.00 an hour, and you can't afford to take a job that pays less than $13.00, it's better to find out ahead of time rather than wasting everyone's time with an interview.

In many cases, the issue of pay in a co-op job or internship is fairly rigid and non-negotiable. Some positions pay a certain figure, period. Others offer varied pay... but the pay only varies depending on your year in school; again, the pay rate is non-negotiable. Some internships don't pay at all, depending on the field and the organization.

In some instances, however, the pay rate is a range that can vary depending on your skills, the employer's alternatives to hiring you, and your desirability as a candidate. The co-op coordinator will usually—but not always—have an accurate sense of what the realm of possibility is with pay. Find out before the interview.

If you *do* know what the pay rate or pay range is, you can acknowledge this in response to the question: *"My understanding is that the job pays something from $13 to $15 an hour. I'd be comfortable with something within that range."*

This kind of response doesn't pigeonhole you as someone seeking a high or low pay rate and indicates that money isn't the most important consideration for you. For a co-op job, you never want to mention money as the reason you want a particular job, or as the main way you will decide between Job A and Job B.

If you *don't* know what the pay range or pay rate is, your best bet is to reply with a question: *"Is there a pay range that you have in mind for the position?"* Usually, there is, and many employers will provide you with a range. When you are told the range, it is best to not show any surprise, positively or negatively.

If you're pressed for a specific dollar figure, another option is to evade the question until an offer is presented: *"Money isn't the main factor in my decision. But I plan to interview with other companies, and if I get more than one excellent opportunity, then money could be a factor. But once you make me a specific offer, I will give you an answer within three business days."*

This kind of response indicates that money is not the top objective. More importantly, it helps you to project yourself as a person who has options and who considers himself or herself to be an attractive candidate. You want to show that you're strongly interested in the job, yes, but not desperate to get it!

Obviously, there are many other possible questions you might be asked in an interview. Several examples can be seen in the box on the next page, which was created by Linnea Basu, a graduate student who has worked extensively in cooperative education at Northeastern. One accounting employer consistently asks job candidates to "define integrity." Some interviewers may ask candidates to name someone that they think of as a hero. We have heard of one employer who asked a job candidate to tell him a joke! In short, you cannot prepare for every specific question that you possibly could be asked.

But when you are asked an unusual question, don't panic: just think, how can I use this question to show that I am THE candidate who is the best MATCH for THIS job description. Whether you're defining integrity or describing your ideal job, this is something that you can focus on.

OTHER TYPICAL INTERVIEW QUESTIONS *by Linnea Basu*

1. Why did you decide to attend *[name of university/college]?*

2. How did you decide to major in *[name of major]?*

3. What's your favorite class? Least favorite?

4. Why do you want this job? Why do you want to work for our organization?

5. What sets you apart from other candidates?

6. Rate your computer skills on a scale of 1-10.

7. Tell me about a time you had to meet a specific deadline and how you met that deadline.

8. How do you organize your time?

9. How would your friends describe you?

10. How would your boss or professors describe you?

11. What kind of a person do you like to work for?

12. Give me an example of a task or project you had to do which required attention to detail.

13. What motivates you to work hard?

14. What's your greatest accomplishment?

15. Tell me about a time when you had to work with a difficult team or group member and how you resolved the situation.

16. What has been your most rewarding college experience?

17. What has been the most difficult part of college life?

18. What's your dream job?

19. Give me an example of a time when you had to learn a skill or information very quickly and how you learned that skill.

20. If you could change one thing about yourself, what would it be?

21. If you could have dinner with any famous person, dead or alive, who would it be and why? What would you ask them?

DEALING WITH DIFFERENT INTERVIEWER STYLES

Another challenge in preparing for an interview is that you may come across many vastly different interviewing styles. Sometimes, students return to the co-op office feeling frustrated because the interviewer never shut up and didn't really give them a chance to sell themselves. Others may have a different frustration: The interviewer barely talked at all, and they felt extremely awkward. So it may be useful to consider how to deal with different types of interviewers.

First of all, keep in mind that many interviewers are NOT experts in interviewing. They may not know the best questions to ask to determine how good a candidate you are. You may find this disappointing, but that's the way it is. You may have to overcome an interviewer's weaknesses or personality if it keeps you from selling yourself. Here are some tips for dealing with several types of interviewers.

Type 1: "The Interrogator"

This interviewer puts job candidates on the spot. The Interrogator asks blunt questions, such as: "Why should we hire YOU for this job?" Or "What makes you think you know computers well enough to work here?" Alternatively, he or she may like to pose a challenge for you: "Here's a set of numbers. Figure out the present value of this sum of money if it's invested for 10 years at 8% interest." One interviewer likes to toss a beeper on the table and ask the potential computer engineering co-op: "How would you go about developing a new operating system for this beeper?" Sales interviewers may pull out a 79-cent pen and say, "You have one minute to sell me this pen."

You should always be prepared for an intense interview. Assume that you're going to be challenged with difficult questions, and that you may be asked to back up your answers with real-life examples.

Most interviewers will not be this tough: particularly with co-op candidates. Still, you have to be prepared for the possibility. And although many job candidates tremble at the thought of facing a high-pressure interviewer, the Interrogator is not the toughest to face. The Interrogator puts you under the microscope and evaluates how you handle tough questions or problems, but this gives you an opportunity to show how you can step up to a challenge and handle it.

Some MIS employers will sit a student down at a computer and have them attempt to fix it. The interviewer sits and notes how the candidate attempts to tackle the problem as much as the result. As the following sidebar box indicates, this kind of "on the spot" challenge is not limited to business students.

Type 2: "The Buddy"

This interviewer is very different from the Interrogator. The Buddy will have more of a conversation with you about the job, asking questions in a non-threatening way, showing interest in who you are as a person, etc. Most students prefer this kind of interviewer, naturally, but you have to be careful. Some wily interviewers

Interviewer Types – A Co-op Professional's Perspective
by Bob Tillman
I do have some strong upper-class jobs that will only interview upper-class students. They want to know if you've had concrete design, if you've had steel design. Not only that, they'll want to see your transcript. I just had one of my former graduate students come back, and they gave him a test: Here's a beam— analyze it. That's the interview.

Bob Tillman is a cooperative education faculty coordinator in Civil Engineering at Northeastern University.

will intentionally take on this friendly tone because they know you are likely to let your guard down. With The Buddy, you might be likely to confide more of your weaknesses, shortcomings, and problems, because their friendliness seems so trustworthy. The Buddy will get you to admit that you got a C- in your accounting class—and will even sound sympathetic—then The Buddy will turn around and nail you when it comes time to pick the best candidate.

If the interviewer is casual and friendly, you should relax too: but be a little cautious. Don't ever forget that you're trying to sell your strengths and show why you're a good match for the job: even if you're doing this with a smile on your face and a more relaxed tone of voice. Friendly conversation can set a nice tone for an interview: Just make sure that your conversation gets beyond small talk.

Type 3: "The Nonstop Talker"

Although The Interrogator may sound like your worst nightmare, The Nonstop Talker is actually the most difficult and frustrating type for most interviewees. You may sit through an interview that feels more like a lecture, barely getting a chance to say anything to this interviewer. At least The Interrogator gives you a chance to say something in your defense!

The Nonstop Talker may not be immediately recognizable. Many good interviewers will begin by telling you a great deal about the job and the organization before asking you questions. The Nonstop Talker may talk about these things, too, in addition to himself or herself, the previous co-op student that worked at the company, and a whole bunch of other topics. Applicants for one job came back and reported with some amazement that the manager talked about his ex-wife! The next thing you know, the interviewer has used up all of the scheduled time, and you've done little but nod a lot. Of course, this is a low-pressure interview, but you run the risk of coming across as part of the office furniture: In other words, this type of interview may mean that they like you and have basically decided to hire you, but it also may mean that you are completely forgotten by the interviewer.

When interviewed by The Nonstop Talker, you have to walk a fine line: Don't interrupt, but DO take advantage of any break in the monologue by asking a question that brings the Talker around to considering you as a candidate. During a pause, you might be able to politely say: "Can I ask you a question? I'm very interested in this job. What would be useful for you to know in order to find out whether I'm the best candidate for the job?" Another strategy is to acknowledge and flatter The Talker's talking while changing the focus of the talk: "I've certainly learned a great deal about you, this job, and the organization. In fact, from what you've said, I think this opportunity would be a great match for my skills because...." At this point, you can tailor your response to what you've learned from the nonstop talking... as long as you were listening carefully!

In short, try to get The Nonstop Talker to focus on you. He or she may still talk a great deal, but at least it might be about you and your ability to do the job.

Type 4: "Silent But Deadly"

This interviewer is the opposite of the talker, but this style can be equally frustrating. The Silent But Deadly interviewer will ask very few questions, and the questions may be very vague or general. So why is this interviewer potentially "deadly?" Basically, he or she gives nervous job candidates every opportunity to hang themselves! Consider the following dialogue:

Interviewer: *"So... tell me about your weaknesses."*

Job Candidate: *"Although I have a good understanding of basic accounting from classwork and my first co-op job, I need to learn more in order to master accounting: specifically, I'm looking forward to learning more about taxes, which is why the job with your company appeals to me."*

Interviewer [nods slowly]: *"Hmmmm......"*

Job Candidate: *"Um, and I guess you want another weakness?"*

Interviewer [nods]: *"Uh-huh..."*

Job Candidate: *"Hmmm.... okay, let me think... Um, I guess I'm not that strong when it comes to debits and credits.... I get my ledger entries confused sometimes..."*

Interviewer [nods, says nothing]:

Job Candidate: *"And.... I suppose that getting a C+ in my last accounting class wasn't that strong."*

Do you see what can happen in this situation? The job candidate started off with a strong answer but then interpreted the interviewer's silence as a negative: The candidate assumed that he or she failed to answer the question adequately. As a result, the candidate supplied more information. In this case, it was information that can only hurt the individual's chances of getting a job.

Most Silent But Deadly interviewers act this way because it reflects their personalities. But some shrewd interviewers may use this as a deliberate strategy to see if you will hang yourself if given enough rope. This is especially common when asking about weaknesses or reasons for leaving a previous job or situation.

Either way, your strategy is simple. If the length of the silence starts to feel awkward, ask a clarifying question: "Does that answer your question?"; "Is there anything else you'd like to ask me?"; "What else would you like to know about me?" Unless you're asked a specific question requesting more information, have faith in your answer; don't assume that silence or apparent indifference means that you have to say something more.

During my last job search, I was interviewed by a very quiet, introverted gentleman. After each of my answers, he would let a solid ten seconds go by; once, he waited for a good 20 seconds, as if he were curious to see how I would handle that. But I believed I had given a strong, definitive answer, so I simply waited. Finally, he said, "Is there anything you'd like to add?" I replied, pleasantly, "I think I covered everything. Was there something else you would like to know?" Ultimately, I was offered the job. Of course, if I were interviewing for a marketing position, I probably would have needed to be more aggressive in that situation. So it just goes to show you: There is seldom one "right" way to handle an interviewing challenge. It's always difficult to feel that you need to carry both sides of any conversation. But if you can take charge of the situation by offering to explain why you're a good match for the job, what you have to offer the organization, and by asking questions that reflect your research, you may succeed in bringing this interviewer out of his or her shell.

Type 5: "The Big Picture Person"
This interviewer is prone to asking very open-ended, general questions, such as:

- Tell me about yourself.

- What do you want to do with your life?

- What are your career goals?

- What kind of person are you?

Students often *hate* these questions because there seems to be no clear-cut way to answer them. Again, though, remember the rule: When asked about something *general*, answer in a way that shows why you are a match for this *specific* job. What kind of person are you? "I have a great deal to offer to a small medical office like this one. I have excellent grades in my anatomy and physiology classes, and I have solid experience working hands-on with people as a volunteer at the small hospital in my hometown. If you hire me, you will be employing a person who has a solid base of experience as well as someone who picks up new things quickly and does work without complaining." If that's the kind of job description in question, that's the right kind of specific answer to a "big picture" question.

Type 6: "The Human Resources Interviewer"

If you are interviewed by someone in an HR department, you may or may not be asked questions relating to your technical skills. An experienced HR person may have enough expertise to ask you about specific tasks, but it is not uncommon to come across an HR interviewer who knows little about engineering, nursing, or social work. Alternatively, the HR interviewer may have the knowledge but decide that such questions are better left to the person who would be your supervisor if you're hired. Either way, the HR interviewer is more likely to ask the classic interview questions as described in the previous section. The questions may be more "warm and fuzzy," as the purpose of this interview may be to "screen" candidates to determine who will go on to the next phase of the interview process. Be prepared for a structured interview, and don't get too technical in your responses unless the interviewer seems to be looking for that. Save your more technical answers for the interviewer who is a network administrator or mechanical engineer—someone who is an expert in your field, whatever it is.

Interviewer Types – A Co-op Professional's Perspective
by Rose Dimarco

Nursing could be different than physical therapy in that nursing may have people in Human Resources to interview you; they may have nurse recruiters interview you. Part of their skill base is knowing how to interview. In physical therapy, you're more apt to be interviewed by the physical therapist—who may have zero skills in interviewing. So if you're going to probably be interviewed by someone who doesn't know how to interview you that well, what do you want to have them remember about you before you walk out? That means when they're walking you down the hall, and they're showing you all the equipment and all the treatment rooms, how are you going to script what you want to say so that you interject what is it about you that you think would fit? If you're being interviewed by someone in Human Resources, and they're more skilled in interviewing, it might be more traditional questions: Tell me about yourself, what are your strengths and weaknesses?

You have to decide: What three things do I want them to remember about me? It's not: 'Oh, what a cute guy—he's trying to get through school; his mom and dad had three jobs.' It's not that kind of remembrance: It's remembrance about what value you bring, and those three things you have to somehow interject. As they talk about things, don't be afraid to say "That reminds me of when I was in high school, and I had to work under pressure because I had x, y, and z to do, and here's how I dealt with it."

Rose Dimarco is a cooperative education faculty coordinator in Physical Therapy at Northeastern University.

Type 7: "The Behavioral-Based Interviewer"

Some organizations swear by the Behavioral-Based Interviewing (BBI) approach, and for good reason: Studies have shown that this style is generally more effective in determining whether someone is a good match for the job. In particular, Big Four accounting firms such as Deloitte and Touche and PricewaterhouseCoopers often use this approach. Microsoft and other corporations also use these questions to determine if you have specific "core competencies" that are considered to be vital to success at the organization in question: drive/results orientation; passion for learning; ability to work in a team; ability to handle conflict effectively; good ethical judgment; etc.

The behavioral-based interview features questions that require specific stories in response. This makes it much more difficult for the interviewee to come up with a slick-sounding, canned answer: Instead, he or she must recount something that they really experienced in the classroom or at work. In answering, the interviewee is urged to walk the interviewer through the specific situation and to detail what they were thinking, feeling, and doing in dealing with it.

Here are some typical BBI questions:

- Tell me specifically what your greatest accomplishment in life thus far has been.

- Tell me about a time when you had to overcome a challenge or obstacle when working as part of a team.

- Tell me about a time when you felt really successful in something at work.

- Describe a situation in which you faced an ethical dilemma and how you dealt with it.

If you're not too forthcoming or struggle initially, the interview may add, "Just walk me through what was going on step-by-step..." or something like that.

The key to these interviews is to have several good, specific stories that you are ready to share. Think long and hard ahead of time about which stories will best showcase multiple positive qualities—some stories are better than others! Describe the situation specifically first, then logically walk the interviewer through how you handled the situation step-by-step, wrapping up with a description of what ended up happening due to your actions.

Practice the telling of your behavioral-based stories ahead of time. Last summer, my nephew interviewed for an engineering position—his first job out of college. Ahead of time, they gave him a list of core competencies that they seek in applicants and told him that they would be looking for him to share some personal experiences related to those competencies. I told him that this was like going for a test where you have been given the questions a week in advance!

However, the first time he told me his stories, they weren't good enough. He had to try out some stories to figure out which ones would be the BEST stories to showcase his strengths. After extensive practice and preparation—and despite limited internship experience—he went in and nailed the interview, and it turned out to be the only offer he got in a tough economy. Without strategizing and practicing for a behavioral-based interview, it may not have happened.

Whether or not you ever have a behavioral-based interview, having extremely vivid and specific examples to share is always a smart idea: It brings alive your ideas and tells employers what you *really* mean when you say that you can learn quickly or work independently or be a strong team player. For a great deal information on behavioral-based interviewing—including several terrific student examples—check out Appendix E in the back of this textbook.

Type 8: "The Olympic Judge"

The Olympic Judge likes to let you know how you're doing throughout the interview. As you might imagine, this can be encouraging, disconcerting, or both. This interviewer may come out and say, "Good answer!" However, this individual may also shake his head or frown or say, "Well, I don't know about that."

Dealing with immediate negative feedback can be very challenging to your confidence. How can you handle it? Most importantly, *don't ignore it.* If an interviewer reacts negatively to one of your answers, ask a clarifying question: "Is there a concern you have about that answer?" Once you understand why the interviewer reacted negatively, try to acknowledge the concern and address it as best as you can. For example, if you're asked to cite your experience in marketing research, and the interviewer reacts negatively to your response, you might handle it like this:

Job candidate: *"I noticed that you had a negative reaction to my answer. What is it about my research experience that concerns you?"*

Interviewer: *"Well, my sense is that your experience is good but extremely limited."*

Job candidate: *"I think it's fair to say that the quantity of experience I've had is limited. But I feel that the quality of experience has been outstanding. My position at Galvinators Unlimited gave me a great opportunity to gain exposure to research..."*

The candidate could then go on to tout some specifics about this research experience. Would this be enough to turn around the Olympic Judge's perception? Maybe not, but it would at least give you a chance. It shows assertiveness, desire to get the job, and sensitivity to the concerns of others.

A variation on the Olympic Judge interviewer is the person who asks *you* to judge yourself: "On a scale of 1 to 10, with 1 being terrible and 10 being fantastic, how would you rate yourself in terms of...." The interviewer then asks you to rate your communication skills, your analytical ability, your interpersonal skills, etc.

This kind of question tests your honesty, realism, and savvy: Rating yourself uniformly high comes off as insincere or unaware, but who will hire you if you give yourself low ratings? When answering this question, make sure you do yourself justice, but make sure to rate yourself lower in certain areas: particularly those that seem less related to the job that you want. Don't rate yourself as a 1 or 2 in something unless you really know nothing about it (i.e., you're asked about C++ programming, and you've never done anything like it). For most generic characteristics, stick between 6 and 10. Bear in mind that your coordinator would not send your resume out for a position if he or she believed that your skills were not a reasonable match for the given job. Have confidence in your skill level, and show it with ratings that are realistic and positive.

TURNING THE TABLES: ASKING THE RIGHT QUESTIONS DURING AN INTERVIEW

Many job candidates think of interviewing as an audition for a part. This perception has some truth to it, but it's not the whole story. In an interview, you *are* trying to show that you're the best person for the job. Additionally, though, you're trying to determine whether the job is a good match for you. In that sense, interviewing should be a two-way street.

The nice thing about asking questions in an interview is that it helps to achieve both of these goals. Asking smart questions is a great way to show the interviewer that you are:

* prepared for the interview in terms of researching the job and the company.

* excited about and interested in the job.

* determined to find out whether *you* think this job is the best match for your considerable talents.

Interviewing – An Employer's Perspective
by Mike Naclerio
The goal of interviewing is to determine a "mutual" fit between the company and potential employee. Too often, candidates view interviews as situations where they have to prove to a company t."interview the company" to see if the company is good enough for them (i.e., does the company have an appropriate level of ethics, will the position be satisfying, what type of people work there, etc.). So, candidates should not lose sight of this opportunity and ask questions!
Mike Naclerio is the Director of Relationship Management at the workplace HELPLINE.

All of these things reflect favorably on you as a job candidate. Likewise, asking questions is a great way for the interviewer to show you whether:

- the job is what it appears to be in the job description.

- the job is something that you will be excited about doing for several months (or at least one year if it's a full-time post-graduation position).

- the job is indeed a good match for someone with your level of skills.

Don't underestimate the importance of determining whether the job is what you really want. More often than not, individuals who end up disliking their jobs failed to ask the right questions during the interview. Basically, they didn't have a realistic sense of what the job requirements would be. As a result, they end up being bored or overwhelmed. But isn't it the employer's fault for failing to communicate this to the job candidate, you might say? True, a great interviewer will do this effectively. However, if an interviewer fails to do so, it's your responsibility to ask if you want to ensure that misunderstandings are avoided.

What questions should I ask?

Many internship and co-op candidates—even many experienced professionals—struggle to come up with good questions. When they are given the opportunity to ask questions during an interview, they will try to think up some on the spot, then decline the opportunity.

Like so many things in interviewing, this element requires preparation. You should have as many as eight to ten questions ready to ask before you even arrive for the interview. Why so many? Because several questions that you had beforehand may be answered during the course of the interview. Most interviewers won't simply ask questions; they'll talk a little about the company and explain a little more about the job. Thus, you need to have numerous questions ready.

What are the "best" questions to ask? In my opinion, the best questions are the ones that:

- force the interviewer to imagine you in the job.

- reflect your attitude and values positively.

Let's consider what this means. If you want the job, it is certainly in your best interest to make the interviewer imagine you in the job. You can do this by using the words "I," "me," and "my" in your question. For example:

- What would my typical day be like in this position?

- Who would train me when I begin this job?

- Would I receive regular feedback about my performance?

These are good questions, but the very best ones are those which also reflect a positive attitude and strong values. Consider these:

- What could I do between now and the first day of co-op to be ready to hit the ground running in this job?

- It's important to me to get an outstanding evaluation in my co-op job: What could I do to really stand out as an exceptional employee in this job?

- I definitely want a job that challenges me and keeps me busy. Given that, can you give me a sense about whether this position would be right for me?

- I would be glad to work part-time after the co-op ends. Do you think that's a possibility?

- If I excel in this job, would I be able to have more responsibilities added to my job description?

Here are some other good questions:

- What would you say is the most challenging part of this job?

- What would you describe as the most rewarding aspect of the job?

- In the research that I did to prepare for today, I noticed that your company is trying to (i.e., implement a new marketing strategy, adopt a new process of providing quality care to patients). How has this development changed things in this department?

- This job involves several different responsibilities: Which do you think would require most of my time?

- Why do YOU like working for this company?

- If everything works out well for this co-op period, would it be possible for me to work here in the future?

- How often do you hire co-ops on a full-time basis after they graduate?

Asking these kinds of questions will show the interviewer that you are serious about the job, and that you value yourself highly enough to know that other options may be more attractive to you than this one. Because this is true, you need to see if the company meets your needs as well as you meet theirs.

One last note: Be sure to *follow up* on your questions. *Listen* to the employer's answer, and *respond* to it positively. Here's an example:

Interviewee:	*"What could I do to earn an outstanding evaluation working here?"*
Interviewer:	*"Well, more than anything we want someone who is willing to do whatever it takes to get the job done—even if that means staying really late or coming in on Saturdays from time."*
Interviewee:	*"That's great to hear. I have no problem putting in extra hours: I just want to be a productive part of the team, whatever it takes. Actually, if you want to call my previous supervisor, she can tell you about my willingness to work overtime or come in on short notice. I think I would stand out in a similar way here."*

ENDING ON A HIGH NOTE

If you have ever taken a psychology class, you may have heard of a phenomenon called the primacy/recency effect. Research has shown that when individuals are presented with a significant amount of information, they tend to best remember what they are exposed to first and last; the middle tends to get hazy.

We already discussed how to get off to a good start. Now let's discuss how you can cap your interview with a strong ending. Here are a few basic guidelines:

Take charge of the transition from asking questions to closing the interview.
Don't wait for the employer to figure out that you have no more questions to ask. The best approach is to bridge from asking questions into closing the interview. After you've had your job-related questions answered, simply say: "I have just one more question. When do you plan to make a hiring decision?"

Ask the interviewer what the next steps will be.
After you learn when the decision will be made, ask the interviewer what his or her preference is regarding next steps: "Would you like me to call you next week about the decision, or should I just wait to hear from you?" If the interviewer says that you can call, make sure to get a business card, or, at least, a phone number you can call.

Thank the interviewer for taking the time to meet with you.
Even if you're not interested in the job, be graceful and polite. Acknowledge the fact that the interviewer has devoted part of his or her day to talk to you. Show some appreciation for the experience, and mention something specific about your conversation that was enlightening. One possibility would be: "Thank you for taking the time to meet with me today. I learned a great deal about the nursing practices in a geriatric care facility. I look forward to hearing from you."

Shake the interviewer's hand before leaving, and make sure that you haven't left behind any personal belongings.
If you have any doubts about whether or not you handled questions well, write them down soon after you leave. Then you can discuss them with your coordinator.

AFTER THE INTERVIEW: FOLLOW-UP STEPS

To some degree, your follow-up steps may vary depending on the employer's needs or preferences. In all circumstances, respect any request that an employer makes of you, whether it's getting a writing sample to her or additional references to him, calling on a particular day, or not calling at all.

Most people would agree that writing a thank-you note or letter or e-mail would be appropriate at this point. But one dilemma is whether a handwritten card is better than a less formal e-mail. My rule is that if a decision is not going to be made within the next two or three days, then it's better to send a brief letter or card if you mail it by the following morning. But if a decision will be made within 24 hours, then opt for an e-mail.

More than anything, though, make sure that any such note or e-mail is absolutely perfect in terms of grammar and spelling... especially when writing the name of the manager or organization. Sending no thank-you letter at all is better than sending one with errors.

Keep your thank-you note simple and professional. A safe approach would include the following steps:

- Thank the interviewer for taking the time to meet with you on Thursday (or whatever day it was).

- Say something positive about the interviewing experience: something you found especially intriguing to learn about the company, its products/ services, the job, etc.

- Briefly reinforce your interest in the position (if you have any) and why you would be a good match for the position.

- Encourage the interviewer to contact you if any additional information is needed.

On the next page is an example of how one might format a thank-you e-mail:

Subject: Thank you for your time

Ms. Maiatico,

Thank you so much for taking the time to meet with me this morning. I very much enjoyed learning more about Deloitte—especially with regard to what would be in store for me if I am hired for a co-op position this January. It sounds like an exciting time for the firm.

I am very interested in the position, and I believe that my bookkeeping experience, attention to detail, and strong academic performance in accounting would make me a strong contributor to your organization.

I look forward to hearing from you soon. Please feel free to contact me if you have any additional questions.

Thanks again,

Kaitlyn Scott

A pleasant and timely thank-you note can't turn a mediocre candidate into a great one. But it can make all the difference if the employer is struggling over the decision or believes that several candidates could do the job.

SPECIAL CONSIDERATIONS FOR MARKETING INTERVIEWS

Generally, most of the information that you have read so far can prove useful when interviewing for any job. As we also have alluded to, however, there are some critical differences between marketing interviews and those for jobs related to other majors.

Why are marketing interviews different? Frequently, marketing employers expect a more aggressive approach. Since sales and marketing are closely related, the marketing employer will closely examine your ability to sell yourself: If you can't persuasively sell yourself in an interview, they believe, how can you be expected to sell that company's products and services? You really have to prepare your "interview presentation" with this in mind. Here are some tips:

* *Generally, it is a good idea to bring notes to a marketing presentation.* As noted earlier, this would be a real no-no for many interviews, but many marketing employers believe that a lack of notes reveals a lack of preparation. Thinking on your feet is one thing, but "winging it" for an important presentation is another one entirely!

   A short section on how to prepare and use notes can be found on page 106.

* *Be aggressive.* There is no room for shyness in a marketing presentation.

Your self-presentation should be energetic, persuasive, and geared toward pushing the employer for a commitment.

- *Ask for the job.* Again, this is something you would not do with most non-marketing employers. But in a marketing interview, conclude your sales pitch with an attempt to close the deal. Your ability to close this deal may reflect your aggressiveness in closing in a selling situation on the job. If you want the job, ask for it. If you can do the job, tell them.

- *Seek closure.* At the end of the interview, ask the interviewer when they expect to make a decision regarding the position. Keeping this information in mind, it is generally recommended that you follow up with the employer after your interview. Be aware that there is a fine line between being persistent and being a nuisance. Some marketing students have failed to get jobs because they failed to follow up with interviewers. Others have been turned down because they called too often and alienated the interviewer.

Accordingly, remember these guidelines:

- *After making clear that you want and can do the job, ask when a hiring decision will be made.* Then plan your follow-up efforts accordingly.

- *If the interviewer tells you when you should call back to follow up, honor their wishes.* If they tell you not to call until next week, then do so.

- *Don't be a pest.* Job candidates have lost jobs because they kept calling until the employer got fed up with it. Limit follow-up calls to one or two per week.

- *Remember that the policy of following up after an interview often doesn't apply if you're interviewing for non-marketing jobs.* Some marketing students pursuing opportunities in finance, accounting, etc. have come across as pushy and obnoxious by repeatedly calling interviewers. If you are interested in opportunities outside of marketing, remember that the recommended follow-up procedure is to simply send a thank-you letter to the interviewer(s).

In any job interview, of course, you need to sell yourself persuasively. In a marketing interview, though, you can do so much more directly. But again, remember this warning for marketing majors who apply for non-marketing jobs: Be sure to tone down your presentation, or you may be perceived as pushy, arrogant, or obnoxious. As always: If in doubt, ask the coordinator who works with the employer about what approach would be most effective.

USING NOTES IN INTERVIEWS

Although there are some potential pitfalls to consider when using a notes page in an interview, I have come around to believing that almost any student could

106

benefit from using notes—if done properly. The single best thing about notes is that they are a safety net if you are concerned about "going blank" due to negative nervous energy. Your notes will not include word-for-word answers, but they will feature enough words to jog your memory if you blank out. And if you don't go blank at all, nothing says that you *have* to use them just because you prepared them.

Of course, there are some major blunders you could make by using notes. The biggest one would be to write out detailed answers to common questions and to bury your head in your notes page during the interview, reading answers to the interviewer. That definitely would come across as being *less* prepared for the interview, and it would cause you significant problems with eye contact, natural speech, and connecting interpersonally with the interviewer.

So let's walk through how to create and use a notes page. How should your notes look? One former colleague suggests having your notes on an 8 ½ x 11-inch piece of paper, which is divided into four quarters:

- One quarter features key strategic points you intend to make about why you are a good match for the job. For example: "Excellent team player." Beneath each point, write words to help you remember a specific example that shows that strength in action (Example: Banana Republic day after Thanksgiving).

- One quarter has key notes about the job or company that you learned by researching the position.

- One quarter has eight or ten questions that you might ask, so you can be sure that all of your questions won't be answered in the course of the interview.

- The last quarter is left blank, so you can use it to take notes on what the interviewer says during the interview.

Write your notes in large print or—if on computer—print them out in a large font, so that they are easy enough to read without having them leave your lap or a tabletop. Don't wave your notes around. Keeping them on one piece of paper will help you from fumbling around during the interview to find what you need. A portfolio can be handy when using notes: You can buy one which has a flap for your resume and references on one side, with a clipboard for your one page of notes on the other side. Hand over a fresh resume and references when sitting down, then fold over the portfolio so your notes page is right in front of you.

A sample of a good notes page can be found on page 109. For this example, let's assume that the candidate is pursuing a PC support job in a corporate environment.

Interviewing – A Student's Perspective
by Gabriel Glasscock

As expected, your first few interviews will be a little nerve-wracking. But that's to be expected. It's impossible to know exactly the type of interviewer you will have. So try not to prepare too much for a certain type of interviewer. Rather, invest your time into knowing as much about the job as possible. Find good potential conversation starters. I found it good to start a conversation on relevant job-related topics (where appropriate). This shows the employer that you are not just interested in the job but the field as a whole, and it also eases some of the tension. Look them in the eye, and use good body language.

Expect the unexpected. One time, I was at Snell Library at 8:30 p.m. in the middle of an intense group session. I got a call from a recruiter for an excellent position in Florida with a Big Five firm. We had been playing phone tag for a few weeks and she was to make a decision the next day on whom to hire: I had to interview over the phone outside the library in the freezing cold of December. I knew this would be my one and only 15-minute chance at this job, and I had to sell myself RIGHT THEN, without any preparation at all. Unlike most interviews, this was not pre-arranged: The interviewer wanted to see how well I could think on my feet.

The main thing is self-confidence. They were looking for a trainer in Java. When she asked the infamous "Why should we hire you?" question, I had to be creative. Although I had no prior experience with Java, I convinced her that my experience with Visual Basic would help greatly with learning Java, as both are object-oriented programming languages. Understanding transferable skills—and knowing how to use and express them—is an essential quality for an interviewee and also one of my favorite parts of this guidebook.

Any time an interviewer gives you the floor to ask questions, ASK QUESTIONS. Always have several prepared. I used the "Why do you like working here?" question with the Big Five recruiter, and she loved talking about that. Ask questions that show you have an interest in working there in your specific job and in being a part of their company.

Gabriel Glasscock was an MIS student at Northeastern University, Class of 2002.

Lastly, what if an employer questions you on why you are using notes? The biggest thing is to avoid being defensive about it. If you try to hide the fact that you have a notes page or come across as if you're doing something wrong, then it will be perceived negatively. Simply say that this interview is important to you and that it is important for you to feel prepared: You wanted to make sure that you got across everything that mattered in terms of why you are a good fit for the job.

SAMPLE NOTES PAGE

STRATEGY/STORIES	QUESTIONS
Point #1: Passion for technology Supporting Story: The Week I built new computer for myself at age 15 Point #2: Ability to learn quickly Supporting Story: Day I fixed dad's crashed computer despite no experience with Macs. Point #3: Customer-service skills Supporting Story: Night I handled eight tables at Applebee's when many called in sick. Point #4: Team player Supporting Story: My role in MIS301 group project on servers.	1. What could I do beween now and January 2 to hit the ground running in this job? 2. How specifically could I earn a great evaluation? 3. Chance of a position after graduation? 4. Any new technological initiatives planned for the coming year? 5. Opportunity to take on additional work?
RESEARCH POINTS	NOTES
--New investment product, Alpha Edge, just released --650 people in Boston office --Previous intern said ability to work Saturdays is a plus --Intern also said transition to MS-Vista is planned --Hiring five co-ops: hardware, software, customer service roles	

HANDLING JOB OFFERS

Right now, you might believe that the least of your problems is how to deal with job offers. Just *getting* a job offer may seem improbable for the time being. However, your job situation can change quickly, and you need to know how to handle job offers. Over the years, I can't believe how many times an employer has called to tell me that they offered a job to someone, only to have the response be a low-energy mumble, indicating only that the person would have to think about it. In extreme cases, I have seen an employer pull back an offer in this situation, figuring that they don't want to hire someone who only wants the job as a last resort.

So don't take this small step for granted! Here are some quick tips.

Be Proactive.
As soon as you get home after an interview, you should write down the pros and cons of accepting a job offer with that company. Without thinking about any other options that you may or may not have, is this a job that you would accept? In other words, start making up your mind BEFORE you get the offer.

ALWAYS Start Out by Thanking the Person for Making You the Job Offer.
If someone is not sure if they want to accept a co-op job, they often quickly state that they'll have to think about it or that they aren't sure. This is impolite, at best. You should be flattered to receive ANY job offer: whether or not you choose to accept it. You also may mention some aspect of the interview that you found enjoyable.

EXAMPLE: *"First, I'd like to thank you for offering me this position. I enjoyed getting the chance to hear what you had to say about working for [ORGANIZATION]."*

AFTER thanking them, gracefully tell them what your situation is.
If you definitely know whether or not you want the job, AND you're clear about the position and pay, this will be easy. The hard part is knowing what to say when you're really not sure what to do or if the job is good but not necessarily your top choice. I suggest handling this situation carefully: You don't want to treat any employer like a second or third choice, but you also don't want to give someone the impression that you probably will take a job when you don't feel that way. Also, you have to be sensitive to the employer's needs. It's not fair to keep an offer dangling for weeks while you make your mind; if you ultimately say "no," then the employer will miss out on other good students. Most coordinators at my university believe that you should make up your mind within THREE BUSINESS DAYS OF RECEIVING AN OFFER. In other words, if a company makes you an offer on Thursday, you will need to say yes or no by the following Tuesday.

Here is the simplest way to keep an offer on hold without making a potential employer feel like you're shopping around for something better:

EXAMPLE: *"I promised my co-op coordinator that I would discuss things with her (or him) before making a final decision, but I definitely will get back to you in no more than three business days, and sooner than that if possible."*

Here is another way to keep an offer on hold without alienating a potential employer:

EXAMPLE: *"Let me tell you what my situation is: I'm considering a few other employers right now, and I want to be fair to those other employers and give them a chance to make me an offer. But I WILL give you my decision within three business days, and sooner than that if possible. Is that okay?"*

An employer has every right to ask you to make a decision faster if possible. However, you also have the right to talk to your coordinator before saying yes or no. If you feel that an employer is trying to corner you into making an on-the-spot answer, let your coordinator know. This generally does not happen and should not happen.

Be clear on what you are being offered.
If the employer has not told you what your hourly pay rate would be, NOW is the time to ask or to confirm what you believe the pay rate to be. Do so before you accept the job to avoid any misunderstandings. Likewise, you should be clear on what hours and days they expect you to work, your start date and end date, and what your responsibilities will be, so everyone is clear about this.

Be careful about pay rate issues.
In many cases, the pay rate will not be open to negotiation: You should know whether or not it is before you bring up the matter. And even if there is some room for negotiation, there are some good reasons to avoid doing so: Pushing for more pay can send the message that you care more about the money than about the learning experience.

When there is some room for negotiation, you probably should not take matters into your own hands. Talk to your coordinator to find out if there is any latitude regarding pay. In some rare cases, a coordinator may be able to negotiate a higher pay rate. This takes skill and experience, however, as handling this the wrong way can backfire quickly.

The same is true in cases when you are offered less than the job description indicated or less than your coordinator told you to expect. If this occurs, thank the employer for the offer, tell him or her that you need to talk to your coordinator before reaching a final decision, and contact your coordinator immediately about the situation. Perhaps the situation has changed, or the company simply has made a mistake. Either way, get your coordinator's advice before proceeding on your own.

If you're not sure what to do, contact your co-op or internship coordinator immediately.
It's hard to predict every dilemma that you may face when getting a job offer. But if in doubt about what to do, seek the advice of your coordinator. In some cases, a coordinator may be able to get a faster response from a second employer if you need to make a decision about an offer from a first employer. If it's a matter of being indecisive, your coordinator probably will not tell you what to do: Instead, she or he may try to help you walk through the different pros and cons of the offer or offers. In the end, though, it's your decision.

Follow up with ALL employers once you have made a decision.
After you have made a timely decision, make sure that you communicate that decision to EACH employer that is waiting to hear as well as to each co-op coordinator that you have worked with to obtain the job.

ALWAYS be polite when turning down a job offer.
Usually, people feel awkward when they have to turn down a job. This is understandable: Employers may be very disappointed to hear about your decision. But usually they are understanding if you are professional and gracious about it (see the sidebar box).

Declining A Job Offer – A Co-op Professional's Perspective
by Rose Dimarco
A student who was in her third year interviewed for a job and she got it, but she felt she was more compatible with a very different experience, so she turned it down. But she sent a thank-you note—even though she rejected the offer. She praised that employer—she did not want to burn that bridge.

It turned out that she eventually interviewed again with that employer. It was the same interviewer, and she remembered—very positively—that rejection. So she ended up with a second chance at the job.

Rose Dimarco is a cooperative education faculty coordinator in
Physical Therapy at Northeastern University.

EXAMPLE: *"I just wanted to let you know that I decided to accept a job with another company. It was a tough decision: I just felt that this other job was a slightly better match for me in my current situation. But I do appreciate your offer, and I hope that you can find a good candidate for your position."*

Once you have accepted a job offer, you CANNOT go on other interviews or consider other job offers.
There are NO exceptions to this rule. Think of it this way: Accepting a job and continuing to interview is like getting engaged and continuing to go on dates. It doesn't make sense, and it's just plain wrong. Or, if you'd like to think of it another way, how about this: How would you feel if a company makes you an offer on November 1st, you accept the offer and stop pursuing other jobs; maybe

112

you even turn down another good job or two. A week or two later, the company calls you up and tells you "Sorry, but somebody else came along who turned out to be a better candidate." Universities would not work with an employer who behaved in this way, and, likewise, career professionals will not work with you if you treat an employer in a similar way.

That said, you absolutely SHOULD call back any employer who is interested in interviewing you, even after you have accepted a job. It's professional and courteous to follow up on any interview request, and it is not hard to get across the situation: "I wanted to thank you for your interest in interviewing me. However, I have accepted a position with another employer, so I am no longer available. But I do wish you luck in finding a good candidate, and I will keep you in mind for a future co-op job."

Once you have accepted the offer, make sure to see your co-op coordinator one last time.
Let your coordinator know as soon as you have a job lined up: That's why 24-hour voice mail exists. Your coordinator generally will ask you to come in to complete an agreement form and to go over success factors for your position.

DRUG TESTING

It's important to know that some employers make offers that are contingent upon the candidate's ability to pass a drug test successfully. Though many employers do not require this, drug testing is on the rise. Two of my large and prominent co-op employers—Procter & Gamble and General Electric—require drug testing for all new hires. Eventually you're likely to encounter this issue.

Why do companies drug test? Generally, it's not a moral issue. People with substance abuse problems can be costly to organizations in terms of absenteeism, tardiness, and turnover. Companies don't want invest time, money, and energy developing a co-op or new employee who may not prove to be a productive worker.

If you do use illegal drugs—or if you use any prescription drugs *without* having a prescription—you may have time to change your behaviors. Many companies now use hair tests to test for drug use—these tests are harder to fool than urine tests. These tests generally will reveal if you have regularly used drugs over the last three or four months. If you're a fall semester sophomore and stop using drugs now, you likely will be able to pass a drug test for a summer/fall job. If you don't want to limit your opportunities, you should consider this choice carefully.

In some fields, drug testing is not just a part of the hiring process—it's an ongoing part of being a professional employee. See the sidebar box on the following page: It's a good example of a situation in which a couple of good

113

students were wise enough to recognize that they'd better not interview for a position for this reason. These situations should lead you think about if you need to make a lifestyle choice—unless using drugs illegally is more important to you than being eligible for as many great opportunities as possible.

Just a few weeks before I revised this section, I had a student get an offer from one of my very best positions—a job that offered an incredible learning experience as well as about $19/hour plus one week of paid vacation. The student failed the drug test because he had smoked marijuana within the last several months. He asked me if the company would let him retake the test in a few weeks—he really wanted the job. Of course, the drug test was a one-shot deal, and he missed out on the opportunity of a lifetime with that employer.

> **Drug Testing – A Co-op Professional's Perspective**
> *by Bob Tillman*
> I'm spending a lot more time on drug testing now. Almost all of my field jobs now require random drug testing, and it doesn't happen when you first start, but it happens within a period of time at all of my municipalities. You can get pulled out for testing at any time because you're around heavy equipment. I had two of my best students come in and see me to tell me that they didn't want to interview at a place. One of them said to me, "Yeah, I have a lot of history in my hair."
> *Bob Tillman is a cooperative education faculty coordinator*
> *in Civil Engineering at Northeastern University.*

FINAL THOUGHTS ON INTERVIEWING

Remember, you can't control many aspects of interviewing. You can worry all you want about the quality of the interviewer or the caliber of the candidates who are competing for the job, but that won't change anything. Your goal should be to walk out of the interview feeling good because you did terrific research, employed a smart and thought-out strategy, answered questions honestly and enthusiastically, and asked provocative questions to wrap up the interview.

It's a terrific feeling to come out of an interview knowing you gave it your all. If, after that, another candidate gets the job because of superior experience, you really can't have any regrets—especially because your effort will pay off for you down the road, probably sooner rather than later.

We had a grad student working in co-op a few years ago who applied for a position as a co-op coordinator. In terms of experience, she was ninth out of the nine among the interviewees. This didn't faze her: She interviewed co-op employers, academic faculty, and students, formulated a great strategy, and wowed the five-person committee. Afterwards, she came down and told me, "That was great. Whatever happens, I did exactly what I set out to do."

Did she get the job? Not quite—she was runner-up to someone with more job experience. But within a month another position opened up in the department, and committee members *urged* her to apply and *recommended* her to the chairman of that committee. She used the same approach to ready herself for that interview and completely blew the competition off the map to get the job.

One great fact is that it's really amazing how little the average person knows about interviewing. Even when we hire co-op faculty at Northeastern, I have often been amazed at how poor some of the interviewees have been. They ask questions that make it obvious that they didn't do one iota of research, and they clearly haven't begun to think strategically about why they would be good for the job and how they would approach the position. And this is for a job in which you must be able to teach students how to interview! In any event, if you can really learn and apply the concepts in this chapter, you'll be way ahead of most interviewees twice your age.

Lastly, give some serious consideration to doing a practice interview. At the very least, stop and think about what interview questions you hate answering, then see if you can practice them with your coordinator. Reviewing your strategy for a specific interview is something that most coordinators can do if a practice interview is not possible. The worst thing you can do is to assume that you have nothing left to learn about interviewing.

CHAPTER 3 REVIEW QUESTIONS

1. If you were researching in preparation for an interview, what are two ways in which you can go beyond the job description to learn more about the job and the organization?

2. Which statement most appropriately captures how to approach an interview?

   A. Be able to summarize your strengths as an individual.
   B. More than anything, be sure to tell the interviewer what he or she hopes to hear.
   C. Try to just relax and be yourself—don't get too worked up about it.
   D. Try to make connections between your background and the job description.
   E. Be sure to give the interviewer plenty of personal background about yourself.

3. Think about the kind of job that you hope to get through your next search: For that job, how you would answer a question about your weaknesses?

4. What does the chapter describe as the most difficult type of interviewer for most interviewees?

   A. The Nonstop Talker
   B. The Silent But Deadly Interviewer
   C. The Olympic Judge
   D. The Big-Picture Person
   E. The Interrogator

5. Write a brief but effective thank-you note that would be appropriate to send to an interviewer as a follow-up step.

6. Name at least two great questions to ask at the end of any job interview.

CHAPTER FOUR
Keys To On-The-Job Success

By the time you have prepared your resume, gone on numerous interviews, and finally accepted a job offer from an employer, you may feel like it's time to kick back and relax and let the money come in from your job. However, nothing could be further from the truth: Accepting a job offer doesn't mean you've reached the end of all your hard work. All it means is that you've reached the end of the beginning.

When you have accepted a job, you need to start thinking about living up to your interview... and then some. In other words, anyone can walk into an interview and state that they are punctual, conscientious, hard-working, willing to learn, and happy to help out with some of the less glamorous tasks associated with a job. But it's very different to actually go out and live up to these statements all day, every day, for three months, six months, or longer.

My goal in this chapter is to point out why your performance matters in your first professional job, and to help you get the best possible evaluation from your co-op employer or internship supervisor when it's time to go back to school. Some of the points we make here may seem like common sense, but we have learned that sense can be rather uncommon when it comes to some behaviors in the workplace. If you follow the guidelines in this chapter, you can prevent most co-op problems before they happen... which is infinitely easier than trying to fix something after it breaks.

WHY YOUR PERFORMANCE MATTERS

The best interns and co-op students realize that there is a great deal at stake when you're working in a job. An "outstanding" or "very good" evaluation from an employer means that:

- *You are a person of integrity who remembers your interview and delivers what you said you could deliver.* You come off as a hypocrite if you say that you are punctual, for example, and you start showing up late to work. Right away, the employer might start wondering what *else* might not be exactly true in what you said in your interview.

- *You are intelligent enough to realize that today's supervisor is tomorrow's reference.* Think about interviewing for a future job: It's nice to say "I'm an excellent worker with a great attitude," but it's highly effective and powerful to be able to say "I'm an excellent worker with a great attitude, and I would encourage you to contact my previous employer if you'd like to confirm this." Some employers may even call your previous employer without telling you: You don't want bad performance to come back and haunt you when seeking future employment.

- *If you are asked about a previous job in an interview, you want to be able to say in all honesty that you did a great job.* Interviewers can often tell how successful you were in a previous job by how you describe it. A common interview question is "If I were to ask your previous supervisor about what kind of employee you were, what would he or she say?" You have to be honest in these situations, and you want to be able to mention many positives.

- *You can feel good about yourself.* It's a lot more fun to do things well than to do things poorly. If you can complete your job with a sense of pride and accomplishment, you will have more confidence and will be better prepared for challenging jobs in the future.

- *You'll learn more and get better work to do.* The harder you work—the more you go "above and beyond" the basic requirements of the job, the more likely you are to learn more and gain valuable exposure to more sophisticated aspects of your field. You'll also show your employer that you're capable of handling bigger and better challenges.

The last point merits some more consideration. I always tell my students that there is often a domino effect while on co-op. When you first start work, you may be given low-level work to do. This is rarely because supervisors believe that you're an idiot until you prove otherwise, so don't look at it that way. Rather, employers know that it's difficult to be a new employee, so they want to make sure that you feel comfortable in the early going by giving you work that will be relatively easy.

What happens next? That depends! If you get those simple tasks done efficiently, effectively, and with a positive attitude, eventually this tends to get noticed... and your manager may start giving you better work to do, tasks that weren't even on your job description.

Of course, this domino effect works the other way occasionally. A few years ago, I visited two co-op students at work. When I met with them, they were irritated: "This is a terrible job," they said. "There's nothing to do; they just give us data entry work that anyone could do. This should not be a co-op job."

This surprised me. Many students had worked for this employer before, and the verdict had been that it was a good job. Yes, there was some downtime, but you were allowed to use that time to teach yourself computer skills using resources that the supervisor made available to you. Of course, some good jobs do turn bad, so I approached the supervisor with an open mind. "How's it going with the co-ops?" I asked. He looked at me and shook his head. "I wish we could get these two to *do* something!"

At first glance, this seemed as if it would be an easy problem to solve: Here we had two bored co-ops with nothing to do and a manager who was itching to get them to work. Naturally, it wasn't that easy. It turned out that these two co-ops were *insulted* by the low-level tasks that they initially were given. How did they respond? They did the work slowly and poorly, so the manager assumed that they weren't able or willing to handle anything more challenging. He continued to give them grunt work, and their performance never improved.

Admittedly, maintaining a strong work ethic and an excellent attitude can be challenging in some work environments. When you go on co-op, you're testing out a field as a possible career. As such, you may learn that you don't want to be an accountant or a computer programmer. That's fine, but bear in mind the following: A mediocre co-op can do a great job in a job that she or he loves, but a great co-op continues to do a great job *even after realizing that he or she is working in the wrong field.*

Sometimes you probably will be asked to do work that is less fun, less interesting, and less educational than you had hoped. In fact, one unpleasant fact you have to accept is that almost *any* job you will ever have may require you to do some things that you don't enjoy. But if you can take on *all* work assignments with a pleasant and cooperative attitude, your employer will remember this and often will reward you with better assignments as well as an excellent evaluation.

I have seen first-time co-ops take what seemed to be an entry-level job, only to have them end up making presentations to senior management by the end of their work term! You never know what doors might open to you if you do a terrific job on whatever you're asked to do.

MAKING THE TRANSITION FROM STUDENT TO EMPLOYEE

Don't underestimate the fact that you're undergoing a significant transition when you go from being a full-time student to being a full-time employee. If you're in a parallel program like the new one at DePaul University—working as a co-op while simultaneously attending classes—you will be continually making the transition from your role as student to your role as employee. In either type of format, it's useful to give some thought to these role changes.

As indicated in the sidebar box below, when you're a student, you're a customer of your college or university. You have a right to expect some level of customer service. You also may believe that you have every right to be late to class: After all, it's your money. Likewise, the student lifestyle can be quite different for some individuals. I'm sure that some of my students stay up till 2 or 3 a.m. more often than not, waking up at the last minute to make a mad dash to their 8 a.m. class or maybe sleeping through it.

From Student To Employee – A Co-op Professional's Perspective
by Bob Tillman

When you're a student, you pay the university for services in your role as a student. What are you paying for, and what do you expect to get out of it? How do you know that you're getting what you're paying for? What are the other amenities that you're paying for? It's a good exercise to think about that. Then I tell them that when you go out on co-op, *that role will exactly reverse itself.* You're being paid for your services now. So let's talk about some of the behaviors that don't work from your perspective as a student: Why do you think they would work as an employee as a part of an engineering team?

Students tend to connect with that pretty well. I want you to shift that role and almost forget that you're a student because it really will bring you down. For example, why do you have to show up on time? Well, if you don't, other work is not getting done; clients aren't getting billed. Let's talk about clients getting the bill, and what that means, as well as all the other people that fit into an engineering environment.

Bob Tillman is a cooperative education faculty coordinator in Civil Engineering at Northeastern University.

Your role becomes more complicated when you're a co-op. Yes, you're still a student and a customer of the university, but that role is trumped by your most important role: You are an employee and a service provider to your employer. This should be obvious when you're drawing a paycheck, but it's also the attitude that you need to take into an unpaid internship or co-op.

Think about the implications of the fact that your supervisor is your customer. It means that you need to figure out what you must do to be sure that you're not only showing up but that you're arriving rested, alert, and ready to put in a full day's work of good quality.

Another way to think of the transition is an analogy to running: The classroom is more of a sprint, while a co-op job is more of a marathon. In the classroom, you may be able to be very successful with periodic bursts of effort at the right time. On co-op, the individuals who do best are those who are able to sustain a consistent effort for several hours, weeks, and months.

Last year I had a student with a 4.0 GPA who was fired from her job, and I have seen many other top academic performers fail. Likewise, we have had many co-op superstars whose GPAs were in the 2.0 to 2.4 range. Once you get your co-op job or internship, you have a clean slate... but you also will have to prove yourself day in and day out. Remembering that the employer is your customer and acting accordingly should help you make this transition effectively.

THE FIRST DAY OF WORK

On your first day of work, you'll probably be excited, nervous, and eager to show that you can be a productive employee. This is perfectly normal. However, bear in mind that few workers—whether co-op or otherwise—can be immediate heroes. Be patient. If you're introduced to people, do your best to come across as positive and agreeable. You're going to want to have good relationships with many people besides your supervisor, and you can cultivate those relationships by making an effort to be friendly. This may include going out to lunch with people even if you'd rather be working, and it definitely includes saying "Good Morning" and "Good Night" at the start and end of the day.

You also may have an orientation or training session to attend. Even though you might be dying to dive into the job itself, take advantage of these sessions. They can help you get acclimated and learn what it may take to be successful in that environment. You'll have plenty of time to work before you know it.

UNCOMMON SENSE: WHAT IS AND ISN'T ACCEPTABLE IN THE WORKPLACE

As stated earlier, there are many aspects of work life that internship and co-op coordinators would *like* to believe are common sense: Things that everyone should know without being told. However, we have found that this is not always the case. As a result, here are some critical recommendations regarding how to avoid problems in the workplace. Some may appear obvious; others are less so. HOWEVER, no one should have to *tell* you these things once you have started your job. It is your responsibility to know these things ahead of time!

1. *You must be on time to work.*
After you have accepted your offer, be very clear about what time you are expected at work. Then make sure you are *always* there at least 15 minutes before that time.

When you become a co-op, intern, or full-time employee, you undergo a tremendous role reversal (see the following sidebar box). As a student, some people may be used to showing up late to classes. This is a bad habit, but you could argue that you're the customer: You have the right to not show up on time for classes. However, when an employer is paying *you* to arrive at a specific time and to work a specific number of hours, you do *not* have that right. Unless an employer specifically tells you that you can come in when you want to, you have to live by that employer's rules. For example, you can't just decide that you'll come in 30 minutes late and then eat your lunch at your desk instead of taking a 30-minute break at noontime.

Another point to remember is that too many interns and co-op students fail to leave any extra time in the morning to allow for possible traffic, parking problems, car trouble, or whatever. If it takes you 25 minutes to get to work, assuming that you catch every train or traffic light just right, then you probably should allow for at least 45 minutes to get to work. If you have to use this kind of excuse more than once over a six-month job, you need to change your habits: These excuses get old very quickly.

Co-op Job Success – A Student's Perspective
by Ted Schneider

⬧ Meet as many people in your workplace as you can. And I do not mean this in only the superficial, "networking" type of way. If your co-workers are willing, do social things with them outside of work. I found that working closely with good friends on co-op was not at all distracting. I actually think that I performed much better when I worked for people who I liked and respected.

⬧ An old one but still so true: Do not ever go to work late if you can help it. I knew people on co-op who were very good at what they did, but would fail to be promoted due to their tardiness. I also find that managers are much more flexible about giving time off if you are on time in the morning.

⬧ Wear the right clothes. Wearing questionable or even semi-questionable attire makes you look like a fool. Enough said.

⬧ Make sure to find a balance between asking for too much help and asking for too little. It's a difficult skill to master - I certainly haven't yet.

Ted Schneider was an Accounting/MIS student at Northeastern University, Class of 2002.

Lastly, remember one critical point: *Just because your co-workers arrive late, don't automatically assume that it's okay for you to do the same.* I recall one memorable student who had been given a warning by his employer because of repeated tardiness. His boss also told me that he sometimes came in by 9 but other times it was more like 10. When I talked to the co-op student about it, he thought that he was being unfairly singled out: "I see quite a few full-time people coming in at 10 or 10:30 every day!"

When I looked into this, it turned out that my student was missing a few key facts: For one, he didn't know that these people were software developers. They had an understanding with management that they could come in late because they often stayed until 8:00 or 9:00 p.m. at night, well after my student left by

5:30! Secondly, the student had misinterpreted something his manager had told him when he was hired. When she said that it was possible to have a "flexible schedule," she meant that you could work from 7:30 to 4:30 with an hour for lunch, from 9 to 6 with an hour for lunch, etc. She did NOT mean that you could change your schedule every day, or that you could start your day later than 9:30. Lastly, I had to tell the student that sometimes policies are not always fair. Sure, the manager could have done a better job upfront about communicating the "unwritten rules" of that workplace, but she didn't. That simply means that the student needed to step up and be sure that his assumptions were correct.

2. If being late or absent is absolutely unavoidable, give your employer as much advance notice as possible.

There may be rare situations in which being late or absent is absolutely unavoidable. These primarily include car accidents, serious illnesses, or deaths in your family. These things can't be avoided at times. However, you need to call your employer *before* the official workday begins. That may mean leaving a voice mail or answering machine message early in the morning before you show up: not in the late morning or afternoon, when everyone has already been wondering where you are for several hours. If you have a flat tire on the way to work, for example, you need to find the nearest possible phone so you can call in and give your estimated time of arrival. Always carry your supervisor's phone number in your wallet just in case something like this happens.

Unless you are completely incapacitated through illness or injury, YOU should be the one to call in: not your roommate, your mother, your roommate's boyfriend's sister's cousin or anyone else. And if you don't say how long you will need to be out, and you remain sick or otherwise unavailable the next day, you need to call your supervisor *again*.

3. Keep personal phone calls to an absolute minimum.

Working in an office with your own phone and phone number does not give you the right to have extended conversations with friends, family, and significant others throughout the workday. Beyond using your phone for business, you should generally use your phone only if you need to contact your co-op/ internship coordinator, your physician, or to contact a family member in the event of an emergency.

One good way to avoid temptation is to not give your work number out to anyone besides your parents, your spouse or partner (if applicable), and your co-op coordinator. If you do need to make a five-minute phone call once or twice a week to arrange for plans after work, that probably would be acceptable in most workplaces. But generally you should avoid it whenever possible.

Over the last several years, cellphones have become incredibly common. As you have undoubtedly noticed, many people don't hesitate to use their cellphones in inappropriate places, including classrooms and—most incredibly in my opinion—restrooms. When you are working in a co-op job, your friends and family obviously will already know your cellphone number, and some people probably won't hesitate to call you during the workday. It's important to remember that making personal phone calls on your cellphone is really just as bad as making such calls through your company line. So unless you specifically need to use your cellphone for job-related purposes—which is not uncommon with PC support jobs, for example—you generally should turn off your cellphone before you walk in the door at work and keep it off until the end of the day. At most, you might check your messages during your lunch break.

Also, watch what you say over any type of phone while at work—even during your lunch break. Employers have accidentally overheard co-op students say the darndest things (e.g., "personal" comments from boyfriend to girlfriend or vice-versa) when the student/caller thinks no one is listening.

4. *Use your computer for work-related activities only.*

Like a telephone, a computer on your desk can be highly tempting to some interns, co-ops, and full-time employees. Most computers have at least some games (such as Minesweeper and Solitaire) on Windows, and more and more computers have Internet access, which can be an irresistible on-line temptation to some—especially those with e-mails accounts through AOL, Yahoo or Hotmail. More recently, AOL Instant Messenger (IM) and similar messaging systems are becoming widely available—many students are logged on to IM almost around the clock when they are in classes, so it's a habit that can be hard to break when you're starting a job. However, it's very important to do so—if you want to juggle your homework with e-mail and IM for hours on end, that's up to you. But when you're role has changed from student to employee, you're generally being paid to be at work, you shouldn't be using personal e-mail or IM on company time. You aren't being paid to chat with friends, after all. Even in an unpaid internship, this sends the wrong message to your co-workers and supervisor.

Unless your supervisor tells you that it's okay for you to practice exploring the Internet or World Wide Web as part of your job, you should avoid using it. If you really want the opportunity to play around on the Web, you could ask your supervisor if it would be okay to come in early or stay late in order to navigate the Internet or send e-mails with a clear conscience.

Several of our students were fired from co-op jobs a few summers ago, primarily because of using the Internet frequently and spending a great deal of time writing e-mails or Instant Messages to friends during the work day. In late 2006, we had our first—but probably not last—students fired for managing their fantasy football teams on their work computers. Try explaining that to a future employer. After all, it's relatively easy for a computer network administrator to be able to see what applications anyone on the system has open, and it is completely legal and easy for organizations to monitor the e-mails that their employees send and receive to determine whether they are appropriate. Entertaining yourself on the computer during work hours certainly doesn't say very much about your initiative, drive, and judgment. Don't take chances—surf the 'net and use AOL IM at home or on campus!

Even if you have a Blackberry or some other Personal Digital Assistant (PDA), don't think of that as a way to "get around" the advisories above. Refrain from using any technological activity that is not work-related. Even if no one sees you doing it, I guarantee that your decreased level of productivity will be noticed eventually if you're unable to curb your technology addiction at work.

I will discuss the specifics of professional e-mail and IM etiquette later in this chapter.

Although this behavior is not excusable, these problems are most likely to arise when there is not enough work to do in a given job. Therefore, we will address that next.

5. If you don't have enough work to keep you busy, talk to your supervisor as soon as possible.

If your supervisor needs to come around and see you playing a game, staring at the ceiling, or talking on the phone in order to find out that you don't have enough work, you already have made a significant mistake. If you anticipate running out of work, try to give your supervisor as much notice as possible. It's perfectly fine to ask your supervisor what you should do if you run out of work: Especially if your supervisor isn't always readily available. Asking for more work when necessary shows that you are mature, that you take initiative, and that you have a good work ethic. All of these things reflect positively on you as an employee. Basically, *learn* from your work environment. Something ALWAYS needs to be done. Be proactive. Say something like, "I've finished 'X'; should I move onto 'Y'?" Your supervisor may be too busy to find a project for you and may be appreciative if you offer suggestions.

One challenge with such a conversation is to make sure that you don't come across as a whiner. Even if you're bored because of a lack of work, it probably won't be productive to go in to your supervisor and say, "I'm bored; I have nothing to do." Try to frame it positively by emphasizing your ability and willingness to take on more challenges on top of your current responsibilities.

As noted earlier, many first-time professionals have begun a job with relatively low-level responsibilities but managed to end up with much more demanding jobs—simply by getting the easy stuff done quickly and correctly and then enthusiastically requesting more work to do. Show that you're hungry for a challenge.

6. If you consistently have MORE work than you can do and do well, you should discuss this with your supervisor.

Most good jobs will keep you very busy all day and all week. But if you find that you are working so hard that it is affecting the quality of your work, your health, and your enthusiasm for the job, you need to discuss this with your supervisor *before* it becomes a major problem.

Obviously, the best way to deal with this problem is to avoid these situations in the first place by using your interview to ask the appropriate questions about workload and expectations. But you can't always anticipate this problem. If talking to your supervisor doesn't improve the situation—or if you're unsure about whether you really are being asked to do more than what could be considered reasonable—call your co-op coordinator and get his or her input. Together, you can determine the best course of action.

7. If you're confused or unsure about how to do one of your assigned tasks, say so. When you are assigned a task or given specific instructions, take careful notes so you won't have to request the same information again.

The worst thing you can do if you're unsure about how to do a task is to just forge ahead and hope for the best. Usually, people are reluctant to ask questions because they are afraid of appearing stupid or ignorant. But remember: appearing ignorant is MUCH better than demonstrating your ignorance by doing your job poorly. Making mistakes on the job can be very costly to a company. Good employers expect you to ask for help when you need it to avoid these costly mistakes. Don't be afraid to ask a supervisor or co-worker to repeat or clarify instructions if you didn't understand the first time.

From Student To Employee – A Co-op Professional's Perspective
by Bob Tillman

I tell students that if you only learn two things when you go out on your first co-op, it's going to be a huge success: If you learn when to ask a question when you should, and when to keep your mouth shut when you should, you're really light years ahead. When you figure out, "This is a problem that I ought to be able to solve on my own" and know "What are the resources that are going to help me do it?" you're way ahead.

Another thing you learn out there is that there's a whole language out there that you haven't been exposed to, and you have to learn it. And the last thing is, "What are the other learning opportunities that are going on around you that aren't directly sitting on your desk?"

In engineering, if you can't do the routine work—checking calculations, adding numbers, checking drawings—you're never going to get more advanced work.

Bob Tillman is a cooperative education faculty coordinator
in Civil Engineering at Northeastern University.

A corresponding point relates to what you do with information or instructions when given to you. A smart employee shows up on the first day of work with a calendar for marking down due dates, deadlines, and meetings. A smart employee also brings a notebook and some writing materials so he or she can jot down specific instructions, guidelines, job requirements, computer procedures, and anything else you need to know. Nothing frustrates an employer more than a student who claims that he or she doesn't need to write things down, and then winds up making mistakes or sheepishly asking for the same information some time in the future.

8. *Always keep your desk and/or work area reasonably neat and well organized.*
This means keeping food and drink to a minimum in your work area. Keeping some mints or granola bars in your desk and a coffee cup on your desk is okay, but leaving food wrappers or food in plain sight at any time other than lunch is something to avoid.

Co-op Job Success – A Student's Perspective
by Mark Moccia
In order to get the most out of your job, you must bring a strong work ethic to the table. Once your employer sees you are willing to work hard, they will be impressed. Then, after you have shown the ability to work hard, you can polish your "working smart" skills: By this I mean getting things done quickly AND more efficiently for the company/department.

It is also important to learn the preferences/personality of your boss immediately. It is important to know whether your boss is the type that wants assignments done in five minutes or 30 minutes. A question I still ask to this day is, "When do you want this done by?" This avoids any confusion as to when you are supposed to finish an assignment and also avoids potential conflicts.

Speaking of conflicts, if you encounter one at work then it is important to alert your immediate supervisor. While fellow co-op students might lend an ear to your problems, they might not always have the best solution because they are just as inexperienced as you. If the conflict is with your supervisor, bring it to the attention of your co-op advisor quickly. I have heard stories of co-op students who feel invincible because they are only on assignment for three or six months and imagine that the company cannot fire them because it would look bad for the company. This could not be further from the truth; if you have direct conflicts with your supervisor or are not performing to your potential, you can be fired just as easily as a full-time employee. I encourage co-op students to use their best judgment in these situations and avoid "blow-ups" at all costs. If you can do this, work hard, and bring a positive contribution to your time on the job, a good reference and evaluation will follow.
Mark Moccia was an Accounting/MIS student at Northeastern University, Class of 2002.

Also try to keep items on your desk well organized. If asked to produce some paperwork, you shouldn't have to do a scavenger hunt in your desk or office to find it. If you're unsure about ways to organize your work materials efficiently, ask your co-workers for advice.

> **Co-op Job Success – An Employer's Perspective**
> *by Steve Sim*
>
> There are two things to keep in mind when coming for an internship/co-op at Microsoft:
>
> 1. *Know your limitations.* This is a fact at MS. There will always be someone who knows more about business, technology, marketing; etc. than you here (especially technology). Knowing your limitations also makes you aware of how these people can help in your development.
>
> 2. *Don't be afraid to fail.* You're here to learn about how we do things. MS is a place where we do things, if anything, for the right to learn how to do that thing better. You'll always be challenged to do something right the first time, and possibly, you do it right the first time. Or did you? Have you tried <u>everything</u> possible? Who's to know that better than you?
>
> *Steve Sim is a Technical Recruiter at the Microsoft Corporation.*

9. Always use good judgment regarding attire and hygiene in the workplace.

You need to convey a professional image every single day that you are employed. The standards may differ from one workplace to another: Some places allow "business casual" attire, for example. But be careful in how you interpret dress codes. Casual attire generally still means that you should wear a collared shirt and nice pants: not blue jeans or shorts. Sometimes you can get away with dressy black sneakers, but not always white sneakers. Women should avoid low-cut blouses, halter tops and tank tops. Open-toed shoes or sandals are a bad idea for men and may or may not be okay for women, depending on the particular office. You should always wear clothing that is clean, wrinkle-free, and without any holes in it. For men in casual environments, you should still shave each day. It's not a bad idea to look at how your co-workers dress, but you want to err on the conservative side—don't assume it's okay to dress a certain way just because one or two co-workers choose to wear extremely informal attire at work!

Another point here: You may think nothing of wearing an eyebrow ring or a nose ring or a tongue stud, but an employer may find these items to be unprofessional. Save your unusual jewelry for after-hours and weekends.

10. Don't misunderstand the meaning of the words "casual work environment."

As stated above, you may be able to wear more comfortable and informal clothing in some work settings. But don't think that "a casual work environment" means that *everything* is casual. Just because the company president wears jeans and jokes around with you when he or she visits your desk or cubicle, it doesn't mean that it's okay for *you* to pop into his office and joke around with him or her. Likewise, a casual work setting is not a place where work is done in a casual, laid-back manner. In fact, there are many very intense organizations that allow casual attire. Remember, casual work environments are just like all other jobs in one important way: You still can get a poor evaluation or get fired by not living up to your interview and by not living up to the company's expectations and standards.

Another point about casual environments: It is *never* acceptable to wear headphones in any workplace unless your boss specifically *suggests* it. This is true regardless even if you are working on your own, doing boring, monotonous work. Wearing headphones on a job sends a clear message that you're not really paying attention to what you're doing and that you don't care if you look unprofessional. Even if co-workers wear headphones, don't make the same mistake.

11. When asked to do something that you don't enjoy, do so without complaining or sulking.

I visited one employer who was Director of MIS for a prestigious organization in Cambridge. He mentioned that a co-op student from another university (not Northeastern, thankfully) complained when he was told to do a fairly monotonous and time-consuming task with the computer system. The employer told me, "The thing that I asked him to do is something that *I* have to do pretty often, and I'm the Director of the whole department! And he tells me that *he* shouldn't have to do it?"

There's a valuable lesson here: Sometimes students are quick to assume that they are given boring tasks to do because they are "only students." This can be an erroneous assumption at times. Sometimes, you may be asked to do something simply because it has to get done, and it doesn't matter who does it. Employers appreciate *any* employee who does routine, unglamorous, necessary tasks without complaining, whining, or sulking.

If an employer asks you if you enjoy doing a certain task, be honest but be pleasant about it. If you don't like doing a given task, you might say, "Well I don't mind doing it, but it's not my favorite part of the job..." Be ready to point out some other tasks that you would be excited about doing.

12. Go above and beyond your basic duties.

One reason some students fail to get great job evaluations is because they basically show up at 9, do their job in a competent, acceptable way, and go home as soon as possible. If you want to get a very good evaluation, you need to go beyond this. You need to be willing to put in extra hours if necessary. You need to show some pride and excitement in what you do: If you're asked to do something, give them even more than they expect in terms of effort, ideas, and attitude. Always think about ways in which you could do your job more efficiently, whether it involves helping your supervisor, your co-workers, or just the tasks you do on your own. The following sidebar box is a great example of this phenomenon.

> **Above and Beyond – A Co-op Professional's Perspective**
> *by Ronnie Porter*
> We had this co-op job that on paper didn't look very exciting. It was doing some computer work for a company that manufactured an instrument that allowed anaesthesiologists to know if a patient undergoing surgery was getting to a level of wakefulness. So there was a lot of data entry—looking at the data, reviewing the data, etc.
> What this person ended up doing was taking this information and learning a tremendous amount about what kinds of drugs were used on what kinds of patients for what kinds of surgeries. He really came to understand the sleep patterns and how all that interrelated. He actually had so many conversations with his co-workers that he got to go to an open-heart surgery and witness an eight-hour surgery along with the person who was teaching the anaesthesiologist how to use this device. He came back and said, "You need to rewrite this job description! It's the most exciting position, and there are so many things you can learn in this job. I didn't really realize that, looking on the surface."
> *Ronnie Porter is a cooperative education faculty coordinator in Biology at Northeastern University.*

13. Understand what an employer's expectations are regarding time off from work.

Before you begin any job, you should make sure you have total clarity regarding your start date and end date as well as time off from work. In many cases, co-ops and interns—or full-time hires for their first six months on the job—have NO vacation time coming to them! So don't assume that it's going to be fine to take a Spring Break if it falls in the middle of your work term; don't imagine that there will be no problem if you want to take a week off in the middle of the summer.

What days do you get to take off? Any days that are official holidays for your employer (i.e., Memorial Day, Labor Day). Technically, that's all that an employer is required to allow you to take. But can there be exceptions to this? Sometimes, yes, but you shouldn't count on it. For example, a student who works in a position that is far away from his or her home may *ask* his or her employer if it would be okay to conclude a work assignment prior to Christmas rather than going home and coming back for three or four days before the assignment technically ends. The employer may or may not grant this request.

What can you do to improve your chances of having a request for unpaid time off granted? Do the following:

- *Keep such requests to an absolute minimum.* If you know you're going to ask for time off after Christmas, for example, don't press your luck by looking for additional time off earlier in the work period.

- *Only ask if you have an excellent reason for requesting time off.* Besides Christmas and other religious holidays, it may be reasonable to ask for a

130

day off to attend an out-of-state wedding, for example. Or if you've been working 12 hours a day for a month during tax season in an accounting job, it may be reasonable to ask for a day off when things slow down once again. Generally, though, you don't want to ask unless it's an absolute necessity. You never know when you might *really* need the time off.

- *Do such an outstanding job during the work period that your employer will be willing to give you time off.* An outstanding worker definitely has a much better chance of having requests for time off granted when necessary. In some cases, an employer even raises the subject to offer a reward to an extremely productive worker.

Look at it this way: If a worker has a bad attitude, is late or absent frequently, does mediocre work, and constantly needs to be supervised, an employer is bound to look at a request for time off as the final insult.

14. Keep your internship or co-op coordinator informed about any major problems, dilemmas, or unpleasant situations that arise.

The majority of students will not have any major problems arise during their work experiences. However, there is always the possibility that you might face problems that are beyond what we expect you to handle without our help. Please call your coordinator as soon as possible if you are:

- the victim of sexual harassment or other abusive behavior from your co-workers or supervisor.

- laid off from your job, regardless of the cause (i.e., budget cuts, buyouts).

- given a warning about being fired.

- fired.

- being paid less than promised.

- having problems with your supervisor that are difficult to discuss.

Additionally, call your coordinator if you have brought up any of the following problems with your supervisor, and the conversation has not produced a change:

- You are given far too much or too little work to do on a regular basis.

- Your job is not what you were led to believe it would be, and you are not having a good learning experience.

- You are stressed out due to the work, your co-workers, or your customers.

Sometimes a problem can be easily fixed if addressed quickly, while it can become a huge issue if ignored. When in doubt about the seriousness of a problem, contact your coordinator.

Co-op Job Success – A Student's Perspective
by Gabriel Glasscock

Don't sit back and say to yourself "I'm just an intern." This is your job, and you have the ability to make the most of it. Some jobs will have downtime; it's just a fact. You can spend that time surfing www.espn.com, and www.boston.com, or you can go to your boss and say "Hey, I have some downtime, is there anything I can do?" In one such situation, I went to my boss, and she ended up shipping me off to a very expensive class on Web development in which I learned an immense amount, and thus had more responsibility at work.

If there is a problem at the job, don't be afraid to talk to your manager. If you're not doing anything stated on your job description, don't go silently. Remember: it's up to you to take charge. Your advisor or boss can't do anything unless they know about it.

Gabriel Glasscock was an MIS student at Northeastern University, Class of 2002

---

15. When faced with ethical dilemmas, make sure that you always act in a way that allows you to maintain your self-respect, integrity, and clean record.

We hope that you won't face too many ethical dilemmas during your practice-oriented work experience. However, any job that you will ever have potentially can present you with tough situations. For example, would you cheat on your timesheet: even if you were sure you could get away with it? Sadly, I have had students caught for falsifying their hours, and they were terminated immediately—all those potential references and resume-building experiences permanently ruined or severely damaged, just for the possibility of a little extra money. This kind of offense also may lead to suspension or expulsion from your college or university.

What would you do if you became aware that another employee was stealing money, supplies, or equipment from the organization? If you make a potentially critical mistake and become aware of it later, should you tell your supervisor or simply hope that no one notices your error?

A few years ago, a student of mine faced a major dilemma. He had been asked to do the back-end work involving in getting antivirus software ready to go on the desktops of a big department. A full-time worker was supposed to take the final steps to get the software operational. When my student followed up with him to see if it was completed, his co-worker said to him, "I had trouble getting it to work, so I basically just decided to forget about it."

My student agonized about whether or not he should go to their mutual boss to report this. If he spoke up, he knew he would feel that he had "squealed" on a co-worker. But if he kept his mouth shot, and a new virus ended up causing significant problems, then he could be getting himself and others in trouble as well. What would you do?

I think he handled it very well. He went to his supervisor and told him about it, but he did so in a way that *assumed the best* of his co-worker. He told his boss that his co-worker had not completed the task, but he also said, "He might have been intending to get back to finishing up once he solved the problem." His boss was grateful, pointing out that the people in that group downloaded things all the time, and a major virus and worm problem would have reflected badly on the whole group.

Ultimately, every individual has to decide for himself or herself how to act in situations when no one—not your coordinator, your supervisor, or your parents—is looking over your shoulder. Basically, it's simple: Do the right thing, and you will save yourself a lot of guilt, fear, and worry about the consequences. If you're not sure about what the right thing is in a given situation, contact your coordinator.

16. Sit down with your manager during the first week of your job to set goals for your co-op work period.

If your program uses a standard work evaluation, you and your manager should review the entire evaluation upfront to know how you will be judged at the end of the work period. Additionally, though—whether or not your program requires it—you should write at least three goals for your work assignment, and you should do this in the first few weeks of your work experience.

What might your goals be for a given work assignment? They could vary dramatically depending on your major, the job, and your level of previous experience. For some first-time student employees, one goal may simply be to learn how a corporation works and how to perform effectively day-in, day-out for six months in a professional environment. Some goals may relate to refining soft skills, such as improving presentation skills, proving to be a dependable employee by arriving at work early every day, or perhaps learning how to multi-task or to prioritize in the face of deadlines or multiple responsibilities. Other goals may be more advanced and/or more geared to specific job skills: "I hope to find out if I'm comfortable working hands-on with patients of all backgrounds as an aspiring physical therapist;" "I intend to learn how to use ASP to make database-linked dynamic websites," or "I want to be immersed in the activities of this cat hospital so I can learn if this veterinary environment is right for me."

With goals in place, you and your manager will have a better mutual understanding of what you are supposed to be accomplishing in your role, and you can both do a better job of tracking your progress toward these objectives as the work period progresses.

Setting Goals – A Co-op Professional's Perspective
by Rose Dimarco
First I would suggest that within the first couple of weeks that you sit down with your boss and talk about expectations to nail down what people expect of you and what you can get out of the position. Always remember that this is typically a paid position, so it's value added that you bring to the employer.

Obviously there will be learning opportunities for you but not at the expense of what you were hired to do. I think a pitfall is when there is some conflict or misunderstanding that you don't bring up with an employer—or an employer doesn't bring up with you—and then it manifests itself and causes tremendous problems with that relationship.

Rose Dimarco is a cooperative education faculty coordinator in Physical Therapy at Northeastern University.

17. Do everything you can to become part of the work team and not "just a student."

To make the most of your job experience, make an effort to integrate yourself as fully as possible in the workplace. This is especially important if you work at a company that employs more than one student. Some students have the tendency to go to lunch with their fellow students, socialize outside of work only with fellow students, and generally avoid significant contact with full-time employees. This is understandable—in a new and strange situation, a person may be tempted to cling to something or someone who is familiar or similar. However, if you fail to make some connections with full-time employees, you're missing out on one of the great things that co-ops, internships, and other practice-oriented roles have to offer.

We recently had problems when we had a few dozen Northeastern co-ops at one employer. With the best of intentions, a few students started an e-mail thread that enabled their fellow students to be aware of social plans for after work and other such events. Over time, though, it became obvious that some people on the list were spending a significant part of their work day reading and responding to these "co-op group" e-mails! Inevitably, many of the students began to be perceived as an outside group of co-op students rather than blending in with the full-time employees. That made it harder for the co-ops to be looked at as true equals at the office.

Initially, talking to full-time people at work will help you learn the "unwritten rules" of that particular workplace regarding what is and is not acceptable and appropriate. Ultimately, your experience can become a chance to rub elbows with people who work professionally in your field as well as other areas of possible future professional interest. Simply joining these people for lunch or for a bite to eat after work, you may pick up invaluable information about:

• how to succeed in your job.

- whether or not you have much in common with people who work professionally in the career that interests you.

- what kinds of coursework, job experiences, or self-study projects will help prepare you for a great career after graduation.

- how people perceive the pros and cons of their own career choices.

Another benefit of getting to know full-time employees is that they will be more likely to think of you as part of their group or team, and therefore more likely to give you tasks to do that are appropriate to your interests, experiences, and skill levels.

Becoming Part of the Work Team
by Marie Sacino

Our computer information systems interns at the Queens Public Library work on the client side, providing 24/7 functionality, troubleshooting, changing hard drives, and ghosting as ongoing support tasks. Interns also work in the field on new PC rollout projects—2,000 new PC installations at branches throughout Queens this past summer.

What does it take to be a successful IT intern? Philip Darsan, Director of Information Technology at Queens Public Library, has some good thoughts. "An intern needs to begin to understand their working environment, to ask more questions, to utilize the department's organizational chart, to be cognizant of naming conventions—firewalls, deployment, DNS, IP," Darsan says. "We need serious students who really want to learn and don't watch the clock. Most IT personnel work 50 to 60 hours a week.

"I try to give the students an opportunity to open their eyes to the technology," adds Darsan. "Just how wide they choose to open them is up to the student. I'm interested in students who have a technician's perspective and who are customer-service oriented. I'll ask a student, 'How well do you communicate?' Without solid communication skills—interpersonal, reading, writing, speaking—there will be little growth for a technical support person."

Marie Sacino is an Associate Professor of Cooperative Education at LaGuardia Community College

---

18. However, be careful about mixing business and pleasure.

Sure, you want to be part of the work team. This can mean going out for lunch with co-workers or going out after work. It's great to fit in and be part of the gang, but you need to be careful when it comes to drinking with co-workers or getting romantically or sexually involved with people at work.

First, let's talk about alcohol. In some organizations, drinking is very much a part of the culture—you may be encouraged to drink at lunchtime before going back to work for the afternoon. In some offices, going out for beers after work is routine—or even having beer or wine brought into the office on a Friday afternoon by the organization itself! What should you do? You have to decide for yourself, but remember a few things. If you're underage to drink in your state, it's simply a bad idea to drink with co-workers—even if they urge you to do so. I had a student years ago who got fired from a prestigious firm because he drank at an office Christmas party. His boss had been proactive—telling him in advance that he could come but he could not drink. At the party itself, though, co-workers twisted his arm and got drinks for him: His boss found out, and he was fired.

Even if you are legal to drink and enjoy doing so, you should be discreet about doing so. I would never recommend that you take the initiative in ordering a drink if you're out with a colleague. If you're with several people who are drinking, it might not be a big deal to have a beer or a glass of wine—but be very moderate at most.

The same goes with getting romantically and/or sexually involved with people at work. In particular, it's never advisable to date a supervisor or someone who works for you. Even if someone is a fellow intern or a co-worker of similar age, you need to proceed with caution. What will you do if you break up with someone, and then you need to keep working closely together? Not a fun situation for either party. At the minimum, the best bet is to wait until after you complete your job before considering any relationship with a co-worker. Remember, also, that making unwanted advances can lead to embarrassing disciplinary issues as well.

One other reminder: When are student employees most likely to forget that it's not such a great idea to get involved with co-workers? You guessed it: When they've been out drinking at lunch or after work! If you're not careful, this issue can be double trouble, and it can affect how people perceive your professionalism at work.

19. If you're on a full-time job, your job performance should be your highest priority.
When you're in classes full-time, that should be your top priority. But when you're on co-op or on a full-time internship, you need to focus the bulk of your energy on performing your co-op job to the best of your ability.

Two factors can interfere with your job performance if you're not careful: First, some students choose to take classes while on co-op or an internship with long hours. To do so, you may need the permission of your co-op employer and your co-op or internship coordinator. Before seeking their permission, however, be honest with yourself: Can you take on one or two classes without jeopardizing your job performance or your academic performance? If in doubt, it is best to avoid taking classes on co-op or to keep them at an absolute minimum. Of course, if you're in a parallel program, you'll have to master the ability to be a student and employee at the same time without compromising your performance level in either role.

Another situation may arise for seniors: Naturally, seniors are concerned with getting full-time jobs after graduation. Sometimes, seniors may be interviewing for full-time jobs and co-op jobs simultaneously. However, once you've started a co-op job, you should keep any full-time interviewing to an absolute minimum. To go on one or two interviews through your Department of Career Services during your co-op job—with your co-op employer's permission, and with the understanding that you will make up for the missed hours—may be acceptable. To miss significant time from work to go on numerous interviews is not acceptable. For that matter, it's not that smart: Many seniors get full-time job offers from their last co-op employers IF they are outstanding performers. Don't jeopardize your co-op job—and a possible future offer—by looking elsewhere for full-time jobs during your work term.

20. If you're working part-time while attending classes full-time, you need to manage your time very effectively.

There are a few possibilities here. In some programs, students regularly juggle a co-op or internship with full-time classes. Likewise, some full-time co-ops opt to stay with their co-op employer on a part-time basis when their co-op experience officially ends. Either way, working part-time poses several challenges. I have had some full-time co-op superstars who absolutely destroyed their reputation with their employer because of their failure to adapt to being a part-time employee.

Here are a few tips to avoid this pitfall:

- *Don't over-commit.* Some students ambitiously promise to work 25-30 hours per week part-time. The employer counts on this resource, only to have the student start to realize that it's too much to balance—so he cuts back to 18 hours…. Then 15. This is all very annoying to the manager. Better to under-promise and over-deliver—don't commit to more than roughly 15 hours of part-time work per week while in full-time classes unless you really, really know you can handle it.

- *Set a regular schedule and stick to it as much as possible.* Committing to 15 hours a week generally doesn't mean that you go in whenever you feel like it in a given week. Look at your course schedule and block out some times that you can regularly do. Maybe one whole day and a couple of half-days; maybe two whole days—it doesn't really matter as long as your supervisor is comfortable with the arrangement and you generally stick to it. If you have voice mail and e-mail at work, make sure to include a message that informs everyone about your hours and what to do in your absence. Likewise, if you have a desk, office, or cubicle of your own, prominently post your part-time schedule so people will know when you will be working next. In scheduling, also remember that coming in for just an hour or two here and there seldom works well.

- *Plan ahead.* As soon as you get your syllabi, note the dates of exams and major due dates on your calendar. Maybe you have a week in which you have three midterms. In that case, you can approach your boss with plenty of notice to let her know that you'll need to be out for a few days. There is really no excuse for calling in the morning to say that you can't come in because you have an exam that day.

Effective Internships – A Co-op Professional's Perspective
by Ronnie Porter

I think in addition to the skill sets, there's a professionalization/socialization piece that doesn't occur as much when you're working on a part-time basis, ten hours a week, as opposed to doing it full-time when you're a member of a team and equally counted on.

I think the important thing is that at the outset you really set some goals for the time period of the job. I think that's really critical in any situation—that students have goals and that employers agree as to what those goals are. I think it's even more critical when you're there on a limited basis—when you're going to have to pick and choose what you do or what you want to learn and still have that coincide with what's needed at the organization. Otherwise, anything could happen. Things might turn out okay, but in other situations they might turn out to be very disappointing with people feeling like they've wasted their time.

Ronnie Porter is a cooperative education faculty
coordinator in Biology at Northeastern University.

---

21. If you are relocating for a job, be careful about how your situation can affect your perceptions of the job.

If you take advantage of an opportunity elsewhere in the country, you may end up living with other students who work for the same employer or with a different employer. As a result, students sometimes end up comparing notes about jobs, employers, supervisors, co-workers, etc. If both students are having a good experience, this is fine. But if one student is having a bad experience, everyone in that living situation needs to make sure that they continue thinking for themselves. In other words, decide for yourself whether or not you are having a good experience: Don't let anyone tell you what you should or shouldn't be thinking about your unique situation. This is true of any roommates who live together while working, but the negative effects can be magnified when you're living a long way from home and perhaps eating, breathing, and sleeping your practice-oriented experience every minute of the day. It's a powerful experience, so you have to make sure you maintain some objectivity.

Working in a different part of the country can be an excellent idea. In a sense, you're guaranteed of having a "double learning experience"—you'll learn on the job, and you'll learn off the job about what it's like to live in a different region. At best, you may find a place you enjoy more than your home city. At worst, you'll appreciate your own region, campus, or home more when you return.

22. Learn to master "cubicle etiquette" if necessary.

Many work environments feature cubicles or other arrangements that blur the lines between what behavior is public and what is private. Basically, a somewhat contradictory but useful rule of thumb is to assume that all of your own behavior is on public display... but also that you need to respect the privacy of others despite the lack of doors.

First, here are some good reminders relating to the fact that your own behavior is quite visible and public:

- Keep your phone ringer on a low volume and your speaking voice relatively low as well. Obviously, avoid speakerphones.

- Be aware that most phone conversations can be overheard.

- Turn off your phone ringer—or forward your calls appropriately—when not in your cubicle.

- E-mail or even instant messaging can be useful in this context to communicate to co-workers without unnecessary noise.

- Keep computer sound levels low.

- Try to avoid eating hot food at your desk. The aromas may distract those who are hungry or disgust those who are not hungry or who don't share your food preferences.

When it comes to respecting the privacy of others in a cubicle environment, here are some more good tips:

- Act as if your co-workers' cubicles have doors. Don't just barge in and start talking: Knock on the cubicle's wall.

- Don't be a "prairie dog," peering over the tops of cubes to see if someone is in or to talk.

- If you go to see someone in their cubicle, and they're on the phone, leave and come back later. Don't hang around where you can readily overhear their conversation.

- Here's a really challenging one: You may overhear a question or comment occasionally and be tempted to respond because you know the right answer. Unless the question is directed to everyone in the area, don't do it! It will bring attention to the fact that you've been eavesdropping, intentionally or not. Wait until someone asks you directly.

- If you have to share a cubicle or workspace with a colleague, you might want to suggest arranging different breaks or lunchtimes so each person gets at least some privacy regularly.

23. Return to school with a network of new contacts.

Lastly, don't miss the golden opportunity of co-ops and internships: When you're working in any position, make sure that you have acquired a network of new contacts before you complete the job! You have the opportunity to earn the respect of many people in your field during your work period. That's great, but make sure you capitalize on that by collecting business cards and/or contact information before you leave. You never know who might be in a position to help you out when you're networking for another job in the future. If you only know one or two people at your worksite, you might be out of luck if those people move on and can't be located.

Assuming you've done all you can to make a positive impression, having plenty of names can pay incredible dividends in the future when it comes time for another job search. Even if those individuals can't directly hire you, they may be in a position to recommend you for other jobs or to give you valuable career advice. Don't miss the boat!

Networking – A Co-op Professional's Perspective
by Bob Tillman
Who did you network with? Can you tell me ten new people who you know now, who know you? People who you could talk to down the road about a job? Because if you didn't, you wasted your time. That was the freebie out there. That's the value added that you don't get someplace else.

Bob Tillman is a cooperative education faculty coordinator in Civil Engineering at Northeastern University.

E-MAIL AND IM ETIQUETTE

I have been working with co-op students since March of 1995. Without question, the biggest change I have seen over the time is the degree to which e-mail has come to dominate business communication. Likewise, the average person is far more likely to be familiar with this form of communication. People love e-mail because of its speed, ease of use, and relative informality. However, all of these characteristics also can lead to blunders in the workplace. So let's review what every professional should know about e-mail.

The 'E' in E-Mail

Most people know that the "e" in e-mail literally stands for electronic. However, it's important to remember that 'e' stands for many other words as well: embarrassing, everlasting, eternal, and evidence.

Because an e-mail seems to disappear into cyberspace, it's easy to imagine that it's less "real" than a hard copy. However, the opposite is true. E-mails have lives of their own, and there is always a chance that once they are sent they will never go away. Maybe you only intended to send it to one person, but who's to say that they won't forward it on? Perhaps you sent something confidential to a friend... but what might happen if that relationship turns sour? You never know when an e-mail you sent might reappear at the worst possible moment.

One terrific student that I had in my class a few years ago recently had an experience that showed how 'e' can be embarrassing. While at work, she fired off a hasty e-mail to her boyfriend, basically implying that she was looking forward to spending a very passionate Sunday with him. But with a few unsent messages open, she accidentally e-mailed the steamy message to her supervisor!

What happened next was rather amazing. The supervisor thought it was funny and forwarded the message to six or seven colleagues in the Boston office, adding a little joke about how he seemed to be making quite an impression on his intern. Those six or seven colleagues passed it along to others in that office... and to colleagues at *another* office in another city. By the time I saw the message, it had been forward to over 60 employees in five cities!

To the student's credit, she owned responsibility for her part in this embarrassing fiasco. Interestingly, though, her manager was reprimanded for passing along the message instead of quietly confronting the co-op to make her aware of her mistake. Still, the co-op could not have enjoyed knowing that her private feelings were now known across the company.

Remember, anything you send as an e-mail is NOT private. I had an IT co-op whose job was "sniffing" e-mails. As a senior, he spoke to my class of first-time co-op students, describing how part of his job was to look through e-mail messages. He often came across porn, illegally downloaded music and videos, and many other incriminating messages. I'll always remember how horrified the class looked as he described what he found and how he reported it to his supervisor, who in turn went to Human Resources. I think that the students were shocked to know that their electronic communications at work were fair game for scrutiny.

Basically, you should be careful about what you send from your laptop or home computer... and maybe even a little paranoid about what you e-mail from your work computer. Don't think you can beat the system by sending questionable e-mail from a hotmail or gmail account: Any e-mail can be traced back to the computer from which it was sent!

If you stop to reflect that e-mail really is everlasting, embarrassing evidence, you'll go a long way toward avoiding problems.

Preparing To Send An E-Mail Or Instant Message
Before you send your first e-mail as a new employee of a professional

organization, there are several factors to consider and steps to take:

1. *Become familiar with your organization's culture regarding e-mails.* Every organization is different when it comes to communication. I deal with employers who almost *never* use e-mails to communicate internally, favoring the telephone or face-to-face interaction. On the other end of the spectrum are companies like Microsoft, where employees may often e-mail individuals who are in the office next door!

    In your early weeks in a new job, pay attention to who e-mails who and for what reason. You may need to e-mail less or more frequently than you ordinarily would to fit in with the new culture. If you're not sure, ask your co-workers or manager how to proceed.

2. *Set up your e-mail account to ensure that your name is obvious to message recipients.* I routinely receive 50-75 e-mails daily during the busiest times of the year. As a result, I end up scrolling through dozens of messages all day long. One minor annoyance is when it's not possible to deduce the sender from the name on my inbox. It may say something like jg1967@hotmail.com, which gives me no clue as to the sender's identity.

    Avoid inflicting this minor bit of inconvenience by setting your e-mail properties up so your name is readily obvious to the recipient. Then that message will appear as coming from Jill Gómez <jg1967@hotmail.com> in the message itself.

3. *Fill in the "To:" field LAST when sending any e-mail message.* Depending on the e-mail application you use, it can be surprisingly easy to send a message before you've finished writing or proofreading it. Therefore, it's a good practice to leave the recipient's e-mail address out until you're definitely ready to hit SEND. Because once you do, that message is not coming back!

4. *Always use a concise, descriptive subject for each e-mail message.* This is another problem area for many young professionals. It's not unusual for students to use problematic subjects when e-mailing me. I had one young man who seemed to think it appropriate to use a complete sentence as a subject: "Mr. Weighart I have some things I need to discuss with you." Another student simply used to write "IMPORTANT" for almost every message... and, believe me, the subject matter never turned out to be all that important. That almost feels like a spam e-mail tactic—using a vague subject that conveys some sense of urgency.

    Keep your subjects concise, but also be sure to give some sense of what the message concerns. Here are some good and bad examples:

__Good e-mail subjects__	__Bad e-mail subjects__
Question regarding Maiatico account	Call me ASAP!
Agenda item for Monday's meeting	Hi!
Quick update on JTC project	This is Henry.
Expense report – January 2008	Hey, how's it going?
Dentist appointment tomorrow	John can you answer these questions for me?
Following up on yesterday's meeting	<no subject>

5. *Don't abuse the "high priority" or "high importance" options.* This e-mail option can become like the story of the boy who cried wolf. If you abuse it in an attempt to get a quick answer to a less-than-urgent question, people will resent it. It leads people to question whether your judgment is good... and eventually they may not take it seriously when something really *is* high priority!

If you're looking for a quick answer to a simple question, you might just indicate that with an e-mail subject that reads "Quick question." Save the high-priority option for situations that truly are emergencies. For example, I use it when a student is at risk of being temporarily withdrawn from the university quite soon due to a paperwork issue. You may never need to utilize this option at all, and consider it carefully. If the matter is that important, you might want to just pick up the phone.

6. *Use an appropriate salutation.* Surprisingly, some of my best co-ops and interns have struggled with this one. I had a top student at Microsoft recently, and she had to e-mail a group of about 50 people with a project update. She knew that introducing the e-mail with something like "Hey guys" would be inappropriate, but a better alternative didn't come to mind immediately.

First, though, let's consider the easier situation. When writing an e-mail to an individual, there are several options that may be appropriate:

Dear Charlie, -- This is a little more formal but fine.

Hi Charlie, -- This is a bit more informal but also acceptable.

Charlie, -- Perhaps a bit more of a down-to-business salutation, but it's fine, too.

If you're writing to someone you don't know as well, go a little more formal, avoiding the assumption of being on a first-name basis:

Dear Mr. Bognanni,

Hi Ms. Shumbata,

Ms. Brady,

It also can be acceptable to exclude any salutation at all and just launch into the body of the message. However, some research shows that people are less likely to respond when there is no personal salutation.

Above all, avoid the salutations that you might see in e-mails from a friend:

Hey Charlie!

Hey, how's it going?

When writing to a group, I would recommend something like this:

Hi everyone,

There are probably other things that would work there—including no salutation at all—but this seems to be the simplest and most effective.

7. *Be wary of the cc and bcc options.* There are times when it's appropriate to use the cc function, which sends an extra copy of your e-mail to another person. Maybe you're updating a colleague on some issue but feel that your supervisor also should hear about it—but more as an FYI rather than as an action item. That's a good time to use the cc function. It can be a good way to keep people informed while also implying that you don't necessarily expect a reply from them.

Unfortunately, though, people get carried away with sending a cc of their e-mails. There are those who overestimate the importance or interest level that their news will generate, and—even worse—there are those who send a cc to show a third party how dumb the original message was and/or to escalate the intensity of the problem. As we'll see when we consider "flaming" e-mails, this can get out of hand in a hurry.

Then there is the bcc, which technically stands for "blind carbon copy." In this case, you're letting a third party see the e-mail without the primary recipient being able to see who else is allowed to see it. There are times when this makes a great deal of sense. Sometimes I write to groups of people but want to make sure that others don't see the individual e-mail addresses, which may be considered private. For example, if ten students are late in getting some done for me, I will e-mail them all at once to save time... but I will bcc them all, as it would be potentially embarrassing for each student to know who else is not getting things done. It's also no one else's business.

But I try to avoid bcc in most cases. Some feel that it's rather unethical—I have heard of a bcc recipient being referred to as a "blind co-conspirator."

144

However, the biggest risk is that the bcc recipient will accidentally hit REPLY TO ALL, and then the primary recipient will become aware that others saw the initial message. If I do want others to see an e-mail that is somewhat sensitive, I may just forward a copy from my Sent folder AFTER sending that initial message.

8. *Beware of REPLY TO ALL.* This connects to the previous point. It's all too easy to click "reply to all" instead of simply "reply" when you receive a group message. What is the impact? At best, you end up sending information to a group that has no need whatsoever to read your response. For example, sometimes invitations to events go out on work e-mails, and recipients are told to reply to the sender to RSVP. Instead, the person hits REPLY TO ALL, and the whole group gets a message indicating that, say, that person will not attend the event because of a dentist appointment. Not a horrible thing to share with a group, but it's basically just another message that needs to be deleted.

   However, there are other situations which can lead to bad feelings, serious embarrassment, or even disciplinary action. A few years ago, I received an e-mail on a nationally distributed list-serv that reached thousands of individuals. One person sent a perfectly fine message to the group. But then a colleague at her own organization hit REPLY TO ALL and informed the e-mail sender that the toilet in their building was clogged yet again! The exchange went back and forth a few times before a recipient finally wrote to say "Do we all really need to read about your bathroom issues?" A mortified apology followed.

   Even worse, though, is another possibility. Let's say that Tom sends an e-mail to his entire work group, noting that there will be a farewell party for Jane, a co-worker who is leaving the company. Then Jack—a very close friend of Tom—intends to send a message back to Tom that is for his eyes only. But he accidentally hits REPLY TO ALL. There are any number of things that he might say that could have terrible consequences. He could ask Tom if he thinks the boss will make another of his stupid speeches at the event, or he could express delight that Jane is leaving the company at last. He could talk about a "hot" co-worker who he plans to ask out for drinks after the event. The possibilities are infinite.

   The moral of the story is to think twice before you put anything in an e-mail which will reflect poorly on you if others see it—either due to it being forwarded, intercepted by someone in IT, or accidentally shared through REPLY TO ALL.

9. *Don't open file attachments unless you're very sure that they can be trusted.* File attachments often contain viruses. Even if a friend or co-worker sends a file attachment, look out for vague messages with file attachments. They may be the result of a virus, worm, or Trojan horse that's infected their

machines. More obviously, don't open files from people you don't know.

10. *Don't forward virus threats, offensive content, or chain letter e-mails.*
Sometimes e-mails claiming to warn people of virus threats actually contain
viruses or worms. Let your IT department stay current on such threats.

Offensive content is very much in the eye of the beholder. What's funny
to one person might offend someone else. In general, stay away from
forwarding jokes—especially when you're new at an organization and
probably not clear about what people will find humorous or even how they
might feel about you spending time at work forwarding jokes. If you're
just there temporarily for a co-op or internship, I would say that you never
should send e-mails to co-workers that have nothing to do with work.

Many people get sucked in by chain letter e-mails. Periodically you may
receive emotional pleas in which, say, a warning of a terrorist act is passed
along or a child dying of cancer wants to see how many e-mails he can
receive from around the world before he or she dies. Sometimes there is a
claim that the American Cancer Society will donate a few cents to cancer
research for everyone who receives the e-mail.

While such appeals may bring out your humanitarian nature, don't be
fooled. More often than not, these e-mails are hoaxes. Sometimes I go
to www.snopes.com to see if e-mails are true or not, as this site reports
diligently on "urban legends." Most of them are hoaxes, so you're often just
wasting your time and that of your friends and co-workers by passing along
such nonsense.

11. *Don't reply to spam e-mail messages.* You may receive quite a few annoying
spam messages, offering everything from discount drugs and loans to
elaborate scams promising you massive amounts of money for helping
some overseas widow get access to a massive inheritance. Unless your
organization has a spam-reporting mechanism to follow, the best thing to
do is to simply delete such messages. Responding to them or clicking on
a link—even when doing so supposedly removes you from a mailing list—
actually can help a spammer *confirm* your e-mail address and may lead to
getting viruses.

12. *Strike when the iron is cold.* Never reply to an e-mail when you are angry,
frustrated, or otherwise not prepared to write a professional, businesslike
message that you can live with forever. I call this "striking when the iron
is cold"—exactly the opposite of the expression "strike when the iron is
hot." As a professional, you want to respond with a rational, constructive
response—even when you are agitated.

It's very easy to blast someone when you are angry, saying things that you
never would say face to face. Sometimes it's best to resist the urge to fire

off a response when you first receive an emotionally charged e-mail. Take a walk, talk about it with someone, maybe sleep on it if you can. Ask yourself what kind of response will reflect you best as an aspiring professional. Then write back when your frame of mind is more positive. Otherwise you'll have a long time to regret responding in the heat of the moment.

The E-Mail Message Itself

Now that we have considered everything that should go into preparing to e-mail, let's go through the writing of the actual message itself. Here are several pointers that will help you write effective e-mails:

1. *Be concise.* Limit your professional e-mails to "need to know" information. Be quick to describe why you are writing, what you need to tell or ask, and what steps, if any, the respondent needs to take in response. Then thank them and end it.

    It's also a good idea to take a moment to reflect on whether an e-mail really is the best way to convey your message. If you can't convey the information in a few short paragraphs—or if the information is complicated and requires additional input—it may be best to use the phone or have a brief meeting.

2. *Create templates if you find yourself writing identical or highly similar e-mails on a regular basis.* Depending on your job, you may need to write highly similar messages repeatedly. Why waste time rewriting them from scratch every time? I keep a Word file of messages that come up constantly. If I get a request for information about the co-op program or about how to set up an appointment with me among other things, I can paste in the appropriate response and add the appropriate salutation on top. That saves hours and hours each year.

3. *Use blank lines to separate paragraphs as opposed to indenting.* Just as in any piece of writing, you want to avoid massive paragraphs with no visual or conceptual break. Getting a 25-line e-mail with no spacing just makes the recipient groan. Try to limit each paragraph to no more than 5-6 sentences or lines, and hit ENTER twice at the end to go to the next paragraph without indenting.

4. *Understand that e-mails are one-way communication.* When you have a face-to-face conversation with a co-worker, you can infer a great deal from the speaker's tone of voice and body language. You also can adjust your message based on how the listener reacts to what you say as the conversation progresses.

    Naturally, all of these helpful cues go out the window in an e-mail message. It can be very difficult to grasp the writer's tone. Sometimes it's hard to tell if someone is angry or just in a hurry as well as whether they're joking, serious, or sarcastic. As a result, it's good to be cautious in drawing conclusions. Ask clarifying questions if need be, and avoid emotional topics.

5. *Use "smilies" or "emoticons" sparingly in professional e-mails.* Smilies and emoticons are small symbols that are sometimes used to compensate for the one-way nature of e-mail and IM communication. There are literally dozens of them out there, but here are some common examples:

:)	Happy
☺	Happy
;)	Winking
:(	Sad
:-o	Surprised

Experts differ as to whether such symbols have any place in professional e-mails. Some believe that it can be helpful to add an emoticon in order to make sure that there is no misunderstanding about whether you're joking. For example, an intern who receives an e-mail informing her that she is going to have much more responsibility going forward might write the following text in response:

Looks like I'll have my hands full for the next month.

If the message is left like that, we're not sure whether her reaction is an expression of complaint, anxiety, or enthusiasm. So writing it this way makes that very clear:

Looks like I'll have my hands full for the next month. :)

The best advice is to use these emoticons sparingly. There are quite a few that will baffle e-mail recipients who don't use them at all. For example, can you even guess what these represent?

:C

*

{}

:\'-)

Respectively, they are supposed to indicate astonishment, a kiss, no comment, and tears of happiness! But you'll baffle most co-workers by using these, so stick with the common ones if you use them at all.

6. *Capitalize appropriately and avoid IM slang.* Many young professionals are experienced e-mail writers and users of AOL's Instant Messenger (IM) or

similar instant message applications. As a result, they bring their highly informal e-mail and IM habits into the workplace. I cringe when I get a professional message in which someone writes something like this:

> can i meet with u 2day? maybe 4 lunch?

Occasionally, I'll get e-mails using other abbreviations, such as LOL (laughing out loud), FWIW (for what it's worth), or IMHO (in my humble opinion). I use these sometimes in my personal e-mail but not in professional e-mail. For the latter, I think it's fine to use FYI (For Your Information) and maybe BTW (by the way), but generally these acronyms should be avoided.

This issue *can* be confusing. You may receive e-mails or IMs at work from very senior people who opt for punctuation-free e-mails with plenty of IM slang and not a single capitalization. However, even though it's obviously faster to ignore capitalization and use "shorthand slang," it can come across as unprofessional. And when you're new to an organization, it may underscore the fact that you are young and inexperienced.

Also understand that it's not just IM slang that is a problem. I had a student who made a serious mistake at work. When I encouraged him to apologize, he wrote an e-mail that included this sentence: "That definitely was my bad." This just infuriated me. You might say "my bad" when you make a bad pass in a pick-up basketball or football game, but you would never use such an expression in any form of professional communication. Basically, if it's not the kind of word or expression that you would use in a term paper, don't use it in an e-mail.

7. *Avoid attaching large files unless absolutely necessary.* Sometimes you may need to forward a Word or Excel document at work. That's fine. However, it can get annoying to get massive audio or video files in one's e-mail account—whether they are humorous or actually have some work relevance. Generally, avoid sending large files. They can be especially annoying if someone is accessing their e-mail account from a slower home computer.

8. *Use threads and quotes sensibly.* Many e-mail applications give you the option of simply hitting "reply" or "reply with history." So what should you do? It depends, but including at least some of that history may be very helpful to your e-mail recipient. Not infrequently I get a response to an e-mail *without* that history. Sometimes I know what the writer is talking about, sometimes not. If the message says, "Yes, it would be great if you could do that for me" and nothing more, I may have to dig through my Sent folder to figure out what the heck the person wants me to do—especially when I have looked at 50 or 100 e-mails in between the new message and the previous one!

Keeping the "thread" of previous responses allows the recipient the luxury of scrolling down to remind himself of what had been said previously. That can be very helpful... and it also can get a little out of control. If you've exchanged many previous messages—including some with file attachments— the e-mail can get to be quite large. In that case, you may want to cut and paste the last two or three exchanges into a new message. Another option would be to just cut and paste small bits of text so the person can see what you're talking about. This can be indicated with a > sign as follows:

> When can you meet on Tuesday?

Any time from 9:30-11:30 works for me.

> Do I need to bring anything?

 Just bring your hard copy of that report.

9. *Don't write "flaming" e-mails or respond in kind if you receive one.* A flaming e-mail is a message that is intended to provoke with inflammatory comments. An example might be the following:

I CANNOT BELIEVE THAT YOU FAILED TO INCLUDE THE COST OF GOODS SOLD ON THAT SPREADSHEET. WHAT WERE YOU THINKING???

Writing an all-uppercase message is something to avoid in general, as is the emotionally charged tone of the e-mail. Faced with such a communication, it may be tempting to get defensive or to go on the warpath in response. Don't engage in the same behavior, though, or you'll regret it. Sometimes it's best to not respond at all via e-mail but to call or see the individual to deflate the tension. Bashing the person in reply may be momentarily satisfying but will not win any points for you in the long run.

10. *Prepare an automatic electronic signature for the end of your e-mail.* It's relatively easy to set up an electronic signature that automatically appears whenever you compose a new e-mail or reply to an existing one. The signature should include your name, title, organization name, phone number, and e-mail address, which may not be obvious from the e-mail itself. Your mailing address at work may be included as well if that will be helpful to your recipients. If you are often not at your desk due to the nature of your job, you might include a cellphone number too. It's a professional courtesy to include this data when e-mailing, so someone can have ready access to your contact information.

Some people include brief quotes with their signatures. These can be nice but also could create problems. They certainly aren't something you need to include in an e-mail signature.

11. *Proofread and spellcheck.* Many e-mail applications can be set up to proofread messages automatically before they are sent. While this can be

useful, remember that spellcheckers are far from foolproof. They often fail to find missing words or words that really are words... but that are not the correct word for that context. So use your spellchecker, but also proofread messages carefully before sending them. This is especially true for those who are prone to spelling errors and typos.

I have an employer who hired a terrific interviewee, only to be horrified at the quality of her e-mails. Now the employer always includes a writing component in the interviewing process. After having his department embarrassed by unprofessional e-mails, he came to realize how important it was to avoid them. I hope that this section will help you do the same.

After You Send An E-Mail
After the e-mail goes out, there are just a couple of things to bear in mind:

1. *Don't "recall" a message.* What if you do send a message that includes a mistake—whether a factual error or a bad typo? Many systems now have the option of allowing you to "recall" an e-mail. This may give you the impression that you can "take back" an e-mail that you now regret for whatever reason. Instead, what happens is that the recipient finds both the original e-mail message in his or her inbox along with another e-mail notifying him or her that the message has been recalled. Being human, I know that the recall makes me immediately curious about what dumb error is in the first e-mail. In other words, it effectively draws more attention to it.

    If you do make a factual error, it's best to send out a correction. In some cases—when you have incorrectly named a time or place for a meeting—you might have an e-mail with an explanatory subject: CORRECTION on meeting location. Don't profusely apologize—just explain the mistake and clarify what the message should have said.

    If a small typo or other stylistic error is made, it's probably best to just let it go. Drawing more attention to it might make it worse.

2. *Be responsive to any e-mail messages that require a reply.* At work, you will receive many group messages that require no reply at all. However, when a message is sent to you individually, it's good to acknowledge receipt of it, briefly. For most professionals, the rule of thumb is to reply to any personal e-mail message within 24 hours if it's a message that requires any sort of response. Responding faster is better if possible and potentially critical if it's a more urgent question.

    Failing to respond quickly to e-mails may start to create unfortunate negative perceptions. Your manager or co-workers may believe that you lack attention to detail, organizational skills, or the ability to manage your time effectively. Responding efficiently and effectively will reinforce the notion that you *do* have these qualities.

SPECIAL CONSIDERATIONS FOR HEALTH SCIENCE PROFESSIONALS

If you're majoring in one of the health sciences—nursing, physical therapy, occupational therapy, pharmacy, athletic training, cardiopulmonary science are some examples—you may do clinical assignments as well as co-op jobs. In both cases, you're working in the world of practice as opposed to the classroom. However, there are some key differences between the two experiences. The following sidebar box addresses them. As you'll see, the contrast can be ironic—some behaviors that are extremely appropriate for a health sciences co-op can be quite out of place on a clinical!

Clinical Versus Co-op – A Health Sciences Co-op Perspective
by Rose Dimarco
Clinical affiliations in the health care professions are a place in the world of work where students have to demonstrate clinical skills that they've learned in the classroom as well as some professional behaviors that are appropriate for that level of student. There is a curriculum; there are objectives that the student must fulfill in the out-of-classroom experience. They are graded on it, and they are supervised by someone from the university—typically in all the health-care professions. Co-op is driven by a job description: Opportunities for learning are there in co-op, but they're not the first thing.

In most cases, clinicals are assigned—there's no interview. But approaching it? Well, I'll tell you a quick story. One of my better students on co-op came back and said, "I'm having a hell of a time on my clinical." And I said, "Abby, how can that be? You just shine in everything you touch." And she said, "Rose, I don't know how to delegate. As a licensed therapist, I have to demonstrate that I know how to delegate to appropriate personnel, and I do it all! As a co-op, I was delegated to, and I don't know how to get out of my own way! So if I need towels, I go get them. If I see a linen closet that needs organizing, I organize it. I make time for it—I stay after work. My clinical advisor at the site would say, "Abby! That's what you should have given the aide to do!"

So that transition is more of a challenge than anything—getting out of that mindset. So a clinical is more student objective-centered, based on a curriculum.
Rose Dimarco is a cooperative education faculty coordinator
in Physical Therapy at Northeastern University.

THE EMPLOYER'S PERSPECTIVE

All of the recommendations listed in this chapter generally reflect the expectations of most managers and organizations. HOWEVER, remember: *Every manager and organization is different.* One of the most important survival and success skills in any job for the rest of your career is to pay close attention to the written and unwritten rules of each workplace. Don't make assumptions about what is or is not okay!

Find out what drives your supervisor crazy and what makes her happy, then make any adjustments accordingly. Some bosses really don't care what time you arrive as long as you do a great job—others are upset if their employees don't arrive *early* every day! In some environments, wearing jeans and a t-shirt is acceptable; in others, wearing anything other than business formalwear is a major mistake. In some organizations, how you dress, speak, and act may have very different rules depending on the department. I visited a small software company in Cambridge a few years ago: The software developers wore ripped jeans and t-shirts and were playing chess at 2:00 in the afternoon. Meanwhile, the marketing personnel were wearing suits and working hard from 9-5 with a brief lunch break, while the accounting personnel were wearing business casual clothes and working fairly flexible hours. All of this was happening in a company of about 40 people. Any co-op student entering that environment would have to be very careful in figuring out what was and was not appropriate behavior.

Regardless of your position, you must begin to think and act like a professional. Professionals remain on the job until a project is completed in a timely accurate manner.

On-The-Job Performance – An Employer's Perspective
by Mike Naclerio

Students can get the most out of their jobs by taking the initiative. Many co-op positions in the business field have heavy administrative functions built into them. Do the administrative part thoroughly and without resentment and find additional opportunities to contribute in the organization. Do not get stuck in the gossip and pity trap of how bad my co-op and/or supervisor is. It is all what you make of it. Ask for more work and if your supervisor doesn't have anything, come back to them with a proposal to fix a major problem they may be facing or overlooking. Do not wait for the company to provide you with the opportunity because many organizations are just too busy to focus. If you come to them with a well thought out plan that addresses a key problem, you are sure to stand out.

As far as dealing with conflict, just deal with it. If you are having a problem with a supervisor or co-worker, ask them if they have a few minutes to talk, go somewhere private and clear the air. There is no time for drama in the workplace and most people should respect the directness.

Mike Naclerio is the Director of Relationship Management at the workplace HELPLINE.

Figuring out what is and is not okay with a given employer can be much trickier than you might imagine. Just because you see a couple of co-workers take a two-hour lunch, you can't assume that it's okay for you to do the same. If you see someone wearing shorts at work, that doesn't mean that this should be your dress code as well. On the whole, you need to keep your eyes open: Don't make the "lowest common denominator" at work become your standard. We have many co-op students who prove to be more motivated and productive than their full-time counterparts. Make sure that you're doing whatever you can to exceed expectations, whether the issue is attire, breaks, effort, or anything else.

Don't worry whether you are being compensated or not for extra work. A marketing manager recently calculated what his salary worked out to be on an hourly rate, only to discover that he was making just a few more dollars per hour than his co-op students!

FINAL THOUGHTS REGARDING ON-THE-JOB SUCCESS

Getting on top of the many details in this chapter obviously has an enormous impact on the job experience. Perhaps the biggest key is *owning the responsibility for your own success.* Sooner or later in your career, you'll have to contend with a poor manager, a difficult co-worker, or a problematic or uninspiring work environment. I've dealt with some high-level managers at Microsoft who like to say, "It's not the situation: It's how you handle it."

One senior manager at Microsoft told me the following: "When I interview people now, I mainly try to weed out the whiners, complainers, and moaners," he said. "Years ago, I sometimes interviewed people who told me that they were held back in their old jobs because of poor managers, a negative work environment, or a lack of resources. I hired some of these people, because I believed that once they got to Microsoft—where we have great managers, a very achievement-oriented work environment, and plentiful resources—they would shine. It didn't happen. Instead they found new excuses. I've learned that good people just learn to overcome obstacles."

By adhering to the principles discussed in this chapter, you will learn to be solution-oriented, preventing problems from arising and building a foundation of success in the workplace that will help you get your next job and excel in it. Above all, if in doubt about what to do and how to do it, ask someone. Then you'll find out how to live up to your interview.

CHAPTER 4 REVIEW QUESTIONS

1. List three different ways in which performing well on your job or internship will benefit you.

2. Depending on traffic or public transportation issues, let's say that it could take you anywhere from 30 to 50 minutes to get to work. If you absolutely have to be at work by 8:30 a.m., what time should you leave?

3. Give three examples of specific goals that you would like to be able to set for your next internship, co-op job, or full-time job.

4. Name four on-the-job situations in which it would be highly advisable to contact your internship or co-op coordinator.

5. Describe three common mistakes students make when trying to juggle a part-time job or internship with full-time coursework.

CHAPTER FIVE
Making Sense of Your Experience

Eventually, your job will end, and you will return to the classroom. Whether your experience was terrific, terrible, or anywhere in between, it would be a missed opportunity to just put it behind you when you return to the classroom. At this point, you need to take the final steps toward getting credit for your co-op as well as figuring out what comes next in your career. At Northeastern, this process includes a) turning in an evaluation and b) completing a reflection requirement. Make sure you find out what's required in your program.

Receiving an evaluation and fulfilling reflection requirements offer you a chance to make sense of what happened while you were on co-op. Because the primary goal of co-op is to learn from anything you experienced at work—whether positive or negative—the evaluation and reflection processes will help you gain some perspective on how you did and what you can take away from the experience. This will help build self-awareness—including a sense of what you need to do to keep growing and improving as a professional in the future. It's not uncommon for a student to emerge from a co-op or internship with a greater sense of urgency about the classroom. For that matter, it's not unusual for students to improve dramatically in their coursework after co-op. In addition to seeing the practical relevance of the material in the "real world," taking classes sometimes feels pretty easy after a demanding work experience!

As the following sidebar box indicates, internships and co-op jobs don't only answer some career questions that you may have—they also may raise new questions regarding about what comes next.

157

> **Returning To The Classroom – A Co-op Professional's Perspective**
> *by Ronnie Porter*
> In my program, students sometimes realize what the theories really meant when they were put into the practice—or sometimes the other way around: They've done things on co-op and then studied the theory and figured out why things were done a certain way. Either way, it just naturally flows into the academics and into thinking about how they want to do things next time around on their co-op.
>
> Through their co-op experience, they may know that they need to take courses to enhance their expertise in a certain area. In Arts and Sciences, the question should not be, say, "Can you give me a list of all the philosophy jobs?" We say, "That's not the right question." We're interested in "Why are you interested in philosophy and what do you want to do with it?" So it's a different approach. There's no list of jobs, rather there are a lot of conversations around what the person wants to do and what their hopes and expectations are about how they're going to use this information that they're learning.
>
> *Ronnie Porter is a cooperative education faculty coordinator in Biology at Northeastern University.*

YOUR EVALUATION

As your co-op job comes to a close, you generally will receive an evaluation. Most programs have a standard form that employers can complete and return to the program coordinator. Often you will be asked to summarize the job and your sense of how it was as an experience, while your supervisor will write up her or his thoughts on your responsibilities, strengths, areas for further professional development, and on your soft skills: interpersonal relationships, dependability, judgment, etc. You also may be given an overall rating, such as outstanding, very good, average, marginal, or unsatisfactory.

Some employers will give you an evaluation form that is typically used for all employees in their organization. These forms can be several pages long and are quite detailed. At some organizations, the format involves asking you and your manager to reflect briefly in writing on how successful you were in reaching your job-related tasks and objectives.

Whatever your evaluation looks like, keep a few things in mind when receiving your first performance evaluation:

1. *Don't take it too personally.* You and your manager may not see eye to eye on how you did in your job—and it won't always be because your supervisor has a higher opinion of your performance than you do! You may receive criticism that you believe to be inaccurate or unfair. Regardless, you want to end your relationship with any employer in a gracious, classy manner—don't blow it because of an impulsive, emotional reaction to evaluation comments.

2. *View the evaluation experience as a learning opportunity.* If you have communicated consistently with your manager throughout your co-op, you should not be too surprised by your evaluation. In any event, your evaluation gives you things to think about and talk about with your co-op coordinator—it can lead to specific goals for personal improvement and success in your next co-op. No one is perfect, and no one is perfectly self-aware of all of her or his strengths and areas requiring further development. Use the evaluation as a tool in your professional development.

3. *If you feel your evaluation is unjust or unfair, take the initiative to discuss it with your coordinator.* Getting evaluated on co-op is hardly an exact science. Some employers may rate students higher than they deserve because they fear that a negative or neutral review will cause undesirable conflict or impair your academic progress. Other employers may have impossibly high standards or just believe that most employees should receive average reviews unless something really astonishing was accomplished. In other situations, you may have a change of manager midway through your co-op, or perhaps you reported to numerous people or maybe even to no one at all. Obviously, any of these developments will affect the fairness or accuracy of your review.

Discuss any of these concerns with your coordinator. We know that these things happen, and it also can be quite challenging for us to figure out the truth amidst many different perceptions. Your coordinator should be able to provide you with a more objective and balanced view of how you did if you're not sure what to think about your review.

4. *After a few months have gone by, review your evaluation again.* It's easy to lose your objectivity when you're immersed in a job for 40 hours or more per week. After you have been out of that specific work environment for a good while, you may find that it's easier for you to consider the positives and negatives of your review more openly and less emotionally. It's also good to reconsider your performance before you begin your next job search, so that you are ready to discuss how your job went with a future employer. This is a good opportunity to show self-awareness and graciousness. Even if you have lingering bad feelings about a previous job or supervisor, you need to move on and take the high road when discussing past events with a potential new boss.

While most co-op students get anxious about their initial performance evaluation, the great majority of our students at Northeastern University do very well in the eyes of employers. Probably at least 90 percent receive very good or outstanding evaluations. Still, everyone always has ways in which they can improve, and it's generally very helpful to get feedback from an experienced manager in the professional world.

PURPOSES OF REFLECTION

As co-op, internships, and other forms of practice-oriented education become a bigger piece of the learning puzzle at many colleges and universities, more schools are beginning to require some form of reflection requirement for students returning to school following co-op. Why do co-op programs require reflection? There are numerous reasons:

1. *Making connections between classroom and the world of practice.* One purpose of co-ops and internships is to give students a practice-oriented element to their educations, making learning "hands-on" instead of just learning about theories. Reflection often requires you to think about how a work experience brought classroom concepts to life, or how practical work experience changed an understanding of something you *thought* you understood in a course. In return, your job experience gives you raw material that you bring with you to class to help you understand new concepts and theories in your field.

Integrating Practice With Coursework – A Co-op Professional's Perspective
by Rose Dimarco
I find that as an undergrad student in health care, you learn quickly when to do something and how to do it. The why you are doing it—why you are doing that range of motion or stretching exercise or providing certain pharmaceutical drugs—comes in the classroom. So it's up to you to take the where and when and connect it with the why. Now you're slowly going to evolve from studying nursing to becoming a nurse—that's going to come from that interchange.
Rose Dimarco is a cooperative education faculty coordinator
in Physical Therapy at Northeastern University.

---

2. *Having an opportunity to compare your experience with those of others.* Going to reflection seminars gives you a chance to hear about where your classmates worked, what they did, and how it all went. It can be useful to hear about how others dealt with challenges that they faced and to hear the thoughts that upperclassmen have about the job experiences after going through the process repeatedly. At best, you may be able to learn from the successes and mistakes of others.

3. *Learning about future job options.* Hearing about other students' experiences may give you some added perspective about where you might want to work in the future as well as jobs or organizations that you may wish to avoid. HOWEVER—Be careful about drawing conclusions from the experiences of others! Just because one industrial engineering student complains bitterly about her internship at Amalgamated Suitcases, does that mean that YOU wouldn't like the same job? Maybe, maybe not. In the same reflection seminar, you may hear another engineering student praising his supply chain management job at an organization called www.advancedlogistics.

com—does that mean this job is great for everyone? Of course not.

Exploring Job Options – A Co-op Professional's Perspective
by Bob Tillman
The discussion now is going to be, "Tell me more about what you're looking for the next time. Are you looking for more of the same but just at a higher level? Is it a new challenge? A career exploration you're looking for? Skill development? Are there certain projects you want to work on? What's the itch? Let's identify that.
Bob Tillman is a cooperative education faculty coordinator in Civil Engineering at Northeastern University.

Whenever I start my reflection seminars, I usually tell the tale of two students who did the exact same job at the same time with the same employer. In one reflection seminar, the first student said, "My PC support job was fantastic—I'd recommend it to anyone. The day goes by really quickly because there's always something new to handle—you're not stuck behind a desk; you're going all over the company to troubleshoot problems. When you go to see end users, they're usually upset about their computer problems, but when you fix the problem, they are SO grateful! What a great job!"

At the next reflection seminar, that student's co-worker complained bitterly about his job: "Don't ever work in PC support! What a bunch of headaches—you come in and try to get a project done, and you keep getting interrupted constantly by end users. They're generally pretty clueless about computers, and they're in a foul mood when you go to see them. Every day I went home with a headache."

Which student is "right"? Both... and neither. The quality of a job experience is very much in the eye of the beholder. When students describe their previous jobs, listen more carefully to their descriptions of the job duties and the reasons why they liked or disliked their jobs. Make up your own mind as to whether that job would be good for you.

4. *Having the opportunity for more detached and objective appraisal of one's experience, after the fact.* Working at an organization full-time is kind of like being in an intense relationship. Whether you're in a romantic relationship, living with a roommate, or working in a job, it can be easy to lose your perspective when you're immersed in the situation. Positively or negatively, you might do things you wouldn't ordinarily do—and then wonder why that happened, after the fact.

Reflection gives you an opportunity to make sense of your experience in a more detached, open way, after you are no longer in the situation. This may lead to new insights and a new appreciation of what it all meant.

Reflection also can be quite surprising for both students and coordinators. One time I was running a reflection seminar for entrepreneurship/small business management students. One student reported that he had worked at a small restaurant but found it frustrating because the entrepreneur was highly secretive about the financial affairs of the business. "My guess is that he didn't want to show me the books because he was cheating on his taxes," the student said. "But I guess that's what you have to do to make it as an entrepreneur."

I managed to hold my tongue and asked if anyone else in the room had another perspective on the situation. A second student raised his hand, "My family has run a business for several generations, and my grandfather *went to jail* for basically thinking the same thing as your boss." It was a powerful moment and a great chance for the group to reflect on the challenges and ethical dilemmas that entrepreneurs face—as well as considering the potential consequences of running a business that is engaged in illegal activity.

FORMS OF REFLECTION

Generally, there are many ways in which you can fulfill your reflection requirement. Which one will you end up doing? It depends partly on what works best for you and partly on what your coordinator finds most advisable given your circumstances. All reflection methods have pros and cons, so let's consider briefly the different forms of reflection.

1. *Small-group seminars*: Most Northeastern students participate in a reflection seminar in a small group—usually no more than 15 students. For the time being, business students are required to go to one 60-minute session with their coordinator and a group of students in their field. On the positive side, this method is fairly quick and painless for most students and coordinators. It also gives students a chance to exchange ideas and experiences with classmates. On the negative side, it's hard to go into serious issues in great depth in a one-time, one-hour session. Also, some students may feel awkward or uncomfortable sharing their job experiences—especially if something unpleasant happened at work. For these students, another reflection method may be preferable.

2. *Writing a reflection paper and/or keeping a journal:* This is another common form of reflection. Your coordinator may provide you with some questions or topics that can be addressed in a paper. Often the focus is not so much on a plot summary of your work experience: instead, the idea usually is to try to make connections between the real world and the classroom and to get across what you learned about yourself and the organizational world while on an internship or co-op—even if that included getting fired from your job! Some students even write weekly journals reflecting on their development through the job experience—it can be quite remarkable to look back at a list of your anxieties and concerns before day one at the end of a six-month full-

time co-op. Here are some questions that might be considered for a paper or journal:

- How has this job experience helped you understand concepts that you previously learned when taking classes in your major? Has this experience changed your attitude toward being in classes and your ability to perform since returning to campus after completing your job? How have liberal arts classes helped you build useful transferable skills for the professional world?

- What was the purpose of your job? How did your job fit into the overall organizational mission?

- How did you learn how to do your job? Formal training? Personal instruction by your supervisor? "Peer-to-peer" learning—did you pick things up from co-workers? Figuring things out for yourself? Break down the various ways you learned about appropriate behaviors as well as work tasks or products.

- What differentiates an excellent manager or supervisor from a poor or average one?

- How and why did your job confirm or change your career direction?

- Describe the organizational culture of where you worked and whether or not this culture is the best for you as a worker.

- What were the norms or "unwritten rules" regarding what was and was not acceptable where you worked? Was it difficult to learn these norms and adjust to them?

- How would you rate the quality of your job as a learning experience?

- What did you learn in this job that had nothing to do with your technical skills or your major/concentration?

- How would you rate your performance in the job, regardless of the job's quality?

- Now that you have had this experience, what are your plans for your next job, whether co-op, internship, clinical, or post-graduate?

  Journals and papers are advantageous in that they provide a chance to really go into depth about what you learned, and they also are a more private form of reflection. The downside is that they are more time-consuming and don't allow you the chance to hear the perspectives of fellow students.

3. *Reflecting via e-mail, online message boards, and the Web.* Some coordinators may set up electronic ways of helping you reflect on the job

while you are still working. You may have questions e-mailed to you for your consideration and response. Sometimes programs like Blackboard, online message boards, or the Web are used in order to create places where students can connect with other students and their coordinator despite being far away from campus. The best thing about these methods is that they help you have opportunities to reflect when there is still time to make changes in your performance or address problem areas at work. The negatives include the time involved and the risk of information getting into the hands of those who are not meant to see it. Additionally, the technology is a hurdle for some co-op programs.

4. *Taking a work-related class DURING your co-op.* In the last few years, some Northeastern students have had the opportunity to take a one-credit course during their co-op. The students who took this course on ethics in the workplace were allowed to have this count toward completing their reflection requirement. The class generally meets only a few times in the early evening, though there are also online assignments and discussions. In addition to getting reflection credit for this course, many students found this to be a great opportunity to discuss ethical issues or concerns while they were in the midst of them in the workplace.

5. *Having a one-on-one meeting with your coordinator.* Occasionally—most often in special circumstances—a coordinator may find it acceptable to meet one-on-one with a student to complete the reflection requirement. This is not typical, as it is a very labor-intensive method for a coordinator who may have over 100 students returning to classes after co-op. If something particularly difficult happened on the job, though, this may be an important and useful option in order to confront problems, learn from mistakes, or to determine if the coordinator has issues that must be addressed with the employer.

GETTING CREDIT FOR YOUR WORK EXPERIENCE

For most students, getting an at least average evaluation and completing a reflection requirement means that they will get a passing grade for their work experience. (Most co-ops and internships are graded on a pass/fail basis, if at all.) Sometimes, though, the outcome is in doubt. Any of the following can jeopardize your ability to get a passing grade for your work experience:

*   failing to notify your coordinator about your job before it begins

*   accepting an offer from one employer, only to renege on your agreement to accept an offer with another employer

*   quitting a job without getting your coordinator's permission first

*   getting fired (or getting a poor evaluation)

- failing to turn in an evaluation in a timely manner

- failing to complete a reflection requirement within two months of returning to school

In the end, your coordinator will determine the grade you receive for your work experience. Make sure you understand the grading criteria. Make sure that you're never in a borderline category by doing a great job and completing all steps with your coordinator! After all, failing your work experience doesn't look so great to future employers who will be reviewing your transcript.

FINAL THOUGHTS ON CO-OP SURVIVAL AND SUCCESS

After reading this much of the guidebook, you should have a good foundation when it comes to understanding workplace survival and success. If you can apply the concepts that we've covered in these pages, you will emerge with greater self-awareness, a sense of accomplishment, and a set of experiences that will entice employers looking to hire new graduates. You also will have a new appreciation for how, why, and where learning happens as you go from one job to the next as well as from the classroom to the world of experience.

For a co-op coordinator, internship director, or career services professional, the most satisfying part of the job is seeing students come in with retail stores and restaurants on their resumes and graduate as professionals with a keen sense of who they are, what they want, and what they are capable of accomplishing through hard work. I have seen students who were barely able to get a low-level administrative job on the first co-op who ultimately graduated with incredible experience and a very attractive job offer. I often tell students that internships and co-op jobs are not sprints: They are marathons that reward those who display persistence and consistent effort over the months of a co-op position.

But perhaps I should let some of our top Northeastern University students tell their stories to give you a better sense of what I mean.

Making Sense of Your Co-op – A Student's Perspective
by Ted Schneider

There is nothing like co-op for turning inexperienced freshmen into successful professionals. The constant transition between class and work is painful, tiring, and repetitive but also extremely exciting, rewarding, and invaluable. After four co-op positions in four terrifically different locations, I "know" that I have had a college experience that cannot be matched by experiences had by those at traditional universities.

When I go home for the holidays, I laugh about my high school friends' nervous questions regarding the interview process. Since freshman year, I have had approximately 25 interviews for "professional positions." Interviewing has become such a commonality for my peers and myself that most of us look forward to it almost as if it is a fun challenge - not to see if we could do well, but to find out if we could do even better than the last time. NU students—or co-op students anywhere I guess—are so far ahead of their traditional-program counterparts when it comes to professionalism that we have a reason to be a little proud.

Ted Schneider was an Accounting/MIS student at Northeastern University, Class of 2002.

Here's another one:

Making Sense of Your Co-op – A Student's Perspective
by Mark Moccia

To be honest, I did not know what to expect from co-op. I heard mostly positives about co-op. However, I was still unsure of how I was going to be treated, the relationships I would have with management, how much work I would receive, and other job-related concerns. The most surprising thing I learned about co-op is that you are, in fact, treated just as a full-time employee. You are expected to work standard hours (and overtime if needed), take your job seriously (and not as a temporary assignment where you can "goof off" for 3-6 months) and contribute in a positive manner. The co-op program is the main reason I attended Northeastern: I would have been making a $100,000 blunder by not getting the most out of co-op. The other amazing advantage of co-op is that if you perform well enough, you have the inside track on a full-time position with the company!

I have always been a great student. However, the co-op program has made me realize that it takes more than excellent grades to be successful. Co-op has taught me that you need to have good transferable skills, such as communication, multi-tasking, time management, and the ability to interact with all levels of the organization. Working with corporations has taught me to take my focus on schoolwork and apply it to the business world, specifically through the co-op program. Without the co-op program, my grades would be just as strong but I would not have the skills and savvy to match it.

Mark Moccia was an Accounting/MIS student at Northeastern University, Class of 2002

166

Here's one more!

Making Sense Of Co-op – A Student's Perspective
by Gabriel Glasscock

When I began my co-op career, my expectations weren't high. I expected to be exposed to the corporate climate and have minimal responsibilities at a few companies, graduating with my foot in the door at a few places. Before I knew it, I was in Tampa, Florida, standing in a classroom in front of 80 over-analytical recent college graduates, giving them lectures on the Java programming language. The most surprising thing I've learned is that you can ride this co-op roller coaster as fast as you want to if you're not afraid to take on challenges.

Co-op has humbled me but also made me aware of my capabilities. It tests your resilience, and helps you realize what you really want to do with the rest of your life. It has helped me mature and exposed me to many things. I now know what it's like to have 12 friends laid off on the same day!

Co-op prepares you mentally for the reality of working and dealing with life after college. I truly consider myself lucky to have had these opportunities. In some areas, I consider myself 100% different, and for the better. Typical four-year programs? Heck no! CO-OP!

Gabriel Glasscock was an MIS student at Northeastern University, Class of 2002.

The rest of the book features appendices that may or may not be useful to you right now. Appendix A covers the job search process through the Co-op Learning Model.

Appendix B is a Skills Identification Worksheet that you can complete and tally up. I've found that this is a real confidence builder when used shortly before beginning work on your first resume. Many fledgling co-ops believe that they have nothing to offer a prospective employer. This exercise will help you realize that you probably have at least 20-30 soft skills that are going to be attractive to employers.

Appendix C details how to write cover letters—whether for obtaining an internship, a co-op job, or your first job after graduation. Generally, you won't need to write a cover letter if you're applying for a job through a co-op or internship program, but sooner or later you will want to learn how to write a cover letter that is every bit as strategic as the interviewing approach described earlier in the book.

Appendix D includes a "bridging" exercise that will help you make connections between your resume and a specific job description. Doing this activity will help you realize how you need to change gears and emphasize different strengths and skills based on the job description at hand.

Appendix E has more in-depth information on behavioral-based interviewing, including several excellent student examples. Being able to rehearse specific, vivid stories that can be used to prove that you really do have a given skill is a great way to prepare for *any* kind of interview, not just a behavioral-based one.

Appendix F features some handouts that I like to use in my Introduction to Co-op course. Some may be useful in helping to fine-tune your resume or interview, while others are thought-provoking scenarios that can be a good basis for written reflection or in-class discussion.

Good luck with your co-op career, and remember: The goal is to shine and not simply survive!

CHAPTER 5 REVIEW QUESTIONS

1. Why do many students start getting better grades in classes after completing a co-op or internship?

2. What are three benefits of attending reflection seminars?

3. Think about the last job that you held. What was the *purpose* of that job? How did it fit into the goals of the organization that employed you?

4. Name three situations that could result in a student not getting credit for a co-op or internship.

5. From the three lengthy student sidebar boxes on the benefits of co-op, which one resonated the most with you? Why?

APPENDIX A
The Co-op/Internship Process

In this book we have covered a great deal of information about co-op. Nonetheless, you may very well be wondering "what do I do next?" Every program has its own rules, regulations, and idiosyncrasies, causing difficulty in making generalizations about the job search process across universities. However, there are enough commonalities to make it worth our while to review them here.

More than anything, though, I want to make sure to preface this information with a warning: *The job search process is always evolving and changing over time. Universities are continually revising the job search process, making changes to computer systems and student requirements such as deadlines for turning in resumes, creating e-portfolios, and changing ways to get referred to employers.* ***As such, ALWAYS stay in touch with your coordinator to be sure of the requirements and deadlines for your specific program!*** If in doubt about when you need to get started, make contact and find out sooner rather than later. Failing to do so could make all the difference between success and failure in your job search.

CO-OP LEARNING MODEL

The Co-op Learning Model is a simple but useful way to understand the three primary phases of the co-op process: preparation; activity; and reflection.

The Preparation Phase
The preparation phase includes all of the activities that you undertake to get ready for your co-op or internship. Contrary to the opinion of a few misinformed students, most programs are not job placement services. In other words, you can't just waltz into your coordinator's office a few weeks before your scheduled

work period begins and—just like that—get "assigned" to a job. The system doesn't work that way. Why not? The most important reason is that we want you to own the responsibility of your job search, so you will understand how to do everything you need to do to get a job for the rest of your professional career! Therefore, most co-op professionals won't write your resume for you, don't tell companies who to hire, and require an employer evaluation to help determine if you should get a passing grade for your work experience.

Because of all of this, preparation takes time! Generally, you will be asked to revise your resume more than once, and some students may go on more than a dozen interviews before getting and accepting an offer.

The Activity Phase
After you get a job, you start working regularly with your employer; the work period is the activity phase. During this phase, your focus should be on understanding and meeting your supervisor's expectations regarding everything from work hours to job responsibilities, setting goals together to ensure that you have a mutual understanding about your level of job performance.

During this phase, it also may be advisable to check in with your coordinator back at school—especially if any concerns or problems arise. The objective is to return to school with the best possible evaluation and reference.

The Reflection Phase
After you return to classes, you need to complete the reflection phase to get credit for your co-op. Basically, you will need to make sure that your coordinator receives your evaluation and find out if any reflection requirement needs to be fulfilled. It's also advisable to update your resume, while the job is still fresh in your mind.

Now that you have an overview of the co-op process, let's take a closer look at the details that may be involved in each step.

WORKING WITH YOUR INTERNSHIP/CO-OP COORDINATOR

As mentioned briefly in Chapter 1, it's critical to build a good working relationship with your co-op coordinator—and with other co-op faculty if necessary. Here are some key pointers:

Stay On Your Coordinator's Radar Screen.
Given that your co-op or internship coordinator works with hundreds of students each year, you can't expect him or her to hold your hand through the process. It's absolutely critical that you own the responsibility for finding out and remembering how early and often you need to come in and what you need to accomplish each step along the way. If you're not sure, call or send an e-mail. "I just didn't have time to get in touch" just doesn't cut it with us—not

when it takes all of one or two minutes to update us with an e-mail or voice mail at whatever hour of the day or night. If you're not in touch with us regularly—especially during the months before you're scheduled to start your job—we have to assume that you're really not that interested in working.

Know How To Determine Your Co-op Coordinator's Availability.

Find out if your co-op coordinator can be seen individually either by appointment or by going to walk-in hours. But how can you find out when a given co-op coordinator is available? See if your coordinator has a calendar—either online or just outside the door of their offices.

If you have trouble finding a time to meet·with your coordinator, you should drop an e-mail or call your coordinator to see if additional times are available. If we don't know that you're trying to meet us, we can't help to accommodate you!

Here are a few other helpful hints about working with co-op and internship coordinators as well as career services professionals. With a little thought and communication, you can avoid considerable frustration.

1. *If you are on a tight schedule in general, try to schedule appointments.* Some students have limited free time available due to classes, part-time jobs, clubs, and varsity sports. If you fit this description, you need to be proactive, scheduling appointments ahead of time and asking your coordinator for ways to ensure regular meetings. Most coordinators and career professionals will schedule meetings at irregular times if a student has legitimate conflicts and is proactive and polite about addressing the situation.

2. *If you prefer to come to walk-in hours, try to come first thing in the morning and/or bring homework or reading material if you must come when it's busy.* During the months leading up to the beginning of a work period, coordinators can be very busy seeing students. Some students end up frustrated because they haven't really thought about how to avoid the walk-in logjam. There are many ways to minimize your waiting time. First, come in early—early in the day and early in the process. Many college students are not early risers, so most coordinators tend to have shorter walk-in lines during the morning hours. Anytime after 11:30 tends to get really busy during the peak times of year. Likewise, if you come in several months before your co-op for that first resume review, you will beat the rush and be in good shape the rest of the way.

   Sometimes, though, you can't avoid a long wait—especially during peak months. With this in mind, bring some homework or reading material. That way you won't sit around feeling impatient if you do need to wait a while.

3. *If you really can't come in every week or so during referral period, you need to stay in contact via e-mail or voice mail.* Some students keep popping by

during a busy afternoon walk-in hour time... only to find that there is a long line. If they get discouraged and leave, the coordinator has no idea that the student has made any effort to get in touch. Thus, you really need to stay in touch by voice mail or e-mail—even if it's just to give a quick update regarding your job search or to let your coordinator know that you're having difficulty coming in during the available times. If you fail to let us know that you're having a problem, then we won't know!

4. *Be reasonable about what you expect your coordinator to be able to do for you in person, on the phone, or by e-mail.* In person, don't expect your coordinator to write or rewrite your resume for you or to describe numerous available jobs to you. You need to do many things for yourself. As for e-mails, bear in mind that they should not replace individual meetings. One of my frustrations is when students e-mail their resume to me and ask me to critique it or correct it. It's incredibly time-consuming to edit a resume this way, as it results in extremely long e-mail replies: "On the fourth line of your second job description, three-quarters of the way across the line, add a comma before the word 'demonstrated.'" Ugh! There may be situations in which long e-mails are unavoidable—for example, when you are facing a major problem at work and can't openly talk about it on the phone or come into the office because you're on the job full-time—but resume reviews are generally not one of those situations. Many situations just require a personal meeting.

5. *When faced with frustration or uncertainty, assume the best of your coordinator.* If your coordinator doesn't reply to your call or e-mail as quickly as you like, assume the best in this situation. It may be because you wrote your e-mail on Monday night, and the coordinator was out visiting companies on Tuesday. Then that coordinator may be welcomed back to the office with a few dozen e-mails, 15-20 voice mails, and a long line of students filling up the whole morning of walk-in hours. It doesn't mean that you have been forgotten or that your coordinator doesn't care. If more than three days go by without hearing back—or sooner if you are facing a real emergency—follow up politely and professionally: "I'm sure you're very busy right now.... I just wanted to follow up to make sure you got my message and to see if there was anything else I should be doing right now. It would be great to hear from you when you get a moment. Thanks!"

This is good practice for when similar situations arise with managers and co-workers on co-op. In either situation, this kind of message goes a long way in terms of getting a quick and professional response.

THE STEP-BY-STEP PROCESS

Preparation Phase

Step 1 – *Become Aware of ALL Deadlines and Requirements As Soon As Possible.*
If you're a first-time student—and especially if you are a transfer student, meet with your coordinator as soon as possible to learn about your options regarding when to start co-op. *Don't assume that you can start your co-op or internship whenever you feel like it!* Co-ops and internships are not guaranteed for all students—if you blow off meeting with your coordinator, the consequences generally will be severe. If you miss deadlines, you may not be allowed to use the resources of the co-op department in finding a job. The student who does this will end up seeking his or her own job and risks getting a failing grade for co-op.

Step 2 – *Have a One-on-One Meeting with your Co-op Coordinator.*
This is a mandatory step in most programs. You will identify and discuss your short-term and long-term co-op and career objectives with your coordinator. You also will bring a hard copy of your resume to your co-op coordinator, so he or she can critique and edit it. Save these edits, and use them to revise your resume accordingly. Bring a hard copy of your revised resume to your coordinator along with the edits, so your resume can be proofread quickly and effectively. It may take a few rounds of corrections, but eventually your coordinator may ask for an electronic copy of the finalized resume to e-mail to employers.

Step 3 – *Review Co-op Job Descriptions and Rank Them.*
Once your finalized resume has been approved by your co-op coordinator, you generally will be allowed to start pursuing jobs. Make sure you understand your school's system—including how to work with computerized job listings.

Study the description and requirements and try to determine which jobs represent good learning experiences for you as well as being within your reach. If you're not sure, ask your coordinator. Many coordinators will require you to print out job descriptions that are of great interest to you—this will help you and your coordinator to determine if the job is a good fit and if you meet the qualifications. Keep the job descriptions in a folder.

Step 4 – *Meet with your Co-op Coordinator to Review your Job Rankings.*
The next step generally is to review your job rankings in an individual meeting with your co-op coordinator. Find out how early you can do this, and also if there is a deadline for making this happen. Bring your folder of printed job descriptions to your co-op coordinator.

Your co-op coordinator will review your rankings. In all probability, he or she will have additional suggestions and also may determine that a given job might be too much of a reach for you. Don't be discouraged—it's part of the process, and sometimes seeing your "reach" jobs can help your co-op coordinator suggest other jobs that are steps in the direction of your "reach" jobs. In many but not all programs, coordinators will limit how many jobs you can pursue simultaneously. Coordinators definitely do not want students to just fling dozens of resumes at employers—they want you to be more selective. This also means that you should really know each job description when you come in: Don't just look at a company name or job title and print out the job description without really thinking about how you match up with the job duties and requirements.

I can tell you that students vary *dramatically* in how they interact with a coordinator. I have had students interrupt a meeting with another student—or a phone call—by walking into my office regardless and saying "Send this to Gillette for me for the such-and-such job." Such behavior says a great deal about a student's professionalism—it's never a good idea to treat a coordinator as if she or he is your servant or administrative assistant.

On the other hand, there have been any number of times when I have been absolutely wowed by a student. If someone comes in and is upbeat, professional, and polite, I'm going to try that much harder to help them. There have been many occasions when such a student came in asking about a job that was already filled—and I was so impressed by them that I encouraged them to apply for other good jobs... and even recommended them to an employer!

Step 5 – *Stay in Touch with your Coordinator Regularly throughout the Process.* After your rankings and referrals have been completed, your resume will start going out to employers. Most coordinators e-mail resumes out at least once per week. At this point, there are many different possibilities. Some students get a few interviews out of their first batch of resumes to go out to employers; others don't get any—especially less experienced students.

If you get an interview, let your coordinator know—even if only by e-mail or voice mail. Ask your coordinator how often you should check in. At some point, your coordinator may be able to fill you in a little. You may be told that a company has not contacted any candidates yet, or you may learn that you are not one of the candidates chosen for an interview. In any case, your coordinator will suggest sooner or later that you select some more jobs and then come in again to discuss the new selections.

The worst thing you can do is to get discouraged by not getting interviews or by getting interviews and no offers. These developments don't always come easily! Some students start on time and do everything right—but then disappear completely after they send a batch of resumes and get no reply! Other students definitely intend to stay on top of things, but then they get distracted by mid-terms or other academic responsibilities. *You have to stay in touch*—even if it's just to say that you haven't received any calls and aren't sure what to do next.

Repeat the process of ranking jobs, getting referrals, and going on interviews as many times as you need to in order to get a job. In a job search, you never know if you're ten percent of the way to getting a job or whether you're incredibly close.

But you always have to assume that you're really close and that with another push of effort it will happen for you.

Step 6 – *Responding to a Job Offer.*
Remember these key points:

- Unless you are in a dire financial situation, money should not be the deciding factor in which job you accept. Money is NOT a motivator! That's been proven in many studies. What WILL motivate you? A job with the following characteristics:

  —You like the work itself
  —You have opportunities for growth and advancement
  —You have opportunities for achievement and recognition

  If you're choosing between a great learning experience that is an unpaid internship, or a mediocre experience that pays $8/hour, which will you choose? Depending on your field and other alternatives, you very well may be better off taking the unpaid position. On the other hand, there's nothing wrong with taking a great job that pays $14/hour over a comparable job that pays $10/hour.

  For most students, my advice is to go after the best learning experience at this point in your career. If you focus on your career development now, the financial rewards will come sooner or later—and you'll be happier in the meantime going to work every day.

- If you are offered a job that is not your first choice, you can ask the employer for a short time to consider the offer—no more than three business days. Chapter 3 details how to put an offer on hold gracefully.

- Once you have accepted a job, meet with your coordinator to do an agreement form and any other paperwork. **If you are an international student (here on F-1 and J-1 visas), it is absolutely critical that you receive work authorization BEFORE starting ANY job in the United States.** After 9/11, the government has become incredibly strict about international students who are working without formal authorization. Deportation is becoming much more common. For all students, though, meeting with your coordinator is a good opportunity to discuss success factors for your co-op job, including how to avoid problems and get the best possible evaluation and reference.

- REMEMBER—do NOT accept a job unless you are prepared to honor your commitment no matter what else happens. It is completely unacceptable to renege on your acceptance if you get another offer later—even if the other offer is a much better offer for significantly more money. Students who don't honor their agreements risk getting a failing grade for co-op. If in doubt,

ALWAYS talk to your coordinator before you accept a job offer.

- That said, be careful about being too fickle when it comes to job offers. Increasingly, we have had students waffling about accepting a perfectly good offer—merely because "I really hoped to have several offers to choose from." Applying for a job is not like applying to college, where you might apply to eight or ten and then have weeks or months to choose between three or four who accept you. You need to make a prompt decision in fairness to other candidates who might accept if you decline.

- Re-read Chapter 4 of this guidebook before starting your job, as this chapter has many good ideas about on-the-job success.

Developing Your Own Job

Chapter 1 goes over the guidelines for developing your own job, so you should re-read them if you have any questions about how the process works. Most importantly, remember that students developing their own jobs still need to be in regular contact with their coordinators. You can't go off and do a job without getting it approved beforehand by your coordinator.

Activity Phase

You are expected to complete the entire work period once you have accepted a job. In other words, you can't do a job for a few weeks and then decide you don't like it and just quit. There may be rare occurrences in which a student may be released from their commitment—for example, if the employer misled the student about the nature of the job, or if harassment is going on. HOWEVER, it is the student's responsibility to bring any problems or concerns to the attention of the co-op coordinator instead of just quitting as soon as a problem arises. Send an e-mail, make a call—anything—just let the co-op or internship coordinator know what's going on and get her or his advice before taking action.

Note that most co-ops and interns rarely get vacation days during their co-op work period: There is no "Spring Break" for students working winter and spring, for example. Likewise, students can't end a full-time co-op job in early December to get an extra long Christmas break: At best, your co-op will end a few days before Christmas. Likewise, students working winter/spring may end their co-op on a Friday and start classes by the following Wednesday!

You are expected to work on any days that the organization is open—meaning that some students will get a day off on Columbus Day, while others will not. Organizations have different policies regarding paying students for holidays, but most often employers simply pay you for whatever hours you work.

Contact your coordinator with any problems that arise on the job.

Reflection Phase

Most of the whys and wherefores regarding reflection can be reviewed in Chapter 5. To get credit for co-op or an internship, most programs require that you:

*   complete your co-op job successfully.

*   turn in a relatively good evaluation form.

*   complete a reflection requirement or some other follow-up activity.

APPENDIX B
Skills Identification Worksheet

Instructions: This worksheet is designed to help make you aware of how many skills you already have—probably more than you realize! Put a check mark in every box that reflects a skill that you have as well as WHERE you have demonstrated that skill. Then add up the total number of skills in each column.

COMMUNICATION	Job experience?	School experience?	Other experience?
Sales/Marketing			
Teaching/Training			
Explaining/Listening			
Public speaking			
Total # of Skills			

ORGANIZATION	Job experience?	School experience?	Other experience?
Anticipating/Planning			
Attention to detail			
Prioritizing			
Researching			
Time Management			
Multi-tasking			
Total # of Skills			

INTERPERSONAL	Job experience?	School experience?	Other experience?
Working in a team			
Advising			
Resolving conflict			
Negotiating			
Total # of Skills			

CREATIVE	Job experience?	School experience?	Other experience?
Designing/Inventing			
Developing solutions			
Out of box thinking			
Conceptualizing			
Total # of Skills			

LEADERSHIP	Job experience?	School experience?	Other experience?
Owning responsibility			
Setting/Reaching goals			
Delegating			
Managing/Supervising			
Total # of Skills			

QUANTITATIVE	Job experience?	School experience?	Other experience?
Bookkeeping			
Budgeting			
Calculating			
Collecting			
Estimating			
Recording			
Total # of Skills			

COMPUTER	Job experience?	School experience?	Other experience?
Data Entry			
MS Word			
MS Excel			
Databases			
Programming			
Web Design			
Total # of Skills			

SOFT SKILLS	Job experience?	School experience?	Other experience?
Ability to learn quickly			
Positive attitude			
Work ethic			
Dependability / Reliability			
Flexibility			
Good judgment			
Total # of Skills			

SKILLS IDENTIFICATION SUMMARY

SKILL	Total Number of Skills
COMMUNICATION	
ORGANIZATION	
INTERPERSONAL	
CREATIVE	
LEADERSHIP	
QUANTITATIVE	
COMPUTER	
SOFT SKILLS	
Grand Total:	

Questions

1. What area would you most like to improve before starting co-op?

2. Name two ways in which you could improve some of these skills before starting your first co-op:

APPENDIX C
Writing Effective Cover Letters

If you're looking for a co-op job with the assistance of a co-op program, you may not need to write any cover letters. It may be enough to submit your resume through a co-op coordinator in order to obtain a job interview. Sooner or later, though, you will need to write an effective cover letter in response to a job listing. I have read thousands of cover letters over the years, and it never fails to amaze me how bad they can be—and how good they can be.

The most common mistake made by job applicants is to write a cover letter that really doesn't say anything useful. The bad cover letter will be extremely short, often saying no more than this:

"In response to your listing (in The Boston Globe, on www.monster.com, etc.) I am writing to be considered for the position of Accounts Payable Coordinator (or Financial Analyst or Desktop Support Manager). As you can see on the enclosed resume, I have a degree in business. I am a hard-working individual who would be a good fit for a company in any number of different accounting and finance roles.

"I am excited about the possibility of working for your organization. If you wish to arrange an interview, please contact me at...".

What's wrong with this approach? It breaks the cardinal rule of cover letters: **You need to think of the cover letter as a bridge connecting your resume to a specific job description.** Far too often, job seekers take the easy way out: They write a simple cover letter that is so general that it can be modified quickly to send to another employer. While this has the advantages of being efficient and convenient, there is no question that this is a short-sighted perspective. When a recruiter or manager reads through dozens of cover letters, inevitably he or she sees quite a few that are just like this. Fairly or unfairly, the reader of the quick

185

and general cover letter will make several assumptions about the candidate. It's easy to conclude that the applicant is probably flinging his resume at dozens of jobs—maybe even sending out a hundred cover letters and resumes in the hopes of getting a small handful of interviews. The potential interviewer has to question whether the applicant has even given any serious consideration to whether he really wants the job in question. It's certainly hard to believe that the candidate really wants this specific job, and why would you ever want to hire someone who doesn't really want the job at hand—even if they have a terrific resume?

On the other hand, a great cover letter will not get you a job—but it can get you in the door for an interview, even if you're not a perfect candidate on paper. At best, the cover letter can make the interview much easier by covering the fundamental, strategic reasons why you are a good match for the job. So let's take a look at what comprises an effective cover letter before walking through some specific examples.

ELEMENTS OF AN EFFECTIVE COVER LETTER

Yes, writing a cover letter is more time-consuming than you might like because of the need to tailor each letter individually for each job that you're pursuing. The good news is that there are numerous elements that can be applied to *all* cover letters. While you can never reduce cover letter writing to a formula, you'll find that they become easier to write because the style issues are quite consistent. Here they are:

Start off with a flush-left heading that gives the appropriate name, job title, and address of the cover letter's recipient. Usually this would look something like this:

Ms. Lenora Fritillary, Human Resources Manager
Schlobotnick Products
123 American Way
Roanoke, VA 33547

You then would begin your cover letter with "Dear Ms. Fritillary,".

At other times, you may not have a name and may have to use a job title:

Network Adminstrator
Byte Size Products
1200 Easy Street
Walla Walla, WA 94239

In this situation, you will have to start your cover letter with the more formal "To Whom It May Concern." That's a little formal, but if the job listing offers no contact name, you have to go with it. If the job is one that you are pursuing

186

without any contact name, you can call up the main number of the organization and ask for the name of the person who is in charge of marketing, human resources, or information systems. It's always better to have a real live person listed as the cover letter's recipient unless the ad obviously indicates that the employer prefers to avoid a personal contact.

Briefly state how you learned of the job opportunity (if there is one) or simply express your interest in potential employment. Just as you always want to target a specific individual when you write your cover letter, you definitely want to write a cover letter with a specific job description in mind whenever possible. Otherwise, you face the challenge of writing a cover letter that implies that you're equally excited about any of a wide range of possible jobs. That's a much tougher sell.

Here are a few ways in which you might describe how you learned about the job at hand:

Example 1: I am writing to express my interest in the Accounts Payable Assistant position, which was advertised in last Sunday's *Boston Globe*.

Example 2: Speaking to my friend Patti O'Furnichoor, who works in sales at your organization, I learned that your organization is looking for a market research analyst.

Example 3: In response to your listing on www.monster.com, I am writing to express my interest in the Human Resources Assistant position.

If you have no choice but to submit a cover letter without knowing what jobs might be available, you are forced to write something more general.

Example 1: I am writing to express my interest in working for your organization. Given that your company is known for their work in financial services, I was wondering if there would be a suitable position available for a finance student with excellent organizational skills and a great academic background in the principles of finance. I have strong analytical skills and would be effective in working in positions involving mutual funds, stocks, and bonds.

Example 2: After doing extensive research on the Internet, I know that your company has 600 employees at your Dedham office. With this in mind, I was wondering if there might be opportunities available in PC/LAN support, database administration, or Web development. I am a quick learner with computers, and I have the flexibility to be effective in any number of IT functions.

Make several strong connections between your resume and the job description at hand whenever possible. At this point, you need to put your resume next to the job description and read the two side by side. Are there specific job requirements that you definitely have? Why would this employer hire you instead of someone else for this job? Why wouldn't this employer hire you? Making these assessments will help you figure out what your strategy should be—for the cover letter as well as for a potential interview. You need to come up with three or four concrete reasons as to why you are excellent candidate to interview.

REMEMBER—the goal is to do more than justify why you thought it was okay to submit your resume! Some cover letters come off as a little defensive or apologetic in this way: "Your job description said that you were looking for someone with an accounting degree who also has strong knowledge of advanced functions in Excel. I hope to receive my accounting degree by the end of 2004. While my knowledge of Excel is not advanced, I am certainly very willing to learn..." If you're writing many sentences like these, you probably just aren't a good enough match to merit consideration.

Another common mistake—both in cover letters and interviews—is to talk too much about why the job would be great for you, rather than why you would be great for the job! This ill-fated applicant might write something like this: "Working for your organization would give me a great opportunity to build my knowledge of human resource management. I would be very excited about enhancing my computer skills in this position as well...." Showing enthusiasm about the job is always a good idea, but not if you're only excited about what the job will do for you. You have to imagine yourself as the person reading a big pile of cover letters and resumes—your goal is to find the person who can best help in your organization in this role: not to find the candidate who most needs your help! As such, the hiring manager is going to pick out some number (probably somewhere between three and ten) of candidates who appear to be the most plausible for the job, based on the cover letter and resume.

We'll consider some full-fledged job descriptions and resumes shortly. In the meantime, here are a few examples of ways in which a good cover letter might make connections between a resume and a job description:

Example 1:   Your job description details the need for candidates to have a strong background in marketing as well as excellent communication skills. I received a grade of A- in my Introduction to Marketing class; in particular, I earned a top grade on an analysis of market segmentation in the automobile industry. Additionally, I have worked in numerous retail positions, honing my customer-service skills and refining my knowledge of merchandising. As for my communication skills, I have obtained considerable presentation experience in my business classes and have augmented this by taking an elective in Public Speaking—a course in which I performed extremely well.

Example 2:   From your ad on www.monster.com, I know that you are seeking a highly trustworthy individual with a solid understanding of accounting principles and Excel for your Accounts Receivable Associate position. Both in the classroom and on the job, I have shown that I possess these qualities. As an accounting concentrator at Northeastern University's College of Business Administration, I had a 3.0 GPA overall—but my GPA in accounting classes was a 3.6. Many of my classmates struggled mightily with Intermediate Accounting in particular, while I received an A- in this rigorous course. As far as being trustworthy, I would encourage you to contact any or all of my previous employers, whose contact information is available on the enclosed reference page. I am confident that each supervisor will indicate that I was entrusted with depositing considerable amounts of cash after closing for the night and locking up the place of business. Additionally, I am proficient with Excel: I am extremely confident and comfortable when creating formulas, charts, and graphs—even pivot tables.

Close the cover letter by reaffirming your interest and noting how you prefer to be contacted. This is fairly straightforward.

Example: I would welcome the opportunity to interview for the position. To arrange an interview, please feel free to contact me via e-mail at brooke.m@neu.edu or by phone at 617-555-8800. I look forward to hearing from you soon.

Revise, edit, and proofread your cover letter and resume with extreme care—then find some other competent people to double-check your work.
I can hardly overstate the importance of this point. When reading cover letters and resumes, managers assume that they are seeing the very best that you have to offer. Intentionally or unintentionally—fairly or unfairly—an employer will infer a great deal from your cover letter. The potential employer will develop perceptions regarding your communication skills, attention to detail, level of interest in the job, self-awareness, and selling skills based on the quality of your cover letter. Accordingly, your cover letter needs to be perfect grammatically and completely free of any typos. I knew of one employer who would simply circle typos with red pen and return the cover letters to applicants, noting that "you clearly lack the attention to detail that we seek in all potential recruits." Most employers won't be that harsh—they simply won't bring you in for an interview.

A COMPLETE EXAMPLE OF CREATING A COVER LETTER

Remember the resume of Meghan Brooke from the sample resumes at the end of Chapter 2 of this book? Because we always must try to match a specific individual to a specific job description, let's use her resume in writing a sample cover letter. As for the job description, let's say Meghan is applying for the following job:

GLAMTONE PUBLISHING

Glamtone Publishing — a leader in the publishing and distribution of medical textbooks and other health-related media products — seeks a PC/LAN Support Associate to assist our 400+ end users with computer-related issues ranging from simple MS-Office issues to Intranet updates and ultimately more technical troubleshooting issues, including assistance with our Windows NT network. Qualifications: All applicants must have familiarity with MS-Office, strong communication skills, and the ability to learn to use new technology quickly. Exposure to the following technologies is a plus but not required: HTML, Symantec Ghost, Windows NT Server, and TCP/IP. Looking for a team player with a great attitude who can handle a high-pressure environment! Compensation: This position pays $36,000-$42,000 depending on experience. To submit a resume, please write to Louise Guardado at Glamtone Publishing, 145 West North Street, Southborough, MA 01234. No phone calls please.

It would appear that Meghan has some chance of getting this position: She believes she has all the required skills and at least one of the "plus" skills. She decides to write a cover letter.

The first step in writing this cover letter would be for Meghan to try to be honest with herself regarding her strengths and weaknesses for this position. Here is a quick checklist of some questions for a candidate to ask herself at this point:

1. *Why would this company hire me rather than someone else?* You want to focus on attributes that might make you stand out from other applicants if at all possible. Lots of MIS students have familiarity with MS-Office, for example, so that might not be the best primary selling point. For Meghan, her best bet might be to concentrate on her high GPA as a reflection of the "ability to learn quickly"—not everyone can say that they have a high GPA. Her customer service experience at two jobs—including the ability to learn quickly at Kohl's—would be worth citing as well.

2. *Why WOULDN'T this employer hire me, and can I do anything about that?* When looking at job descriptions, you can't just consider what jobs are attractive to you—you have to ask yourself how you can make yourself most attractive to the employer. You have to be honest with yourself—for example, could Meghan be beaten out by someone who has more of the preferred skills listed in this job description? Absolutely. Can she do anything about that? Maybe. If she really wants this job and has the time to do some additional research, she could take a few days to try to ramp up on the skills she lacks. She certainly could learn enough about Symantec Ghost to be able to mention it briefly in the cover letter and discuss it intelligently in the interview. Reading a *Networking for Dummies* book or something shorter about Windows NT Server and TCP/IP obviously could make an impact.

But isn't that a lot of extra work in light of the fact that she doesn't even have an interview yet? Of course it is. You have to be judicious about how much time you are willing and able to invest in each cover letter. However, if Meghan is completely sure that she wants a PC/LAN Support job, then doing some extra research on software applications is bound to pay off sooner or later. Doing research on the company also can help—though that would definitely be the kind of extra effort that is more of a one-shot deal.

3. *Is there anything I can reasonably do that will help get me inside information about the job?* If you were referred to the job by someone, you definitely should pump that person for information about the organization. If you're lucky, maybe they will even be able to tell you some useful facts about the organization's culture, the supervisor and/or interviewer, and the job itself. What do people really like and dislike about this job, this department, this organization? If you know some of these things, you may able to tailor your cover letter accordingly. At the very least, you could check out the company website or drop by the company and tell the receptionist that you intend to apply for a job—is there any general information available about the company. Taking any of these steps can reflect your willingness to go the extra mile as well as your sincere interest in the job.

Once you have made this kind of self-assessment and done what you can do regarding your "fatal flaws," you can write the cover letter itself. On the following page, you can see what Meghan's finished cover letter might look like.

191

March 24, 2008

Ms. Louise Guardado
Glamtone Publishing
145 West North Street
Southborough, MA 01234

Dear Ms. Guardado,

I am writing to express my interest in the PC/LAN Support Associate position, which your organization posted with the job listings made available on Northeastern University's HuskyCareerLink system.

As you can see on the enclosed resume, I have numerous skills and qualities that make me a great fit for this position. Despite challenging myself with a double concentration in MIS and Marketing, I have managed to maintain a 3.6 GPA at Northeastern University. I believe that my excellent academic record reflects my ability to learn quickly—a critical soft skill for any new hire in a technology-oriented position. In my previous job experience, I have an outstanding record of providing patient and effective customer service. This experience should prove invaluable when providing PC support to Glamtone's end users.

While I have not had the opportunity to work with Symantec Ghost or with Local Area Networks, I have done extensive reading on these areas since reviewing your job description. As a result, I have a good but basic sense of how to re-image a computer as well as an understanding of networking fundamentals.

I would be delighted to come in for an interview at your earliest convenience. From my research on Glamtone Publishing, I know that you are a young, fast-growing publisher with a reputation for producing highly professional medical materials. After talking to Beth Shawerma in your Human Resources Department, I would say that I especially would enjoy working in the fast-paced environment at Glamtone.

Please feel free to contact me via e-mail at brooke.m@neu.edu or by phone at 617-555-8800 to arrange an interview. For your convenience, I am also enclosing my references—I urge you to contact them to verify anything on my resume or to ask any questions about my work and academic history. I look forward to hearing from you soon.

Sincerely,

Meghan Brooke

WRITING A COVER LETTER AS A CO-OP STUDENT

In some instances, students also may write cover letters when attempting to find a co-op job—most often with a co-op employer who is not currently involved with a co-op program. When writing this kind of cover letter, you will need to provide a brief explanation of what you are seeking as well as why hiring a co-op student would be a good move for the employer.

With this in mind, let's revise the previous letter. In this case, let's assume that Meghan is a co-op student seeking an MIS position for six months. We also will use this example to show how to write a more general cover letter. As noted earlier, you also want to write the cover letter with a specific job description in mind. If that is not possible, however, this might be a good approach.

Look at the following page to see this co-op job search cover letter in its entirety.

March 24, 2008

Human Resources Manager
Glamtone Publishing
145 West North Street
Southborough, MA 01234

To Whom It May Concern:

As a current student at Northeastern University, I am writing to express my interest in seeking a computer-related co-op position. In my academic program, I go to classes full-time for the first half of the calendar year. Then I am available to work full-time hours for over six full months, starting work this year on Monday, June 15 and continuing through December. I am willing to consider any position that involves computers—some examples would include PC/LAN support, database design/development maintenance, Web page design and maintenance, QA testing, or positions that use computers to help other functional areas such as marketing and finance.

From your perspective as an employer, there are many benefits to hiring a co-op student. In these economically uncertain times, co-op student workers represent a relatively short-term commitment. Co-ops are cost-effective and benefit-free human resources. Co-op students are trying to build great resumes and references for future employment, so they are highly motivated workers as well. Lastly, co-op hires are a good way to keep a recruiting pipeline active in anticipation of brighter economic times in the future.

As you can see on the enclosed resume, I have numerous skills and qualities that make me a great fit for a computer-related position. Despite challenging myself with a double concentration in MIS and Marketing, I have managed to maintain a 3.6 GPA at Northeastern University. I believe that my excellent academic record reflects my ability to learn quickly—a critical soft skill for any new hire in a technology-oriented position. In my previous job experience, I have an outstanding record of providing patient and effective customer service. This experience would prove invaluable if your Network Administrator needs assistance in providing PC support to Glamtone's end users.

I would be delighted to come in for an interview at your earliest convenience. From my research on Glamtone Publishing, I know that you are a young, fast-growing publisher with a reputation for producing highly professional medical materials. After talking to Beth Shawerma in your Human Resources Department, I would say that I especially would enjoy working in the fast-paced environment at Glamtone.

Please feel free to contact me via e-mail at brooke.m@neu.edu or by phone at 617-555-8800 to arrange an interview. For your convenience, I am also enclosing my references—I urge you to contact them to verify anything on my resume or to ask any questions about my work and academic history. I look forward to hearing from you soon.

Sincerely,

Meghan Brooke

FINAL THOUGHTS ON WRITING A COVER LETTER

You may never have to write a cover letter during your co-op career, but sooner or later you will have to know how to write one effectively. Even when you learn about job opportunities through friends, family, fellow students, or former employers, you frequently will be asked to write a cover letter when submitting your resume.

Given that cover letters are time-consuming, there is nothing inherently wrong with having a few cover letters that you re-use to some degree—certain elements might remain the same across quite a few letters. However, don't EVER send out a cover letter without making sure that you have changed ANY customized references! Imagine how well it would go over if Meghan took her Glamtone cover letter and reworked it for another position—but then left the reference to Glamtone in the final paragraph!! All of a sudden, the first impression that the other employer has of Meghan is of someone who lacks attention to detail and who may indeed be flinging dozens of cover letters at jobs with only slight modifications.

Because organizations listing jobs may get tons of replies—especially in a tough economy—a little persistence can't hurt. If you hear nothing from an employer within a few weeks, you might try writing a brief, upbeat note to reaffirm your interest—particularly if you think the job is a great fit.

Several years ago, I replied to a *Boston Globe* ad listing a position that appeared to be an unusually good match for me at that time. Two weeks passed, and I heard nothing. I wrote a follow-up letter and politely acknowledged that I was sure that the company was very busy—particularly given that they were a small company listing a position emphasizing their need for a medical writer/project manager. I reaffirmed my interest in the position and briefly recapitulated why I was a great match. Then I just said the honest truth—I was only a few weeks away from needing to make a commitment regarding a teaching position that was available to me. If the position was filled or if they were uninterested, I understood completely. If not, I urged them to arrange an interview as soon as possible.

Within three days of mailing the letter, I received a call to arrange the interview. Three interviews later, I got the offer and accepted it. I often wondered if that would have happened if I had simply waited however long it might have taken for them to acknowledge my first attempt. After the second letter, they definitely knew that I was seriously interested. I don't know any organization that wants to hire someone who only wants the job a little!

APPENDIX D
Bridging Exercise

Many individuals are strong job candidates, but they are hurt by failing to tailor their answers to the job for which they are applying. When they get asked general questions such as "Tell me about yourself," they always give the same generic response. This exercise attempts to counter that tendency, forcing individuals to see how different their answers might be to open-ended questions in one interview versus another.

This is useful as a prep class assignment or for students who want extra practice in connecting their qualifications to a specific job description. For instructors, I recommend running through several resume/job description combinations in front of the class, so students can begin to see how different responses can be when job candidates are devising customized, strategic answers.

DIRECTIONS FOR BRIDGING EXERCISE

Step 1
Print out a copy of your resume.

Step 2
From your school's job listings—or from any other source of job descriptions—print out a job description that interests you. Try to pick out a job that lists many qualifications, including some soft skills (i.e., ability to multi-task).

Step 3
Referring to your resume to some degree, write out a detailed answer to the question "TELL ME ABOUT YOURSELF." Your answer should include the three or four top reasons why YOU are good match for THIS job description, making sure to emphasize your most important reason. One good trick that will help

you ensure that you have a *strategic* answer to "tell me about yourself" is to start off your answer by saying "I'm excited to be here at [*name of company*] today because I know you're looking for someone who…" Then proceed to list three or four specific soft skills, technical skills, job experiences, or classroom credentials that make you a great candidate for the job at hand. Refer to the guidebook if you need assistance in determining what an EXCELLENT answer to this question would be.

Step 4
Write out TWO specific stories about yourself that support two different strategic elements that you presented in your answer to "Tell Me About Yourself." For example, if you touted your ability to work in a fast-paced environment as one trait that makes you a good fit for the job, give us a specific story that shows you at your best in demonstrating that quality in a job, in a specific academic situation, or in an extracurricular experience. These stories should have enough details to be vivid and believable. Usually, they start out with a specific situation, challenge, problem, or conflict. Walk through that, and then tell, step-by-step, what you said or did to bring about a positive outcome. Do that with two different elements of your "Tell me about yourself" answer.

So if you answered your Tell Me About Yourself question by touting your customer-service skills, your organizational skills, and your ability to learn quickly, you would need to come up with two specific stories that show two of those skills "in action." These stories could come from an experience in a job, in the classroom, or in your personal life. **Be sure to label your story to indicate which trait or skill you're intending to showcase with that story.**

EXAMPLE OF A GOOD STORY
Here's a story I might use to back up my claim that I'm a self-starter:

Story #1 – Self-Starter
"One summer I was doing temp jobs in offices, and I ended up in a state government agency, covering for an employee who was on a two-week vacation. Within a couple of days, I was surprised to find that I could complete her whole day's worth of work in under two hours.

"My co-workers encouraged me to take it easy—no one seemed to work hard in that office, goofing off was a part of the culture. For me, though, the day dragged if I wasn't doing much, and I wanted to feel like I was earning my pay. I started asking people if they had work for me to do.

"Soon the word got around: 'Hey, there's a guy on the fifth floor who will do your work for you! And he does it really well, too!' People from as far as three floors away brought me tons of work with spreadsheets and reports. It was maybe a little bit of a ridiculous situation from an organizational standpoint, but the bottom line was that I learned a great deal about a variety of jobs; I kept busy and had a much better time. By the end of my two weeks, my supervisor urged me to take the civil service exam so he could keep me there full time. I declined—not my kind of work culture—but I was flattered."

The great thing about using stories like this is as follows: You use a story to prove that you have one quality—in this case, being a self-starter—but you end up proving that you have many other good qualities. In my example, I could use this story to show that I'm efficient, a quick learner, and a strong enough person to not be influenced by unmotivated co-workers.

Step 5
Staple together your finalized resume, the job description that you picked for this exercise, your typed answer to "tell me about yourself," and your two typed stories—each of which should be labeled to indicate what soft skill, trait, or quality that you're trying to demonstrate through each story.

APPENDIX E
Behavioral-Based Interviewing

In Chapter 3, I touched on Behavioral-Based Interviewing (BBI). Having taught BBI to my preparation class over the last four semesters, however, I have come to believe that interviewees should devote much more time to preparing BBI stories for interviews. The good news is that this has come to be the favorite part of the class. Putting some energy into planning what stories you will use and writing them out is incredibly valuable. Once you have a handful of BBI stories, believe me, you'll find opportunities to work them into ANY type of interview!

Behavioral-based interviewing is an increasingly common interviewing method. Many large companies use it, including Microsoft and many consulting firms. Just recently, Johnson & Johnson had a new interviewer come to campus and ask students for stories as a major component of the interview—stories about making the transition from high school to college, stories about previous jobs, and so forth. Some interviewers almost exclusively use this approach, while others may ask one or two BBI questions as part of an otherwise conventional interview. Although all interview methods are far from perfect in predicting future job performance, behavioral-based interviews generally are considered the most valid tool available. Why would that be? Probably because BBI questions require that you use true stories instead of scripted answers that sound good. Unless you're a pathological liar, it's quite difficult to make up a vivid, believable story with considerable detail.

But what if your interviews prove to be entirely conventional? Well, I've come to believe that ALL interview candidates should be prepared for BBI questions. Even when interviewers use the conventional approach to questioning, it's always helpful to be able to tell a couple of specific and vivid stories. After all, anyone can start off an interview by touting their excellent interpersonal skills or ability to juggle multiple tasks: But just *saying* that is not proving that you really have those traits. You need to *show* what you really mean, and it needs to be a true story for it to be credible and believable. In any interview, your strategy is your foundation, but BBI stories are a great way to build on that foundation.

Characteristics of Behavioral-Based Interview Questions

BBI questions are pretty easy to spot. The interviewer will often start questions by saying "Tell me about a time when....," before going on to ask you about a specific instance in which you demonstrated one of any number of qualities: customer service skills; ability to multi-task; organizational skills; ability to be a good team player; willingness to go the extra mile; ability to overcome adversity; passion for technology; etc. Here are some examples:

- Tell me about a specific time when you encountered adversity working in a group. Describe the group's goals, the nature of the adversity, what your role was in the group, and how the situation turned out.

- What would you say has been the greatest achievement of your life thus far? Walk me through how you accomplished it.

- Please give me an example of a time when you failed at something and how you handled that.

- Tell me about a time when you went above and beyond expectations in a school or work situation.

- Describe a specific situation in which you took an unpopular stand.

From these questions, you might imagine that the interviewee ends up doing most of the talking in these interviews. If so, you would be correct. After setting the stage with the question, the interviewer probably will listen and take notes, occasionally stepping in with a clarifying question.

When faced with a behavioral-based interview, most candidates find it difficult to come up with a great and relevant story off the top of their heads. Sometimes the first answer that comes to mind may not be the best one to illustrate a given quality. You need to think in advance about the situations that truly show you at your very best.

Answering Behavioral-Based Interviewing Questions

Many career professionals favor an approach called STAR (Situation, Task, Actions, Results) in answering these questions. While this is a memorable acronym, I think that it perhaps oversimplifies the approach to answering these questions. With that in mind, here are my principles:

1. *Think STORY, not EXAMPLE.* What's the difference between a story and an example? When asked to give an example, many interviewees fall into the trap of responding too generally: "When I worked at Papa Gino's, we always had to juggle multiple tasks. We usually had many tables to handle at once, and more often than not we had a packed restaurant...."

202

Right away, this answer is off to a bad start. If you find yourself saying things like "always" or "usually" or similar words, you're being much too general. If you're asked a BBI question in an interview, and you respond with a general overview of a job or classroom experience, the interviewer often will follow up by saying, "Okay, but can you tell me about a *specific* time when you [had to handle conflict, overcome adversity in a team, etc.]?" Often the interviewer will keep pushing until you do.

Here are some good questions to ask yourself when attempting to come up with the best possible stories:

- What was my very best day in that job? What was the hardest day or week?

- What was my most challenging task or customer or problem I had to overcome? What was the biggest crisis I faced?

Unlike an example, a story starts at one moment in time—maybe it's Tuesday, July 19 at about 10:30 a.m. Think in terms of a good book or movie. Usually any good story starts at a moment of conflict or crisis or challenge. Sure, a very quick overview may be appropriate, but make sure to get to that moment of truth very soon. Next, remember that you are the protagonist. Therefore, we are most interested in YOUR actions, thoughts, and emotions—be sure to convey them. Lastly, many a good story has been spoiled by a dissatisfying end. Be sure to RESOLVE the conflict by briefly describing the outcome, impact, or aftermath of the story.

2. *When you use a really good story to prove you have one particular soft skill, you will end up proving that you have three or four other soft skills.* BBI stories are usually rich in material. You usually have to convey so much detail to prove that you have a given quality that you end up showcasing other positive traits as well. Therefore, it's always great to use BBI stories—even when you're not in a BBI interview.

Here's a terrific example of this phenomenon. I did a practice interview many years ago with one student, and I used a mostly conventional style. Her interview was absolutely mediocre: I wasn't getting any sense of what made this woman unique or why I might have any interest in her as a potential employee. So in an attempt to see if I could pull more out of her, I asked her a BBI question: "What, specifically, would you say has been the greatest achievement of your life?"

She thought about it for several seconds, and then she blew me away with her reply. "When I was very young, there were some sudden deaths in my immediate family. As a result, I grew up feeling very terrified of death and of any possible medical emergency. But one day when I was in high school, I just got fed up with being that way. I decided to get CPR training, and then

I joined a Rescue Squad in my hometown. Now I know that if anything were to happen to a loved one, I wouldn't be powerless to help."

Wow! All of a sudden I saw many admirable qualities in this woman. Here was someone who had self-awareness and who had the courage to tackle a weakness head-on. Here was someone who certainly was able and willing to learn and who had training in handling high-pressure situations. More than anything, though, I think I saw her as a multidimensional, sympathetic human being for the first time. At the end of the interview, I told her that I wanted her to push that story to the beginning of her interview—using it as soon as she was given any open-ended question, such as "Tell me about yourself" or "What are your strengths?" I also reminded her that she could tap into these experiences for any number of other BBI or "specific example" types of questions. It didn't take long for her to have a dynamic interview.

3. *Make sure to walk through the story step by step.* After you've identified a pretty specific day or week or job task, then walk through it step by step:

    A. Give a quick, brief overview of the job or situation. Ideally, use the overview to help the interviewer understand what is really "at stake" in the story.
    B. Pick a specific moment in time when something caused a problem or conflict.
    C. Walk through the situation step by step: What did you do in response? What were you thinking as you dealt with it? What were you feeling? What was the final outcome?

    That's a good rule of thumb if you feel like your stories lack depth or meat: Dig deeper into your actions, thoughts, and feelings to help us understand HOW you got through this situation. Some interviewers will pull your thoughts and feelings and specific actions out of you, but it's much easier if you can just lay them out without being asked.

4. *Focus on YOUR role in the situation.* There's an old cliché that "There is no 'I' in TEAM." Well, that's not true in behavioral-based interviewing. In fact, there are FOUR "I"s in BEHAVIORAL-BASED INTERVIEWING! When you're telling a story about a work or school team, make sure to describe YOUR individual role on the team—not just the team as a collective. There are many ways to contribute to a team: describe what KIND of team player you are by spelling out roles in a team situation.

5. *Don't "use up" a job in just one story!* Another problem with the more general stories is that you can use up a job in just one story... and you may need more stories later in the interview. If it's a job you've done well, there should be MANY stories from various days, customers, tasks, projects, and so forth. Odds are that these stories can be used to highlight many, many transferable skills.

6. *Be sure to pick a high-stakes story if you have one.* Stories about doing something simple to turn around a slightly disgruntled customer or solving a fairly minor problem at work or school aren't terrible, but they do make one wonder if this is really the individual's best achievement. If it isn't, the person made an error in judgment in picking that story. If it is, maybe the person just isn't all that impressive. Start off by thinking about some of the proudest moments in your life—overcoming a major weakness or fear or failure, or maybe just something where you blew away people's expectations in a situation. Dig deep and give this some thought in coming up with more great stories.

A few years ago Microsoft asked this question: "Tell me about a specific time when you failed at something and how you responded to that failure." A couple of students talked about getting a D or F on a first paper and then responding by working harder and getting, say, a C+ in the course. That's not too inspiring. Maybe it was the best story they had, but I have to think that with more planning they could have come up with something that would be more impressive. In contrast, another candidate talked about failing accounting despite going to office hours, getting tutoring, working harder, and so on. The interviewers were impressed because he was able to convey his emotions about all of this—what stood out was how much this failure upset him. They were even more impressed when he talked about taking his accounting textbook to work every day the following summer so he could study during breaks. He wrapped up by telling them that he finally retook the class and got a B+. That was a great story: He showed that he DID care about his grades, and he also showed the soft skills of persistence, initiative, and overcoming adversity. I might add that he just graduated and has accepted a job at Microsoft.

7. *Vivid details make the stories come alive.* One good mnemonic device is ABC, as it helps remind you to inject *affective, behavioral, and cognitive* elements—emotions, actions, and thoughts—into your stories. Just like in a good novel, I want to get inside your head—especially when you get to that "moment of truth" in your story. For every major plot twist in your story, try telling me what was going through your mind at those critical moments. Quantitative details also make the story come alive.

8. *Be careful about too little information—or too much!* When there was a problem with story length, often the stories were too short. If it's something you can tell in three or four sentences and less than 30 seconds, the story probably lacks depth. Microsoft talks about interviewees failing to "drill down into the details."

One analogy that may be helpful is to think of your stories the way a novelist or film director would think of them. There are times in movies or novels where we skip over the action quickly... and there are times when we have that extreme close-up, that tight focus when we really see and hear everything that the protagonist is doing. Give us a quick overview, but be sure to have that extreme close-up, too.

Conversely, some stories are too long. Avoid any information that is not "need to know." Some details may be entertaining, but if they aren't really showcasing your skills or traits, they aren't helping you. Even in BBI, a good story can be told in about 60 seconds, maybe 90 at most... and remember that you don't want to speak too fast in an interview! If you're not sure if you've gone on too long, try timing yourself while speaking at a reasonable pace.

9. *Life lesson stories also can work.* In my days in fiction-writing workshops, I learned that there are rules... but sometimes they can be broken. This came home to me again just this semester. As you'll see with one of the following stories, it is indeed possible to have a story in which you learned something not so much from something you *did* but from something that happened to you. You have to be careful with this kind of story, as you don't want to come off as a passive person as opposed to a change agent in life. But if you can frame the life lesson in a way that shows how that experience helped you learn, grow, and change as an individual, it CAN work!

10. *What have you done for me lately?* When one prominent interviewer came to class recently, he reported afterwards that his BBI questions yielded some good answers... but that some candidates had no stories at all from their college years. So while you may have accomplished something great as a child or back in junior high, you want to make sure that you have at least some stories that reflect accomplishments in the last year or two. If you don't believe that you *have* any great successes from your college years, you need to think harder... or to start working toward the kind of performances in the classroom or in jobs that will result in some great success stories!

Here's an assignment that I recommend: Write up three stories that show you at your best. Then, for each story, write up at least three soft skills or marketable qualities that each story could be used to illustrate.

Each story should incorporate the following steps: What challenge or problem or situation did you face? What did you think, say, and do in addressing that problem, step-by-step? What were the positive outcomes and results of your actions?

To give you some excellent examples of how to do this, here are some of the best stories that my students submitted in response to the bridging assignment in Appendix D. I've taken each story a step further by mentioning three or more additional soft skills that the story could be used to show.

GREAT STORIES – STUDENT EXAMPLES

1. *Ali Ciccariello wrote up this story to prove that she has analytical and multi-tasking skills:*

    "During the time I worked at the Fruit Center Marketplace, I was eventually promoted to a managerial position in the front-end department. Being in a supervising position was a great experience for me, allowing me to recognize store priorities and multi-task different problems. I consider myself to be very analytical, so when I came across a particular store problem I enjoyed finding a solution.

    "I can remember one particular Saturday when everything in the store seemed to be going wrong. The Fruit Center had just received new cash registers, and my fellow bosses and I were still trying to figure out all the new "kinks" in the system. The registers had been working normally all day, until suddenly one register froze and wouldn't turn on. Believe it or not, it is a huge problem when even one register stops working on a high-volume day.

    "Immediately, I tried to prioritize the problems I had to deal with. I knew customer satisfaction was the main goal of the Fruit Center, so I calmly and politely explained to the customers in that particular line what was occurring and suggested moving to another line for business. Because I had clearly explained the situation to the customers and apologized for it, they were willing to move to another line without incident. I then dealt with the cash register malfunction. I called the computer company that serviced the register, and their support staff walked me through the steps necessary to deal with the register problem. Although it was a stressful situation, I was able to work well under pressure and still manage to prioritize what needed to be done."

    ~ Alexandra Ciccariello, Northeastern University Class of 2008

Did Ali prove that she had strong multi-tasking and analytical skills? Absolutely! But there are several other skills that are displayed here: customer-service skills; problem-solving skills; ability to stay calm under pressure; and ability to prioritize. That's a pretty amazing assortment of skills!

I think that the power of this story is that it pinpoints the focus on one specific day while still giving a little background for that day. The more you tighten your focus on "one moment in time," the more likely you are to make the situation really come alive. When that happens, the interviewer can see all kinds of great qualities that you have—even ones that you're not trying to display!

The other bonus from a rich story is that Ali not only has a powerful story up her sleeve; she also has a story that can be used to showcase different qualities in different interviews. My students find that once they have done the heavy lifting of writing the story, they manage to find opportunities to work it into conventional interviews—not just BBIs.

2. *For her job description, Aimee Stupak needed to show dedication:*

"Last summer, I took a new position in the West Hartford Building Department as a temporary Office Assistant. I was eager to experience a new position with more responsibility. I quickly learned to dress in more businesslike attire and to wake up two hours earlier than I used to for my previous job. I learned to appreciate the office setting very quickly as well, and given the fact that initiative is the number one thing my boss was looking for, I excelled immediately.

"From the first day, I took the initiative to understand the filing system and to help organize the files in a new way, so as to simplify the process of finding files for anyone in the office who needed to. I set up new labels for the cabinets and was instantly shown appreciation from the secretaries that I was working for.

"After only a week, the head supervisor and main building inspector asked me if I'd be interested in attempting a job they had been trying to find someone to do for a while. He brought me into "the Vault" which is full of barrels that contain building plans for single-family homes, stores, and apartment complexes all over the Town of West Hartford. Unfortunately, the barrels were dated back so far that "the Vault" was becoming overfilled and impossible to work with. No one, however, was willing to do the "dirty work." My supervisor explained that I would need to search through each barrel, and weed out only the plans that applied to single-family homes. After collecting these plans, he asked me to send them back to the home to which they applied.

"I started the job immediately, completing my daily responsibilities and entering "the Vault" at any point in the day that there was some downtime. I made a lot of progress and ended up cleaning out a very large portion of the space. When my last day came at the job because of the upcoming semester, I was thanked by all and told that my motivation and intense dedication to the job would be greatly missed."

~ Aimee Stupak, Northeastern University Class of 2008

This story shows dedication but many other qualities as well: willingness to do whatever asked without complaint; positive attitude; persistence; and organizational skills. I'm fond of this story because it's a good reminder that most students have had high-school jobs that included a good amount of "gruntwork." As a result, many students believe that they don't have interesting experiences to use for a BBI, as they haven't done anything "important" enough. Yet a story about taking on the task that nobody else wanted is a great way to show off some very attractive qualities in an entry-level professional.

3. *Here's a story that Nat Stevens used in an attempt to prove that he has strong organizational skills:*

"As the day lagged on at TextHELP Systems, I thought about how it was already 3:30 p.m., and that I only had an hour and a half left to finish up the logs. Just then the phone rang. I picked it up to hear the lovely voice of one of our sales reps on the west coast. She started off by saying, 'You're going to hate me,' so I knew that something challenging was coming. She added, 'I need you to get a mailing out to about five counties in Texas, by tonight. I didn't realize it until now.' I thought to myself about how difficult this would be, but I told her it wouldn't be a problem and I would gladly get it done.

"I started my work. First, I had to pull the names of all the directors from these counties that she wanted me to mail information to. The final list came to about 441 people. Next I had to print all the labels. In the meantime, I used two copy machines to make sure the first page of two of the press releases for the mailing were on letterhead. Then I had to make sure that the following pages were correlated appropriately. Finally, I had to fill each envelope, stamp them, and label them. Needless to say, although I had intended to leave at 5:00 pm, I did not step out of the office until 8:00 pm. The sense of accomplishment for completing the job provided me with much more satisfaction than I had originally anticipated."

~ Nat Stevens, Northeastern University Class of 2008

Here Nat attempts to prove that he has strong organizational skills, and he succeeds. However, a good story always ends up showing much more than one skill or quality! Nat could use this story to show many other valued traits: positive attitude, dedication, willingness to go above and beyond... maybe even customer-service skills if we think of the salesperson as an internal customer.

4. *Jared Yee's story below proves a useful point: Many first-time job seekers take their retail experiences for granted. If you reflect on them, you're bound to come up with an impressive incident. Note how he jumps right in the phrase "One time..."—a good hint that we're about to get a story of one especially challenging or interesting day or incident.*

"One time at BJ's Wholesale Club where I worked, it was incredibly busy. All the lines at the registers were filled almost to the middle of the store. My supervisors were busy helping customers and the managers were too busy to assist customers. My supervisor told me to take over some of her responsibilities. She told me one of the freezers with dairy products was broken and that I needed to find one of the managers to fix the problem. She told me afterwards to help a customer with a problem she was having. I went to the produce section but the manager was busy. He told me to get another manager to handle the situation. This manager however, was also unavailable to fix the freezer.

"I realized that the freezer would not get fixed for possibly hours. I took matters in to my own hands. I got three carriages from the parking lot, filled them with all the dairy products from the broken freezer, and brought them into the storage section of a nearby freezer. After that was resolved, I found the very frustrated customer who was trying to buy a computer and was in a rush because she had to pick up her daughter. The computer she wanted was not on the shelf but she wanted the one on display. I had dealt with a situation like this before but with a supervisor's help.

"However, due to the chaos within the store I was told to handle the situation on my own. I wrote down the codes of the computer she wanted, being unable to look it up on the system's computer because it was being used. I then went to the storage room and looked for the empty box with the same code. I found it, went back down to the display shelf, and packed it along with all its parts in the box. I then assisted the customer bringing the computer to my register line, since all the others were filled and she was in a rush. The manager said this was alright to do because she had been waiting for a long time. After ringing up the customer's computer, she thanked me and said that I had "saved her from a terrible day."

~ Jared Yee, Northeastern University Class of 2009

Jared picked this story because he wanted to show the ability to handle multiple projects at one time—a qualification for a job with Deloitte and Touche. However, Deloitte also seeks an excellent team player who is highly organized—two other qualities that this story captures. It also could be used to show an ability to work independently, perseverance, and customer service—to name just a few qualities!

5. *The next story is by Rebecca Harkess. As you read it, remember that the ultimate goal is to be able to write a story FIRST, and then to list at least THREE soft skills that the story could be used to prove about yourself. So as you read this story, try to think of all the different soft skills or qualities that Rebecca could use this story to prove during an interview:*

"At my high school they take their yearbook very seriously. The book is over 400 pages long, has an annual budget of over $200,000, and has won numerous national awards. There is typically an editorial staff of two editors-in-chief and eight section editors, along with a staff of 30. My senior year our advisor asked if I would be willing to take on the position of Editor in Chief by myself as she did not feel anyone else was qualified for the job. I agreed and spent the summer before preparing the layout of the book, setting up our office, and buying new equipment.

"Our first deadline of around 80 pages was due in mid-October. I decided to tell the staff the deadline was at the end of September so we would have adequate editing time. The due date I set came and I went to collect layouts from my staff and found that only half had completed their layouts and even those were only mediocre. I went home that night feeling that I had already failed. I had nothing to work with and yet in a few weeks I was responsible for turning in 80 pages. No one had listened to the revisions I had made and I felt powerless.

"I decided that I couldn't give up; I was going to get this book done and done right because I had been given the responsibility to do so. I stayed up almost the whole night and wrote a two-page speech to deliver to my staff the next morning. I knew I had to be careful to balance coming off as angry to get my point across that I was serious, but at the same time I did not want everyone to think that I was on a power trip, especially because a lot of these students were in my same grade and people I considered friends. On the way to class that day I stopped at the grocery store to buy some doughnuts for the staff as I knew this was a way to show that I really cared about them and that I wanted this to be an enjoyable experience.

"I then sat everyone down and explained to them how very disappointed I was with the results I had seen and that they were unacceptable. I outlined a plan of how I wanted the layouts to get done including showing them new forms that I had created so that each student could review his or her own work before turning it in to me. I stressed the fact that I believed in the ability of each one of them and that I truly believed we could have a lot of fun and produce a book that we would all be really proud of. I could tell when I was done that everyone seemed much more motivated, they really wanted to work hard as a team and get this done.

"Every deadline after that I almost always received layouts on time and in near perfect form. In addition, our staff really bonded throughout the year and we had a really great time. When the book came out at the end of the year we heard from countless students that of all the years this was their favorite yearbook. I felt so proud of the book and my staff."

~ *Rebecca Harkess, Northeastern University Class of 2010*

Rebecca's story is one of the best BBI stories that I've seen in a long time. Consider some of the elements: Even when she is giving background/ overview to set up the critical moment of the story, we learn some things that are impressive about her. Due to the quantitative and qualitative details, we see that her editorial position was a high-stakes role.

211

The next great thing about this story is how well it conveys her thoughts, emotions, and actions as she encounters a major obstacle. We really know what it was like to be her in this role, and we have an appreciation for how seriously she took the failure that she faced. She proceeds to walk us through her thought process and actions in addressing the problem and carries it right through to the outcome. Just wonderful.

Better still, the story is one that Rebecca will have up her sleeve in case she needs to prove any number of qualities or soft skills: leadership, responsibility, conflict management, results orientation, and interpersonal skills to name just a few!

6. *The next story is from Cheyenne Olinde. This story is an almost fiendishly clever story for a Supply Chain Management (SCM) major to use in an interview. Cheyenne has never worked in corporate SCM... but this story absolutely will resonate with SCM professionals: After all, it entails meeting a logistical challenge—one that required consideration of manpower, equipment capabilities, delivery time, and so forth. So while the story illustrates many soft skills—see if you can spy them as you read—it is particularly smart in showing that he has an appreciation for what a SCM interviewer may want to know.*

"As a combat photographer, I have been fortunate enough to document every aspect the Marine Corps has to offer. I have documented everything from aerial reconnaissance to autopsies. I have been deployed to Cuba, Spain, Seychelles, Malta, Greece, Italy, Puerto Rico, Djibouti Africa, and Wisconsin. The one thing that all my missions had in common was that I was serving a customer. Whether it was a Captain for a routine passport photo, or aerial photographs of a military base's security weakness for a General, I have always interacted with clients. Many times my customers would want certain photographs that were impractical and I would have to tactfully explain why their request would not work and offer a solution to solve their problem. Other times, I would get a call from an important client who needs an exceptional amount of work done in a very short window of time.

"When our Marines were preparing to go to Afghanistan, we had to provide them with the tools to help teach their Marines basic Arabic. Their request was for over 1,000 instructional Arabic CDs, needed in less than seven days on top of the other 30 jobs we currently had. My shop had neither the manpower nor the equipment to handle the request, and the customer did not have the funds to go elsewhere. I had to make it work.

"The original CDs were provided; we just needed to make the copies. We only had the capability to copy 20 CDs an hour, plus the work could not interfere with our other jobs requested by my other customers.

"I implemented a split schedule of three eight and a half-hour shifts, operating non-stop. This allowed for the constant copying of CDs, and the continuous work on other current productions. Not only did we meet the goal in less than three days, we made an extra 500 copies for future operations and completed all the current productions in house.

"I approached my commanding officer and requested time off for the team after the hard work and dedication my Marines showed. I then had them all come over to my house and treated them to a BBQ to thank them. After that, there was nothing my Marines would not do for me, and superiors knew that there was no challenge too large I couldn't handle."

~ Cheyenne Olinde, Northeastern University Class of 2010

If I remember correctly, Cheyenne used this story to prove that he had good customer-service skills. While it does so, it also could be rolled out to illustrate problem-solving skills, leadership, and time management skills.

7. *This story is from Jake Thaler, and it shows how a story about athletics can be very effective. Pay special attention to how he works his thoughts and emotions into the story.*

"Let me tell you of a time when I proved to be self-motivated. Upon being recruited for hockey at Northeastern, I received a packet for strength and conditioning. I was planning on showing up on campus in the best shape of my life. I had begun my first week of the workout when I experienced a great deal of pain in my left knee. I learned that I tore my meniscus and was forced to undergo surgery. Frustration overcame me as I learned that most of my hard work getting to the point of being recruited was going to waste. After repairing the torn cartilage, I was told that I had to slowly rehab my knee for a full three months without heavily working out. A feeling of bitterness took control of me, and I knew that this was going to be a huge setback for me in the long run. My dream of playing college hockey increased in difficulty but I knew I could come back from it.

"After a summer of tedious rehab sessions I was finally cleared to play by the school. My excitement took over and adrenaline flowed through my body before my first workout with the team. In a matter of seconds, my joy turned to a heart-stopping experience when I heard the same "pop" that indicated my knee was not fully repaired. The first thought that went through my head was that I completed three months of rehab for nothing. After this initial thought, my conscience took over and I realized that I had wanted to play at this level ever since I watched my first hockey game. Another surgery was necessary, and this time they partially removed the cartilage, letting me recover much faster. After not being able to skate and work out for months, I had been eagerly waiting to catch up. I felt aggravated from my hiatus as I needed to acclimate myself to the position again.

213

"As the season drew close to the end, I still had yet to play in a game although our team had been riding an unsuccessful year. I kept on thinking that the next game was going to be the one where I'd get my shot. The last weekend of the year we played two games against Boston University—the third-ranked team in the nation and two days before we played them my coach told me I had the start. All of the obstacles I had to overcome to get my shot and I finally had my chance to show what I could do. Our team battled hard and lost both games that weekend, but I surprised myself and a lot of other doubtful people that I could play at this level. Although we had lost, I had felt that I demonstrated a winning attitude that was driven by motivation."

--Jake Thaler, Northeastern University Class of 2010

In addition to self-motivation, this story could be used to show persistence, ability to handle frustration and adversity, being goal-oriented (literally!), and patience. That's a lot of mileage for one story!

Remember my rule: Use a specific, vivid story to prove that you have one great quality, and you'll wind up proving you have at least three other great qualities!

As described earlier in this appendix, write three stories showing you at your best. Then, read over your stories, and list three different transferable skills that each story could be used to prove.

As you look at a job description's qualifications, think of stories you might use to prove that you have those qualities. However, it's also worth your while to come up with situations that show you at your best, and THEN figure out various ways in which you could apply them in job interview situations. It's always smart to find opportunities to tell your best stories.

Once you have done this successfully, you should have a good collection of stories to bring your interview to life!

APPENDIX F
Additional Resources

In this last section of the book, I have included a few different materials that I have found useful in teaching our Introduction to Co-op courses at Northeastern University as well as sheets that I have developed for working with my graduate assistants and students over the years.

Fine-Tuning Your Resume may be useful for students wishing to do a spot-check of their resume or for instructors who want to tip off students to common errors. I developed **Common Interview Problems and How To Solve Them** after conducting over 250 practice interviews. It's easy to tell if an interview is good, bad, or somewhere in between, but it can be difficult to articulate exactly *why* an interview is lacking. I have given this to my graduate assistants when training them, but it also can be helpful for co-op and career services professionals in their efforts to get beyond *symptoms* of interview difficulties to identify the root problems. The problems are listed in approximate order of frequency, and each is paired with plausible solutions to the problem. The **Interviewing Scenarios, Job Search Scenarios,** and **On-The-Job Performance Scenarios** can be provocative for classroom discussion in small or large groups; I also use these as make-up assignments for students who miss classes. Lastly, **You Make The Call! Decide What To Do If YOU Were The Co-op Coordinator** is an exercise designed to make students walk in our shoes as career professionals. Understanding the roles of all constituencies—student, co-op/intern, co-worker, supervisor, internship/co-op coordinator, and career services professional—is critical to becoming successful as a developing student employee. This exercise may help students appreciate the delicate balance that co-op and career professionals must maintain when providing services to numerous students and employers.

FINE-TUNING YOUR RESUME

Is your resume REALLY all set? Here are a few elements to double-check. They represent solutions to the most common mistakes on business co-op resumes!

1. Make sure to include your month and year of graduation (i.e., May 2012).

2. Add *References Provided Upon Request* as last line.

3. If appropriate, consider adding *Financing ___% of Education Through Part-Time and Cooperative Education Employment* to bottom of education section.

4. Write out your degree: Say "Bachelor of Science Degree in Business Administration" NOT "B.S. Degree in Marketing" (or "Studying Psychology," etc.).

5. Have start and end dates for all jobs.

6. Add computer skills section if missing.

7. Add interests section if missing.

8. Differentiate between majors, concentrations, and minors if necessary.

9. Make sure jobs are in reverse chronological order (with some exceptions).

10. Add GPA if at least 3.0.

11. At most, list GPA to two decimal places (3.25); it's okay to round up or down (i.e., 3.072 can be written as 3.1).

12. Write out all numbers that are ten or smaller. Unless beginning a sentence, write 11 or higher as a number (i.e., 15, not fifteen).

13. Use bold and italic fonts to improve aesthetic quality of resume and add variety. Consider using something other than Times New Roman to be different (i.e., Arial, Garamond, Century).

14. Make sure each sentence or bullet point has a verb—almost without exception.

15. Avoid passive phrases such as "Responsibilities included."

16. In job descriptions, don't just list transferable skills: each sentence/bullet point should include an aspect of what you actually did.

17. Add quantitative and qualitative details to bring your job description to life.

18. Go beyond summarizing your duties: What were your *accomplishments* in the job?

19. Follow a format from this guidebook: NOT a MS-Word template or the advice of your brother's girlfriend's cousin's friend who is really good at resumes!

20. Be consistent in font, capitalization of words, and bolding; be consistent in the use of periods at the end of sentences and with abbreviations—especially for months and street addresses..

21. Use a consistent format for city and state (i.e., San Diego, CA).

22. Spell-check **and** proofread!

COMMON INTERVIEW PROBLEMS AND HOW TO SOLVE THEM

	PROBLEM	SOLUTION
1.	Being "interviewer dependent" (Quality of your interview depends on quality of interviewer)	• Answer general questions with specifics. • Use specific stories and examples. • Make interview a "conversation with a purpose."
2.	Lacking a strategy	• Write down three reasons why YOU should be hired for THIS specific job. • Discuss these reasons ASAP in interview (i.e., when answering open-ended questions).
3.	Inadequate research	• Prepare as if your life depended on it! • Weave your research into answers and end-of-interview questions.
4.	Answers aren't helpful	• Always tie answers to company's needs according to the job description.
5.	Negative nervous energy	• Preparation. • Practice. • Put energy into presentation. • Maintain external focus.
6.	Weak opening and/or closing	• Don't rehash resume. • Articulate strategy early. • Prepare ten good questions. • Bridge to close of interview.
7.	Getting stuck; blanking out	• Ask clarifying question. • Don't be afraid to pause. • Use notes page (carefully).
8.	Raising flags for interviewer (making statements that raise concerns about whether you are appropriate for the job)	• Preparation • Focus on positives, always. • If negatives must be discussed, choose ones that won't hurt you.
9.	Insensitivity to interviewer --Talking too fast --Lack of "active listening" --Digressing from the point	• Practice speaking style. • Pause, especially after key points. • Respond to verbal/non-verbal cues. • Stick to what he or she needs to know.

INTERVIEWING SCENARIOS

Scenario 1
You're asked what pay rate you'd be seeking for a job. What would you say?

Scenario 2
A person from a company calls to invite you in for an interview. You set up an interview for 10:00 a.m. on Friday. "Oh, by the way," the interviewer says. "It's Casual Day here on Friday, so no need for you to get dressed up." How do you dress for the interview?

Scenario 3
You agree to have an interview at 11:45 a.m. on Tuesday. But then one of your professors announces that there will be a review session at the same time, and you know it will hurt you to miss it. What do you do?

Scenario 4
You don't have a car now, but you will have one in time for your co-op or internship. You have the opportunity to interview for a great job that's about 25 miles outside of the city. Describe three different ways you could get to the company for the interview.

Scenario 5
You arrive 15 minutes early for a 9:00 a.m. interview. You had to get up early to be there on time, so you are annoyed when the interviewer doesn't appear until 9:20. How would you pass the time while waiting? What do you say about the interviewer being late?

Scenario 6
You are an international student. At some point in the interview, you are asked: "Do you plan to stay in the U.S. after graduation, or will you return home?" How do you respond?

Scenario 7
It is Monday, May 8, and you don't have a job lined up for the summer or fall. You are hoping to get an offer from Cornell Products but know you probably won't hear from them until early in the next week. The phone rings, and you get an offer from Carew Software. It's not a bad job but definitely one that you would turn down if you had an offer from Cornell. What do you say to the person from Carew Software?

Scenario 8
You accept a job offer from Pandolfo Hospital in mid-May and feel pleased that you lined up your co-op job so early. Two weeks later, though, you get a surprise offer from The Drury Rehabilitation Center that had interviewed you in early May; you had given up on getting an offer from them, but now they are offering you more money and a better job than the one at Pandolfo. What do you do?

JOB SEARCH SCENARIOS

1. You're looking for a job for January. You meet with your co-op or internship coordinator and agree on six jobs for which your resume will be sent. Two weeks later, you haven't heard anything at all, and there's a job with Boston Beer Company that you really wanted in that group. What do you do?

2. You come home and you get the following message from an employer: "This is [indecipherable name] from John Hancock, and we'd like to have you in for an interview. Can you contact us as soon as possible to arrange an interview for Monday?" You applied for three different jobs at Hancock and have no idea which job the employer is referring to. You call the number on your caller ID, but you get a message indicating that the number is not a working number; it's only used for outgoing calls. What do you do?

3. An employer calls you and wants to schedule you for an interview in two days: "What's your availability?" The problem is that you don't have your schedule handy. How do you handle the situation?

4. You know that resumes have already started going out, and you're freaking out because whenever you try to see your coordinator during her walk-in hours, there are impossibly long lines. There are no other times on her schedule for appointments or walk-ins that work for you, and you can't wait around because you have a class. What do you do?

5. You have an interview scheduled for Monday with RSA for their E-Commerce Analyst position. You know that you're a "reach candidate." What do you do to prepare in order to give yourself the best chance for an offer?

6. It's November 12, and you get an offer for a very entry-level position doing general office work. You are lukewarm about accepting the offer, but the fact is that you have no corporate experience, no other interviews scheduled, and no other possible offers at this point. You're supposed to start work on January 2. What do you do?

7. You have a friend who is currently on co-op for State Street Bank. He tells you to forward your resume to him; he will pass it along to his manager and put in a good word for you. It's a great job, and you're excited to hear that you may have an "in" with the company. What do you do?

8. You get two job offers, and you're struggling in attempting to decide which one to accept. Job A has really nice people and a great work environment, and it's also a very easy commute of about 15 minutes. However, the job itself is very easy. You're not sure if you would learn very much. In contrast, job B would be very stressful at first. It's in a very fast-paced environment, and it's obvious that you'll be thrown in at the deep end of the pool to sink or swim. It's also a 45-minute commute. But you know that

you would learn much more in this job, as it's significantly more challenging. Which job would you accept? Would you change your mind if the other job paid significantly more than your first choice?

ON-THE-JOB PERFORMANCE SCENARIOS

Scenario 1

Jeff is interviewed by a large company for a finance job. The job description is vague and mentions little more than the need for a 2.0 GPA and dependability. The interviewer asks only one or two questions; at the end of the interview, Jeff asks a question about the hours. Jeff is surprised to receive an offer two days later. He accepts. After two weeks on the job, he finds he is very bored. Assisting the finance department, he spends most of his time filing and faxing and photocopying. He does a little data entry each day, but this is not difficult to master. Though he has agreed to work for six months, he thinks he will go crazy doing this kind of work for that long. What should he do now? Should he have done anything differently?

Scenario 2

Lucinda is feeling a little annoyed about her job. It seems like her boss is picking on her about everything she does. First, her boss complained that Lucinda would just sit at her desk when she ran out of work, instead of asking for more. Then the boss gave Lucinda a hard time because Lucinda thought she should double-check on how to do a bookkeeping procedure that she was trained to do a week before. Today, she is especially irritated because her boss gave her a hard time about being late a couple times this week. Lucinda had come in only five or ten minutes late: Several full-time employees did that, but she didn't see the boss talking to them about it! At 11:00 a.m., Lucinda puts aside the spreadsheet work that she has been asked to get done as soon as possible, and she calls her co-op coordinator to complain. What would you say to her if you were her co-op coordinator? Do you think Lucinda is being treated unfairly?

Scenario 3

Ya-hui is asked to back up all of the voice mail systems on the tape. It is a long and tedious job, and it is not her favorite thing to do. Yet her job for the most part is good: she is learning a lot about networks, databases, and hardware. Her boss comes in as she is finishing up with the voice mail back-up process. "Do you like doing this sort of work, Ya-hui?" the supervisor asks. How should she reply?

Scenario 4

Steven is an Arts and Sciences student studying communications. He lands an internship with an advertising agency. He is excited about the job. During the interview, the manager told him that he would be working on an important event and get to use his writing skills on developing some promotional materials. Three weeks into the job, he finds that all he ever does is clerical work such as faxing or sorting through file cabinets to throw out dated material. He feels that the employer hasn't kept their promise, and he is tempted to simply up and quit. How should he handle this situation?

222

Scenario 5

Oliver, a sophomore, is hired to do a fairly low-level job at an animal hospital. He knows it is not the best job, but he wants to get a good evaluation. What are some suggestions that you would give him?

Scenario 6

Sarah is feeling uncomfortable about a situation at work. As one of three co-ops working in an accounting group during tax season, Sarah has enjoyed her job—especially the opportunity to work overtime hours for good pay. However, she finds it odd that she is usually the only co-op asked to work overtime. A few days ago, her manager praised Sarah's work and offered to give her a ride home because it was dark. This morning he suggested taking her out to dinner to thank her for putting in all the overtime hours without complaint. Nothing has "happened," but she feels uncomfortable about being asked out to dinner by her boss. What should see do? If you were her co-op coordinator, and Sarah told you about the situation, what would your response be?

Scenario 7

Upon being hired for a co-op job, Max is told by an HR person that his hours are 8:45-5:00 Monday-Friday, including 45 minutes for lunch. His pay will be $12/hour, which multiplies out to $450/week before taxes. Max hits it off with a couple of full-time co-workers during the first few weeks of the job. One Friday they tell Max that they're going way across town for a long lunch—does he want to come? It's obvious that they'll be gone for a couple of hours. "Don't worry about it," one of the co-workers says. "The boss won't be back today, and HR will never know." Max isn't sure. At times it does seem like he's the only one who's usually taking just 45 minutes for lunch, and he's definitely the only one carefully tabulating his hours to submit on Monday morning. What should he do?

Scenario 8

Here is what one student wrote after being fired from a co-op job a few years ago: "I am currently a fourth-year student at NU. I recently was let go from a co-op position that I held for more than a year. The reason for my dismissal was because I received an e-mail that was deemed unacceptable by my employer. I was let go on the same day that I received this e-mail and forwarded it to my NU account.

"The purpose of e-mail in a co-op environment is as a way to conduct corporate communication—not for the social benefit of the co-op student. This is the lesson that I hope you take from this case. Actually, I think I was lucky—the situation could have been more serious. When I opened the e-mail, someone could have seen the letter and been offended—maybe offended enough to charge me with sexual harassment. Or I could have forwarded the e-mail to a co-worker by accident.

"Here are my suggestions for future co-ops: Use e-mail only for work purposes, and if you must send e-mail to friends, then keep it simple. Ask them what time they want to meet after work, for example. Also, you may want to make sure that your friends do not have access to your e-mail address at work. Additionally, don't check your other e-mail accounts while at work if at all possible: You never know what someone might send to your personal e-mail account."

QUESTIONS FOR DISCUSSION

1. Do you think the employer was ethically and/or legally right in choosing to terminate this student? More specifically, is it ethical and/or legal for an employer to read a co-op student's e-mail?

2. What would be some examples of an "inappropriate" e-mail?

3. Besides e-mail, list other examples of ways in which a student could be doing something "inappropriate" at work.

YOU MAKE THE CALL!

Decide What To Do If YOU Were The Co-op Coordinator

In the following scenarios, assume that you are the internship or co-op coordinator. As such, you are the go-between working with both students and employers, trying to do what is fair and right in all situations. You also are trying to ensure that your students are learning to become professionals, which includes being responsible for their actions. With all of this in mind, how would you handle the following scenarios?

Scenario 1

Co-op was scheduled to start on September 21, and Alex came to your office for the first time on September 17. When asked why he started so late, Alex said, "I was real busy, and then I had to drive to Florida." When you ask if he can get the guidebook today and bring in a resume tomorrow, he says, "I can buy the guidebook, but I have to go to Delaware tomorrow for the weekend. I can come in Tuesday." When he comes in Tuesday with a resume—two hours late for his 9:00 a.m. appointment—you go over it and make many corrections. Alex says, "Since it's so late, can I call you at home tonight to go over the revisions?" You say no, and he accepts this.

You help him get a job at Premium Life Insurance in the suburbs. He is pleased because it is near his house. But less than two weeks later, he calls you in an irate mood because he has been fired. "They screwed me over!" he says repeatedly. "I was late ONCE because I had a flat tire... what am I supposed to do about that? And they said I used the Internet too much, and I only went on it TWICE, when there was NOTHING to do. My supervisor thought I was great...It was HER boss that fired me. I think he doesn't like co-ops."

You call his immediate supervisor. She says that Alex was 1) on time twice during just eight days of employment—generally five to 15 minutes late; 2) using the Internet after being specifically warned not to do so until he had mastered all the basics of customer service, which he had not done; 3) accidentally hanging up on customers after keeping them on hold for a long time, then denying that he did it; and 4) coming in very tired, wearing wrinkled clothing, etc. She had tried to work with him but others had become fed up and demanded that he should be terminated. She found it hard to object.

The two versions of this story differ dramatically. Alex is coming to your office shortly. He has already said he wants to talk to another of your employers about a co-op job, as they had wanted to interview him but had been unable to because he accepted the job with Premium Life. How would you deal with Alex? What would you say to him? Would you send his resume out to another employer?

Scenario 2

Tarek is a student looking for an internship starting in early January. It is early December, and you have not seen him for months. He comes into your office with a resume and says he wants to interview for a position at Raytheon that just became available. You look at the resume for the first time. It has several typos, and the format doesn't match the guidebook, but these are mistakes that could be fixed fairly quickly. And you see that he actually has much more experience than the seven or eight students who have been looking for jobs since referrals began in mid-October. There's a good chance he would get the Raytheon job. How would you handle the situation? Would you refer his resume to Raytheon? Whether you would or would not, what would you say to this student?

Scenario 3

It is mid-November, and you are incredibly busy with employers on campus, students making decisions on offers, and other students who are at various stages of the process. The phone has been ringing like crazy, maybe 40 to 50 times today alone. On top of everything, there is a long line of students waiting to see you this afternoon during walk-in hours. You are trying to deal with each student efficiently, but you also need to keeping things moving along.

Around 4:00 p.m., a student named Samantha from another coordinator comes into your office. As she sits down, she says, "I've been sitting here waiting to see you for over an hour." You tell her that you're sorry for the inconvenience and point out that it is an extremely busy time of day and time of year.

Samantha says, "You're never available. I've come in every afternoon this week, and you're either not in your office or there's a long line ahead of me. Everybody else is getting jobs, and you haven't even seen my resume yet. This isn't fair."

Checking your files, you see that Samantha contacted you just once this quarter. Three weeks ago, she left a message saying that she needed to see you as soon as possible. You left a voice mail for her indicating a few days and times that you were available. There has been no contact since then.

You have some good employers coming in over the next week or so to interview students. It would be easy enough to put Samantha on a few interview schedules. What would you say or do?

Scenario 4

A new employer has interviewed four of your students for a new position with a small company. "I don't know who to hire," the employer says. "Why don't you tell me who the best one is? I'll just offer the job to whoever you think."

You consider the candidates: **Carol** was in your Introduction to Co-op class last year and came to all the classes but otherwise doesn't stand out in memory. **Henry** is a transfer student who has made a good impression on you so far in terms of his attitude and professionalism. **Mark** has the most relevant job experience on his resume, but he strikes you as being difficult: He made a stink over needing to revise his resume repeatedly. What would you say to the employer about whom to hire?

Scenario 5

You receive an evaluation for Nkeche Adebiyi, who recently completed a position with your second-largest employer. It's an extremely negative evaluation, giving her low rankings almost across the board. You ask Nkeche about it, and she says, "Oh, it's just because my immediate supervisor didn't like me for some reason. But her boss thought I was terrific, and we were great friends."

You call up her boss. The boss acknowledges that she thought Nkeche was okay for a while, but she now thinks that they just weren't aware of her shortcomings because the company admittedly did a poor job of giving her structured work in the first two months on the job. After that, though, the boss was amazed at how seemingly uninterested Nkeche was in doing the work. Nkeche apparently has told co-workers that she really doesn't like this type of work—she just does it because the pay is good. There also were issues with her making many personal phone calls, apparently to her boyfriend.

Nkeche basically denies all of this when you confront her with these new facts. She says that this manager now has it in for her because she received such negative information from her immediate supervisor. You tell Nkeche that you're concerned about referring her out to another employer; she pleads with you to give her another chance. You're not sure: It's a bad economy, and you can't afford to alienate any more employers. What do you do?

Scenario 6

A company in Florida calls you up in December looking for a co-op student to work for six months in their Florida office. It's a great job, and they are willing to hire up to four students to start in January.

You only have 12 students still available. While they all need jobs, some are stronger than others. There are only two candidates whom you are fairly positive would do a very good job in this situation. The others started looking late and/or have come across as having attitude problems, difficult personalities, and a questionable work ethic. If you send all 12 resumes, the chances are that three or four students will be hired, and that you will be very nervous about a couple of them. A highly successful performance by one or two co-ops likely will increase the number of jobs available in the future. But if even one student goes down to Florida and performs poorly, the company may never hire another student from your program. Would you send all the resumes?